Count Hannibal
A Romance of the Court of France

by
Stanley John Weyman

Count Hannibal
A Romance of the Court of France
by Stanley John Weyman

Copyright © 2024

All Rights reserved.

No part of this publication may be reproduced, stored in a retrieval system, or transmitted in any form or by any means, electronic, mechanical, photocopying or Otherwise, without the written permission of the publisher.
The author/editor asserts the moral right to be identified as the author/editor of this work.

ISBN: 978-93-63052-22-2

Published by
DOUBLE 9 BOOKS
2/13-B, Ansari Road
Daryaganj, New Delhi – 110002
info@double9books.com
www.double9books.com
Tel. 011-40042856

This book is under public domain

ABOUT THE AUTHOR

Stanley John Weyman 7 August 1855 – 10 April 1928) was an English historical romance writer. His most successful novels, written between 1890 and 1895, were set in late 16th and early 17th-century France. They were quite successful at the time, but are now largely forgotten. Stanley John Weyman was born on August 7, 1855, in Ludlow, Shropshire, as the second son of an attorney. He attended Shrewsbury School and Christ Church, Oxford, and graduated in 1877 with a degree in Modern History. Following a year of teaching at the King's School in Chester, he returned to Ludlow in December 1879 to live with his widowed mother. Weyman was called to the law in 1881 but struggled as a barrister due to his shyness, nervousness, and soft-spokenness. However, the lack of briefs provided him time to write. His short story "King Pippin and Sweet Clive" was published in the Cornhill Magazine, but its editor, James Payn, a novelist himself, advised Weyman that it would be simpler to make a career by writing novels. Weyman saw himself as a historian, so he was particularly pleased by excellent feedback on an article he wrote about Oliver Cromwell that appeared in the English Historical Review.

CONTENTS

CHAPTER I
CRIMSON FAVOURS 9

CHAPTER II
HANNIBAL DE SAULX, COMTE DE TAVANNES 18

CHAPTER III
THE HOUSE NEXT THE GOLDEN MAID 27

CHAPTER IV
THE EVE OF THE FEAST 32

CHAPTER V
ROUGH WOOING 39

CHAPTER VI
WHO TOUCHES TAVANNES? 47

CHAPTER VII
IN THE AMPHITHEATRE 54

CHAPTER VIII
TWO HENS AND AN EGG 62

CHAPTER IX
UNSTABLE 70

CHAPTER X
MADAME ST. LO 75

CHAPTER XI
A BARGAIN 83

CHAPTER XII
IN THE HALL OF THE LOUVRE 91

CHAPTER XIII
DIPLOMACY 100

CHAPTER XIV
TOO SHORT A SPOON 110

CHAPTER XV
THE BROTHER OF ST. MAGLOIRE 117

CHAPTER XVI
AT CLOSE QUARTERS 124

CHAPTER XVII
THE DUEL 129

CHAPTER XVIII
ANDROMEDA, PERSEUS BEING ABSENT 139

CHAPTER XIX
IN THE ORLÉANNAIS 147

CHAPTER XX
ON THE CASTLE HILL 154

CHAPTER XXI
SHE WOULD, AND WOULD NOT 161

CHAPTER XXII
PLAYING WITH FIRE 168

CHAPTER XXIII
A MIND, AND NOT A MIND 176

CHAPTER XXIV
AT THE KING'S INN 184

CHAPTER XXV
THE COMPANY OF THE BLEEDING HEART 192

CHAPTER XXVI
TEMPER 198

CHAPTER XXVII
THE BLACK TOWN 204

CHAPTER XXVIII
IN THE LITTLE CHAPTER-HOUSE 215

CHAPTER XXIX
THE ESCAPE 222

CHAPTER XXX
SACRILEGE! 232

CHAPTER XXXI
   THE FLIGHT FROM ANGERS 237
CHAPTER XXXII
   THE ORDEAL BY STEEL 244
CHAPTER XXXIII
   THE AMBUSH 249
CHAPTER XXXIV
   WHICH WILL YOU, MADAME? 258
CHAPTER XXXV
   AGAINST THE WALL 267
CHAPTER XXXVI
   HIS KINGDOM 275

CHAPTER I
CRIMSON FAVOURS

M. de Tavannes smiled. Mademoiselle averted her eyes, and shivered; as if the air, even of that close summer night, entering by the door at her elbow, chilled her. And then came a welcome interruption.

"Tavannes!"

"Sire!"

Count Hannibal rose slowly. The King had called, and he had no choice but to obey and go. Yet he hung a last moment over his companion, his hateful breath stirring her hair.

"Our pleasure is cut short too soon, Mademoiselle," he said, in the tone, and with the look, she loathed. "But for a few hours only. We shall meet to-morrow. Or, it may be—earlier."

She did not answer, and "Tavannes!" the King repeated with violence. "Tavannes! Mordieu!" his Majesty continued, looking round furiously. "Will no one fetch him? Sacré nom, am I King, or a dog of a—"

"I come, sire!" the Count cried hastily. For Charles, King of France, Ninth of the name, was none of the most patient; and scarce another in the Court would have ventured to keep him waiting so long. "I come, sire; I come!" Tavannes repeated, as he moved from Mademoiselle's side.

He shouldered his way through the circle of courtiers, who barred the road to the presence, and in part hid her from observation. He pushed past the table at which Charles and the Comte de Rochefoucauld had been playing primero, and at which the latter still sat, trifling idly with the cards. Three more paces, and he reached the King, who stood in the *ruelle* with Rambouillet and the Italian Marshal. It was the latter who, a moment before, had summoned his Majesty from his game.

Mademoiselle, watching him go, saw so much; so much, and the King's roving eyes and haggard face, and the four figures, posed apart in the fuller light of the upper half of the Chamber. Then the circle of courtiers came together before her, and she sat back on her stool. A fluttering, long-drawn sigh escaped her. Now, if she could slip out and make her escape! Now—she looked round. She was not far from the door; to withdraw seemed easy. But a staring, whispering knot of gentlemen and pages blocked the way; and the girl, ignorant of the etiquette of the Court, and with no more than a week's experience of Paris, had not the courage to rise and pass alone through the group.

She had come to the Louvre this Saturday evening under the wing of Madame d'Yverne, her *fiancé's* cousin. By ill-hap Madame had been summoned to the Princess Dowager's closet, and perforce had left her. Still, Mademoiselle had her betrothed, and in his charge had sat herself down to wait, nothing loth, in the great gallery, where all was bustle and gaiety and entertainment. For this, the seventh day of the fêtes, held to celebrate the marriage of the King of Navarre and Charles's sister—a marriage which was to reconcile the two factions of the Huguenots and the Catholics, so long at war—saw the Louvre as gay, as full, and as lively as the first of the fête days had found it; and in the humours of the throng, in the ceaseless passage of masks and maids of honour, guards and bishops, Swiss in the black, white, and green of Anjou, and Huguenot nobles in more sombre habits, the country-bred girl had found recreation and to spare. Until gradually the evening had worn away and she had begun to feel nervous; and M. de Tignonville, her betrothed, placing her in the embrasure of a window, had gone to seek Madame.

She had waited for a time without much misgiving; expecting each moment to see him return. He would be back before she could count a hundred; he would be back before she could number the leagues that separated her from her beloved province, and the home by the Biscay Sea, to which even in that brilliant scene her thoughts turned fondly. But the minutes had passed, and passed, and he had not returned. Worse, in his place Tavannes—not the Marshal, but his brother, Count Hannibal—had found her; he, whose odious court, at once a menace and an insult, had subtly enveloped her for a week past. He had sat down beside her, he had taken possession of her, and, profiting by her inexperience, had played on her fears and smiled at her dislike. Finally, whether she would or no, he had swept her with him into the Chamber. The rest had been an obsession, a nightmare, from which only the King's voice summoning Tavannes to his side had relieved her.

Her aim now was to escape before he returned, and before another, seeing her alone, adopted his *rôle* and was rude to her. Already the courtiers about her were beginning to stare, the pages to turn and titter and whisper. Direct her gaze as she might, she met some eye watching her, some couple enjoying her confusion. To make matters worse, she presently discovered that she was the only woman in the Chamber; and she conceived the notion that she had no right to be there at that hour. At the thought her cheeks burned, her eyes dropped; the room seemed to buzz with her name, with gross words and jests, and gibes at her expense.

At last, when the situation had grown nearly unbearable, the group before the door parted, and Tignonville appeared. The girl rose with a cry of relief, and he came to her. The courtiers glanced at the two and smiled.

He did not conceal his astonishment at finding her there. "But, Mademoiselle, how is this?" he asked, in a low voice. He was as conscious of the attention they attracted as she was, and as uncertain on the point of her right to be there. "I left you in the gallery. I came back, missed you, and—"

She stopped him by a gesture. "Not here!" she muttered, with suppressed impatience. "I will tell you outside. Take me—take me out, if you please, Monsieur, at once!"

He was as glad to be gone as she was to go. The group by the doorway parted; she passed through it, he followed. In a moment the two stood in the great gallery, above the Salle des Caryatides. The crowd which had paraded here an hour before was gone, and the vast echoing apartment, used at that date as a guard-room, was well-nigh empty. Only at rare intervals, in the embrasure of a window or the recess of a door, a couple talked softly. At the farther end, near the head of the staircase which led to the hall below, and the courtyard, a group of armed Swiss lounged on guard. Mademoiselle shot a keen glance up and down, then she turned to her lover, her face hot with indignation.

"Why did you leave me?" she asked. "Why did you leave me, if you could not come back at once? Do you understand, sir," she continued, "that it was at your instance I came to Paris, that I came to this Court, and that I look to you for protection?"

"Surely," he said. "And—"

"And do you think Carlat and his wife fit guardians for me? Should I have come or thought of coming to this wedding, but for your promise, and Madame your cousin's? If I had not deemed myself almost your wife," she continued warmly, "and secure of your protection, should I have come within a hundred miles of this dreadful city? To which, had I my will, none of our people should have come."

"Dreadful? Pardieu, not so dreadful," he answered, smiling, and striving to give the dispute a playful turn. "You have seen more in a week than you would have seen at Vrillac in a lifetime, Mademoiselle."

"And I choke!" she retorted; "I choke! Do you not see how they look at us, at us Huguenots, in the street? How they, who live here, point at us and curse us? How the very dogs scent us out and snarl at our heels, and the babes cross themselves when we go by? Can you see the Place des Gastines and not think what stood there? Can you pass the Grève at night and not fill the air above the river with screams and wailings and horrible cries— the cries of our people murdered on that spot?" She paused for breath, recovered herself a little, and in a lower tone, "For me," she said, "I think of Philippa de Luns by day and by night! The eaves are a threat to me; the tiles would fall on us had they their will; the houses nod to—to—"

"To what, Mademoiselle?" he asked, shrugging his shoulders and assuming a tone of cynicism.

"To crush us! Yes, Monsieur, to crush us!"

"And all this because I left you for a moment?"

"For an hour—or well-nigh an hour," she answered more soberly.

"But if I could not help it?"

"You should have thought of that—before you brought me to Paris, Monsieur. In these troublous times."

He coloured warmly. "You are unjust, Mademoiselle," he said. "There are things you forget; in a Court one is not always master of one's self."

"I know it," she answered dryly, thinking of that through which she had gone.

"But you do not know what happened!" he returned with impatience. "You do not understand that I am not to blame. Madame d'Yverne, when I reached the Princess Dowager's closet, had left to go to the Queen of Navarre. I hurried after her, and found a score of gentlemen in the King of Navarre's chamber. They were holding a council, and they begged, nay, they compelled me to remain."

"And it was that which detained you so long?"

"To be sure, Mademoiselle."

"And not—Madame St. Lo?"

M. de Tignonville's face turned scarlet. The thrust in tierce was unexpected. This, then, was the key to Mademoiselle's spirt of temper.

"I do not understand you," he stammered.

"How long were you in the King of Navarre's chamber, and how long with Madame St. Lo?" she asked with fine irony. "Or no, I will not tempt you," she went on quickly, seeing him hesitate. "I heard you talking to Madame St. Lo in the gallery while I sat within. And I know how long you were with her."

"I met Madame as I returned," he stammered, his face still hot, "and I asked her where you were. I did not know, Mademoiselle, that I was not to speak to ladies of my acquaintance."

"I was alone, and I was waiting."

"I could not know that—for certain," he answered, making the best of it. "You were not where I left you. I thought, I confess—that you had gone. That you had gone home."

"With whom? With whom?" she repeated pitilessly. "Was it likely? With whom was I to go? And yet it is true, I might have gone home had I pleased—with M. de Tavannes! Yes," she continued, in a tone of keen reproach, and with the blood mounting to her forehead, "it is to that, Monsieur, you expose me! To be pursued, molested, harassed by a man whose look terrifies me, and whose touch I—I detest! To be addressed wherever I go by a man whose every word proves that he thinks me game for the hunter, and you a thing he may neglect. You are a man and you do not know, you cannot know what I suffer! What I have suffered this week past whenever you have left my side!"

Tignonville looked gloomy. "What has he said to you?" he asked, between his teeth.

"Nothing I can tell you," she answered, with a shudder. "It was he who took me into the Chamber."

"Why did you go?"

"Wait until he bids you do something," she answered. "His manner, his smile, his tone, all frighten me. And to-night, in all these there was a something worse, a hundred times worse than when I saw him last—on Thursday! He seemed to—to gloat on me," the girl stammered, with a flush of shame, "as if I were his! Oh, Monsieur, I wish we had not left our Poitou! Shall we ever see Vrillac again, and the fishers' huts about the port, and the sea beating blue against the long brown causeway?"

He had listened darkly, almost sullenly; but at this, seeing the tears gather in her eyes, he forced a laugh.

"Why, you are as bad as M. de Rosny and the Vidame!" he said. "And they are as full of fears as an egg is of meat! Since the Admiral was wounded by that scoundrel on Friday, they think all Paris is in a league against us."

"And why not?" she asked, her cheek grown pale, her eyes reading his eyes.

"Why not? Why, because it is a monstrous thing even to think of!" Tignonville answered, with the confidence of one who did not use the argument for the first time. "Could they insult the King more deeply than by such a suspicion? A Borgia may kill his guests, but it was never a practice of the Kings of France! Pardieu, I have no patience with them! They may lodge where they please, across the river, or without the walls if they choose, the Rue de l'Arbre Sec is good enough for me, and the King's name sufficient surety!"

"I know you are not apt to be fearful," she answered, smiling; and she looked at him with a woman's pride in her lover. "All the same, you will not desert me again, sir, will you?"

He vowed he would not, kissed her hand, looked into her eyes; then melting to her, stammering, blundering, he named Madame St. Lo. She stopped him.

"There is no need," she said, answering his look with kind eyes, and refusing to hear his protestations. "In a fortnight will you not be my husband? How should I distrust you? It was only that while she talked, I waited—I waited; and—and that Madame St. Lo is Count Hannibal's cousin. For a moment I was mad enough to dream that she held you on purpose. You do not think it was so?"

"She!" he cried sharply; and he winced, as if the thought hurt him. "Absurd! The truth is, Mademoiselle," he continued with a little heat, "you are like so many of our people! You think a Catholic capable of the worst."

"We have long thought so at Vrillac," she answered gravely.

"That's over now, if people would only understand. This wedding has put an end to all that. But I'm harking back," he continued awkwardly; and he stopped. "Instead, let me take you home."

"If you please. Carlat and the servants should be below."

He took her left hand in his right after the wont of the day, and with his other hand touching his sword-hilt, he led her down the staircase, that by a single turn reached the courtyard of the palace. Here a mob of armed servants, of lacqueys, and footboys, some bearing torches, and some carrying their masters' cloaks and *galoshes*, loitered to and fro. Had M. de Tignonville been a little more observant, or a trifle less occupied with his own importance, he might have noted more than one face which looked darkly on him; he might have caught more than one overt sneer at his expense. But in the business of summoning Carlat—Mademoiselle de Vrillac's steward and major-domo—he lost the contemptuous "Christaudins!" that hissed from a footboy's lips, and the "Southern dogs!" that died in the moustachios of a bully in the livery of the King's brother. He was engaged in finding the steward, and in aiding him to cloak his mistress; then with a ruffling air, a new acquirement, which he had picked up since he came to Paris, he made a way for her through the crowd. A moment, and the three, followed by half a dozen armed servants, bearing pikes and torches, detached themselves from the throng, and crossing the courtyard, with its rows of lighted windows, passed out by the gate between the Tennis Courts, and so into the Rue des Fosses de St. Germain.

Before them, against a sky in which the last faint glow of evening still contended with the stars, the spire and pointed arches of the church of St. Germain rose darkly graceful. It was something after nine: the heat of the August day brooded over the crowded city, and dulled the faint distant ring of arms and armour that yet would make itself heard above the hush; a hush which was not silence so much as a subdued hum. As Mademoiselle passed the closed house beside the Cloister of St. Germain, where only the day before Admiral Coligny, the leader of the Huguenots, had been wounded, she pressed her escort's hand, and involuntarily drew nearer to him. But he laughed at her.

"It was a private blow," he said, answering her unspoken thought. "It is like enough the Guises sped it. But they know now what is the King's will, and they have taken the hint and withdrawn themselves. It will not happen again, Mademoiselle. For proof, see the guards"—they were passing the end of the Rue Bethizy, in the corner house of which, abutting on the Rue de l'Arbre Sec, Coligny had his lodgings—"whom the King has placed for his security. Fifty pikes under Cosseins."

"Cosseins?" she repeated. "But I thought Cosseins—"

"Was not wont to love us!" Tignonville answered, with a confident chuckle. "He was not. But the dogs lick where the master wills, Mademoiselle. He was not, but he does. This marriage has altered all."

"I hope it may not prove an unlucky one!" she murmured. She felt impelled to say it.

"Not it!" he answered confidently. "Why should it?"

They stopped, as he spoke, before the last house, at the corner of the Rue St. Honoré opposite the Croix du Tiroir; which rose shadowy in the middle of the four ways. He hammered on the door.

"But," she said softly, looking in his face, "the change is sudden, is it not? The King was not wont to be so good to us!"

"The King was not King until now," he answered warmly. "That is what I am trying to persuade our people. Believe me, Mademoiselle, you may sleep without fear; and early in the morning I will be with you. Carlat, have a care of your mistress until morning, and let Madame lie in her chamber. She is nervous to-night. There, sweet, until morning! God keep you, and pleasant dreams!"

He uncovered, and bowing over her hand, kissed it; and the door being open he would have turned away. But she lingered as if unwilling to enter.

"There is—do you hear it—a stir in *that* quarter?" she said, pointing across the Rue St. Honoré. "What lies there?"

"Northward? The markets," he answered. "'Tis nothing. They say, you know, that Paris never sleeps. Good night, sweet, and a fair awakening!"

She shivered as she had shivered under Tavannes' eye. And still she lingered, keeping him.

"Are you going to your lodging at once?" she asked—for the sake, it seemed, of saying something.

"I?" he answered a little hurriedly. "No, I was thinking of paying Rochefoucauld the compliment of seeing him home. He has taken a new lodging to be near the Admiral; a horrid bare place in the Rue Bethizy, without furniture, but he would go into it to-day. And he has a sort of claim on my family, you know."

"Yes," she said simply. "Of course. Then I must not detain you. God keep you safe," she continued, with a faint quiver in her tone; and her lip trembled. "Good night, and fair dreams, Monsieur."

He echoed the words gallantly. "Of you, sweet!" he cried; and turning away with a gesture of farewell, he set off on his return.

He walked briskly, nor did he look back, though she stood awhile gazing after him. She was not aware that she gave thought to this; nor that it hurt her. Yet when bolt and bar had shot behind her, and she had mounted the cold, bare staircase of that day—when she had heard the dull echoing footsteps of her attendants as they withdrew to their lairs and sleeping-places, and still more when she had crossed the threshold of her chamber, and signed to Madame Carlat and her woman to listen—it is certain she felt a lack of something.

Perhaps the chill that possessed her came of that lack, which she neither defined nor acknowledged. Or possibly it came of the night air, August though it was; or of sheer nervousness, or of the remembrance of Count Hannibal's smile. Whatever its origin, she took it to bed with her and long after the house slept round her, long after the crowded quarter of the Halles had begun to heave and the Sorbonne to vomit a black-frocked band, long after the tall houses in the gabled streets, from St. Antoine to Montmartre and from St. Denis on the north to St. Jacques on the south, had burst into rows of twinkling lights—nay, long after the Quarter of the Louvre alone remained dark, girdled by this strange midnight brightness—she lay awake. At length she too slept, and dreamed of home and the wide skies of Poitou, and her castle of Vrillac washed day and night by the Biscay tides.

CHAPTER II
HANNIBAL DE SAULX, COMTE DE TAVANNES

"Tavannes!"

"Sire."

Tavannes, we know, had been slow to obey the summons. Emerging from the crowd, he found that the King, with Retz and Rambouillet, his Marshal des Logis, had retired to the farther end of the Chamber; apparently Charles had forgotten that he had called. His head a little bent—he was tall and had a natural stoop—the King seemed to be listening to a low but continuous murmur of voices which proceeded from the door of his closet. One voice frequently raised was beyond doubt a woman's; a foreign accent, smooth and silky, marked another; a third, that from time to time broke in, wilful and impetuous, was the voice of Monsieur, the King's brother, Catherine de Médicis' favourite son. Tavannes, waiting respectfully two paces behind the King, could catch little that was said; but Charles, something more, it seemed, for on a sudden he laughed, a violent, mirthless laugh. And he clapped Rambouillet on the shoulder.

"There!" he said, with one of his horrible oaths, "'tis settled! 'Tis settled! Go, man, and take your orders! And you, M. de Retz," he continued, in a tone of savage mockery, "go, my lord, and give them!"

"I, sire?" the Italian Marshal answered, in accents of deprecation. There were times when the young King would show his impatience of the Italian ring, the Retzs and Biragues, the Strozzis and Gondys, with whom his mother surrounded him.

"Yes, you!" Charles answered. "You and my lady mother! And in God's name answer for it at the day!" he continued vehemently. "You will have it! You will not let me rest till you have it! Then have it, only see to it, it be done thoroughly! There shall not be one left to cast it in the King's teeth and cry, 'Et tu, Carole!' Swim, swim in blood if you will," he continued, with growing wildness. "Oh, 'twill be a merry night! And it's true so far, you may kill fleas all day, but burn the coat, and there's an end. So burn it, burn it, and—" He broke off with a start as he discovered Tavannes at his elbow. "God's death, man!" he cried roughly, "who sent for you?"

"Your Majesty called me," Tavannes answered; while, partly urged by the King's hand, and partly anxious to escape, the others slipped into the closet and left them together.

"I sent for you? I called your brother, the Marshal!"

"He is within, sire," Tavannes answered, indicating the closet. "A moment ago I heard his voice."

Charles passed his shaking hand across his eyes. "Is he?" he muttered. "So he is! I heard it too. And—and a man cannot be in two places at once!" Then, while his haggard gaze, passing by Tavannes, roved round the Chamber, he laid his hand on Count Hannibal's breast. "They give me no peace, Madame and the Guises," he whispered, his face hectic with excitement. "They will have it. They say that Coligny—they say that he beards me in my own palace. And—and, *mordieu*," with sudden violence, "it's true. It's true enough! It was but to-day he was for making terms with me! With me, the King! Making terms! So it shall be, by God and Devil, it shall! But not six or seven! No, no. All! All! There shall not be one left to say to me, 'You did it!'"

"Softly, sire," Tavannes answered; for Charles had gradually raised his voice. "You will be observed."

For the first time the young King—he was but twenty-two years old, God pity him!—looked at his companion.

"To be sure," he whispered; and his eyes grew cunning. "Besides, and after all, there's another way, if I choose. Oh, I've thought and thought, I'd have you know." And shrugging his shoulders, almost to his ears, he raised and lowered his open hands alternately, while his back hid the movement from the Chamber. "See-saw! See-saw!" he muttered. "And the King between the two, you see. That's Madame's king-craft. She's shown me that a hundred times. But look you, it is as easy to lower the one as the other," with a cunning glance at Tavannes' face, "or to cut off the right as the left. And—and the Admiral's an old man and will pass; and for the matter of that I like to hear him talk. He talks well. While the others, Guise and his kind, are young, and I've thought, oh, yes, I've thought—but there," with a sudden harsh laugh, "my lady mother will have it her own way. And for this time she shall, but, All! All! Even Foucauld, there! Do you mark him. He's sorting the cards. Do you see him—as he will be to-morrow, with the slit in his throat and his teeth showing? Why, God!" his voice rising almost to a scream, "the candles by him are burning blue!" And with a shaking hand, his face convulsed, the young King clutched his companion's arm, and pinched it.

Count Hannibal shrugged his shoulders, but answered nothing.

"D'you think we shall see them afterwards?" Charles resumed, in a sharp, eager whisper. "In our dreams, man? Or when the watchman cries, and we awake, and the monks are singing lauds at St. Germain, and—and the taper is low?"

Tavannes' lip curled. "I don't dream, sire," he answered coldly, "and I seldom wake. For the rest, I fear my enemies neither alive nor dead."

"Don't you? By G-d, I wish I didn't," the young man exclaimed. His brow was wet with sweat. "I wish I didn't. But there, it's settled. They've settled it, and I would it were done! What do you think of—of it, man? What do you think of it, yourself?"

Count Hannibal's face was inscrutable. "I think nothing, sire," he said dryly. "It is for your Majesty and your council to think. It is enough for me that it is the King's will."

"But you'll not flinch?" Charles muttered, with a quick look of suspicion. "But there," with a monstrous oath, "I know you'll not! I believe you'd as soon kill a monk—though, thank God," and he crossed himself devoutly, "there is no question of that—as a man. And sooner than a maiden."

"Much sooner, sire," Tavannes answered grimly. "If you have any orders in the monkish direction—no? Then your Majesty must not talk to me longer. M. de Rochefoucauld is beginning to wonder what is keeping your Majesty from your game. And others are marking you, sire."

"By the Lord!" Charles exclaimed, a ring of wonder mingled with horror in his tone, "if they knew what was in our minds they'd mark us more! Yet, see Nançay there beside the door? He is unmoved. He looks to-day as he looked yesterday. Yet he has charge of the work in the palace—"

For the first time Tavannes allowed a movement of surprise to escape him.

"In the palace?" he muttered. "Is it to be done here, too, sire?"

"Would you let some escape, to return by-and-by and cut our throats?" the King retorted, with a strange spirt of fury; an incapacity to maintain the same attitude of mind for two minutes together was the most fatal weakness of his ill-balanced nature. "No. All! All!" he repeated with vehemence. "Didn't Noah people the earth with eight? But I'll not leave eight! My cousins, for they are blood-royal, shall live if they will recant. And my old nurse, whether or no. And Paré, for no one else understands my complexion. And—"

"And Rochefoucauld, doubtless, sire?"

The King, whose eye had sought his favourite companion, withdrew it. He darted a glance at Tavannes.

"Foucauld? Who said so?" he muttered jealously. "Not I! But we shall see. We shall see! And do you see that you spare no one, M. le Comte, without an order. That is your business."

"I understand, sire," Tavannes answered coolly. And after a moment's silence, seeing that the King had done with him, he bowed low and withdrew; watched by the circle, as all about a King were watched in the days when a King's breath meant life or death, and his smile made the fortunes of men. As he passed Rochefoucauld, the latter looked up and nodded.

"What keeps brother Charles?" he muttered. "He's madder than ever to-night. Is it a masque or a murder he is planning?"

"The vapours," Tavannes answered, with a sneer. "Old tales his old nurse has stuffed him withal. He'll come by-and-by, and 'twill be well if you can divert him."

"I will, if he come," Rochefoucauld answered, shuffling the cards. "If not 'tis Chicot's business, and he should attend to it. I'm tired, and shall to bed."

"He will come," Tavannes answered, and moved, as if to go on. Then he paused for a last word. "He will come," he muttered, stooping and speaking under his breath, his eyes on the other's face. "But play him lightly. He is in an ugly mood. Please him, if you can, and it may serve."

The eyes of the two met an instant, and those of Foucauld—so the King called his Huguenot favourite—betrayed some surprise; for Count Hannibal and he were not intimate. But seeing that the other was in earnest, he raised his brows in acknowledgment. Tavannes nodded carelessly in return, looked an instant at the cards on the table, and passed on, pushed his way through the circle, and reached the door. He was lifting the curtain to go out, when Nançay, the Captain of the Guard, plucked his sleeve.

"What have you been saying to Foucauld, M. de Tavannes?" he muttered.

"I?"

"Yes," with a jealous glance, "you, M. le Comte."

Count Hannibal looked at him with the sudden ferocity that made the man a proverb at Court.

"What I chose, M. le Capitaine des Suisses!" he hissed. And his hand closed like a vice on the other's wrist. "What I chose, look you! And remember, another time, that I am not a Huguenot, and say what I please."

"But there is great need of care," Nançay protested, stammering and flinching. "And—and I have orders, M. le Comte."

"Your orders are not for me," Tavannes answered, releasing his arm with a contemptuous gesture. "And look you, man, do not cross my path tonight. You know our motto? Who touches my brother, touches Tavannes! Be warned by it."

Nançay scowled. "But the priests say, 'If your hand offend you, cut it off!'" he muttered.

Tavannes laughed, a sinister laugh. "If you offend me I'll cut your throat," he said; and with no ceremony he went out, and dropped the curtain behind him.

Nançay looked after him, his face pale with rage. "Curse him!" he whispered, rubbing his wrist. "If he were any one else I would teach him! But he would as soon run you through in the presence as in the Pré aux Clercs! And his brother, the Marshal, has the King's ear! And Madame Catherine's too, which is worse!"

He was still fuming, when an officer in the colours of Monsieur, the King's brother, entered hurriedly, and keeping his hand on the curtain, looked anxiously round the Chamber. As soon as his eye found Nançay, his face cleared.

"Have you the reckoning?" he muttered.

"There are seventeen Huguenots in the palace besides their Highnesses," Nançay replied, in the same cautious tone. "Not counting two or three who are neither the one thing nor the other. In addition, there are the two Montmorencies; but they are to go safe for fear of their brother, who is not in the trap. He is too like his father, the old Bench-burner, to be lightly wronged! And, besides, there is Paré, who is to go to his Majesty's closet as soon as the gates are shut. If the King decides to save any one else, he will send him to his closet. So 'tis all clear and arranged here. If you are forward outside, it will be well! Who deals with the gentleman with the tooth-pick?"

"The Admiral? Monsieur, Guise, and the Grand Prior; Cosseins and Besme have charge. 'Tis to be done first. Then the Provost will raise the town. He will have a body of stout fellows ready at three or four rendezvous, so that the fire may blaze up everywhere at once. Marcel, the ex-provost, has the same commission south of the river. Orders to light the town as for a frolic have been given, and the Halles will be ready."

Nançay nodded, reflected a moment, and then with an involuntary shudder—

"God!" he exclaimed, "it will shake the world!"

"You think so?"

"Ay, will it not!" His next words showed that he bore Tavannes' warning in mind. "For me, my friend, I go in mail to-night," he said. "There will be many a score paid before morning, besides his Majesty's. And many a left-handed blow will be struck in the *mêlée*!"

The other crossed himself. "Grant none light here!" he said devoutly. And with a last look he nodded and went out.

In the doorway he jostled a person who was in the act of entering. It was M. de Tignonville, who, seeing Nançay at his elbow, saluted him, and stood looking round. The young man's face was flushed, his eyes were bright with unwonted excitement.

"M. de Rochefoucauld?" he asked eagerly. "He has not left yet?"

Nançay caught the thrill in his voice, and marked the young man's flushed face and altered bearing. He noted, too, the crumpled paper he carried half-hidden in his hand; and the Captain's countenance grew dark. He drew a step nearer, and his hand reached softly for his dagger. But his voice, when he spoke, was smooth as the surface of the pleasure-loving Court, smooth as the externals of all things in Paris that summer evening.

"He is here still," he said. "Have you news, M. de Tignonville?"

"News?"

"For M. de Rochefoucauld?"

Tignonville laughed. "No," he said. "I am here to see him to his lodging, that is all. News, Captain? What made you think so?"

"That which you have in your hand," Nançay answered, his fears relieved.

The young man blushed to the roots of his hair. "It is not for him," he said.

"I can see that, Monsieur," Nançay answered politely. "He has his successes, but all the billets-doux do not go one way."

The young man laughed, a conscious, flattered laugh. He was handsome, with such a face as women love, but there was a lack of ease in the way he wore his Court suit. It was a trifle finer, too, than accorded with Huguenot taste; or it looked the finer for the way he wore it, even as Teligny's and Foucauld's velvet capes and stiff brocades lost their richness and became but the adjuncts, fitting and graceful, of the men. Odder still, as Tignonville laughed, half hiding and half revealing the dainty scented paper in his hand, his clothes seemed smarter and he more awkward than usual.

"It is from a lady," he admitted. "But a bit of badinage, I assure you, nothing more!"

"Understood!" M. de Nançay murmured politely. "I congratulate you."

"But—"

"I say I congratulate you!"

"But it is nothing."

"Oh, I understand. And see, the King is about to rise. Go forward, Monsieur," he continued benevolently. "A young man should show himself. Besides, his Majesty likes you well," he added, with a leer. He had an unpleasant sense of humour, had his Majesty's Captain of the Guard; and this evening somewhat more than ordinary on which to exercise it.

Tignonville held too good an opinion of himself to suspect the other of badinage; and thus encouraged, he pushed his way to the front of the circle. During his absence with his betrothed, the crowd in the Chamber had grown thin, the candles had burned an inch shorter in the sconces. But though many who had been there had left, the more select remained, and the King's return to his seat had given the company a fillip. An air of feverish gaiety, common in the unhealthy life of the Court, prevailed. At a table abreast of the King, Montpensier and Marshal Cossé were dicing and disputing, with now a yell of glee, and now an oath, that betrayed which way fortune inclined. At the back of the King's chair, Chicot, his gentleman-jester, hung over Charles's shoulder, now scanning his cards, and now making hideous faces that threw the on-lookers into fits of laughter. Farther up the Chamber, at the end of the alcove, Marshal Tavannes—our Hannibal's brother—occupied a low stool, which was set opposite the open door of the closet. Through this doorway a slender foot, silk-clad, shot now and again into sight; it came, it vanished, it came again, the gallant Marshal striving at each appearance to rob it of its slipper, a dainty jewelled thing of crimson velvet. He failed thrice, a peal of laughter greeting each failure. At the fourth essay, he upset his stool and fell to the floor, but held the slipper. And not the slipper only, but the foot. Amid a flutter of silken skirts and dainty laces—while the hidden beauty shrilly protested—he dragged first the ankle, and then a shapely leg into sight. The circle applauded; the lady, feeling herself still drawn on, screamed loudly and more loudly. All save the King and his opponent turned to look. And then the sport came to a sudden end. A sinewy hand appeared, interposed, released; for an instant the dark, handsome face of Guise looked through the doorway. It was gone as soon as seen; it was there a second only. But more than one recognised it, and wondered. For was not the young Duke in evil odour with the King by reason of the attack on the Admiral? And had he not been chased from Paris only that morning and forbidden to return?

They were still wondering, still gazing, when abruptly—as he did all things—Charles thrust back his chair.

"Foucauld, you owe me ten pieces!" he cried with glee, and he slapped the table. "Pay, my friend; pay!"

"To-morrow, little master; to-morrow!" Rochefoucauld answered in the same tone. And he rose to his feet.

"To-morrow!" Charles repeated. "To-morrow?" And on the word his jaw fell. He looked wildly round. His face was ghastly.

"Well, sire, and why not?" Rochefoucauld answered in astonishment. And in his turn he looked round, wondering; and a chill fell on him. "Why not?" he repeated.

For a moment no one answered him: the silence in the Chamber was intense. Where he looked, wherever he looked, he met solemn, wondering eyes, such eyes as gaze on men in their coffins.

"What has come to you all?" he cried, with an effort. "What is the jest, for faith, sire, I don't see it?"

The King seemed incapable of speech, and it was Chicot who filled the gap.

"It is pretty apparent," he said, with a rude laugh. "The cock will lay and Foucauld will pay—to-morrow!"

The young nobleman's colour rose; between him and the Gascon gentleman was no love lost.

"There are some debts I pay to-day," he cried haughtily. "For the rest, farewell my little master! When one does not understand the jest it is time to be gone."

He was halfway to the door, watched by all, when the King spoke.

"Foucauld!" he cried, in an odd, strangled voice. "Foucauld!" And the Huguenot favourite turned back, wondering. "One minute!" the King continued, in the same forced voice. "Stay till morning—in my closet. It is late now. We'll play away the rest of the night!"

"Your Majesty must excuse me," Rochefoucauld answered frankly. "I am dead asleep."

"You can sleep in the Garde-Robe," the King persisted.

"Thank you for nothing, sire!" was the gay answer. "I know that bed! I shall sleep longer and better in my own."

The King shuddered, but strove to hide the movement under a shrug of his shoulders. He turned away.

"It is God's will!" he muttered. He was white to the lips.

Rochefoucauld did not catch the words. "Good night, sire," he cried. "Farewell, little master." And with a nod here and there, he passed to the door, followed by Mergey and Chamont, two gentlemen of his suite.

Nançay raised the curtain with an obsequious gesture. "Pardon me, M. le Comte," he said, "do you go to his Highness's?"

"For a few minutes, Nançay."

"Permit me to go with you. The guards may be set."

"Do so, my friend," Rochefoucauld answered. "Ah, Tignonville, is it you?"

"I am come to attend you to your lodging," the young man said. And he ranged up beside the other, as, the curtain fallen behind them, they walked along the gallery.

Rochefoucauld stopped and laid his hand on Tignonville's sleeve.

"Thanks, dear lad," he said, "but I am going to the Princess Dowager's. Afterwards to his Highness's. I may be detained an hour or more. You will not like to wait so long."

M. de Tignonville's face fell ludicrously. "Well, no," he said. "I—I don't think I could wait so long—to-night."

"Then come to-morrow night," Rochefoucauld answered, with good nature.

"With pleasure," the other cried heartily, his relief evident. "Certainly. With pleasure." And, nodding good night, they parted.

While Rochefoucauld, with Nançay at his side and his gentlemen attending him, passed along the echoing and now empty gallery, the younger man bounded down the stairs to the great hall of the Caryatides, his face radiant. He for one was not sleepy.

CHAPTER III
THE HOUSE NEXT THE GOLDEN MAID

We have it on record that before the Comte de la Rochefoucauld left the Louvre that night he received the strongest hints of the peril which threatened him; and at least one written warning was handed to him by a stranger in black, and by him in turn was communicated to the King of Navarre. We are told further that when he took his final leave, about the hour of eleven, he found the courtyard brilliantly lighted, and the three companies of guards—Swiss, Scotch, and French—drawn up in ranked array from the door of the great hall to the gate which opened on the street. But, the chronicler adds, neither this precaution, sinister as it appeared to some of his suite, nor the grave farewell which Rambouillet, from his post at the gate, took of one of his gentlemen, shook that chivalrous soul or sapped its generous confidence.

M. de Tignonville was young and less versed in danger than the Governor of Rochelle; with him, had he seen so much, it might have been different. But he left the Louvre an hour earlier—at a time when the precincts of the palace, gloomy-seeming to us in the light cast by coming events, wore their wonted aspect. His thoughts, moreover, as he crossed the courtyard, were otherwise employed. So much so, indeed, that though he signed to his two servants to follow him, he seemed barely conscious what he was doing; nor did he shake off his reverie until he reached the corner of the Rue Baillet. Here the voices of the Swiss who stood on guard opposite Coligny's lodgings, at the end of the Rue Bethizy, could be plainly heard. They had kindled a fire in an iron basket set in the middle of the road, and knots of them were visible in the distance, moving to and fro about their piled arms.

Tignonville paused before he came within the radius of the firelight, and, turning, bade his servants take their way home. "I shall follow, but I have business first," he added curtly.

The elder of the two demurred. "The streets are not too safe," he said. "In two hours or less, my lord, it will be midnight. And then—"

"Go, booby; do you think I am a child?" his master retorted angrily. "I've my sword and can use it. I shall not be long. And do you hear, men, keep a still tongue, will you?"

The men, country fellows, obeyed reluctantly, and with a full intention of sneaking after him the moment he had turned his back. But he suspected them of this, and stood where he was until they had passed the fire, and could no longer detect his movements. Then he plunged quickly into the Rue Baillet, gained through it the Rue du Roule, and traversing that also, turned to the right into the Rue Ferronerie, the main thoroughfare, east and west, of Paris. Here he halted in front of the long, dark outer wall of the Cemetery of the Innocents, in which, across the tombstones and among the sepulchres of dead Paris, the living Paris of that day, bought and sold, walked, gossiped, and made love.

About him things were to be seen that would have seemed stranger to him had he been less strange to the city. From the quarter of the markets north of him, a quarter which fenced in the cemetery on two sides, the same dull murmur proceeded, which Mademoiselle de Vrillac had remarked an hour earlier. The sky above the cemetery glowed with reflected light, the cause of which was not far to seek, for every window of the tall houses that overlooked it, and the huddle of booths about it, contributed a share of the illumination. At an hour late even for Paris, an hour when honest men should have been sunk in slumber, this strange brilliance did for a moment perplex him; but the past week had been so full of fêtes, of masques and frolics, often devised on the moment and dependent on the King's whim, that he set this also down to such a cause, and wondered no more.

The lights in the houses did not serve the purpose he had in his mind, but beside the closed gate of the cemetery, and between two stalls, was a votive lamp burning before an image of the Mother and Child. He crossed to this, and assuring himself by a glance to right and left that he stood in no danger from prowlers, he drew a note from his breast. It had been slipped into his hand in the gallery before he saw Mademoiselle to her lodging; it had been in his possession barely an hour. But brief as its contents were, and easily committed to memory, he had perused it thrice already.

"At the house next the Golden Maid, Rue Cinq Diamants, an hour before midnight, you may find the door open should you desire to talk farther with C. St. L."

As he read it for the fourth time the light of the lamp fell athwart his face; and even as his fine clothes had never seemed to fit him worse than when he faintly denied the imputations of gallantry launched at him by Nançay, so his features had never looked less handsome than they did now. The glow of vanity which warmed his cheek as he read the message, the smile of conceit which wreathed his lips, bespoke a nature not of the most noble; or the lamp did him less than justice. Presently he kissed the note, and hid it. He waited until the clock of St. Jacques struck the hour before midnight; and then moving forward, he turned to the right by way of the narrow neck leading to the Rue Lombard. He walked in the kennel here, his sword in his hand and his eyes looking to right and left; for the place was notorious for robberies. But though he saw more than one figure lurking in a doorway or under the arch that led to a passage, it vanished on his nearer approach. In less than a minute he reached the southern end of the street that bore the odd title of the Five Diamonds.

Situate in the crowded quarter of the butchers, and almost in the shadow of their famous church, this street—which farther north was continued in the Rue Quimcampoix—presented in those days a not uncommon mingling of poverty and wealth. On one side of the street a row of lofty gabled houses, built under Francis the First, sheltered persons of good condition; on the other, divided from these by the width of the road and a reeking kennel, a row of peat-houses, the hovels of cobblers and sausage-makers, leaned against shapeless timber houses which tottered upwards in a medley of sagging roofs and bulging gutters. Tignonville was strange to the place, and nine nights out of ten he would have been at a disadvantage. But, thanks to the tapers that to-night shone in many windows, he made out enough to see that he need search only the one side; and with a beating heart he passed along the row of newer houses, looking eagerly for the sign of the Golden Maid.

He found it at last; and then for a moment he stood puzzled. The note said, next door to the Golden Maid, but it did not say on which side. He scrutinised the nearer house, but he saw nothing to determine him; and he was proceeding to the farther, when he caught sight of two men, who, ambushed behind a horse-block on the opposite side of the roadway, seemed to be watching his movements. Their presence flurried him; but much to his relief his next glance at the houses showed him that the door of the farther one was unlatched. It stood slightly ajar, permitting a beam of light to escape into the street.

He stepped quickly to it—the sooner he was within the house the better—pushed the door open and entered. As soon as he was inside he tried to close the entrance behind him, but he found he could not; the door would not shut. After a brief trial he abandoned the attempt and passed quickly on, through a bare lighted passage which led to the foot of a staircase, equally bare. He stood at this point an instant and listened, in the hope that Madame's maid would come to him. At first he heard nothing save his own breathing; then a gruff voice from above startled him.

"This way, Monsieur," it said. "You are early, but not too soon!"

So Madame trusted her footman! M. de Tignonville shrugged his shoulders; but after all, it was no affair of his, and he went up. Halfway to the top, however, he stood, an oath on his lips. Two men had entered by the open door below—even as he had entered! And as quietly!

The imprudence of it! The imprudence of leaving the door so that it could not be closed! He turned, and descended to meet them, his teeth set, his hand on his sword, one conjecture after another whirling in his brain. Was he beset? Was it a trap? Was it a rival? Was it chance? Two steps he descended; and then the voice he had heard before cried again, but more imperatively—

"No, Monsieur, this way! Did you not hear me? This way, and be quick, if you please. By-and-by there will be a crowd, and then the more we have dealt with the better!"

He knew now that he had made a mistake, that he had entered the wrong house; and naturally his impulse was to continue his descent and secure his retreat. But the pause had brought the two men who had entered face to face with him, and they showed no signs of giving way. On the contrary.

"The room is above, Monsieur," the foremost said, in a matter-of-fact tone, and with a slight salutation. "After you, if you please," and he signed to him to return.

He was a burly man, grim and truculent in appearance, and his follower was like him. Tignonville hesitated, then turned and ascended. But as soon as he had reached the landing where they could pass him, he turned again.

"I have made a mistake, I think," he said. "I have entered the wrong house."

"Are you for the house next the Golden Maid, Monsieur?"

"Yes."

"Rue Cinq Diamants, Quarter of the Boucherie?"

"Yes."

"No mistake, then," the stout man replied firmly. "You are early, that is all. You have arms, I see. Maillard!"—to the person whose voice Tignonville had heard at the head of the stairs—"A white sleeve, and a cross for Monsieur's hat, and his name on the register. Come, make a beginning! Make a beginning, man."

"To be sure, Monsieur. All is ready."

"Then lose no time, I say. Here are others, also early in the good cause. Gentlemen, welcome! Welcome all who are for the true faith! Death to the heretics! 'Kill, and no quarter!' is the word to-night!"

"Death to the heretics!" the last comers cried in chorus. "Kill and no quarter! At what hour, M. le Prévot?"

"At daybreak," the Provost answered importantly. "But have no fear, the tocsin will sound. The King and our good man M. de Guise have all in hand. A white sleeve, a white cross, and a sharp knife shall rid Paris of the vermin! Gentlemen of the quarter, the word of the night is 'Kill, and no quarter! Death to the Huguenots!'"

"Death! Death to the Huguenots! Kill, and no quarter!" A dozen—the room was beginning to fill—waved their weapons and echoed the cry.

Tignonville had been fortunate enough to apprehend the position—and the peril in which he stood—before Maillard advanced to him bearing a white linen sleeve. In the instant of discovery his heart had stood a moment, the blood had left his cheeks; but with some faults, he was no coward, and he managed to hide his emotion. He held out his left arm, and suffered the beadle to pass the sleeve over it and to secure the white linen above the elbow. Then at a gesture he gave up his velvet cap, and saw it decorated with a white cross of the same material.

"Now the register, Monsieur," Maillard continued briskly; and waving him in the direction of a clerk, who sat at the end of the long table, having a book and a ink-horn before him, he turned to the next comer.

Tignonville would fain have avoided the ordeal of the register, but the clerk's eye was on him. He had been fortunate so far, but he knew that the least breath of suspicion would destroy him, and summoning his wits together he gave his name in a steady voice. "Anne Desmartins." It was his mother's maiden name, and the first that came into his mind.

"Of Paris?"

"Recently; by birth, of the Limousin."

"Good, Monsieur," the clerk answered, writing in the name. And he turned to the next. "And you, my friend?"

CHAPTER IV
THE EVE OF THE FEAST

It was Tignonville's salvation that the men who crowded the long white-walled room, and exchanged vile boasts under the naked flaring lights, were of all classes. There were butchers, natives of the surrounding quarter whom the scent of blood had drawn from their lairs; and there were priests with hatchet faces, who whispered in the butchers' ears. There were gentlemen of the robe, and plain mechanics, rich merchants in their gowns, and bare-armed ragpickers, sleek choristers, and shabby led-captains; but differ as they might in other points, in one thing all were alike. From all, gentle or simple, rose the same cry for blood, the same aspiration to be first equipped for the fray. In one corner a man of rank stood silent and apart, his hand on his sword, the working of his face alone betraying the storm that reigned within. In another, a Norman horse-dealer talked in low whispers with two thieves. In a third, a gold-wire drawer addressed an admiring group from the Sorbonne; and meantime the middle of the floor grew into a seething mass of muttering, scowling men, through whom the last comers, thrust as they might, had much ado to force their way.

And from all under the low ceiling rose a ceaseless hum, though none spoke loud. "Kill! kill! kill!" was the burden; the accompaniment such profanities and blasphemies as had long disgraced the Paris pulpits, and day by day had fanned the bigotry—already at a white heat—of the Parisian populace. Tignonville turned sick as he listened, and would fain have closed his ears. But for his life he dared not. And presently a cripple in a beggar's garb, a dwarfish, filthy creature with matted hair, twitched his sleeve, and offered him a whetstone.

"Are you sharp, noble sir?" he asked, with a leer. "Are you sharp? It's surprising how the edge goes on the bone. A cut and thrust? Well, every man to his taste. But give me a broad butcher's knife and I'll ask no help, be it man, woman, or child!"

A bystander, a lean man in rusty black, chuckled as he listened.

"But the woman or the child for choice, eh, Jehan?" he said. And he looked to Tignonville to join in the jest.

"Ay, give me a white throat for choice!" the cripple answered, with horrible zest. "And there'll be delicate necks to prick to-night! Lord, I think I hear them squeal! You don't need it, sir?" he continued, again proffering the whetstone. "No? Then I'll give my blade another whet, in the name of our Lady, the Saints, and good Father Pezelay!"

"Ay, and give me a turn!" the lean man cried, proffering his weapon. "May I die if I do not kill one of the accursed for every finger of my hands!"

"And toe of my feet!" the cripple answered, not to be outdone. "And toe of my feet! A full score!"

"'Tis according to your sins!" the other, who had something of the air of a Churchman, answered. "The more heretics killed, the more sins forgiven. Remember that, brother, and spare not if your soul be burdened! They blaspheme God and call Him paste! In the paste of their own blood," he continued ferociously, "I will knead them and roll them out, saith the good Father Pezelay, my master!"

The cripple crossed himself. "Whom God keep," he said. "He is a good man. But you are looking ill, noble sir?" he continued, peering curiously at the young Huguenot.

"'Tis the heat," Tignonville muttered. "The night is stifling, and the lights make it worse. I will go nearer the door."

He hoped to escape them; he had some hope even of escaping from the room and giving the alarm. But when he had forced his way to the threshold, he found it guarded by two pikemen; and glancing back to see if his movements were observed—for he knew that his agitation might have awakened suspicion—he found that the taller of the two whom he had left, the black-garbed man with the hungry face, was watching him a-tiptoe, over the shoulders of the crowd.

With that, and the sense of his impotence, the lights began to swim before his eyes. The catastrophe that overhung his party, the fate so treacherously prepared for all whom he loved and all with whom his fortunes were bound up, confused his brain almost to delirium. He strove to think, to calculate chances, to imagine some way in which he might escape from the room, or from a window might cry the alarm. But he could not bring his mind to a point. Instead, in lightning flashes he foresaw what must happen: his betrothed in the hands of the murderers; the fair face that had smiled on him frozen with terror; brave men, the fighters of Montauban, the defenders of Angely, strewn dead through the dark lanes of the city. And now a gust of passion, and now a shudder of fear, seized him; and in any other assembly his agitation must have led to detection. But in that room were many twitching faces and trembling hands. Murder, cruel, midnight, and most foul, wrung even from the murderers her toll of horror. While some, to hide the nervousness they felt, babbled of what they would do, others betrayed by the intentness with which they awaited the signal, the dreadful anticipations that possessed their souls.

Before he had formed any plan, a movement took place near the door. The stairs shook beneath the sudden trampling of feet, a voice cried "De par le Roi! De par le Roi!" and the babel of the room died down. The throng swayed and fell back on either hand, and Marshal Tavannes entered, wearing half armour, with a white sash; he was followed by six or eight gentlemen in like guise. Amid cries of "Jarnac! Jarnac!" — for to him the credit of that famous fight, nominally won by the King's brother, was popularly given — he advanced up the room, met the Provost of the merchants, and began to confer with him. Apparently he asked the latter to select some men who could be trusted on a special mission, for the Provost looked round and beckoned to his side one or two of higher rank than the herd, and then one or two of the most truculent aspect.

Tignonville trembled lest he should be singled out. He had hidden himself as well as he could at the rear of the crowd by the door; but his dress, so much above the common, rendered him conspicuous. He fancied that the Provost's eye ranged the crowd for him; and to avoid it and efface himself he moved a pace to his left.

The step was fatal. It saved him from the Provost, but it brought him face to face and eye to eye with Count Hannibal, who stood in the first rank at his brother's elbow. Tavannes stared an instant as if he doubted his eyesight. Then, as doubt gave slow place to certainty, and surprise to amazement, he smiled. And after a moment he looked another way.

Tignonville's heart gave a great bump and seemed to stand still. The lights whirled before his eyes, there was a roaring in his ears. He waited for the word that should denounce him. It did not come. And still it did not come; and Marshal Tavannes was turning. Yes, turning, and going; the Provost, bowing low, was attending him to the door; his suite were opening on either side to let him pass. And Count Hannibal? Count Hannibal was following also, as if nothing had occurred. As if he had seen nothing!

The young man caught his breath. Was it possible that he had imagined the start of recognition, the steady scrutiny, the sinister smile? No; for as Tavannes followed the others, he hung an instant on his heel, their eyes met again, and once more he smiled. In the next breath he was gone through the doorway, his spurs rang on the stairs; and the babel of the crowd, checked by the great man's presence, broke out anew, and louder.

Tignonville shuddered. He was saved as by a miracle; saved, he did not know how. But the respite, though its strangeness diverted his thoughts for a while, brought short relief. The horrors which impended over others surged afresh into his mind, and filled him with a maddening sense of impotence. To be one hour, only one short half-hour without! To run through the sleeping streets, and scream in the dull ears which a King's flatteries had stopped as with wool! To go up and down and shake into life the guests whose royal lodgings daybreak would turn to a shambles reeking with their blood! They slept, the gentle Teligny, the brave Pardaillan, the gallant Rochefoucauld, Piles the hero of St. Jean, while the cruel city stirred rustling about them, and doom crept whispering to the door. They slept, they and a thousand others, gentle and simple, young and old; while the half-mad Valois shifted between two opinions, and the Italian woman, accursed daughter of an accursed race, cried, "Hark!" at her window, and looked eastwards for the dawn.

And the women? The woman he was to marry? And the others? In an access of passion he thrust aside those who stood between, he pushed his way, disregarding complaints, disregarding opposition, to the door. But the pikes lay across it, and he could not utter a syllable to save his life. He would have flung himself on the doorkeepers, for he was losing control of himself; but as he drew back for the spring, a hand clutched his sleeve, and a voice he loathed hummed in his ear.

"No, fair play, noble sir; fair play!" the cripple Jehan muttered, forcibly drawing him aside. "All start together, and it's no man's loss. But if there is any little business," he continued, lowering his tone and peering with a cunning look into the other's face, "of your own, noble sir, or your friends', anything or anybody you want despatched, count on me. It were better, perhaps, you didn't appear in it yourself, and a man you can trust—"

"What do you mean?" the young man cried, recoiling from him.

"No need to look surprised, noble sir," the lean man, who had joined them, answered in a soothing tone. "Who kills to-night does God service, and who serves God much may serve himself a little. 'Thou shalt not muzzle the ox that treadeth out the corn,' says good Father Pezelay."

"Hear, hear!" the cripple chimed in eagerly, his impatience such that he danced on his toes. "He preaches as well as the good father his master! So frankly, noble sir, what is it? What is it? A woman grown ugly? A rich man grown old, with perchance a will in his chest? Or a young heir that stands in my lord's way? Whichever it be, or whatever it be, trust me and our friend here, and my butcher's gully shall cut the knot."

Tignonville shook his head.

"But something there is," the lean man persisted obstinately; and he cast a suspicious glance at Tignonville's clothes. It was evident that the two had discussed him, and the motives of his presence there. "Have the dice proved fickle, my lord, and are you for the jewellers' shops on the bridge to fill your purse again? If so, take my word, it were better to go three than one, and we'll enlist."

"Ay, we know shops on the bridge where you can plunge your arm elbow-deep in gold," the cripple muttered, his eyes sparkling greedily. "There's Baillet's, noble sir! There's a shop for you! And there's the man's shop who works for the King. He's lame like me. And I know the way to all. Oh, it will be a merry night if they ring before the dawn. It must be near daybreak now. And what's that?"

Ay, what was it? A score of voices called for silence; a breathless hush fell on the crowd. A moment the fiercest listened, with parted lips and starting eyes. Then, "It was the bell!" cried one, "let us out!" "It was not!" cried another. "It was a pistol shot!" "Anyhow let us out!" the crowd roared in chorus; "let us out!" And they pressed in a furious mass towards the door, as if they would force it, signal or no signal.

But the pikemen stood fast, and the throng, checked in their first rush, turned on one another, and broke into wrangling and disputing; boasting, and calling Heaven and the saints to witness how thoroughly, how pitilessly, how remorselessly they would purge Paris of this leprosy when the signal did sound. Until again above the babel a man cried "Silence!" and again they listened. And this time, dulled by walls and distance, but unmistakable by the ears of fear or hate, the heavy note of a bell came to them on the hot night air. It was the boom, sullen and menacing, of the death signal.

The doorkeepers lowered their pikes, and with a wild rush, as of wolves swarming on their prey, the band stormed the door, and thrust and struggled and battled a way down the narrow staircase, and along the narrow passage. "A bas les Huguenots! Mort aux Huguenots!" they shouted; and shrieking, sweating, spurning with vile hands, viler faces, they poured pell-mell into the street, and added their clamour to the boom of the tocsin that, as by magic and in a moment, turned the streets of Paris into a hell of blood and cruelty. For as it was here, so it was in a dozen other quarters.

Quickly as they streamed out—and to have issued more quickly would have been impossible—fiercely as they pushed and fought and clove their way, Tignonville was of the foremost. And for a moment, seeing the street clear before him and almost empty, the Huguenot thought that he might do something. He might outstrip the stream of rapine, he might carry the alarm; at worst he might reach his betrothed before harm befell her. But when he had sped fifty yards, his heart sank. True, none passed him; but under the spell of the alarm-bell the stones themselves seemed to turn to men. Houses, courts, alleys, the very churches vomited men. In a twinkling the street was alive with men, roared with them as with a rushing tide, gleamed with their lights and weapons, thundered with the volume of their thousand voices. He was no longer ahead, men were running before him, behind him, on his right hand and on his left. In every side-street, every passage, men were running; and not men only, but women, children, furious creatures without age or sex. And all the time the bell tolled overhead, tolled faster and faster, and louder and louder; and shots and screams, and the clash of arms, and the fall of strong doors began to swell the maelstrom of sound.

 He was in the Rue St. Honoré now, and speeding westward. But the flood still rose with him, and roared abreast of him. Nay, it outstripped him. When he came, panting, within sight of his goal, and lacked but a hundred paces of it, he found his passage barred by a dense mass of people moving slowly to meet him. In the heart of the press the light of a dozen torches shone on half as many riders mailed and armed; whose eyes, as they moved on, and the furious gleaming eyes of the rabble about them, never left the gabled roofs on their right. On these from time to time a white-clad figure showed itself, and passed from chimney-stack to chimney-stack, or, stooping low, ran along the parapet. Every time that this happened, the men on horseback pointed upwards and the mob foamed with rage.

 Tignonville groaned, but he could not help. Unable to go forward, he turned, and with others hurrying, shouting, and brandishing weapons, he pressed into the Rue du Roule, passed through it, and gained the Bethizy. But here, as he might have foreseen, all passage was barred at the Hôtel Ponthieu by a horde of savages, who danced and yelled and sang songs round the Admiral's body, which lay in the middle of the way; while to right and left men were bursting into houses and forcing new victims into the street. The worst had happened there, and he turned panting, regained the Rue St. Honoré, and, crossing it and turning left-handed, darted through side streets until he came again into the main thoroughfare a little beyond the Croix du Tiroir, that marked the corner of Mademoiselle's house.

 Here his last hope left him. The street swarmed with bands of men hurrying to and fro as in a sacked city. The scum of the Halles, the rabble of the quarter poured this way and that, here at random, there swayed and directed by a few knots of men-at-arms, whose corselets reflected the glare of a hundred torches. At one time and within sight, three or four houses were being stormed. On every side rose heart-rending cries, mingled with brutal laughter, with savage jests, with cries of "To the river!" The most cruel of cities had burst its bounds and was not to be stayed; nor would be stayed until the Seine ran red to the sea, and leagues below, in pleasant Normandy hamlets, men, for fear of the pestilence, pushed the corpses from the bridges with poles and boat-hooks.

All this Tignonville saw, though his eyes, leaping the turmoil, looked only to the door at which he had left Mademoiselle a few hours earlier. There a crowd of men pressed and struggled; but from the spot where he stood he could see no more. That was enough, however. Rage nerved him, and despair; his world was dying round him. If he could not save her he would avenge her. Recklessly he plunged into the tumult; blade in hand, with vigorous blows he thrust his way through, his white sleeve and the white cross in his hat gaining him passage until he reached the fringe of the band who beset the door. Here his first attempt to pass failed; and he might have remained hampered by the crowd, if a squad of archers had not ridden up. As they spurred to the spot, heedless over whom they rode, he clutched a stirrup, and was borne with them into the heart of the crowd. In a twinkling he stood on the threshold of the house, face to face and foot to foot with Count Hannibal, who stood also on the threshold, but with his back to the door, which, unbarred and unbolted, gaped open behind him.

CHAPTER V
ROUGH WOOING

The young man had caught the delirium that was abroad that night. The rage of the trapped beast was in his heart, his hand held a sword. To strike blindly, to strike without question the first who withstood him was the wild-beast instinct; and if Count Hannibal had not spoken on the instant, the Marshal's brother had said his last word in the world.

Yet as he stood there, a head above the crowd, he seemed unconscious alike of Tignonville and the point that all but pricked his breast. Swart and grim-visaged, his harsh features distorted by the glare which shone upon him, he looked beyond the Huguenot to the sea of tossing arms and raging faces that surged about the saddles of the horsemen. It was to these he spoke.

"Begone, dogs!" he cried, in a voice that startled the nearest, "or I will whip you away with my stirrup-leathers! Do you hear? Begone! This house is not for you! Burn, kill, plunder where you will, but go hence!"

"But 'tis on the list!" one of the wretches yelled. "'Tis on the list!" And he pushed forward until he stood at Tignonville's elbow.

"And has no cross!" shrieked another, thrusting himself forward in his turn. "See you, let us by, whoever you are! In the King's name, kill! It has no cross!"

"Then," Tavannes thundered, "will I nail you for a cross to the front of it! No cross, say you? I will make one of you, foul crow!"

And as he spoke, his arm shot out; the man recoiled, his fellow likewise. But one of the mounted archers took up the matter.

"Nay, but, my lord," he said—he knew Tavannes—"it is the King's will there be no favour shown to-night to any, small or great. And this house is registered, and is full of heretics."

"And has no cross!" the rabble urged in chorus. And they leapt up and down in their impatience, and to see the better. "And has no cross!" they persisted. They could understand that. Of what use crosses, if they were not to kill where there was no cross? Daylight was not plainer. Tavannes' face grew dark, and he shook his finger at the archer who had spoken.

"Rogue," he cried, "does the King's will run here only? Are there no other houses to sack or men to kill, that you must beard me? And favour? You will have little of mine, if you do not budge and take your vile tail with you! Off! Or must I cry 'Tavannes!' and bid my people sweep you from the streets?"

The foremost rank hesitated, awed by his manner and his name; while the rearmost, attracted by the prospect of easier pillage, had gone off already. The rest wavered; and another and another broke away. The archer who had put himself forward saw which way the wind was blowing, and he shrugged his shoulders.

"Well, my lord, as you will," he said sullenly. "All the same I would advise you to close the door and bolt and bar. We shall not be the last to call to-day." And he turned his horse in ill-humour, and forced it, snorting and plunging, through the crowd.

"Bolt and bar?" Tavannes cried after him in fury. "See you my answer to that!" And turning on the threshold, "Within there!" he cried. "Open the shutters and set lights, and the table! Light, I say; light! And lay on quickly, if you value your lives! And throw open, for I sup with your mistress to-night, if it rain blood without! Do you hear me, rogues? Set on!"

He flung the last word at the quaking servants; then he turned again to the street. He saw that the crowd was melting, and, looking in Tignonville's face, he laughed aloud.

"Does Monsieur sup with us?" he said. "To complete the party? Or will he choose to sup with our friends yonder? It is for him to say. I confess, for my part," with an awful smile, "their hospitality seems a trifle crude, and boisterous."

Tignonville looked behind him and shuddered. The same horde which had so lately pressed about the door had found a victim lower down the street, and, as Tavannes spoke, came driving back along the roadway, a mass of tossing lights and leaping, running figures, from the heart of which rose the screams of a creature in torture. So terrible were the sounds that Tignonville leant half swooning against the door-post; and even the iron heart of Tavannes seemed moved for a moment.

For a moment only: then he looked at his companion, and his lip curled.

"You'll join us, I think?" he said, with an undisguised sneer. "Then, after you, Monsieur. They are opening the shutters. Doubtless the table is laid, and Mademoiselle is expecting us. After you, Monsieur, if you please. A few hours ago I should have gone first, for you, in this house"—with a sinister smile—"were at home! Now, we have changed places."

Whatever he meant by the gibe—and some smack of an evil jest lurked in his tone—he played the host so far as to urge his bewildered companion along the passage and into the living-chamber on the left, where he had seen from without that his orders to light and lay were being executed. A dozen candles shone on the board, and lit up the apartment. What the house contained of food and wine had been got together and set on the table; from the low, wide window, beetle-browed and diamond-paned, which extended the whole length of the room and looked on the street at the height of a man's head above the roadway, the shutters had been removed—doubtless by trembling and reluctant fingers. To such eyes of passers-by as looked in, from the inferno of driving crowds and gleaming weapons which prevailed outside—and not outside only, but throughout Paris—the brilliant room and the laid table must have seemed strange indeed!

To Tignonville, all that had happened, all that was happening, seemed a dream: a dream his entrance under the gentle impulsion of this man who dominated him; a dream Mademoiselle standing behind the table with blanched face and stony eyes; a dream the cowering servants huddled in a corner beyond her; a dream his silence, her silence, the moment of waiting before Count Hannibal spoke.

When he did speak it was to count the servants. "One, two, three, four, five," he said. "And two of them women. Mademoiselle is but poorly attended. Are there not"—and he turned to her—"some lacking?"

The girl opened her lips twice, but no sound issued. The third time—

"Two went out," she muttered in a hoarse, strangled voice, "and have not returned."

"And have not returned?" he answered, raising his eyebrows. "Then I fear we must not wait for them. We might wait long!" And turning sharply to the panic-stricken servants, "Go you to your places! Do you not see that Mademoiselle waits to be served?"

The girl shuddered and spoke.

"Do you wish me," she muttered, in the same strangled tone, "to play this farce—to the end?"

"The end may be better, Mademoiselle, than you think," he answered, bowing. And then to the miserable servants, who hung back afraid to leave the shelter of their mistress's skirts, "To your places!" he cried. "Set Mademoiselle's chair. Are you so remiss on other days? If so," with a look of terrible meaning, "you will be the less loss! Now, Mademoiselle, may I have the honour? And when we are at table we can talk."

He extended his hand, and, obedient to his gesture, she moved to the place at the head of the table, but without letting her fingers come into contact with his. He gave no sign that he noticed this, but he strode to the place on her right, and signed to Tignonville to take that on her left.

"Will you not be seated?" he continued. For she kept her feet.

She turned her head stiffly, until for the first time her eyes looked into his. A shudder more violent than the last shook her.

"Had you not better—kill us at once?" she whispered. The blood had forsaken even her lips. Her face was the face of a statue—white, beautiful, lifeless.

"I think not," he said gravely. "Be seated, and let us hope for the best. And you, sir," he continued, turning to Carlat, "serve your mistress with wine. She needs it."

The steward filled for her, and then for each of the men, his shaking hand spilling as much as it poured. Nor was this strange. Above the din and uproar of the street, above the crash of distant doors, above the tocsin that still rang from the reeling steeple of St. Germain's, the great bell of the Palais on the island had just begun to hurl its note of doom upon the town. A woman crouching at the end of the chamber burst into hysterical weeping, but, at a glance from Tavannes' terrible eye, was mute again.

Tignonville found voice at last. "Have they—killed the Admiral?" he muttered, his eyes on the table.

"M. Coligny? An hour ago."

"And Teligny?"

"Him also."

"M. de Rochefoucauld?"

"They are dealing with M. le Comte now, I believe," Tavannes answered. "He had his chance and cast it away." And he began to eat.

The man at the table shuddered. The woman continued to look before her, but her lips moved as if she prayed. Suddenly a rush of feet, a roar of voices surged past the window; for a moment the glare of the torches, which danced ruddily on the walls of the room, showed a severed head borne above the multitude on a pike. Mademoiselle, with a low cry, made an effort to rise, but Count Hannibal grasped her wrist, and she sank back half fainting. Then the nearer clamour sank a little, and the bells, unchallenged, flung their iron tongues above the maddened city. In the east the dawn was growing; soon its grey light would fall on cold hearths, on battered doors and shattered weapons, on hordes of wretches drunk with greed and hate.

When he could be heard, "What are you going to do with us?" the man asked hoarsely.

"That depends," Count Hannibal replied, after a moment's thought.

"On what?"

"On Mademoiselle de Vrillac."

The other's eyes gleamed with passion. He leaned forward.

"What has she to do with it?" he cried. And he stood up and sat down again in a breath.

Tavannes raised his eyebrows with a blandness that seemed at odds with his harsh visage.

"I will answer that question by another question," he replied. "How many are there in the house, my friend?"

"You can count."

Tavannes counted again. "Seven?" he said. Tignonville nodded impatiently.

"Seven lives?"

"Well?"

"Well, Monsieur, you know the King's will?"

"I can guess it," the other replied furiously. And he cursed the King, and the King's mother, calling her Jezebel.

"You can guess it?" Tavannes answered; and then with sudden heat, as if that which he had to say could not be said even by him in cold blood, "Nay, you know it! You heard it from the archer at the door. You heard him say, 'No favour, no quarter for man, for woman, or for child. So says the King.' You heard it, but you fence with me. Foucauld, with whom his Majesty played to-night, hand to hand and face to face—Foucauld is dead! And you think to live? You?" he continued, lashing himself into passion. "I know not by what chance you came where I saw you an hour gone, nor by what chance you came by that and that"—pointing with accusing finger to the badges the Huguenot wore. "But this I know! I have but to cry your name from yonder casement, nay, Monsieur, I have but to stand aside when the mob go their rounds from house to house, as they will go presently, and you will perish as certainly as you have hitherto escaped!"

For the second time Mademoiselle turned and looked at him.

"Then," she whispered, with white lips, "to what end this—mockery?"

"To the end that seven lives may be saved, Mademoiselle," he answered, bowing.

"At a price?" she muttered.

"At a price," he answered. "A price which women do not find it hard to pay—at Court. 'Tis paid every day for pleasure or a whim, for rank or the *entrée*, for robes and gewgaws. Few, Mademoiselle, are privileged to buy a life; still fewer, seven!"

She began to tremble. "I would rather die—seven times!" she cried, her voice quivering. And she tried to rise, but sat down again.

"And these?" he said, indicating the servants.

"Far, far rather!" she repeated passionately.

"And Monsieur? And Monsieur?" he urged with stern persistence, while his eyes passed lightly from her to Tignonville and back to her again, their depths inscrutable. "If you love Monsieur, Mademoiselle, and I believe you do—"

"I can die with him!" she cried.

"And he with you?"

She writhed in her chair.

"And he with you?" Count Hannibal repeated, with emphasis; and he thrust forward his head. "For that is the question. Think, think, Mademoiselle. It is in my power to save from death him whom you love; to save you; to save this *canaille*, if it so please you. It is in my power to save him, to save you, to save all; and I will save all—at a price! If, on the other hand, you deny me that price, I will as certainly leave all to perish, as perish they will, before the sun that is now rising sets to-night!"

Mademoiselle looked straight before her, the flicker of a dreadful prescience in her eyes.

"And the price?" she muttered. "The price?"

"You, Mademoiselle."

"I?"

"Yes, you! Nay, why fence with me?" he continued gently. "You knew it, you have said it. You have read it in my eyes these seven days."

She did not speak, or move, or seem to breathe. As he said, she had foreseen, she had known the answer. But Tignonville, it seemed, had not. He sprang to his feet.

"M. de Tavannes," he cried, "you are a villain!"

"Monsieur?"

"You are a villain! But you shall pay for this!" the young man continued vehemently. "You shall not leave this room alive! You shall pay for this insult!"

"Insult?" Tavannes answered in apparent surprise; and then, as if comprehension broke upon him, "Ah! Monsieur mistakes me," he said, with a broad sweep of the hand. "And Mademoiselle also, perhaps? Oh! be content, she shall have bell, book, and candle; she shall be tied as tight as Holy Church can tie her! Or, if she please, and one survive, she shall have a priest of her own church—you call it a church? She shall have whichever of the two will serve her better. 'Tis one to me! But for paying me, Monsieur," he continued, with irony in voice and manner; "when, I pray you? In Eternity? For if you refuse my offer, you have done with time. Now? I have but to sound this whistle"—he touched a silver whistle which hung at his breast—"and there are those within hearing will do your business before you make two passes. Dismiss the notion, sir, and understand. You are in my power. Paris runs with blood, as noble as yours, as innocent as hers. If you would not perish with the rest, decide! And quickly! For what you have seen are but the forerunners, what you have heard are but the gentle whispers that predict the gale. Do not parley too long; so long that even I may no longer save you."

"I would rather die!" Mademoiselle moaned, her face covered. "I would rather die!"

"And see him die?" he answered quietly. "And see these die? Think, think, child!"

"You will not do it!" she gasped. She shook from head to foot.

"I shall do nothing," he answered firmly. "I shall but leave you to your fate, and these to theirs. In the King's teeth I dare save my wife and her people; but no others. You must choose—and quickly."

One of the frightened women—it was Mademoiselle's tiring-maid, a girl called Javette—made a movement, as if to throw herself at her mistress's feet. Tignonville drove her to her place with a word. He turned to Count Hannibal.

"But, M. le Comte," he said, "you must be mad! Mad, to wish to marry her in this way! You do not love her. You do not want her. What is she to you more than other women?"

"What is she to you more than other women?" Tavannes retorted, in a tone so sharp and incisive that Tignonville started, and a faint touch of colour crept into the wan cheek of the girl, who sat between them, the prize of the contest. "What is she more to you than other women? Is she more? And yet—you want her!"

"She is more to me," Tignonville answered.

"Is she?" the other retorted, with a ring of keen meaning. "Is she? But we bandy words and the storm is rising, as I warned you it would rise. Enough for you that I *do* want her. Enough for you that I *will* have her. She shall be the wife, the willing wife, of Hannibal de Tavannes—or I leave her to her fate, and you to yours!"

"Ah, God!" she moaned. "The willing wife!"

"Ay, Mademoiselle, the willing wife," he answered sternly. "Or no man's wife!"

CHAPTER VI
WHO TOUCHES TAVANNES?

In saying that the storm was rising Count Hannibal had said no more than the truth. A new mob had a minute before burst from the eastward into the Rue St. Honoré; and the roar of its thousand voices swelled louder than the importunate clangour of the bells. Behind its moving masses the dawn of a new day—Sunday, the 24th of August, the feast of St. Bartholomew—was breaking over the Bastille, as if to aid the crowd in its cruel work. The gabled streets, the lanes, and gothic courts, the stifling wynds, where the work awaited the workers, still lay in twilight; still the gleam of the torches, falling on the house-fronts, heralded the coming of the crowd. But the dawn was growing, the sun was about to rise. Soon the day would be here, giving up the lurking fugitive whom darkness, more pitiful, had spared, and stamping with legality the horrors that night had striven to hide.

And with day, with the full light, killing would grow more easy, escape more hard. Already they were killing on the bridge where the rich goldsmiths lived, on the wharves, on the river. They were killing at the Louvre, in the courtyard under the King's eyes, and below the windows of the Médicis. They were killing in St. Martin and St. Denis and St. Antoine; wherever hate, or bigotry, or private malice impelled the hand. From the whole city went up a din of lamentation, and wrath, and foreboding. From the Cour des Miracles, from the markets, from the Boucherie, from every haunt of crime and misery, hordes of wretched creatures poured forth; some to rob on their own account, and where they listed, none gainsaying; more to join themselves to one of the armed bands whose business it was to go from street to street, and house to house, quelling resistance, and executing through Paris the high justice of the King.

It was one of these swollen bands which had entered the street while Tavannes spoke; nor could he have called to his aid a more powerful advocate. As the deep "A bas! A bas!" rolled like thunder along the fronts of the houses, as the more strident "Tuez! Tuez!" drew nearer and nearer, and the lights of the oncoming multitude began to flicker on the shuttered gables, the fortitude of the servants gave way. Madame Carlat, shivering in every limb, burst into moaning; the tiring-maid, Javette, flung herself in terror at Mademoiselle's knees, and, writhing herself about them, shrieked to her to save her, only to save her! One of the men moved forward on impulse, as if he would close the shutters; and only old Carlat remained silent, praying mutely with moving lips and a stern, set face.

And Count Hannibal? As the glare of the links in the street grew brighter, and ousted the sickly daylight, his form seemed to dilate. He stilled the shrieking woman by a glance.

"Choose! Mademoiselle, and quickly!" he said. "For I can only save my wife and her people! Quick, for the pinch is coming, and 'twill be no boy's play."

A shot, a scream from the street, a rush of racing feet before the window seconded his words.

"Quick, Mademoiselle!" he cried. And his breath came a little faster. "Quick, before it be too late! Will you save life, or will you kill?"

She looked at her lover with eyes of agony, dumbly questioning him. But he made no sign, and only Tavannes marked the look.

"Monsieur has done what he can to save himself," he said, with a sneer. "He has donned the livery of the King's servants; he has said, 'Whoever perishes, I will live!' But—"

"Curse you!" the young man cried, and, stung to madness, he tore the cross from his cap and flung it on the ground. He seized his white sleeve and ripped it from shoulder to elbow. Then, when it hung by the string only, he held his hand.

"Curse you!" he cried furiously. "I will not at your bidding! I may save her yet! I *will* save her!"

"Fool!" Tavannes answered—but his words were barely audible above the deafening uproar. "Can you fight a thousand? Look! Look!" and seizing the other's wrist he pointed to the window.

The street glowed like a furnace in the red light of torches, raised on poles above a sea of heads; an endless sea of heads, and gaping faces, and tossing arms which swept on and on, and on and by. For a while it seemed that the torrent would flow past them and would leave them safe. Then came a check, a confused outcry, a surging this way and that; the torches reeled to and fro, and finally, with a dull roar of "Open! Open!" the mob faced about to the house and the lighted window.

For a second it seemed that even Count Hannibal's iron nerves shook a little. He stood between the sullen group that surrounded the disordered table and the maddened rabble, that gloated on the victims before they tore them to pieces. "Open! Open!" the mob howled: and a man dashed in the window with his pike.

In that crisis Mademoiselle's eyes met Tavannes' for the fraction of a second. She did not speak; nor, had she retained the power to frame the words, would they have been audible. But something she must have looked, and something of import, though no other than he marked or understood it. For in a flash he was at the window and his hand was raised for silence.

"Back!" he thundered. "Back, knaves!" And he whistled shrilly. "Do what you will," he went on in the same tone, "but not here! Pass on! Pass on!—do you hear?"

But the crowd were not to be lightly diverted. With a persistence brutal and unquestioning they continued to howl, "Open! Open!" while the man who had broken the window the moment before, Jehan, the cripple with the hideous face, seized the lead-work, and tore away a great piece of it. Then, laying hold of a bar, he tried to drag it out, setting one foot against the wall below. Tavannes saw what he did, and his frame seemed to dilate with the fury and violence of his character.

"Dogs!" he shouted, "must I call out my riders and scatter you? Must I flog you through the streets with stirrup-leathers? I am Tavannes; beware of me! I have claws and teeth and I bite!" he continued, the scorn in his words exceeding even the rage of the crowd, at which he flung them. "Kill where you please, rob where you please, but not where I am! Or I will hang you by the heels on Montfaucon, man by man! I will flay your backs. Go! Go! I am Tavannes!"

But the mob, cowed for a moment by the thunder of his voice, by his arrogance and recklessness, showed at this that their patience was exhausted. With a yell which drowned his tones they swayed forward; a dozen thundered on the door, crying, "In the King's name!" As many more tore out the remainder of the casement, seized the bars of the window, and strove to pull them out or to climb between them. Jehan, the cripple, with whom Tignonville had rubbed elbows at the rendezvous, led the way.

Count Hannibal watched them a moment, his harsh face bent down to them, his features plain in the glare of the torches. But when the cripple, raised on the others' shoulders, and emboldened by his adversary's inactivity, began to squeeze himself through the bars, Tavannes raised a pistol, which he had held unseen behind him, cocked it at leisure, and levelled it at the foul face which leered close to his. The dwarf saw the weapon and tried to retreat; but it was too late. A flash, a scream, and the wretch, shot through the throat, flung up his hands, and fell back into the arms of a lean man in black who had lent him his shoulder to ascend.

For a few seconds the smoke of the pistol filled the window and the room. There was a cry that the Huguenots were escaping, that the Huguenots were resisting, that it was a plot; and some shouted to guard the back and some to watch the roof, and some to be gone. But when the fumes cleared away, the mob saw, with stupor, that all was as it had been. Count Hannibal stood where he had stood before, a grim smile on his lips.

"Who comes next?" he cried in a tone of mockery. "I have more pistols!" And then with a sudden change to ferocity, "You dogs!" he went on. "You scum of a filthy city, sweepings of the Halles! Do you think to beard me? Do you think to frighten me or murder me? I am Tavannes, and this is my house, and were there a score of Huguenots in it, you should not touch one, nor harm a hair of his head! Begone, I say again, while you may! Seek women and children, and kill them. But not here!"

For an instant the mingled scorn and brutality of his words silenced them. Then from the rear of the crowd came an answer—the roar of an arquebuse. The ball whizzed past Count Hannibal's head, and, splashing the plaster from the wall within a pace of Tignonville, dropped to the ground.

Tavannes laughed. "Bungler!" he cried. "Were you in my troop I would dip your trigger-finger in boiling oil to teach you to shoot! But you weary me, dogs. I must teach you a lesson, must I?" And he lifted a pistol and levelled it. The crowd did not know whether it was the one he had discharged or another, but they gave back with a sharp gasp. "I must teach you, must I?" he continued with scorn. "Here, Bigot, Badelon, drive me these blusterers! Rid the street of them! A Tavannes! A Tavannes!"

Not by word or look had he before this betrayed that he had supports. But as he cried the name, a dozen men armed to the teeth, who had stood motionless under the Croix du Tiroir, fell in a line on the right flank of the crowd. The surprise for those nearest them was complete. With the flash of the pikes before their eyes, with the cold steel in fancy between their ribs, they fled every way, uncertain how many pursued, or if any pursuit there was. For a moment the mob, which a few minutes before had seemed so formidable that a regiment might have quailed before it, bade fair to be routed by a dozen pikes.

And so, had all in the crowd been what he termed them, the rabble and sweepings of the streets, it would have been. But in the heart of it, and felt rather than seen, were a handful of another kidney; Sorbonne students and fierce-eyed priests, with three or four mounted archers, the nucleus that, moving through the streets, had drawn together this concourse. And these with threats and curse and gleaming eyes stood fast, even Tavannes' daredevils recoiling before the tonsure. The check thus caused allowed those who had budged a breathing space. They rallied behind the black robes, and began to stone the pikes; who in their turn withdrew until they formed two groups, standing on their defence, the one before the window, the other before the door.

Count Hannibal had watched the attack and the check, as a man watches a play; with smiling interest. In the panic, the torches had been dropped or extinguished, and now between the house and the sullen crowd which hung back, yet grew moment by moment more dangerous, the daylight fell cold on the littered street and the cripple's huddled form prone in the gutter. A priest raised on the shoulders of the lean man in black began to harangue the mob, and the dull roar of assent, the brandished arms which greeted his appeal, had their effect on Tavannes' men. They looked to the window, and muttered among themselves. It was plain that they had no stomach for a fight with the Church, and were anxious for the order to withdraw.

But Count Hannibal gave no order, and, much as his people feared the cowls, they feared him more. Meanwhile the speaker's eloquence rose higher; he pointed with frenzied gestures to the house. The mob groaned, and suddenly a volley of stones fell among the pikemen, whose corselets rattled under the shower. The priest seized that moment. He sprang to the ground, and to the front. He caught up his robe and waved his hand, and the rabble, as if impelled by a single will, rolled forward in a huge one-fronted thundering wave, before which the two handfuls of pikemen—afraid to strike, yet afraid to fly—were swept away like straws upon the tide.

But against the solid walls and oak-barred door of the house the wave beat, only to fall back again, a broken, seething mass of brandished arms and ravening faces. One point alone was vulnerable, the window, and there in the gap stood Tavannes. Quick as thought he fired two pistols into the crowd; then, while the smoke for a moment hid all, he whistled.

Whether the signal was a summons to his men to fight their way back—as they were doing to the best of their power—or he had resources still unseen, was not to be known. For as the smoke began to rise, and while the rabble before the window, cowed by the fall of two of their number, were still pushing backward instead of forward, there rose behind them strange sounds—yells, and the clatter of hoofs, mingled with screams of alarm. A second, and into the loose skirts of the crowd came charging helter-skelter, pell-mell, a score of galloping, shrieking, cursing horsemen, attended by twice as many footmen, who clung to their stirrups or to the tails of the horses, and yelled and whooped, and struck in unison with the maddened riders.

"On! on!" the foremost shrieked, rolling in his saddle, and foaming at the mouth. "Bleed in August, bleed in May! Kill!" And he fired a pistol among the rabble, who fled every way to escape his rearing, plunging charger.

"Kill! Kill!" cried his followers, cutting the air with their swords, and rolling to and fro on their horses in drunken emulation. "Bleed in August, bleed in May!"

"On! On!" cried the leader, as the crowd which beset the house fled every way before his reckless onset. "Bleed in August, bleed in May!"

The rabble fled, but not so quickly but that one or two were ridden down, and this for an instant checked the riders. Before they could pass on—

"Ohé!" cried Count Hannibal from his window. "Ohé!" with a shout of laughter, "ride over them, dear brother! Make me a clean street for my wedding!"

Marshal Tavannes—for he, the hero of Jarnac, was the leader of this wild orgy—turned that way, and strove to rein in his horse.

"What ails them?" he cried, as the maddened animal reared upright, its iron hoofs striking fire from the slippery pavement.

"They are rearing like thy Bayard!" Count Hannibal answered. "Whip them, whip them for me! Tavannes! Tavannes!"

"What? This canaille?"

"Ay, that canaille!"

"Who touches my brother, touches Tavannes!" the Marshal replied, and spurred his horse among the rabble, who had fled to the sides of the street and now strove hard to efface themselves against the walls. "Begone, dogs; begone!" he cried, still hunting them. And then, "You would bite, would you?" And snatching another pistol from his boot, he fired it among them, careless whom he hit. "Ha! ha! That stirs you, does it!" he continued, as the wretches fled headlong. "Who touches my brother, touches Tavannes! On! On!"

Suddenly, from a doorway near at hand, a sombre figure darted into the roadway, caught the Marshal's rein, and for a second checked his course. The priest—for a priest it was, Father Pezelay, the same who had addressed the mob—held up a warning hand.

"Halt!" he cried, with burning eyes. "Halt, my lord! It is written, thou shalt not spare the Canaanitish woman. 'Tis not to spare the King has given command and a sword, but to kill! 'Tis not to harbour, but to smite! To smite!"

"Then smite I will!" the Marshal retorted, and with the butt of his pistol struck the zealot down. Then, with as much indifference as he would have treated a Huguenot, he spurred his horse over him, with a mad laugh at his jest. "Who touches my brother, touches Tavannes!" he yelled. "Touches Tavannes! On! On! Bleed in August, bleed in May!"

"On!" shouted his followers, striking about them in the same desperate fashion. They were young nobles who had spent the night feasting at the Palace, and, drunk with wine and mad with excitement, had left the Louvre at daybreak to rouse the city. "A Jarnac! A Jarnac!" they cried, and some saluted Count Hannibal as they passed. And so, shouting and spurring and following their leader, they swept away down the now empty street, carrying terror and a flame wherever their horses bore them that morning.

Tavannes, his hands on the ledge of the shattered window, leaned out laughing, and followed them with his eyes. A moment, and the mob was gone, the street was empty; and one by one, with sheepish faces, his pikemen emerged from the doorways and alleys in which they had taken refuge. They gathered about the three huddled forms which lay prone and still in the gutter: or, not three—two. For even as they approached them, one, the priest, rose slowly and giddily to his feet. He turned a face bleeding, lean, and relentless towards the window at which Tavannes stood. Solemnly, with the sign of the cross, and with uplifted hands, he cursed him in bed and at board, by day and by night, in walking, in riding, in standing, in the day of battle, and at the hour of death. The pikemen fell back appalled, and hid their eyes; and those who were of the north crossed themselves, and those who came from the south bent two fingers horse-shoe fashion. But Hannibal de Tavannes laughed; laughed in his moustache, his teeth showing, and bade them move that carrion to a distance, for it would smell when the sun was high. Then he turned his back on the street, and looked into the room.

CHAPTER VII
IN THE AMPHITHEATRE

The movements of the women had overturned two of the candles; a third had guttered out. The three which still burned, contending pallidly with the daylight that each moment grew stronger, imparted to the scene the air of a debauch too long sustained. The disordered board, the wan faces of the servants cowering in their corner, Mademoiselle's frozen look of misery, all increased the likeness; which a common exhaustion so far strengthened that when Tavannes turned from the window, and, flushed with his triumph, met the others' eyes, his seemed the only vigour, and he the only man in the company. True, beneath the exhaustion, beneath the collapse of his victims, there burned passions, hatreds, repulsions, as fierce as the hidden fires of the volcano; but for the time they smouldered ash-choked and inert.

He flung the discharged pistols on the table. "If yonder raven speak truth," he said, "I am like to pay dearly for my wife, and have short time to call her wife. The more need, Mademoiselle, for speed, therefore. You know the old saying, 'Short signing, long seisin'? Shall it be my priest, or your minister?"

M. de Tignonville started forward. "She promised nothing!" he cried. And he struck his hand on the table.

Count Hannibal smiled, his lip curling. "That," he replied, "is for Mademoiselle to say."

"But if she says it? If she says it, Monsieur? What then?"

Tavannes drew forth a comfit-box, such as it was the fashion of the day to carry, as men of a later time carried a snuff-box. He slowly chose a prune.

"If she says it?" he answered. "Then M. de Tignonville has regained his sweetheart. And M. de Tavannes has lost his bride."

"You say so?"

"Yes. But—"

"But what?"

"But she will not say it," Tavannes replied coolly.

"Why not?"

"Why not?"

"Yes, Monsieur, why not?" the younger man repeated, trembling.

"Because, M. de Tignonville, it is not true."

"But she did not speak!" Tignonville retorted, with passion—the futile passion of the bird which beats its wings against a cage. "She did not speak. She could not promise, therefore."

Tavannes ate the prune slowly, seemed to give a little thought to its flavour, approved it a true Agen plum, and at last spoke.

"It is not for you to say whether she promised," he returned dryly, "nor for me. It is for Mademoiselle."

"You leave it to her?"

"I leave it to her to say whether she promised."

"Then she must say No!" Tignonville cried in a tone of triumph and relief. "For she did not speak. Mademoiselle, listen!" he continued, turning with outstretched hands and appealing to her with passion. "Do you hear? Do you understand? You have but to speak to be free! You have but to say the word, and Monsieur lets you go! In God's name, speak! Speak then, Clotilde! Oh!" with a gesture of despair, as she did not answer, but continued to sit stony and hopeless, looking straight before her, her hands picking convulsively at the fringe of her girdle. "She does not understand! Fright has stunned her! Be merciful, Monsieur. Give her time to recover, to know what she does. Fright has turned her brain."

Count Hannibal smiled. "I knew her father and her uncle," he said, "and in their time the Vrillacs were not wont to be cowards. Monsieur forgets, too," he continued with fine irony, "that he speaks of my betrothed."

"It is a lie!"

Tavannes raised his eyebrows. "You are in my power," he said. "For the rest, if it be a lie, Mademoiselle has but to say so."

"You hear him?" Tignonville cried. "Then speak, Mademoiselle! Clotilde, speak! Say you never spoke, you never promised him!"

The young man's voice quivered with indignation, with rage, with pain; but most, if the truth be told, with shame—the shame of a position strange and unparalleled. For in proportion as the fear of death instant and violent was lifted from him, reflection awoke, and the situation in which he stood took uglier shape. It was not so much love that cried to her, love that suffered, anguished by the prospect of love lost; as in the highest natures it might have been. Rather it was the man's pride which suffered: the pride of a high spirit which found itself helpless between the hammer and the anvil, in a position so false that hereafter men might say of the unfortunate that he had bartered his mistress for his life. He had not! But he had perforce to stand by; he had to be passive under stress of circumstances, and by the sacrifice, if she consummated it, he would in fact be saved.

There was the pinch. No wonder that he cried to her in a voice which roused even the servants from their lethargy of fear.

"Say it!" he cried. "Say it, before it be too late. Say, you did not promise!"

Slowly she turned her face to him. "I cannot," she whispered; "I cannot. Go," she continued, a spasm distorting her features. "Go, Monsieur. Leave me. It is over."

"What?" he exclaimed. "You promised him?"

She bowed her head.

"Then," the young man cried, in a transport of resentment, "I will be no part of the price. See! There! And there!" He tore the white sleeve wholly from his arm, and, rending it in twain, flung it on the floor and trampled on it. "It shall never be said that I stood by and let you buy my life! I go into the street and I take my chance." And he turned to the door.

But Tavannes was before him. "No!" he said; "you will stay here, M. de Tignonville!" And he set his back against the door.

The young man looked at him, his face convulsed with passion.

"I shall stay here?" he cried. "And why, Monsieur? What is it to you if I choose to perish?"

"Only this," Tavannes retorted. "I am answerable to Mademoiselle now, in an hour I shall be answerable to my wife—for your life. Live, then, Monsieur; you have no choice. In a month you will thank me—and her."

"I am your prisoner?"

"Precisely."

"And I must stay here—to be tortured?" Tignonville cried.

Count Hannibal's eyes sparkled. Sudden stormy changes, from indifference to ferocity, from irony to invective, were characteristic of the man.

"Tortured!" he repeated grimly. "You talk of torture while Piles and Pardaillan, Teligny and Rochefoucauld lie dead in the street! While your cause sinks withered in a night, like a gourd! While your servants fall butchered, and France rises round you in a tide of blood! Bah!"—with a gesture of disdain—"you make me also talk, and I have no love for talk, and small time. Mademoiselle, you at least act and do not talk. By your leave I return in an hour, and I bring with me—shall it be my priest, or your minister?"

She looked at him with the face of one who awakes slowly to the full horror, the full dread, of her position. For a moment she did not answer. Then—

"A minister," she muttered, her voice scarcely audible.

He nodded. "A minister," he said lightly. "Very well, if I can find one." And walking to the shattered, gaping casement—through which the cool morning air blew into the room and gently stirred the hair of the unhappy girl—he said some words to the man on guard outside. Then he turned to the door, but on the threshold he paused, looked with a strange expression at the pair, and signed to Carlat and the servants to go out before him.

"Up, and lie close above!" he growled. "Open a window or look out, and you will pay dearly for it! Do you hear? Up! Up! You, too, old crop-ears. What! would you?"—with a sudden glare as Carlat hesitated—"that is better! Mademoiselle, until my return."

He saw them all out, followed them, and closed the door on the two; who, left together, alone with the gaping window and the disordered feast, maintained a strange silence. The girl, gripping one hand in the other as if to quell her rising horror, sat looking before her, and seemed barely to breathe. The man, leaning against the wall at a little distance, bent his eyes, not on her, but on the floor, his face gloomy and distorted.

His first thought should have been of her and for her; his first impulse to console, if he could not save her. His it should have been to soften, were that possible, the fate before her; to prove to her by words of farewell, the purest and most sacred, that the sacrifice she was making, not to save her own life but the lives of others, was appreciated by him who paid with her the price.

And all these things, and more, may have been in M. de Tignonville's mind; they may even have been uppermost in it, but they found no expression. The man remained sunk in a sombre reverie. He had the appearance of thinking of himself, not of her; of his own position, not of hers. Otherwise he must have looked at her, he must have turned to her;

he must have owned the subtle attraction of her unspoken appeal when she drew a deep breath and slowly turned her eyes on him, mute, asking, waiting what he should offer.

Surely he should have! Yet it was long before he responded. He sat buried in thought of himself, and his position, the vile, the unworthy position in which her act had placed him. At length the constraint of her gaze wrought on him, or his thoughts became unbearable; and he looked up and met her eyes, and with an oath he sprang to his feet.

"It shall not be!" he cried, in a tone low, but full of fury. "You shall not do it! I will kill him first! I will kill him with this hand! Or—" a step took him to the window, a step brought him back—ay, brought him back exultant, and with a changed face. "Or better, we will thwart him yet. See, Mademoiselle, do you see? Heaven is merciful! For a moment the cage is open!" His eye shone with excitement, the sweat of sudden hope stood on his brow as he pointed to the unguarded casement. "Come! it is our one chance!" And he caught her by her arm and strove to draw her to the window.

But she hung back, staring at him. "Oh no, no!" she cried.

"Yes, yes! I say!" he responded. "You do not understand. The way is open! We can escape, Clotilde, we can escape!"

"I cannot! I cannot!" she wailed, still resisting him.

"You are afraid?"

"Afraid?" she repeated the word in a tone of wonder. "No, but I cannot. I promised him. I cannot. And, O God!" she continued, in a sudden outburst of grief, as the sense of general loss, of the great common tragedy broke on her and whelmed for the moment her private misery. "Why should we think of ourselves? They are dead, they are dying, who were ours, whom we loved! Why should we think to live? What does it matter how it fares with us? We cannot be happy. Happy?" she continued wildly. "Are any happy now? Or is the world all changed in a night? No, we could not be happy. And at least you will live, Tignonville. I have that to console me."

"Live!" he responded vehemently. "I live? I would rather die a thousand times. A thousand times rather than live shamed! Than see you sacrificed to that devil! Than go out with a brand on my brow, for every man to point at me! I would rather die a thousand times!"

"And do you think that I would not?" she answered, shivering. "Better, far better die than—than live with him!"

"Then why not die?"

She stared at him, wide-eyed, and a sudden stillness possessed her. "How?" she whispered. "What do you mean?"

"That!" he said. As he spoke, he raised his hand and signed to her to listen. A sullen murmur, distant as yet, but borne to the ear on the fresh morning air, foretold the rising of another storm. The sound grew in intensity, even while she listened; and yet for a moment she misunderstood him. "O God!" she cried, out of the agony of nerves overwrought, "will that bell never stop? Will it never stop? Will no one stop it?"

"'Tis not the bell!" he cried, seizing her hand as if to focus her attention. "It is the mob you hear. They are returning. We have but to stand a moment at this open window, we have but to show ourselves to them, and we need live no longer! Mademoiselle! Clotilde!—if you mean what you say, if you are in earnest, the way is open!"

"And we shall die—together!"

"Yes, together. But have you the courage?"

"The courage?" she cried, a brave smile lighting the whiteness of her face. "The courage were needed to live. The courage were needed to do that. I am ready, quite ready. It can be no sin! To live with that in front of me were the sin! Come!" For the moment she had forgotten her people, her promise, all! It seemed to her that death would absolve her from all. "Come!"

He moved with her under the impulse of her hand until they stood at the gaping window. The murmur, which he had heard indistinctly a moment before, had grown to a roar of voices. The mob, on its return eastward along the Rue St. Honoré, was nearing the house. He stood, his arm supporting her, and they waited, a little within the window. Suddenly he stooped, his face hardly less white than hers: their eyes met; he would have kissed her.

She did not withdraw from his arm, but she drew back her face, her eyes half shut.

"No!" she murmured. "No! While I live I am his. But we die together, Tignonville! We die together. It will not last long, will it? And afterwards—"

She did not finish the sentence, but her lips moved in prayer, and over her features came a far-away look; such a look as that which on the face of another Huguenot lady, Philippa de Luns—vilely done to death in the Place Maubert fourteen years before—silenced the ribald jests of the lowest rabble in the world. An hour or two earlier, awed by the abruptness of the outburst, Mademoiselle had shrunk from her fate; she had known fear. Now that she stood out voluntarily to meet it, she, like many a woman before and since, feared no longer. She was lifted out of and above herself.

But death was long in coming. Some cause beyond their knowledge stayed the onrush of the mob along the street. The din, indeed, persisted, deafened, shook them; but the crowd seemed to be at a stand a few doors down the Rue St. Honoré. For a half-minute, a long half-minute, which appeared an age, it drew no nearer. Would it draw nearer? Would it come on? Or would it turn again?

The doubt, so much worse than despair, began to sap that courage of the man which is always better fitted to do than to suffer. The sweat rose on Tignonville's brow as he stood listening, his arm round the girl—as he stood listening and waiting. It is possible that when he had said a minute or two earlier that he would rather die a thousand times than live thus shamed, he had spoken beyond the mark. Or it is possible that he had meant his words to the full. But in this case he had not pictured what was to come, he had not gauged correctly his power of passive endurance. He was as brave as the ordinary man, as the ordinary soldier; but martyrdom, the apotheosis of resignation, comes more naturally to women than to men, more hardly to men than to women. Yet had the crisis come quickly he might have met it. But he had to wait, and to wait with that howling of wild beasts in his ears; and for this he was not prepared. A woman might be content to die after this fashion; but a man? His colour went and came, his eyes began to rove hither and thither. Was it even now too late to escape? Too late to avoid the consequences of the girl's silly persistence? Too late to—? Her eyes were closed, she hung half lifeless on his arm. She would not know, she need not know until afterwards. And afterwards she would thank him! Afterwards—meantime the window was open, the street was empty, and still the crowd hung back and did not come.

He remembered that two doors away was a narrow passage, which leaving the Rue St. Honoré turned at right angles under a beetling archway, to emerge in the Rue du Roule. If he could gain that passage unseen by the mob! He *would* gain it. With a swift movement, his mind made up, he took a step forward. He tightened his grasp of the girl's waist, and, seizing with his left hand the end of the bar which the assailants had torn from its setting in the window jamb, he turned to lower himself. One long step would land him in the street.

At that moment she awoke from the stupor of exaltation. She opened her eyes with a startled movement; and her eyes met his.

He was in the act of stepping backwards and downwards, dragging her after him. But it was not this betrayed him. It was his face, which in an instant told her all, and that he sought not death, but life! She struggled upright and strove to free herself. But he had the purchase of the bar, and by this time he was furious as well as determined. Whether she would or no, he would save her, he would drag her out. Then, as consciousness fully returned, she, too, took fire.

"No!" she cried, "I will not!" and she struggled more violently.

"You shall!" he retorted between his teeth. "You shall not perish here."

But she had her hands free, and as he spoke she thrust him from her passionately, desperately, with all her strength. He had his one foot in the air at the moment, and in a flash it was done. With a cry of rage he lost his balance, and, still holding the bar, reeled backwards through the window; while Mademoiselle, panting and half fainting, recoiled—recoiled into the arms of Hannibal de Tavannes, who, unseen by either, had entered the room a long minute before. From the threshold, and with a smile, all his own, he had watched the contest and the result.

CHAPTER VIII
TWO HENS AND AN EGG

M. de Tignonville was shaken by the fall, and in the usual course of things he would have lain where he was, and groaned. But when a man has once turned his back on death he is apt to fancy it at his shoulder. He has small stomach for surprises, and is in haste to set as great a distance as possible between the ugly thing and himself. So it was with the Huguenot. Shot suddenly into the full publicity of the street, he knew that at any instant danger might take him by the nape; and he was on his legs and glancing up and down before the clatter of his fall had travelled the length of three houses.

The rabble were still a hundred paces away, piled up and pressed about a house where men were being hunted as men hunt rats. He saw that he was unnoted, and apprehension gave place to rage. His thoughts turned back hissing hot to the thing that had happened, and in a paroxysm of shame he shook his fist at the gaping casement and the sneering face of his rival, dimly seen in the background. If a look would have killed Tavannes—and her—it had not been wanting.

For it was not only the man M. de Tignonville hated at this moment; he hated Mademoiselle also, the unwitting agent of the other's triumph. She had thrust him from her; she had refused to be guided by him; she had resisted, thwarted, shamed him. Then let her take the consequences. She willed to perish: let her perish!

He did not acknowledge even to himself the real cause of offence, the proof to which she had put his courage, and the failure of that courage to stand the test. Yet it was this, though he had himself provoked the trial, which burned up his chivalry, as the smuggler's fire burns up the dwarf heath upon the Landes. It was the discovery that in an heroic hour he was no hero that gave force to his passionate gesture, and next moment sent him storming down the beetling passage to the Rue du Roule, his heart a maelstrom of fierce vows and fiercer menaces.

He had reached the further end of the alley and was on the point of entering the street before he remembered that he had nowhere to go. His lodgings were no longer his, since his landlord knew him to be a Huguenot, and would doubtless betray him. To approach those of his faith whom he had frequented was to expose them to danger; and, beyond the religion, he had few acquaintances and those of the newest. Yet the streets were impossible. He walked them on the utmost edge of peril; he lurked in them under the blade of an impending axe. And, whether he walked or lurked, he went at the mercy of the first comers bold enough to take his life.

The sweat stood on his brow as he paused under the low arch of the alley-end, tasting the bitter forlornness of the dog banned and set for death in that sunlit city. In every window of the gable end which faced his hiding-place he fancied an eye watching his movements; in every distant step he heard the footfall of doom coming that way to his discovery. And while he trembled, he had to reflect, to think, to form some plan.

In the town was no place for him, and short of the open country no safety. And how could he gain the open country? If he succeeded in reaching one of the gates—St. Antoine, or St. Denis, in itself a task of difficulty—it would only be to find the gate closed, and the guard on the alert. At last it flashed on him that he might cross the river; and at the notion hope awoke. It was possible that the massacre had not extended to the southern suburb; possible, that if it had, the Huguenots who lay there—Frontenay, and Montgomery, and Chartres, with the men of the North—might be strong enough to check it, and even to turn the tables on the Parisians.

His colour returned. He was no coward, as soldiers go; if it came to fighting he had courage enough. He could not hope to cross the river by the bridge, for there, where the goldsmiths lived, the mob were like to be most busy. But if he could reach the bank he might procure a boat at some deserted point, or, at the worst, he might swim across.

From the Louvre at his back came the sound of gunshots; from every quarter the murmur of distant crowds, or the faint lamentable cries of victims. But the empty street before him promised an easy passage, and he ventured into it and passed quickly through it. He met no one, and no one molested him; but as he went he had glimpses of pale faces that from behind the casements watched him come and turned to watch him go; and so heavy on his nerves was the pressure of this silent ominous attention, that he blundered at the end of the street. He should have taken the southerly turning; instead he held on, found himself in the Rue Ferronerie, and a moment later was all but in the arms of a band of city guards, who were making a house-to-house visitation.

He owed his safety rather to the condition of the street than to his presence of mind. The Rue Ferronerie, narrow in itself, was so choked at this date by stalls and bulkheads, that an edict directing the removal of those which abutted on the cemetery had been issued a little before. Nothing had been done on it, however, and this neck of Paris, this main thoroughfare between the east and the west, between the fashionable quarter of the Marais and the fashionable quarter of the Louvre, was still a devious huddle of sheds and pent-houses. Tignonville slid behind one of these, found that it masked the mouth of an alley, and, heedless whither the passage led, ran hurriedly along it. Every instant he expected to hear the hue and cry behind him, and he did not halt or draw breath until he had left the soldiers far in the rear, and found himself astray at the junction of four noisome lanes, over two of which the projecting gables fairly met. Above the two others a scrap of sky appeared, but this was too small to indicate in which direction the river lay.

Tignonville hesitated, but not for long; a burst of voices heralded a new danger, and he shrank into a doorway. Along one of the lanes a troop of children, the biggest not twelve years old, came dancing and leaping round something which they dragged by a string. Now one of the hindmost would burl it onward with a kick, now another, amid screams of childish laughter, tripped headlong over the cord; now at the crossways they stopped to wrangle and question which way they should go, or whose turn it was to pull and whose to follow. At last they started afresh with a whoop, the leader singing and all plucking the string to the cadence of the air. Their plaything leapt and dropped, sprang forward, and lingered like a thing of life. But it was no thing of life, as Tignonville saw with a shudder when they passed him. The object of their sport was the naked body of a child, an infant!

His gorge rose at the sight. Fear such as he had not before experienced chilled his marrow. This was hate indeed, a hate before which the strong man quailed; the hate of which Mademoiselle had spoken when she said that the babes crossed themselves at her passing, and the houses tottered to fall upon her!

He paused a minute to recover himself, so deeply had the sight moved him; and as he stood, he wondered if that hate already had its cold eye fixed on him. Instinctively his gaze searched the opposite wall, but save for two small double-grated windows it was blind; time-stained and stone-built, dark with the ordure of the city lane, it seemed but the back of a house, which looked another way. The outer gates of an arched doorway were open, and a loaded haycart, touching either side and brushing the arch above, blocked the passage. His gaze, leaving the windows, dropped to this—he scanned it a moment; and on a sudden he stiffened. Between the hay and the arch a hand flickered an instant, then vanished.

Tignonville stared. At first he thought his eyes had tricked him. Then the hand appeared again, and this time it conveyed an unmistakable invitation. It is not from the unknown or the hidden that the fugitive has aught to fear, and Tignonville, after casting a glance down the lane—which revealed a single man standing with his face the other way—slipped across and pushed between the hay and the wall. He coughed.

A voice whispered to him to climb up; a friendly hand clutched him in the act, and aided him. In a second he was lying on his face, tight squeezed between the hay and the roof of the arch. Beside him lay a man whose features his eyes, unaccustomed to the gloom, could not discern. But the man knew him and whispered his name.

"You know me?" Tignonville muttered in astonishment.

"I marked you, M. de Tignonville, at the preaching last Sunday," the stranger answered placidly.

"You were there?"

"I preached."

"Then you are M. la Tribe!"

"I am," the clergyman answered quietly. "They seized me on my threshold, but I left my cloak in their hands and fled. One tore my stocking with his point, another my doublet, but not a hair of my head was injured. They hunted me to the end of the next street, but I lived and still live, and shall live to lift up my voice against this wicked city."

The sympathy between the Huguenot by faith and the Huguenot by politics was imperfect. Tignonville, like most men of rank of the younger generation, was a Huguenot by politics; and he was in a bitter humour. He felt, perhaps, that it was men such as this who had driven the other side to excesses such as these; and he hardly repressed a sneer.

"I wish I felt as sure!" he muttered bluntly. "You know that all our people are dead?"

"He can save by few or by many," the preacher answered devoutly. "We are of the few, blessed be God, and shall see Israel victorious, and our people as a flock of sheep!"

"I see small chance of it," Tignonville answered contemptuously.

"I know it as certainly as I knew before you came, M. de Tignonville, that you would come!"

"That *I* should come?"

"That some one would come," La Tribe answered, correcting himself. "I knew not who it would be until you appeared and placed yourself in the doorway over against me, even as Obadiah in the Holy Book passed before the hiding-place of Elijah."

The two lay on their faces side by side, the rafters of the archway low on their heads. Tignonville lifted himself a little, and peered anew at the other. He fancied that La Tribe's mind, shaken by the horrors of the morning and his narrow escape, had given way.

"You rave, man," he said. "This is no time for visions."

"I said naught of visions," the other answered.

"Then why so sure that we shall escape?"

"I am certified of it," La Tribe replied. "And more than that, I know that we shall lie here some days. The time has not been revealed to me, but it will be days and a day. Then we shall leave this place unharmed, as we entered it, and, whatever betide others, we shall live."

Tignonville shrugged his shoulders. "I tell you, you rave, M. la Tribe," he said petulantly. "At any moment we may be discovered. Even now I hear footsteps."

"They tracked me well-nigh to this place," the minister answered placidly.

"The deuce they did!" Tignonville muttered, with irritation. He dared not raise his voice. "I would you had told me that before I joined you, Monsieur, and I had found some safer hiding-place! When we are discovered—"

"Then," the other continued calmly, "you will see."

"In any case we shall be better farther back," Tignonville retorted. "Here, we are within an ace of being seen from the lane." And he began to wriggle himself backwards.

The minister laid his hand on him. "Have a care!" he muttered. "And do not move, but listen. And you will understand. When I reached this place—it would be about five o'clock this morning—breathless, and expecting each minute to be dragged forth to make my confession before men, I despaired as you despair now. Like Elijah under the juniper tree, I said, 'It is enough, O Lord! Take my soul also, for I am no better than my fellows!' All the sky was black before my eyes, and my ears were filled with the wailings of the little ones and the lamentations of women. 'O Lord, it is enough,' I prayed. 'Take my soul, or, if it be Thy will, then, as the angel was sent to take the cakes to Elijah, give me also a sign that I shall live.'"

For a moment he paused, struggling with overpowering emotion. Even his impatient listener, hitherto incredulous, caught the infection, and in a tone of awe murmured—

"Yes? And then, M. la Tribe!"

"The sign was given me. The words were scarcely out of my mouth when a hen flew up, and, scratching a nest in the hay at my feet, presently laid an egg."

Tignonville stared. "It was timely, I admit," he said. "But it is no uncommon thing. Probably it has its nest here and lays daily."

"Young man, this is new-mown hay," the minister answered solemnly. "This cart was brought here no further back than yesterday. It smells of the meadow, and the flowers hold their colour. No, the fowl was sent. To-morrow it will return, and the next, and the next, until the plague be stayed and I go hence. But that is not all. A while later a second hen appeared, and I thought it would lay in the same nest. But it made a new one, on the side on which you lie and not far from your foot. Then I knew that I was to have a companion, and that God had laid also for him a table in the wilderness."

"It did lay, then?"

"It is still on the nest, beside your foot."

Tignonville was about to reply when the preacher grasped his arm and by a sign enjoined silence. He did so not a moment too soon. Preoccupied by the story, narrator and listener had paid no heed to what was passing in the lane, and the voices of men speaking close at hand took them by surprise. From the first words which reached them, it was clear that the speakers were the same who had chased La Tribe as far as the meeting of the four ways, and, losing him there, had spent the morning in other business. Now they had returned to hunt him down; and but for a wrangle which arose among them and detained them, they had stolen on their quarry before their coming was suspected.

"'Twas this way he ran!" "No, 'twas the other!" they contended; and their words, winged with vile threats and oaths, grew noisy and hot. The two listeners dared scarcely to breathe. The danger was so near, it was so certain that if the men came three paces farther, they would observe and search the haycart, that Tignonville fancied the steel already at his throat. He felt the hay rustle under his slightest movement, and gripped one hand with the other to restrain the tremor of overpowering excitement. Yet when he glanced at the minister he found him unmoved, a smile on his face. And M. de Tignonville could have cursed him for his folly.

For the men were coming on! An instant, and they perceived the cart, and the ruffian who had advised this route pounced on it in triumph.

"There! Did I not say so?" he cried. "He is curled up in that hay, for the Satan's grub he is! That is where he is, see you!"

"Maybe," another answered grudgingly, as they gathered before it. "And maybe not, Simon!"

"To hell with your maybe not!" the first replied. And he drove his pike deep into the hay and turned it viciously.

The two on the top controlled themselves. Tignonville's face was livid; of himself he would have slid down amongst them and taken his chance, preferring to die fighting, to die in the open, rather than to perish like a rat in a stack. But La Tribe had gripped his arm and held him fast.

The man whom the others called Simon thrust again, but too low and without result. He was for trying a third time, when one of his comrades who had gone to the other side of the lane announced that the men were on the top of the hay.

"Can you see them?"

"No, but there's room and to spare."

"Oh, a curse on your room!" Simon retorted. "Well, you can look."

"If that's all, I'll soon look!" was the answer. And the rogue, forcing himself between the hay and the side of the gateway, found the wheel of the cart, and began to raise himself on it.

Tignonville, who lay on that hand, heard, though he could not see his movements. He knew what they meant, he knew that in a twinkling he must be discovered; and with a last prayer he gathered himself for a spring.

It seemed an age before the intruder's head appeared on a level with the hay; and then the alarm came from another quarter. The hen which had made its nest at Tignonville's feet, disturbed by the movement or by the newcomer's hand, flew out with a rush and flutter as of a great firework. Upsetting the startled Simon, who slipped swearing to the ground, it swooped scolding and clucking over the heads of the other men, and reaching the street in safety, scuttled off at speed, its outspread wings sweeping the earth in its rage.

They laughed uproariously as Simon emerged, rubbing his elbow.

"There's for you! There's your preacher!" his opponent jeered.

"D---n her! she gives tongue as fast as any of them!" gibed a second. "Will you try again, Simon? You may find another love-letter there!"

"Have done!" a third cried impatiently. "He'll not be where the hen is! Let's back! Let's back! I said before that it wasn't this way he turned! He's made for the river."

"The plague in his vitals!" Simon replied furiously. "Wherever he is, I'll find him!" And, reluctant to confess himself wrong, he lingered, casting vengeful glances at the hay.

But one of the other men cursed him for a fool; and presently, forced to accept his defeat or be left alone, he rejoined his fellows. Slowly the footsteps and voices receded along the lane; slowly, until silence swallowed them, and on the quivering strained senses of the two who remained behind, descended the gentle influence of twilight and the sweet scent of the new-mown hay on which they lay.

La Tribe turned to his companion, his eyes shining. "Our soul is escaped," he murmured, "even as a bird out of the snare of the fowler. The snare is broken and we are delivered!" His voice shook as he whispered the ancient words of triumph.

But when they came to look in the nest at Tignonville's feet there was no egg!

CHAPTER IX
UNSTABLE

And that troubled M. la Tribe no little, although he did not impart his thoughts to his companion. Instead they talked in whispers of the things which had happened; of the Admiral, of Teligny, whom all loved, of Rochefoucauld the accomplished, the King's friend; of the princes in the Louvre whom they gave up for lost, and of the Huguenot nobles on the farther side of the river, of whose safety there seemed some hope. Tignonville—he best knew why—said nothing of the fate of his betrothed, or of his own adventures in that connection. But each told the other how the alarm had reached him, and painted in broken words his reluctance to believe in treachery so black. Thence they passed to the future of the cause, and of that took views as opposite as light and darkness, as Papegot and Huguenot. The one was confident, the other in despair. And some time in the afternoon, worn out by the awful experiences of the last twelve hours, they fell asleep, their heads on their arms, the hay tickling their faces; and, with death stalking the lane beside them, slept soundly until after sundown.

When they awoke hunger awoke with them, and urged on La Tribe's mind the question of the missing egg. It was not altogether the prick of appetite which troubled him, but regarding the hiding-place in which they lay as an ark of refuge providentially supplied, protected and victualled, he could not refrain from asking reverently what the deficiency meant. It was not as if one hen only had appeared; as if no farther prospect had been extended. But up to a certain point the message was clear. Then when the Hand of Providence had shown itself most plainly, and in a manner to melt the heart with awe and thankfulness, the message had been blurred. Seriously the Huguenot asked himself what it portended.

To Tignonville, if he thought of it at all, the matter was the matter of an egg, and stopped there. An egg might alleviate the growing pangs of hunger; its non-appearance was a disappointment, but he traced the matter no farther. It must be confessed, too, that the haycart was to him only a haycart—and not an ark; and the sooner he was safely away from it the better he would be pleased. While La Tribe, lying snug and warm beside him, thanked God for a lot so different from that of such of his fellows as had escaped—whom he pictured crouching in dank cellars, or on roof-trees exposed to the heat by day and the dews by night—the young man grew more and more restive.

Hunger pricked him, and the meanness of the part he had played moved him to action. About midnight, resisting the dissuasions of his companion, he would have sallied out in search of food if the passage of a turbulent crowd had not warned him that the work of murder was still proceeding. He curbed himself after that and lay until daylight. But, ill content with his own conduct, on fire when he thought of his betrothed, he was in no temper to bear hardship cheerfully or long; and gradually there rose before his mind the picture of Madame St. Lo's smiling face, and the fair hair which curled low on the white of her neck.

He would, and he would not. Death that had stalked so near him preached its solemn sermon. But death and pleasure are never far apart; and at no time and nowhere have they jostled one another more familiarly than in that age, wherever the influence of Italy and Italian art and Italian hopelessness extended. Again, on the one side, La Tribe's example went for something with his comrade in misfortune; but in the other scale hung relief from discomfort, with the prospect of a woman's smiles and a woman's flatteries, of dainty dishes, luxury, and passion. If he went now, he went to her from the jaws of death, with the glamour of adventure and peril about him; and the very going into her presence was a lure. Moreover, if he had been willing while his betrothed was still his, why not now when he had lost her?

It was this last reflection—and one other thing which came on a sudden into his mind—which turned the scale. About noon he sat up in the hay, and, abruptly and sullenly, "I'll lie here no longer," he said; and he dropped his legs over the side. "I shall go."

The movement was so unexpected that La Tribe stared at him in silence. Then, "You will run a great risk, M. de Tignonville," he said gravely, "if you do. You may go as far under cover of night as the river, or you may reach one of the gates. But as to crossing the one or passing the other, I reckon it a thing impossible."

"I shall not wait until night," Tignonville answered curtly, a ring of defiance in his tone. "I shall go now! I'll lie here no longer!"

"Now?"

"Yes, now."

"You will be mad if you do," the other replied. He thought it the petulant outcry of youth tired of inaction; a protest, and nothing more.

He was speedily undeceived. "Mad or not, I am going!" Tignonville retorted. And he slid to the ground, and from the covert of the hanging fringe of hay looked warily up and down the lane. "It is clear, I think," he said. "Good-bye." And with no more, without one upward glance or a gesture of the hand, with no further adieu or word of gratitude, he walked out into the lane, turned briskly to the left, and vanished.

The minister uttered a cry of surprise, and made as if he would descend also.

"Come back, sir!" he called, as loudly as he dared. "M. de Tignonville, come back! This is folly or worse!"

But M. de Tignonville was gone.

La Tribe listened a while, unable to believe it, and still expecting his return. At last, hearing nothing, he slid, greatly excited, to the ground and looked out. It was not until he had peered up and down the lane and made sure that it was empty that he could persuade himself that the other had gone for good. Then he climbed slowly and seriously to his place again, and sighed as he settled himself.

"Unstable as water thou shalt not excel!" he muttered. "Now I know why there was only one egg."

Meanwhile Tignonville, after putting a hundred yards between himself and his bedfellow, plunged into the first dark entry which presented itself. Hurriedly, and with a frowning face, he cut off his left sleeve from shoulder to wrist; and this act, by disclosing his linen, put him in possession of the white sleeve which he had once involuntarily donned, and once discarded. The white cross on the cap he could not assume, for he was bareheaded. But he had little doubt that the sleeve would suffice, and with a bold demeanour he made his way northward until he reached again the Rue Ferronerie.

Excited groups were wandering up and down the street, and, fearing to traverse its crowded narrows, he went by lanes parallel with it as far as the Rue St. Denis, which he crossed. Everywhere he saw houses gutted and doors burst in, and traces of a cruelty and a fanaticism almost incredible. Near the Rue des Lombards he saw a dead child, stripped stark and hanged on the hook of a cobbler's shutter. A little farther on in the same street he stepped over the body of a handsome young woman, distinguished by the length and beauty of her hair. To obtain her bracelets, her captors had cut off her hands; afterwards—but God knows how long afterwards—a passer-by, more pitiful than his fellows, had put her out of her misery with a spit, which still remained plunged in her body.

M. de Tignonville shuddered at the sight, and at others like it. He loathed the symbol he wore, and himself for wearing it; and more than once his better nature bade him return and play the nobler part. Once he did turn with that intention. But he had set his mind on comfort and pleasure, and the value of these things is raised, not lowered, by danger and uncertainty. Quickly his stoicism oozed away; he turned again. Barely avoiding the rush of a crowd of wretches who were bearing a swooning victim to the river, he hurried through the Rue des Lombards, and reached in safety the house beside the Golden Maid.

He had no doubt now on which side of the Maid Madame St. Lo lived; the house was plain before him. He had only to knock. But in proportion as he approached his haven, his anxiety grew. To lose all, with all in his grasp, to fail upon the threshold, was a thing which bore no looking at; and it was with a nervous hand and eyes cast fearfully behind him that he plied the heavy iron knocker which adorned the door.

He could not turn his gaze from a knot of ruffians, who were gathered under one of the tottering gables on the farther side of the street. They seemed to be watching him, and he fancied—though the distance rendered this impossible—that he could see suspicion growing in their eyes. At any moment they might cross the roadway, they might approach, they might challenge him. And at the thought he knocked and knocked again. Why did not the porter come?

Ay, why? For now a score of contingencies came into the young man's mind and tortured him. Had Madame St. Lo withdrawn to safer quarters and closed the house? Or, good Catholic as she was, had she given way to panic, and determined to open to no one? Or was she ill? Or had she perished in the general disorder? Or—

And then, even as the men began to slink towards him, his heart leapt. He heard a footstep heavy and slow move through the house. It came nearer and nearer. A moment, and an iron-grated Judas-hole in the door slid open, and a servant, an elderly man, sleek and respectable, looked out at him.

Tignonville could scarcely speak for excitement. "Madame St. Lo?" he muttered tremulously. "I come to her from her cousin the Comte de Tavannes. Quick! quick! if you please. Open to me!"

"Monsieur is alone?"

"Yes! Yes!"

The man nodded gravely and slid back the bolts. He allowed M. de Tignonville to enter, then with care he secured the door, and led the way across a small square court, paved with red tiles and enclosed by the house, but open above to the sunshine and the blue sky. A gallery which ran round the upper floor looked on this court, in which a great quiet reigned, broken only by the music of a fountain. A vine climbed on the wooden pillars which supported the gallery, and, aspiring higher, embraced the wide carved eaves, and even tapestried with green the three gables that on each side of the court broke the skyline. The grapes hung nearly ripe, and amid their clusters and the green lattice of their foliage Tignonville's gaze sought eagerly but in vain the laughing eyes and piquant face of his new mistress. For with the closing of the door, and the passing from him of the horrors of the streets, he had entered, as by magic, a new and smiling world; a world of tennis and roses, of tinkling voices and women's wiles, a world which smacked of Florence and the South, and love and life; a world which his late experiences had set so far away from him, his memory of it seemed a dream. Now, as he drank in its stillness and its fragrance, as he felt its safety and its luxury lap him round once more, he sighed. And with that breath he rid himself of much.

The servant led him to a parlour, a cool shady room on the farther side of the tiny quadrangle, and, muttering something inaudible, withdrew. A moment later a frolicsome laugh, and the light flutter of a woman's skirt as she tripped across the court, brought the blood to his cheeks. He went a step nearer to the door, and his eyes grew bright.

CHAPTER X
MADAME ST. LO

So far excitement had supported Tignonville in his escape. It was only when he knew himself safe, when he heard Madame St. Lo's footstep in the courtyard and knew that in a moment he would see her, that he knew also that he was failing for want of food. The room seemed to go round with him; the window to shift, the light to flicker. And then again, with equal abruptness, he grew strong and steady and perfectly master of himself. Nay, never had he felt a confidence in himself so overwhelming or a capacity so complete. The triumph of that which he had done, the knowledge that of so many he, almost alone, had escaped, filled his brain with a delicious and intoxicating vanity. When the door opened, and Madame St. Lo appeared on the threshold, he advanced holding out his arms. He expected that she would fall into them.

But Madame only backed and curtseyed, a mischievous light in her eyes.

"A thousand thanks, Monsieur!" she said, "but you are more ready than I!" And she remained by the door.

"I have come to you through all!" he cried, speaking loudly because of a humming in his ears. "They are lying in the streets! They are dying, are dead, are hunted, are pursued, are perishing! But I have come through all to you!"

She curtseyed anew. "So I see, Monsieur!" she answered. "I am flattered!" But she did not advance, and gradually, light-headed as he was, he began to see that she looked at him with an odd closeness. And he took offence.

"I say, Madame, I have come to you!" he repeated. "And you do not seem pleased!"

She came forward a step and looked at him still more oddly.

"Oh yes," she said. "I am pleased, M. de Tignonville. It is what I intended. But tell me how you have fared. You are not hurt?"

"Not a hair!" he cried boastfully. And he told her in a dozen windy sentences of the adventure of the haycart and his narrow escape. He wound up with a foolish meaningless laugh.

"Then you have not eaten for thirty-six hours?" she said. And when he did not answer, "I understand," she continued, nodding and speaking as to a child. And she rang a silver handbell and gave an order.

She addressed the servant in her usual tone, but to Tignonville's ear her voice seemed to fall to a whisper. Her figure—she was small and fairy-like—began to sway before him; and then in a moment, as it seemed to him, she was gone, and he was seated at a table, his trembling fingers grasping a cup of wine which the elderly servant who had admitted him was holding to his lips. On the table before him were a spit of partridges and a cake of white bread. When he had swallowed a second mouthful of wine—which cleared his eyes as by magic—the man urged him to eat. And he fell to with an appetite that grew as he ate.

By-and-by, feeling himself again, he became aware that two of Madame's women were peering at him through the open doorway. He looked that way and they fled giggling into the court; but in a moment they were back again, and the sound of their tittering drew his eyes anew to the door. It was the custom of the day for ladies of rank to wait on their favourites at table; and he wondered if Madame were with them, and why she did not come and serve him herself.

But for a while longer the savour of the roasted game took up the major part of his thoughts; and when prudence warned him to desist, and he sat back, satisfied after his long fast, he was in no mood to be critical. Perhaps—for somewhere in the house he heard a lute—Madame was entertaining those whom she could not leave? Or deluding some who might betray him if they discovered him?

From that his mind turned back to the streets and the horrors through which he had passed; but for a moment and no more. A shudder, an emotion of prayerful pity, and he recalled his thoughts. In the quiet of the cool room, looking on the sunny, vine-clad court, with the tinkle of the lute and the murmurous sound of women's voices in his ears, it was hard to believe that the things from which he had emerged were real. It was still more unpleasant, and as futile, to dwell on them. A day of reckoning would come, and, if La Tribe were right, the cause would rally, bristling with pikes and snorting with war-horses, and the blood spilled in this wicked city would cry aloud for vengeance. But the hour was not yet. He had lost his mistress, and for that atonement must be exacted. But in the present another mistress awaited him, and as a man could only die once, and might die at any minute, so he could only live once, and in the present. Then *vogue la galère!*

As he roused himself from this brief reverie and fell to wondering how long he was to be left to himself, a rosebud tossed by an unseen hand struck him on the breast and dropped to his knees. To seize it and kiss it gallantly, to spring to his feet and look about him were instinctive movements. But he could see no one; and, in the hope of surprising the giver, he stole to the window. The sound of the lute and the distant tinkle of laughter persisted. The court, save for a page, who lay asleep on a bench in the gallery, was empty. Tignonville scanned the boy suspiciously; a male disguise was often adopted by the court ladies, and if Madame would play a prank on him, this was a thing to be reckoned with. But a boy it seemed to be, and after a while the young man went back to his seat.

Even as he sat down, a second flower struck him more sharply in the face, and this time he darted not to the window but to the door. He opened it quickly and looked out, but again he was too late.

"I shall catch you presently, *ma reine!*" he murmured tenderly, with intent to be heard. And he closed the door. But, wiser this time, he waited with his hand on the latch until he heard the rustling of a skirt, and saw the line of light at the foot of the door darkened by a shadow. That moment he flung the door wide, and, clasping the wearer of the skirt in his arms, kissed her lips before she had time to resist.

Then he fell back as if he had been shot! For the wearer of the skirt, she whom he had kissed, was Madame St. Lo's woman, and behind her stood Madame herself, laughing, laughing, laughing with all the gay abandonment of her light little heart.

"Oh, the gallant gentleman!" she cried, and clapped her hands effusively. "Was ever recovery so rapid? Or triumph so speedy? Suzanne, my child; you surpass Venus. Your charms conquer before they are seen!"

M. de Tignonville had put poor Suzanne from him as if she burned; and hot and embarrassed, cursing his haste, he stood looking awkwardly at them.

"Madame," he stammered at last, "you know quite well that—"

"Seeing is believing!"

"That I thought it was you!"

"Oh, what I have lost!" she replied. And she looked archly at Suzanne, who giggled and tossed her head.

He was growing angry. "But, Madame," he protested, "you know—"

"I know what I know, and I have seen what I have seen!" Madame answered merrily. And she hummed,

> "'Ce fut le plus grand jour d'esté
> Que m'embrassa la belle Suzanne!'

Oh yes, I know what I know!" she repeated. And she fell again to laughing immoderately; while the pretty piece of mischief beside her hung her head, and, putting a finger in her mouth, mocked him with an affectation of modesty.

The young man glowered at them between rage and embarrassment. This was not the reception, nor this the hero's return to which he had looked forward. And a doubt began to take form in his mind. The mistress he had pictured would not laugh at kisses given to another; nor forget in a twinkling the straits through which he had come to her, the hell from which he had plucked himself! Possibly the court ladies held love as cheap as this, and lovers but as playthings, butts for their wit, and pegs on which to hang their laughter. But—but he began to doubt, and, perplexed and irritated, he showed his feelings.

"Madame," he said stiffly, "a jest is an excellent thing. But pardon me if I say that it is ill played on a fasting man."

Madame desisted from laughter that she might speak. "A fasting man?" she cried. "And he has eaten two partridges!"

"Fasting from love, Madame."

Madame St. Lo held up her hands. "And it's not two minutes since he took a kiss!"

He winced, was silent a moment, and then seeing that he got nothing by the tone he had adopted he cried for quarter.

"A little mercy, Madame, as you are beautiful," he said, wooing her with his eyes. "Do not plague me beyond what a man can bear. Dismiss, I pray you, this good creature—whose charms do but set off yours as the star leads the eye to the moon—and make me the happiest man in the world by so much of your company as you will vouchsafe to give me."

"That may be but a very little," she answered, letting her eyes fall coyly, and affecting to handle the tucker of her low ruff. But he saw that her lip twitched; and he could have sworn that she mocked him to Suzanne, for the girl giggled.

Still by an effort he controlled his feelings. "Why so cruel?" he murmured, in a tone meant for her alone, and with a look to match. "You were not so hard when I spoke with you in the gallery, two evenings ago, Madame."

"Was I not?" she asked. "Did I look like this? And this?" And, languishing, she looked at him very sweetly after two fashions.

"Something."

"Oh, then I meant nothing!" she retorted with sudden vivacity. And she made a face at him, laughing under his nose. "I do that when I mean nothing, Monsieur! Do you see? But you are Gascon, and given, I fear, to flatter yourself."

Then he saw clearly that she played with him: and resentment, chagrin, pique got the better of his courtesy.

"I flatter myself?" he cried, his voice choked with rage. "It may be I do now, Madame, but did I flatter myself when you wrote me this note?" And he drew it out and flourished it in her face. "Did I imagine when I read this? Or is it not in your hand? It is a forgery, perhaps," he continued bitterly. "Or it means nothing? Nothing, this note bidding me be at Madame St. Lo's at an hour before midnight—it means nothing? At an hour before midnight, Madame!"

"On Saturday night? The night before last night?"

"On Saturday night, the night before last night! But Madame knows nothing of it? Nothing, I suppose?"

She shrugged her shoulders and smiled cheerfully on him. "Oh yes, I wrote it," she said. "But what of that, M. de Tignonville?"

"What of that?"

"Yes, Monsieur, what of that? Did you think it was written out of love for you?"

He was staggered for the moment by her coolness. "Out of what, then?" he cried hoarsely. "Out of what, then, if not out of love?"

"Why, out of pity, my little gentleman!" she answered sharply. "And trouble thrown away, it seems. Love!" And she laughed so merrily and spontaneously it cut him to the heart. "No; but you said a dainty thing or two, and smiled a smile; and like a fool, and like a woman, I was sorry for the innocent calf that bleated so prettily on its way to the butcher's! And I would lock you up, and save your life, I thought, until the blood-letting was over. Now you have it, M. de Tignonville, and I hope you like it."

Like it, when every word she uttered stripped him of the selfish illusions in which he had wrapped himself against the blasts of ill-fortune? Like it, when the prospect of her charms had bribed him from the path of fortitude, when for her sake he had been false to his mistress, to his friends, to his faith, to his cause? Like it, when he knew as he listened that all was lost, and nothing gained, not even this poor, unworthy, shameful compensation? Like it? No wonder that words failed him, and he glared at her in rage, in misery, in shame.

"Oh, if you don't like it," she continued, tossing her head after a momentary pause, "then you should not have come! It is of no profit to glower at me, Monsieur. You do not frighten me."

"I would—I would to God I had not come!" he groaned.

"And, I dare say, that you had never seen me—since you cannot win me!"

"That too," he exclaimed.

She was of an extraordinary levity, and at that, after staring at him a moment, she broke into shrill laughter.

"A little more, and I'll send you to my cousin Hannibal!" she said. "You do not know how anxious he is to see you. Have you a mind," with a waggish look, "to play bride's man, M. de Tignonville? Or will you give away the bride? It is not too late, though soon it will be!"

He winced, and from red grew pale. "What do you mean?" he stammered; and, averting his eyes in shame, seeing now all the littleness, all the baseness of his position, "Has he—married her?" he continued.

"Ho, ho!" she cried in triumph. "I've hit you now, have I, Monsieur? I've hit you!" And mocking him, "Has he—married her?" she lisped. "No; but he will marry her, have no fear of that! He will marry her. He waits but to get a priest. Would you like to see what he says?" she continued, playing with him as a cat plays with a mouse. "I had a note from him yesterday. Would you like to see how welcome you'll be at the wedding?" And she flaunted a piece of paper before his eyes.

"Give it me," he said.

She let him seize it the while she shrugged her shoulders. "It's your affair, not mine," she said. "See it if you like, and keep it if you like. Cousin Hannibal wastes few words."

That was true, for the paper contained but a dozen or fifteen words, and an initial by way of signature.

"I may need your shaveling to-morrow afternoon. Send him, and Tignonville in safeguard if he come.—H."

"I can guess what use he has for a priest," she said. "It is not to confess him, I warrant. It's long, I fear, since Hannibal told his beads."

M. de Tignonville swore. "I would I had the confessing of him!" he said between his teeth.

She clapped her hands in glee. "Why should you not?" she cried. "Why should you not? 'Tis time yet, since I am to send to-day and have not sent. Will you be the shaveling to go confess or marry him?" And she laughed recklessly. "Will you, M. de Tignonville? The cowl will mask you as well as another, and pass you through the streets better than a cut sleeve. He will have both his wishes, lover and clerk in one then. And it will be pull monk, pull Hannibal with a vengeance."

Tignonville gazed at her, and as he gazed courage and hope awoke in his eyes. What if, after all, he could undo the past? What if, after all, he could retrace the false step he had taken, and place himself again where he had been—by *her* side?

"If you meant it!" he exclaimed, his breath coming fast. "If you only meant what you say, Madame."

"If?" she answered, opening her eyes. "And why should I not mean it?"

"Because," he replied slowly, "cowl or no cowl, when I meet your cousin—"

"'Twill go hard with him?" she cried, with a mocking laugh. "And you think I fear for him. That is it, is it?"

He nodded.

"I fear just *so much* for him!" she retorted with contempt. "Just so much!" And coming a step nearer to Tignonville she snapped her small white fingers under his nose. "Do you see? No, M. de Tignonville," she continued, "you do not know Count Hannibal if you think that he fears, or that any fear for him. If you will beard the lion in his den, the risk will be yours, not his!"

The young man's face glowed. "I take the risk!" he cried. "And I thank you for the chance; that, Madame, whatever betide. But—"

"But what?" she asked, seeing that he hesitated and that his face fell.

"If he afterwards learn that you have played him a trick," he said, "will he not punish you?"

"Punish me?"

He nodded.

Madame laughed her high disdain. "You do not yet know Hannibal de Tavannes," she said. "He does not war with women."

CHAPTER XI
A BARGAIN

It is the wont of the sex to snatch at an ell where an inch is offered, and to press an advantage in circumstances in which a man, acknowledging the claims of generosity, scruples to ask for more. The habit, now ingrained, may have sprung from long dependence on the male, and is one which a hundred instances, from the time of Judith downwards, prove to be at its strongest where the need is greatest.

When Mademoiselle de Vrillac came out of the hour-long swoon into which her lover's defection had cast her, the expectation of the worst was so strong upon her that she could not at once credit the respite which Madame Carlat hastened to announce. She could not believe that she still lay safe, in her own room above stairs; that she was in the care of her own servants, and that the chamber held no presence more hateful than that of the good woman who sat weeping beside her.

As was to be expected, she came to herself sighing and shuddering, trembling with nervous exhaustion. She looked for *him*, as soon as she looked for any; and even when she had seen the door locked and double-locked, she doubted—doubted, and shook and hid herself in the hangings of the bed. The noise of the riot and rapine which prevailed in the city, and which reached the ear even in that locked room—and although the window, of paper, with an upper pane of glass, looked into a courtyard—was enough to drive the blood from a woman's cheeks. But it was fear of the house, not of the street, fear from within, not from without, which impelled the girl into the darkest corner and shook her wits. She could not believe that even this short respite was hers, until she had repeatedly heard the fact confirmed at Madame Carlat's mouth.

"You are deceiving me!" she cried more than once. And each time she started up in fresh terror. "He never said that he would not return until to-morrow!"

"He did, my lamb, he did!" the old woman answered with tears. "Would I deceive you?"

"He said he would not return?"

"He said he would not return until to-morrow. You had until to-morrow, he said."

"And then?"

"He would come and bring the priest with him," Madame Carlat replied sorrowfully.

"The priest? To-morrow!" Mademoiselle cried. "The priest!" and she crouched anew with hot eyes behind the hangings of the bed, and, shivering, hid her face.

But this for a time only. As soon as she had made certain of the respite, and that she had until the morrow, her courage rose, and with it the instinct of which mention has been made. Count Hannibal had granted a respite; short as it was, and no more than the barest humanity required, to grant one at all was not the act of the mere butcher who holds the trembling lamb, unresisting, in his hands. It was an act—no more, again be it said, than humanity required—and yet an act which bespoke an expectation of some return, of some correlative advantage. It was not in the part of the mere brigand. Something had been granted. Something short of the utmost in the captor's power had been exacted. He had shown that there were things he would not do.

Then might not something more be won from him? A further delay, another point; something, no matter what, which could be turned to advantage? With the brigand it is not possible to bargain. But who gives a little may give more; who gives a day may give a week; who gives a week may give a month. And a month? Her heart leapt up. A month seemed a lifetime, an eternity, to her who had but until to-morrow!

Yet there was one consideration which might have daunted a spirit less brave. To obtain aught from Tavannes it was needful to ask him, and to ask him it was needful to see him; and to see him *before* that to-morrow which meant so much to her. It was necessary, in a word, to run some risk; but without risk the card could not be played, and she did not hesitate. It might turn out that she was wrong, that the man was not only pitiless and without bowels of mercy, but lacked also the shred of decency for which she gave him credit, and on which she counted. In that case, if she sent for him—but she would not consider that case.

The position of the window, while it increased the women's safety, debarred them from all knowledge of what was going forward, except that which their ears afforded them. They had no means of judging whether Tavannes remained in the house or had sallied forth to play his part in the work of murder. Madame Carlat, indeed, had no desire to know anything. In that room above stairs, with the door double-locked, lay a hope of safety in the present, and of ultimate deliverance; there she had a respite from terror, as long as she kept the world outside. To her, therefore, the notion of sending for Tavannes, or communicating with him, came as a thunderbolt. Was her mistress mad? Did she wish to court her fate? To reach Tavannes they must apply to his riders, for Carlat and the men-servants were confined above. Those riders were grim, brutal men, who might resort to rudeness on their own account. And Madame, clinging in a paroxysm of terror to her mistress, suggested all manner of horrors, one on top of the other, until she increased her own terror tenfold. And yet, to do her justice, nothing that even her frenzied imagination suggested exceeded the things which the streets of Paris, fruitful mother of horrors, were witnessing at that very hour. As we now know.

For it was noon—or a little more—of Sunday, August the twenty-fourth, "a holiday, and therefore the people could more conveniently find leisure to kill and plunder." From the bridges, and particularly from the stone bridge of Notre Dame—while they lay safe in that locked room, and Tignonville crouched in his haymow—Huguenots less fortunate were being cast, bound hand and foot, into the Seine. On the river bank Spire Niquet, the bookman, was being burnt over a slow fire, fed with his own books. In their houses, Ramus the scholar and Goujon the sculptor—than whom Paris has neither seen nor deserved a greater—were being butchered like sheep; and in the Valley of Misery, now the Quai de la Megisserie, seven hundred persons who had sought refuge in the prisons were being beaten to death with bludgeons. Nay, at this hour—a little sooner or a little later, what matters it?—M. de Tignonville's own cousin, Madame d'Yverne, the darling of the Louvre the day before, perished in the hands of the mob; and the sister of M. de Taverny, equally ill-fated, died in the same fashion, after being dragged through the streets.

Madame Carlat, then, went not a whit beyond the mark in her argument. But Mademoiselle had made up her mind, and was not to be dissuaded.

"If I am to be Monsieur's wife," she said with quivering nostrils, "shall I fear his servants?"

And opening the door herself, for the others would not, she called. The man who answered was a Norman; and short of stature, and wrinkled and low-browed of feature, with a thatch of hair and a full beard, he seemed the embodiment of the women's apprehensions. Moreover, his *patois* of the cider-land was little better than German to them; their southern, softer tongue was sheer Italian to him. But he seemed not ill-disposed, or Mademoiselle's air overawed him; and presently she made him understand, and with a nod he descended to carry her message.

Then Mademoiselle's heart began to beat; and beat more quickly when she heard *his* step—alas! she knew it already, knew it from all others—on the stairs. The table was set, the card must be played, to win or lose. It might be that with the low opinion he held of women he would think her reconciled to her lot; he would think this an overture, a step towards kinder treatment, one more proof of the inconstancy of the lower and the weaker sex, made to be men's playthings. And at that thought her eyes grew hot with rage. But if it were so, she must still put up with it. She must still put up with it! She had sent for him, and he was coming—he was at the door!

He entered, and she breathed more freely. For once his face lacked the sneer, the look of smiling possession, which she had come to know and hate. It was grave, expectant, even suspicious; still harsh and dark, akin, as she now observed, to the low-browed, furrowed face of the rider who had summoned him. But the offensive look was gone, and she could breathe.

He closed the door behind him, but he did not advance into the room.

"At your pleasure, Mademoiselle?" he said simply. "You sent for me, I think."

She was on her feet, standing before him with something of the submissiveness of Roxana before her conqueror.

"I did," she said; and stopped at that, her hand to her side as if she could not continue. But presently in a low voice, "I have heard," she went on, "what you said, Monsieur, after I lost consciousness."

"Yes?" he said; and was silent. Nor did he lose his watchful look.

"I am obliged to you for your thought of me," she continued in a faint voice, "and I shall be still further obliged—I speak to you thus quickly and thus early—if you will grant me a somewhat longer time."

"Do you mean—if I will postpone our marriage?"

"Yes, Monsieur."

"It is impossible!"

"Do not say that," she cried, raising her voice impulsively. "I appeal to your generosity. And for a short, a very short, time only."

"It is impossible," he answered quietly. "And for reasons, Mademoiselle. In the first place, I can more easily protect my wife. In the second, I am even now summoned to the Louvre, and should be on my way thither. By to-morrow evening, unless I am mistaken in the business on which I am required, I shall be on my way to a distant province with royal letters. It is essential that our marriage take place before I go."

"Why?" she asked stubbornly.

He shrugged his shoulders. "Why?" he repeated. "Can you ask, Mademoiselle, after the events of last night? Because, if you please, I do not wish to share the fate of M. de Tignonville. Because in these days life is uncertain, and death too certain. Because it was our turn last night, and it may be the turn of your friends—to-morrow night!"

"Then some have escaped?" she cried.

He smiled. "I am glad to find you so shrewd," he replied. "In an honest wife it is an excellent quality. Yes, Mademoiselle; one or two."

"Who? Who? I pray you tell me."

"M. de Montgomery, who slept beyond the river, for one; and the Vidame, and some with him. M. de Biron, whom I count a Huguenot, and who holds the Arsenal in the King's teeth, for another. And a few more. Enough, in a word, Mademoiselle, to keep us wakeful. It is impossible, therefore, for me to postpone the fulfilment of your promise."

"A promise on conditions!" she retorted, in rage that she could win no more. And every line of her splendid figure, every tone of her voice flamed sudden, hot rebellion. "I do not go for nothing! You gave me the lives of all in the house, Monsieur! Of all!" she repeated with passion. "And all are not here! Before I marry you, you must show me M. de Tignonville alive and safe!"

He shrugged his shoulders. "He has taken himself off," he said. "It is naught to me what happens to him now."

"It is all to me!" she retorted.

At that he glared at her, the veins of his forehead swelling suddenly. But after a seeming struggle with himself he put the insult by, perhaps for future reckoning and account.

"I did what I could," he said sullenly. "Had I willed it he had died there and then in the room below. I gave him his life. If he has risked it anew and lost it, it is naught to me."

"It was his life you gave me," she repeated stubbornly. "His life—and the others. But that is not all," she continued; "you promised me a minister."

He nodded, smiling sourly to himself, as if this confirmed a suspicion he had entertained.

"Or a priest," he said.

"No, a minister."

"If one could be obtained. If not, a priest."

"No, it was to be at my will; and I will a minister! I will a minister!" she cried passionately. "Show me M. de Tignonville alive, and bring me a minister of my faith, and I will keep my promise, M. de Tavannes. Have no fear of that. But otherwise, I will not."

"You will not?" he cried. "You will not?"

"No!"

"You will not marry me?"

"No!"

The moment she had said it fear seized her, and she could have fled from him, screaming. The flash of his eyes, the sudden passion of his face, burned themselves into her memory. She thought for a second that he would spring on her and strike her down. Yet though the women behind her held their breath, she faced him, and did not quail; and to that, she fancied, she owed it that he controlled himself.

"You will not?" he repeated, as if he could not understand such resistance to his will—as if he could not credit his ears. "You will not?" But after that, when he had said it three times, he laughed; a laugh, however, with a snarl in it that chilled her blood.

"You bargain, do you?" he said. "You will have the last tittle of the price, will you? And have thought of this and that to put me off, and to gain time until your lover, who is all to you, comes to save you? Oh, clever girl! clever! But have you thought where you stand—woman? Do you know that if I gave the word to my people they would treat you as the commonest baggage that tramps the Froidmantel? Do you know that it rests with me to save you, or to throw you to the wolves whose ravening you hear?" And he pointed to the window. "Minister? Priest?" he continued grimly. "*Mon Dieu*, Mademoiselle, I stand astonished at my moderation. You chatter to me of ministers and priests, and the one or the other, when it might be neither! When you are as much and as hopelessly in my power to-day as the wench in my kitchen! You! You flout me, and make terms with me! You!"

And he came so near her with his dark harsh face, his tone rose so menacing on the last word, that her nerves, shattered before, gave way, and, unable to control herself, she flinched with a low cry, thinking he would strike her.

He did not follow, nor move to follow; but he laughed a low laugh of content. And his eyes devoured her.

"Ho! ho!" he said. "We are not so brave as we pretend to be, it seems. And yet you dared to chaffer with me? You thought to thwart me—Tavannes! *Mon Dieu*, Mademoiselle, to what did you trust? To what did you trust? Ay, and to what do you trust?"

She knew that by the movement which fear had forced from her she had jeopardized everything. That she stood to lose all and more than all which she had thought to win by a bold front. A woman less brave, of a spirit less firm, would have given up the contest, and have been glad to escape so. But this woman, though her bloodless face showed that she knew what cause she had for fear, and though her heart was indeed sick with terror, held her ground at the point to which she had retreated. She played her last card.

"To what do I trust?" she muttered with trembling lips.

"Yes, Mademoiselle," he answered between his teeth. "To what do you trust—that you play with Tavannes?"

"To his honour, Monsieur," she answered faintly. "And to your promise."

He looked at her with his mocking smile. "And yet," he sneered, "you thought a moment ago that I should strike you. You thought that I should beat you! And now it is my honour and my promise! Oh, clever, clever, Mademoiselle! 'Tis so that women make fools of men. I knew that something of this kind was on foot when you sent for me, for I know women and their ways. But, let me tell you, it is an ill time to speak of honour when the streets are red! And of promises when the King's word is 'No faith with a heretic!'"

"Yet you will keep yours," she said bravely.

He did not answer at once, and hope which was almost dead in her breast began to recover; nay, presently sprang up erect. For the man hesitated, it was evident; he brooded with a puckered brow and gloomy eyes; an observer might have fancied that he traced pain as well as doubt in his face. At last—

"There is a thing," he said slowly and with a sort of glare at her, "which, it may be, you have not reckoned. You press me now, and will stand on your terms and your conditions, your *ifs* and your *unlesses*! You will have the most from me, and the bargain and a little beside the bargain! But I would have you think if you are wise. Bethink you how it will be between us when you are my wife—if you press me so now, Mademoiselle. How will it sweeten things then? How will it soften them? And to what, I pray you, will you trust for fair treatment then, if you will be so against me now?"

She shuddered. "To the mercy of my husband," she said in a low voice. And her chin sank on her breast.

"You will be content to trust to that?" he answered grimly. And his tone and the lifting of his brow promised little clemency. "Bethink you! 'Tis your rights now, and your terms, Mademoiselle! And then it will be only my mercy—Madame."

"I am content," she muttered faintly.

"And the Lord have mercy on my soul, is what you would add," he retorted, "so much trust have you in my mercy! And you are right! You are right, since you have played this trick on me. But as you will. If you will have it so, have it so! You shall stand on your conditions now; you shall have your pennyweight and full advantage, and the rigour of the pact. But afterwards—afterwards, Madame de Tavannes—"

He did not finish his sentence, for at the first word which granted her petition, Mademoiselle had sunk down on the low wooden window-seat beside which she stood, and, cowering into its farthest corner, her face hidden on her arms, had burst into violent weeping. Her hair, hastily knotted up in the hurry of the previous night, hung in a thick plait to the curve of her waist; the nape of her neck showed beside it milk-white. The man stood awhile contemplating her in silence, his gloomy eyes watching the pitiful movement of her shoulders, the convulsive heaving of her figure. But he did not offer to touch her, and at length he turned about. First one and then the other of her women quailed and shrank under his gaze; he seemed about to add something. But he did not speak. The sentence he had left unfinished, the long look he bent on the weeping girl as he turned from her, spoke more eloquently of the future than a score of orations.

"*Afterwards, Madame de Tavannes!*"

CHAPTER XII
IN THE HALL OF THE LOUVRE

It is a strange thing that love—or passion, if the sudden fancy for Mademoiselle which had seized Count Hannibal be deemed unworthy of the higher name—should so entirely possess the souls of those who harbour it that the greatest events and the most astounding catastrophes, even measures which set their mark for all time on a nation, are to them of importance only so far as they affect the pursuit of the fair one.

As Tavannes, after leaving Mademoiselle, rode through the paved lanes, beneath the gabled houses, and under the shadow of the Gothic spires of his day, he saw a score of sights, moving to pity, or wrath, or wonder. He saw Paris as a city sacked; a slaughter-house, where for a week a masque had moved to stately music; blood on the nailed doors and the close-set window bars; and at the corners of the ways strewn garments, broken weapons, the livid dead in heaps. But he saw all with eyes which in all and everywhere, among living and dead, sought only Tignonville; Tignonville first, and next a heretic minister, with enough of life in him to do his office.

Probably it was to this that one man hunted through Paris owed his escape that day. He sprang from a narrow passage full in Tavannes' view, and, hair on end, his eyes starting from his head, ran blindly—as a hare will run when chased—along the street to meet Count Hannibal's company. The man's face was wet with the dews of death, his lungs seemed cracking, his breath hissed from him as he ran. His pursuers were hard on him, and, seeing him headed by Count Hannibal's party, yelled in triumph, holding him for dead. And dead he would have been within thirty seconds had Tavannes played his part. But his thoughts were elsewhere. Either he took the poor wretch for Tignonville, or for the minister on whom his mind was running; anyway he suffered him to slip under the belly of his horse; then, to make matters worse, he wheeled to follow him in so untimely and clumsy a fashion that his horse blocked the way and stopped the pursuers in their tracks. The quarry slipped into an alley and vanished. The hunters stood and blasphemed, and even for a moment seemed inclined to resent the mistake. But Tavannes smiled; a broader smile lightened the faces of the six iron-clad men behind him; and for some reason the gang of ruffians thought better of it and slunk aside.

There are hard men, who feel scorn of the things which in the breasts of others excite pity. Tavannes' lip curled as he rode on through the streets, looking this way and that, and seeing what a King twenty-two years old had made of his capital. His lip curled most of all when he came, passing between the two tennis-courts, to the east gate of the Louvre, and found the entrance locked and guarded, and all communication between city and palace cut off. Such a proof of unkingly panic, in a crisis wrought by the King himself, astonished him less a few minutes later, when, the keys having been brought and the door opened, he entered the courtyard of the fortress.

Within and about the door of the gatehouse some three-score archers and arquebusiers stood to their arms; not in array, but in disorderly groups, from which the babble of voices, of feverish laughter, and strained jests rose without ceasing. The weltering sun, of which the beams just topped the farther side of the quadrangle, fell slantwise on their armour, and heightened their exaggerated and restless movements. To a calm eye they seemed like men acting in a nightmare. Their fitful talk and disjointed gestures, their sweating brows and damp hair, no less than the sullen, brooding silence of one here and there, bespoke the abnormal and the terrible. There were livid faces among them, and twitching cheeks, and some who swallowed much; and some again who bared their crimson arms and bragged insanely of the part they had played. But perhaps the most striking thing was the thirst, the desire, the demand for news, and for fresh excitement. In the space of time it took him to pass through them, Count Hannibal heard a dozen rumours of what was passing in the city; that Montgomery and the gentlemen who had slept beyond the river had escaped on horseback in their shirts; that Guise had been shot in the pursuit; that he had captured the Vidame de Chartres and all the fugitives; that he had never left the city; that he was even then entering by the Porte de Bucy. Again that Biron had surrendered the Arsenal, that he had threatened to fire on the city, that he was dead, that with the Huguenots who had escaped he was marching on the Louvre, that—

And then Tavannes passed out of the blinding sunshine, and out of earshot of their babble, and had plain in his sight across the quadrangle, the new façade, Italian, graceful, of the Renaissance; which rose in smiling contrast with the three dark Gothic sides that now, the central tower removed, frowned unimpeded at one another. But what was this which lay along the foot of the new Italian wall? This, round which some stood, gazing curiously, while others strewed fresh sand about it, or after long downward-looking glanced up to answer the question of a person at a window?

Death; and over death—death in its most cruel aspect—a cloud of buzzing, whirling flies, and the smell, never to be forgotten, of much spilled blood. From a doorway hard by came shrill bursts of hysterical laughter; and with the laughter plumped out, even as Tavannes crossed the court, a young girl, thrust forth it seemed by her fellows, for she turned about and struggled as she came. Once outside she hung back, giggling and protesting, half willing, half unwilling; and meeting Tavannes' eye thrust her way in again with a whirl of her petticoats, and a shriek. But before he had taken four paces she was out again.

He paused to see who she was, and his thoughts involuntarily went back to the woman he had left weeping in the upper room. Then he turned about again and stood to count the dead. He identified Piles, identified Pardaillan, identified Soubise—whose corpse the murderers had robbed of the last rag—and Touchet and St. Galais. He made his reckoning with an unmoved face, and with the same face stopped and stared, and moved from one to another; had he not seen the slaughter about *"le petit homme"* at Jarnac, and the dead of three pitched fields? But when a bystander, smirking obsequiously, passed him a jest on Soubise, and with his finger pointed the jest, he had the same hard unmoved face for the gibe as for the dead. And the jester shrank away, abashed and perplexed by his stare and his reticence.

Halfway up the staircase to the great gallery or guard-room above, Count Hannibal found his brother, the Marshal, huddled together in drunken slumber on a seat in a recess. In the gallery to which he passed on without awakening him, a crowd of courtiers and ladies, with arquebusiers and captains of the quarters, walked to and fro, talking in whispers; or peeped over shoulders towards the inner end of the hall, where the querulous voice of the King rose now and again above the hum. As Tavannes moved that way, Nançay, in the act of passing out, booted and armed for the road, met him and almost jostled him.

"Ah, well met, M. le Comte," he sneered, with as much hostility as he dared betray. "The King has asked for you twice."

"I am going to him. And you? Whither in such a hurry, M. Nançay?"

"To Chatillon."

"On pleasant business?"

"Enough that it is on the King's!" Nançay replied, with unexpected temper. "I hope that you may find yours as pleasant!" he added with a grin. And he went on.

The gleam of malice in the man's eye warned Tavannes to pause. He looked round for some one who might be in the secret, saw the Provost of the Merchants, and approached him.

"What's amiss, M. le Charron?" he asked. "Is not the affair going as it should?"

"'Tis about the Arsenal, M. le Comte," the Provost answered busily. "M. de Biron is harbouring the vermin there. He has lowered the portcullis and pointed his culverins over the gate and will not yield it or listen to reason. The King would bring him to terms, but no one will venture himself inside with the message. Rats in a trap, you know, bite hard, and care little whom they bite."

"I begin to understand."

"Precisely, M. le Comte. His Majesty would have sent M. de Nançay. But he elected to go to Chatillon, to seize the young brood there. The Admiral's children, you comprehend."

"Whose teeth are not yet grown! He was wise."

"To be sure, M. de Tavannes, to be sure. But the King was annoyed, and on top of that came a priest with complaints, and if I may make so bold as to advise you, you will not—"

But Tavannes fancied that he had caught the gist of the difficulty, and with a nod he moved on; and so he missed the warning which the other had it in his mind to give. A moment and he reached the inner circle, and there halted, disconcerted, nay taken aback. For as soon as he showed his face, the King, who was pacing to and fro like a caged beast, before a table at which three clerks knelt on cushions, espied him, and stood still. With a glare of something like madness in his eyes, Charles raised his hand, and with a shaking finger singled him out.

"So, by G-d, you are there!" he cried, with a volley of blasphemy. And he signed to those about Count Hannibal to stand away from him. "You are there, are you? And you are not afraid to show your face? I tell you, it's you and such as you bring us into contempt! so that it is said everywhere Guise does all and serves God, and we follow because we must! It's you, and such as you, are stumbling-blocks to our good folk of Paris! Are you traitor, sirrah?" he continued with passion, "or are you of our brother Alençon's opinions, that you traverse our orders to the damnation of your soul and our discredit? Are you traitor? Or are you heretic? Or what are you? God in heaven, will you answer me, man, or shall I send you where you will find your tongue?"

"I know not of what your Majesty accuses me," Count Hannibal answered, with a scarcely perceptible shrug of the shoulders.

"I? 'Tis not I," the King retorted. His hair hung damp on his brow, and he dried his hands continually; while his gestures had the ill-measured and eccentric violence of an epileptic. "Here, you! Speak, father, and confound him!"

Then Tavannes discovered on the farther side of the circle the priest whom his brother had ridden down that morning. Father Pezelay's pale hatchet-face gleamed paler than ordinary; and a great bandage hid one temple and part of his face. But below the bandage the flame of his eyes was not lessened, nor the venom of his tongue. To the King he had come—for no other would deal with his violent opponent; to the King's presence! and, as he prepared to blast his adversary, now his chance was come, his long lean frame, in its narrow black cassock, seemed to grow longer, leaner, more baleful, more snake-like. He stood there a fitting representative of the dark fanaticism of Paris, which Charles and his successor—the last of a doomed line—alternately used as tool or feared as master; and to which the most debased and the most immoral of courts paid, in its sober hours, a vile and slavish homage. Even in the midst of the drunken, shameless courtiers—who stood, if they stood for anything, for that other influence of the day, the Renaissance—he was to be reckoned with; and Count Hannibal knew it. He knew that in the eyes not of Charles only, but of nine out of ten who listened to him, a priest was more sacred than a virgin, and a tonsure than all the virtues of spotless innocence.

"Shall the King give with one hand and withdraw with the other?" the priest began, in a voice hoarse yet strident, a voice borne high above the crowd on the wings of passion. "Shall he spare of the best of the men and the maidens whom God hath doomed, whom the Church hath devoted, whom the King hath given? Is the King's hand shortened or his word annulled that a man does as he forbiddeth and leaves undone what he commandeth? Is God mocked? Woe, woe unto you," he continued, turning swiftly, arms uplifted, towards Tavannes, "who please yourself with the red and white of their maidens and take of the best of the spoil, sparing where the King's word is 'Spare not'! Who strike at Holy Church with the sword! Who—"

"Answer, sirrah!" Charles cried, spurning the floor in his fury. He could not listen long to any man. "Is it so? Is it so? Do you do these things?"

Count Hannibal shrugged his shoulders and was about to answer, when a thick, drunken voice rose from the crowd behind him.

"Is it what? Eh! Is it what?" it droned. And a figure with bloodshot eyes, disordered beard, and rich clothes awry, forced its way through the obsequious circle. It was Marshal Tavannes. "Eh, what? You'd beard the King, would you?" he hiccoughed truculently, his eyes on Father Pezelay, his hand on his sword. "Were you a priest ten times—"

"Silence!" Charles cried, almost foaming with rage at this fresh interruption. "It's not he, fool! 'Tis your pestilent brother."

"Who touches my brother touches Tavannes!" the Marshal answered with a menacing gesture. He was sober enough, it appeared, to hear what was said, but not to comprehend its drift; and this caused a titter, which immediately excited his rage. He turned and seized the nearest laugher by the ear. "Insolent!" he cried. "I will teach you to laugh when the King speaks! Puppy! Who laughs at his Majesty or touches my brother has to do with Tavannes!"

The King, in a rage that almost deprived him of speech, stamped the floor twice.

"Idiot!" he cried. "Imbecile! Let the man go! 'Tis not he! 'Tis your heretic brother, I tell you! By all the Saints! By the body of—" and he poured forth a flood of oaths. "Will you listen to me and be silent! Will you—your brother—"

"If he be not your Majesty's servant, I will kill him with this sword!" the irrepressible Marshal struck in. "As I have killed ten to-day! Ten!" And, staggering back, he only saved himself from falling by clutching Chicot about the neck.

"Steady, my pretty Maréchale!" the jester cried, chucking him under the chin with one hand, while with some difficulty he supported him with the other—for he, too, was far from sober—

"Pretty Margot, toy with me,
Maiden bashful—"

"Silence!" Charles cried, darting forth his long arms in a fury of impatience. "God, have I killed every man of sense? Are you all gone mad? Silence! Do you hear? Silence! And let me hear what he has to say," with a movement towards Count Hannibal. "And look you, sirrah," he continued with a curse, "see that it be to the purpose!"

"If it be a question of your Majesty's service," Tavannes answered, "and obedience to your Majesty's orders, I am deeper in it than he who stands there!" with a sign towards the priest. "I give my word for that. And I will prove it."

"How, sir?" Charles cried. "How, how, how? How will you prove it?"

"By doing for you, sire, what he will not do!" Tavannes answered scornfully. "Let him stand out, and if he will serve his Church as I will serve my King—"

"Blaspheme not!" cried the priest.

"Chatter not!" Tavannes retorted hardily, "but do! Better is he," he continued, "who takes a city than he who slays women! Nay, sire," he went on hurriedly, seeing the King start, "be not angry, but hear me! You would send to Biron, to the Arsenal? You seek a messenger, sire? Then let the good father be the man. Let him take your Majesty's will to Biron, and let him see the Grand Master face to face, and bring him to reason. Or, if he will not, I will! Let that be the test!"

"Ay, ay!" cried Marshal de Tavannes, "you say well, brother! Let him!"

"And if he will not, I will!" Tavannes repeated. "Let that be the test, sire."

The King wheeled suddenly to Father Pezelay. "You hear, father?" he said. "What say you?"

The priest's face grew sallow, and more sallow. He knew that the walls of the Arsenal sheltered men whose hands no convention and no order of Biron's would keep from his throat, were the grim gate and frowning culverins once passed; men who had seen their women and children, their wives and sisters immolated at his word, and now asked naught but to stand face to face and eye to eye with him and tear him limb from limb before they died! The challenge, therefore, was one-sided and unfair; but for that very reason it shook him. The astuteness of the man who, taken by surprise, had conceived this snare filled him with dread. He dared not accept, and he scarcely dared to refuse the offer. And meantime the eyes of the courtiers, who grinned in their beards, were on him. At length he spoke, but it was in a voice which had lost its boldness and assurance.

"It is not for me to clear myself," he cried, shrill and violent, "but for those who are accused, for those who have belied the King's word, and set at nought his Christian orders. For you, Count Hannibal, heretic, or no better than heretic, it is easy to say 'I go.' For you go but to your own, and your own will receive you!"

"Then you will not go?" with a jeer.

"At your command? No!" the priest shrieked with passion. "His Majesty knows whether I serve him."

"I know," Charles cried, stamping his foot in a fury, "that you all serve me when it pleases you! That you are all sticks of the same faggot, wood of the same bundle, hell-babes in your own business, and sluggards in mine! You kill to-day and you'll lay it to me to-morrow! Ay, you will! you will!" he repeated frantically, and drove home the asseveration with a fearful oath. "The dead are as good servants as you! Foucauld was better! Foucauld? Foucauld? Ah, my God!"

And abruptly in presence of them all, with the sacred name, which he so often defiled, on his lips, Charles turned, and covering his face burst into childish weeping; while a great silence fell on all—on Bussy with the blood of his cousin Resnel on his point, on Fervacques, the betrayer of his friend, on Chicot, the slayer of his rival, on Cocconnas the cruel—on men with hands unwashed from the slaughter, and on the shameless women who lined the walls; on all who used this sobbing man for their stepping-stone, and, to attain their ends and gain their purposes, trampled his dull soul in blood and mire.

One looked at another in consternation. Fear grew in eyes that a moment before were bold; cheeks turned pale that a moment before were hectic. If *he* changed as rapidly as this, if so little dependence could be placed on his moods or his resolutions, who was safe? Whose turn might it not be to-morrow? Or who might not be held accountable for the deeds done this day? Many, from whom remorse had seemed far distant a while before, shuddered and glanced behind them. It was as if the dead who lay stark without the doors, ay, and the countless dead of Paris, with whose shrieks the air was laden, had flocked in shadowy shape into the hall; and there, standing beside their murderers, had whispered with their cold breath in the living ears, "A reckoning! A reckoning! As I am, thou shalt be!"

It was Count Hannibal who broke the spell and the silence, and with his hand on his brother's shoulder stood forward.

"Nay, sire," he cried, in a voice which rang defiant in the roof, and seemed to challenge alike the living and the dead, "if all deny the deed, yet will not I! What we have done we have done! So be it! The dead are dead! So be it! For the rest, your Majesty has still one servant who will do your will, one soldier whose life is at your disposition! I have said I will go, and I go, sire. And you, churchman," he continued, turning in bitter scorn to the priest, "do you go too—to church! To church, shaveling! Go, watch and pray for us! Fast and flog for us! Whip those shoulders, whip them till the blood runs down! For it is all, it seems, you will do for your King!"

Charles turned. "Silence, railer!" he said in a broken voice. "Sow no more troubles! Already," a shudder shook his tall ungainly form, "I see blood, blood, blood everywhere! Blood? Ah, God, shall I from this time see anything else? But there is no turning back. There is no undoing. So, do you go to Biron. And do you," he went on, sullenly addressing Marshal Tavannes, "take him and tell him what it is needful he should know."

"'Tis done, sire!" the Marshal cried, with a hiccough. "Come, brother!"

But when the two, the courtiers making quick way for them, had passed down the hall to the door, the Marshal tapped Hannibal's sleeve.

"It was touch and go," he muttered; it was plain he had been more sober than he seemed. "Mind you, it does not do to thwart our little master in his fits! Remember that another time, or worse will come of it, brother. As it is, you came out of it finely and tripped that black devil's heels to a marvel! But you won't be so mad as to go to Biron?"

"Yes," Count Hannibal answered coldly. "I shall go."

"Better not! Better not!" the Marshal answered. "'Twill be easier to go in than to come out—with a whole throat! Have you taken wild cats in the hollow of a tree? The young first, and then the she-cat? Well, it will be that! Take my advice, brother. Have after Montgomery, if you please, ride with Nançay to Chatillon—he is mounting now—go where you please out of Paris, but don't go there! Biron hates us, hates me. And for the King, if he do not see you for a few days, 'twill blow over in a week."

Count Hannibal shrugged his shoulders. "No," he said, "I shall go."

The Marshal stared a moment. "Morbleu!" he said, "why? 'Tis not to please the King, I know. What do you think to find there, brother?"

"A minister," Hannibal answered gently. "I want one with life in him, and they are scarce in the open. So I must to covert after him." And, twitching his sword-belt a little nearer to his hand, he passed across the court to the gate, and to his horses.

The Marshal went back laughing, and, slapping his thigh as he entered the hall, jostled by accident a gentleman who was passing out.

"What is it?" the Gascon cried hotly; for it was Chicot he had jostled.

"Who touches my brother touches Tavannes!" the Marshal hiccoughed. And, smiting his thigh anew, he went off into another fit of laughter.

CHAPTER XIII
DIPLOMACY

Where the old wall of Paris, of which no vestige remains, ran down on the east to the north bank of the river, the space in the angle between the Seine and the ramparts beyond the Rue St. Pol wore at this date an aspect typical of the troubles of the time. Along the waterside the gloomy old Palace of St. Pol, once the residence of the mad King Charles the Sixth—and his wife, the abandoned Isabeau de Bavière—sprawled its maze of mouldering courts and ruined galleries; a dreary monument of the Gothic days which were passing from France. Its spacious curtilage and dark pleasaunces covered all the ground between the river and the Rue St. Antoine; and north of this, under the shadow of the eight great towers of the Bastille, which looked, four outward to check the stranger, four inward to bridle the town, a second palace, beginning where St. Pol ended, carried the realm of decay to the city wall.

This second palace was the Hôtel des Tournelles, a fantastic medley of turrets, spires, and gables, that equally with its neighbour recalled the days of the English domination; it had been the abode of the Regent Bedford. From his time it had remained for a hundred years the town residence of the kings of France; but the death of Henry II., slain in its lists by the lance of the same Montgomery who was this day fleeing for his life before Guise, had given his widow a distaste for it. Catherine de Médicis, her sons, and the Court had abandoned it; already its gardens lay a tangled wilderness, its roofs let in the rain, rats played where kings had slept; and in "our palace of the Tournelles" reigned only silence and decay. Unless, indeed, as was whispered abroad, the grim shade of the eleventh Louis sometimes walked in its desolate precincts.

In the innermost angle between the ramparts and the river, shut off from the rest of Paris by the decaying courts and enceintes of these forsaken palaces, stood the Arsenal. Destroyed in great part by the explosion of a powder-mill a few years earlier, it was in the main new; and by reason of its river frontage, which terminated at the ruined tower of Billy, and its proximity to the Bastille, it was esteemed one of the keys of Paris. It was the appanage of the Master of the Ordnance, and within its walls M. de

Biron, a Huguenot in politics, if not in creed, who held the office at this time, had secured himself on the first alarm. During the day he had admitted a number of refugees, whose courage or good luck had led them to his gate; and as night fell—on such a carnage as the hapless city had not beheld since the great slaughter of the Armagnacs, one hundred and fifty-four years earlier—the glow of his matches through the dusk, and the sullen tramp of his watchmen as they paced the walls, indicated that there was still one place in Paris where the King's will did not run.

In comparison of the disorder which prevailed in the city, a deadly quiet reigned here; a stillness so chill that a timid man must have stood and hesitated to approach. But a stranger who about nightfall rode down the street towards the entrance, a single footman running at his stirrup, only nodded a stern approval of the preparations. As he drew nearer he cast an attentive eye this way and that; nor stayed until a hoarse challenge brought him up when he had come within six horses' lengths of the Arsenal gate. He reined up then, and raising his voice, asked in clear tones for M. de Biron.

"Go," he continued boldly, "tell the Grand Master that one from the King is here, and would speak with him."

"From the King of France?" the officer on the gate asked.

"Surely! Is there more than one king in France?"

A curse and a bitter cry of "King? King Herod!" were followed by a muttered discussion that, in the ears of one of the two who waited in the gloom below, boded little good. The two could descry figures moving to and fro before the faint red light of the smouldering matches; and presently a man on the gate kindled a torch, and held it so as to fling its light downward. The stranger's attendant cowered behind the horse.

"Have a care, my lord!" he whispered. "They are aiming at us!"

If so the rider's bold front and unmoved demeanour gave them pause. Presently, "I will send for the Grand Master" the man who had spoken before announced. "In whose name, monsieur?"

"No matter," the stranger answered. "Say, one from the King."

"You are alone?"

"I shall enter alone."

The assurance seemed to be satisfactory, for the man answered "Good!" and after a brief delay a wicket in the gate was opened, the portcullis creaked upward, and a plank was thrust across the ditch. The horseman waited until the preparations were complete; then he slid to the ground, threw his rein to the servant, and boldly walked across. In an instant he left behind him the dark street, the river, and the sounds of outrage, which the night breeze bore from the farther bank, and found himself within the vaulted gateway, in a bright glare of light, the centre of a ring of gleaming eyes and angry faces.

The light blinded him for a few seconds; but the guards, on their side, were in no better case. For the stranger was masked; and in their ignorance who it was looked at them through the slits in the black velvet they stared, disconcerted, and at a loss. There were some there with naked weapons in their hands who would have struck him through had they known who he was; and more who would have stood aside while the deed was done. But the uncertainty—that and the masked man's tone paralyzed them. For they reflected that he might be anyone. Condé, indeed, stood too small, but Navarre, if he lived, might fill that cloak; or Guise, or Anjou, or the King himself. And while some would not have scrupled to strike the blood royal, more would have been quick to protect and avenge it. And so before the dark uncertainty of the mask, before the riddle of the smiling eyes which glittered through the slits, they stared irresolute; until a hand, the hand of one bolder than his fellows, was raised to pluck away the screen.

The unknown dealt the fellow a buffet with his fist. "Down, rascal!" he said hoarsely. "And you"—to the officer—"show me instantly to M. de Biron!"

But the lieutenant, who stood in fear of his men, looked at him doubtfully.

"Nay," he said, "not so fast!" And one of the others, taking the lead, cried, "No! We may have no need of M. de Biron. Your name, monsieur, first."

With a quick movement the stranger gripped the officer's wrist.

"Tell your master," he said, "that he who clasped his wrist *thus* on the night of Pentecost is here, and would speak with him! And say, mark you, that I will come to him, not he to me!"

The sign and the tone imposed upon the boldest. Two-thirds of the watch were Huguenots, who burned to avenge the blood of their fellows; and these, overriding their officer, had agreed to deal with the intruder, if a Papegot, without recourse to the Grand Master, whose moderation they dreaded. A knife-thrust in the ribs, and another body in the ditch—why not, when such things were done outside? But even these doubted now; and M. Peridol, the lieutenant, reading in the eyes of his men the suspicions which he had himself conceived, was only anxious to obey, if they would let him. So gravely was he impressed, indeed, by the bearing of the unknown that he turned when he had withdrawn, and came back to assure himself that the men meditated no harm in his absence; nor until he had exchanged a whisper with one of them would he leave them and go.

While he was gone on his errand the envoy leaned against the wall of the gateway, and, with his chin sunk on his breast and his mind fallen into reverie, seemed unconscious of the dark glances of which he was the target. He remained in this position until the officer came back, followed by a man with a lanthorn. Their coming roused the unknown, who, invited to follow Peridol, traversed two courts without remark, and in the same silence entered a building in the extreme eastern corner of the enceinte abutting on the ruined Tour de Billy. Here, in an upper floor, the Governor of the Arsenal had established his temporary lodging.

The chamber into which the stranger was introduced betrayed the haste in which it had been prepared for its occupant. Two silver lamps which hung from the beams of the unceiled roof shed light on a medley of arms and inlaid armour, of parchments, books and steel caskets, which encumbered not the tables only, but the stools and chests that, after the fashion of that day, stood formally along the arras. In the midst of the disorder, on the bare floor, walked the man who, more than any other, had been instrumental in drawing the Huguenots to Paris—and to their doom. It was no marvel that the events of the day, the surprise and horror, still rode his mind; nor wonderful that even he, who passed for a model of stiffness and reticence, betrayed for once the indignation which filled his breast. Until the officer had withdrawn and closed the door he did, indeed, keep silence; standing beside the table and eyeing his visitor with a lofty porte and a stern glance. But the moment he was assured that they were alone he spoke.

"Your Highness may unmask now," he said, making no effort to hide his contempt. "Yet were you well advised to take the precaution, since you had hardly come at me in safety without it. Had those who keep the gate seen you, I would not have answered for your Highness's life. The more shame," he continued vehemently, "on the deeds of this day which have compelled the brother of a king of France to hide his face in his own capital and in his own fortress. For I dare to say, Monsieur, what no other will say, now the Admiral is dead. You have brought back the days of the Armagnacs. You have brought bloody days and an evil name on France, and I pray God that you may not pay in your turn what you have exacted. But if you continue to be advised by M. de Guise, this I will say, Monsieur"—and his voice fell low and stern. "Burgundy slew Orleans, indeed; but he came in his turn to the Bridge of Montereau."

"You take me for Monsieur?" the unknown asked. And it was plain that he smiled under his mask.

Biron's face altered. "I take you," he answered sharply, "for him whose sign you sent me."

"The wisest are sometimes astray," the other answered with a low laugh. And he took off his mask.

The Grand Master started back, his eyes sparkling with anger.

"M. de Tavannes?" he cried, and for a moment he was silent in sheer astonishment. Then, striking his hand on the table, "What means this trickery?" he asked.

"It is of the simplest," Tavannes answered coolly. "And yet, as you just now said, I had hardly come at you without it. And I had to come at you. No, M. de Biron," he added quickly, as Biron in a rage laid his hand on a bell which stood beside him on the table, "you cannot that way undo what is done."

"I can at least deliver you," the Grand Master answered, in heat, "to those who will deal with you as you have dealt with us and ours."

"It will avail you nothing," Count Hannibal replied soberly. "For see here, Grand Master, I come from the King. If you are at war with him, and hold his fortress in his teeth, I am his ambassador and sacrosanct. If you are at peace with him and hold it at his will, I am his servant, and safe also."

"At peace and safe?" Biron cried, his voice trembling with indignation. "And are those safe or at peace who came here trusting to *his* word, who lay in his palace and slept in his beds? Where are they, and how have they fared, that you dare appeal to the law of nations, or he to the loyalty of Biron? And for you to beard me, whose brother to-day hounded the dogs of this vile city on the noblest in France, who have leagued yourself with a crew of foreigners to do a deed which will make our country stink in the nostrils of the world when we are dust! You, to come here and talk of peace and safety! M. de Tavannes"—and he struck his hand on the table—"you are a bold man. I know why the King had a will to send you, but I know not why you had the will to come."

"That I will tell you later," Count Hannibal answered coolly. "For the King, first. My message is brief, M. de Biron. Have you a mind to hold the scales in France?"

"Between?" Biron asked contemptuously.

"Between the Lorrainers and the Huguenots."

The Grand Master scowled fiercely. "I have played the go-between once too often," he growled.

"It is no question of going between, it is a question of holding between," Tavannes answered coolly. "It is a question—but, in a word, have you a mind, M. de Biron, to be Governor of Rochelle? The King, having dealt the blow that has been struck to-day, looks to follow up severity, as a wise ruler should, with indulgence. And to quiet the minds of the Rochellois he would set over them a ruler at once acceptable to them—or war must come of it—and faithful to his Majesty. Such a man, M. de Biron, will in such a post be Master of the Kingdom; for he will hold the doors of Janus, and as he bridles his sea-dogs, or unchains them, there will be peace or war in France."

"Is all that from the King's mouth?" Biron asked with sarcasm. But his passion had died down. He was grown thoughtful, suspicious; he eyed the other intently as if he would read his heart.

"The offer is his, and the reflections are mine," Tavannes answered dryly. "Let me add one more. The Admiral is dead. The King of Navarre and the Prince of Condé are prisoners. Who is now to balance the Italians and the Guises? The Grand Master—if he be wise and content to give the law to France from the citadel of Rochelle."

Biron stared at the speaker in astonishment at his frankness.

"You are a bold man," he cried at last. "But *timeo Danaos et dona ferentes*," he continued bitterly. "You offer, sir, too much."

"The offer is the King's."

"And the conditions? The price?"

"That you remain quiet, M. de Biron."

"In the Arsenal?"

"In the Arsenal. And do not too openly counteract the King's will. That is all."

The Grand Master looked puzzled. "I will give up no one," he said. "No one! Let that be understood."

"The King requires no one."

A pause. Then, "Does M. de Guise know of the offer?" Biron inquired; and his eye grew bright. He hated the Guises and was hated by them. It was *there* he was a Huguenot.

"He has gone far to-day," Count Hannibal answered dryly. "And if no worse come of it should be content. Madame Catherine knows of it."

The Grand Master was aware that Marshal Tavannes depended on the Queen-mother; and he shrugged his shoulders.

"Ay, 'tis like her policy," he muttered. "'Tis like her!" And pointing his guest to a cushioned chest which stood against the wall, he sat down in a chair beside the table and thought awhile, his brow wrinkled, his eyes dreaming. By-and-by he laughed sourly. "You have lighted the fire," he said, "and would fain I put it out."

"We would have you hinder it spreading."

"You have done the deed and are loth to pay the blood-money. That is it, is it?"

"We prefer to pay it to M. de Biron," Count Hannibal answered civilly.

Again the Grand Master was silent awhile. At length he looked up and fixed Tavannes with eyes keen as steel.

"What is behind?" he growled. "Say, man, what is it? What is behind?"

"If there be aught behind, I do not know it," Tavannes answered steadfastly.

M. de Biron relaxed the fixity of his gaze. "But you said that you had an object?" he returned.

"I had—in being the bearer of the message."

"What was it?"

"My object? To learn two things."

"The first, if it please you?" The Grand Master's chin stuck out a little, as he spoke.

"Have you in the Arsenal a M. de Tignonville, a gentleman of Poitou?"

"I have not," Biron answered curtly. "The second?"

"Have you here a Huguenot minister?"

"I have not. And if I had I should not give him up," he added firmly.

Tavannes shrugged his shoulders. "I have a use for one," he said carelessly. "But it need not harm him."

"For what, then, do you need him?"

"To marry me."

The other stared. "But you are a Catholic," he said.

"But she is a Huguenot," Tavannes answered.

The Grand Master did not attempt to hide his astonishment.

"And she sticks on that?" he exclaimed. "To-day?"

"She sticks on that. To-day."

"To-day? *Nom de Dieu*! To-day! Well," brushing the matter aside after a pause of bewilderment, "any way, I cannot help her. I have no minister here. If there be aught else I can do for her—"

"Nothing, I thank you," Tavannes answered. "Then it only remains for me to take your answer to the King?" And he rose politely, and taking his mask from the table prepared to assume it.

M. de Biron gazed at him a moment without speaking, as if he pondered on the answer he should give. At length he nodded, and rang the bell which stood beside him.

"The mask!" he muttered in a low voice as footsteps sounded without. And, obedient to the hint, Tavannes disguised himself. A second later the officer who had introduced him opened the door and entered.

"Peridol," M. de Biron said—he had risen to his feet—"I have received a message which needs confirmation; and to obtain this I must leave the Arsenal. I am going to the house—you will remember this—of Marshal Tavannes, who will be responsible for my person; in the mean time this gentleman will remain under strict guard in the south chamber upstairs. You will treat him as a hostage, with all respect, and will allow him to preserve his *incognito*. But if I do not return by noon to-morrow, you will deliver him to the men below, who will know how to deal with him."

Count Hannibal made no attempt to interrupt him, nor did he betray the discomfiture which he undoubtedly felt. But as the Grand Master paused—

"M. de Biron," he said, in a voice harsh and low, "you will answer to me for this!" And his eyes glittered through the slits in the mask.

"Possibly, but not to-day or to-morrow!" Biron replied, shrugging his shoulders contemptuously. "Peridol! see the gentleman bestowed as I have ordered, and then return to me. Monsieur," with a bow, half courteous, half ironical, "let me commend to you the advantages of silence and your mask." And he waved his hand in the direction of the door.

A moment Count Hannibal hesitated. He was in the heart of a hostile fortress where the resistance of a single man armed to the teeth must have been futile; and he was unarmed, save for a poniard. Nevertheless, for a moment the impulse to spring on Biron, and with the dagger at his throat to make his life the price of a safe passage, was strong. Then—for with the warp of a harsh and passionate character were interwrought an odd shrewdness and some things little suspected—he resigned himself. Bowing gravely, he turned with dignity, and in silence followed the officer from the room.

Peridol had two men in waiting at the door. From one of these the lieutenant took a lanthorn, and, with an air at once sullen and deferential, led the way up the stone staircase to the floor over that in which M. de Biron had his lodging. Tavannes followed; the two guards came last, carrying a second lanthorn. At the head of the staircase, whence a bare passage ran, north and south, the procession turned right-handed, and, passing two doors, halted before the third and last, which faced them at the end of the passage. The lieutenant unlocked it with a key which he took from a hook beside the doorpost. Then, holding up his light, he invited his charge to enter.

The room was not small, but it was low in the roof, and prison-like, it had bare walls and smoke-marks on the ceiling. The window, set in a deep recess, the floor of which rose a foot above that of the room, was unglazed; and through the gloomy orifice the night wind blew in, laden even on that August evening with the dank mist of the river flats. A table, two stools, and a truckle bed without straw or covering made up the furniture; but Peridol, after glancing round, ordered one of the men to fetch a truss of straw and the other to bring up a pitcher of wine. While they were gone Tavannes and he stood silently waiting, until, observing that the captive's eyes sought the window, the lieutenant laughed.

"No bars?" he said. "No, Monsieur, and no need of them. You will not go by that road, bars or no bars."

"What is below?" Count Hannibal asked carelessly. "The river?"

"Yes, Monsieur," with a grin; "but not water. Mud, and six feet of it, soft as Christmas porridge, but not so sweet. I've known two puppies thrown in under this window that did not weigh more than a fat pullet apiece. One was gone before you could count fifty, and the other did not live thrice as long—nor would have lasted that time, but that it fell on the first and clung to it."

Tavannes dismissed the matter with a shrug, and, drawing his cloak about him, set a stool against the wall and sat down. The men who brought in the wine and the bundle of straw were inquisitive, and would have loitered, scanning him stealthily; but Peridol hurried them away. The lieutenant himself stayed only to cast a glance round the room, and to mutter that he would return when his lord returned; then, with a "Good night" which said more for his manners than his good will, he followed them out. A moment later the grating of the key in the lock and the sound of the bolts as they sped home told Tavannes that he was a prisoner.

CHAPTER XIV
TOO SHORT A SPOON

Count Hannibal remained seated, his chin sunk on his breast, until his ear assured him that the three men had descended the stairs to the floor below. Then he rose, and, taking the lanthorn from the table, on which Peridol had placed it, he went softly to the door, which, like the window, stood in a recess—in this case the prolongation of the passage. A brief scrutiny satisfied him that escape that way was impossible, and he turned, after a cursory glance at the floor and ceiling, to the dark, windy aperture which yawned at the end of the apartment. Placing the lanthorn on the table, and covering it with his cloak, he mounted the window recess, and, stepping to the unguarded edge, looked out.

He knew, rather than saw, that Peridol had told the truth. The smell of the aguish flats which fringed that part of Paris rose strong in his nostrils. He guessed that the sluggish arm of the Seine which divided the Arsenal from the Île des Louviers crawled below; but the night was dark, and it was impossible to discern land from water. He fancied that he could trace the outline of the island—an uninhabited place, given up to wood piles; but the lights of the college quarter beyond it, which rose feebly twinkling to the crown of St. Genevieve, confused his sight and rendered the nearer gloom more opaque. From that direction and from the Cité to his right came sounds which told of a city still heaving in its blood-stained sleep, and even in its dreams planning further excesses. Now a distant shot, and now a faint murmur on one of the bridges, or a far-off cry, raucous, sudden, curdled the blood. But even of what was passing under cover of the darkness, he could learn little; and after standing awhile with a hand on either side of the window he found the night air chill. He stepped back, and, descending to the floor, uncovered the lanthorn and set it on the table. His thoughts travelled back to the preparations he had made the night before with a view to securing Mademoiselle's person, and he considered, with a grim smile, how little he had foreseen that within twenty-four hours he would himself be a prisoner. Presently, finding his mask oppressive, he removed it, and, laying it on the table before him, sat scowling at the light.

Biron had jockeyed him cleverly. Well, the worse for Armand de Gontaut de Biron if after this adventure the luck went against him! But in the mean time? In the mean time his fate was sealed if harm befell Biron. And what the King's real mind in Biron's case was, and what the Queen-Mother's, he could not say; just as it was impossible to predict how far, when they had the Grand Master at their mercy, they would resist the temptation to add him to the victims. If Biron placed himself at once in Marshal Tavannes' hands, all might be well. But if he ventured within the long arm of the Guises, or went directly to the Louvre, the fact that with the Grand Master's fate Count Hannibal's was bound up, would not weigh a straw. In such crises the great sacrificed the less great, the less great the small, without a scruple. And the Guises did not love Count Hannibal; he was not loved by many. Even the strength of his brother the Marshal stood rather in the favour of the King's heir, for whom he had won the battle of Jarnac, than intrinsically; and, durable in ordinary times, might snap in the clash of forces and interests which the desperate madness of this day had let loose on Paris.

It was not the peril in which he stood, however—though, with the cold clear eye of the man who had often faced peril, he appreciated it to a nicety—that Count Hannibal found least bearable, but his enforced inactivity. He had thought to ride the whirlwind and direct the storm, and out of the danger of others to compact his own success. Instead he lay here, not only powerless to guide his destiny, which hung on the discretion of another, but unable to stretch forth a finger to further his plans.

As he sat looking darkly at the lanthorn, his mind followed Biron and his riders through the midnight streets along St. Antoine and La Verrerie, through the gloomy narrows of the Rue la Ferronerie, and so past the house in the Rue St. Honoré where Mademoiselle sat awaiting the morrow—sat awaiting Tignonville, the minister, the marriage! Doubtless there were still bands of plunderers roaming to and fro; at the barriers troops of archers stopping the suspected; at the windows pale faces gazing down; at the gates of the Temple, and of the walled enclosures which largely made up the city, strong guards set to prevent invasion. Biron would go with sufficient to secure himself; and unless he encountered the bodyguard of Guise his passage would quiet the town. But was it so certain that *she* was safe? He knew his men, and while he had been free he had not hesitated to leave her in their care. But now that he could not go, now that he could not raise a hand to help, the confidence which had not failed him in straits more dangerous grew weak. He pictured the things which might happen, at which, in his normal frame of mind, he would have laughed. Now they troubled him so that he started at a shadow, so that he quailed at a thought. He, who last night, when free to act, had timed his coming and her rescue to a minute! Who had rejoiced in the peril, since with the glamour of such things foolish women were taken! Who had not flinched when the crowd roared most fiercely for her blood!

Why had he suffered himself to be trapped? Why indeed? And thrice in passion he paced the room. Long ago the famous Nostradamus had told him that he would live to be a king, but of the smallest kingdom in the world. "Every man is a king in his coffin," he had answered. "The grave is cold and your kingdom shall be warm," the wizard had rejoined. On which the courtiers had laughed, promising him a Moorish island and a black queen. And he had gibed with the rest, but secretly had taken note of the sovereign counties of France, their rulers and their heirs. Now he held the thought in horror, foreseeing no county, but the cage under the stifling tiles at Loches, in which Cardinal Balue and many another had worn out their hearts.

He came to that thought not by way of his own peril, but of Mademoiselle's; which affected him in so novel a fashion that he wondered at his folly. At last, tired of watching the shadows which the draught set dancing on the wall, he drew his cloak about him and lay down on the straw. He had kept vigil the previous night, and in a few minutes, with a campaigner's ease, he was asleep.

Midnight had struck. About two the light in the lanthorn burned low in the socket, and with a soft sputtering went out. For an hour after that the room lay still, silent, dark; then slowly the grey dawn, the greyer for the river mist which wrapped the neighbourhood in a clammy shroud, began to creep into the room and discover the vague shapes of things. Again an hour passed, and the sun was rising above Montreuil, and here and there the river began to shimmer through the fog. But in the room it was barely daylight when the sleeper awoke, and sat up, his face expectant. Something had roused him. He listened.

His ear, and the habit of vigilance which a life of danger instils, had not deceived him. There were men moving in the passage; men who shuffled their feet impatiently. Had Biron returned? Or had aught happened to him, and were these men come to avenge him? Count Hannibal rose and stole across the boards to the door, and, setting his ear to it, listened.

He listened while a man might count a hundred and fifty, counting slowly. Then, for the third part of a second, he turned his head, and his eyes travelled the room. He stooped again and listened more closely, scarcely breathing. There were voices as well as feet to be heard now; one voice—he thought it was Peridol's—which held on long, now low, now rising into violence. Others were audible at intervals, but only in a growl or a bitter exclamation, that told of minds made up and hands which would not be restrained. He caught his own name, *Tavannes*—the mask was useless, then! And once a noisy movement which came to nothing, foiled, he fancied, by Peridol.

He knew enough. He rose to his full height, and his eyes seemed a little closer together; an ugly smile curved his lips. His gaze travelled over the objects in the room, the bare stools and table, the lanthorn, the wine-pitcher; beyond these, in a corner, the cloak and straw on the low bed. The light, cold and grey, fell cheerlessly on the dull chamber, and showed it in harmony with the ominous whisper which grew in the gallery; with the stern-faced listener who stood, his one hand on the door. He looked, but he found nothing to his purpose, nothing to serve his end, whatever his end was; and with a quick light step he left the door, mounted the window recess, and, poised on the very edge, looked down.

If he thought to escape that way his hope was desperate. The depth to the water-level was not, he judged, twelve feet. But Peridol had told the truth. Below lay not water, but a smooth surface of viscid slime, here luminous with the florescence of rottenness, there furrowed by a tiny runnel of moisture which sluggishly crept across it to the slow stream beyond. This quicksand, vile and treacherous, lapped the wall below the window, and more than accounted for the absence of bars or fastenings. But, leaning far out, he saw that it ended at the angle of the building, at a point twenty feet or so to the right of his position.

He sprang to the floor again, and listened an instant; then, with guarded movements—for there was fear in the air, fear in the silent room, and at any moment the rush might be made, the door burst in—he set the lanthorn and wine-pitcher on the floor, and took up the table in his arms. He began to carry it to the window, but, halfway thither, his eye told him that it would not pass through the opening, and he set it down again and glided to the bed. Again he was thwarted; the bed was screwed to the floor. Another might have despaired at that, but he rose with no sign of dismay, and listening, always listening, he spread his cloak on the floor, and deftly, with as little noise and rustling as might be, be piled the straw in it, compressed the bundle, and, cutting the bed-cords with his dagger, bound all together with them. In three steps he was in the embrasure of the window, and, even as the men in the passage thrust the lieutenant aside and with a sudden uproar came down to the door, he flung the bundle lightly and carefully to the right—so lightly and carefully, and with so nice and deliberate a calculation, that it seemed odd it fell beyond the reach of an ordinary leap.

An instant and he was on the floor again. The men had to unlock, to draw back the bolts, to draw back the door which opened outwards; their numbers, as well as their savage haste, impeded them. When they burst in at last, with a roar of "To the river! To the river!"—burst in a rush of struggling shoulders and lowered pikes, they found him standing, a solitary figure, on the further side of the table, his arms folded. And the sight of the passive figure for a moment stayed them.

"Say your prayers, child of Satan!" cried the leader, waving his weapon. "We give you one minute!"

"Ay, one minute!" his followers chimed in. "Be ready!"

"You would murder me?" he said with dignity. And when they shouted assent, "Good!" he answered. "It is between you and M. de Biron, whose guest I am. But"—with a glance which passed round the ring of glaring eyes and working features—"I would leave a last word for some one. Is there any one here who values a safe-conduct from the King? 'Tis for two men coming and going for a fortnight." And he held up a slip of paper.

The leader cried, "To hell with his safe-conduct! Say your prayers!"

But all were not of his mind. On one or two of the savage faces—the faces, for the most part, of honest men maddened by their wrongs—flashed an avaricious gleam. A safe-conduct? To avenge, to slay, to kill—and to go safe! For some minds such a thing has an invincible fascination. A man thrust himself forward.

"Ay, I'll have it!" he cried. "Give it here!"

"It is yours," Count Hannibal answered, "if you will carry ten words to Marshal Tavannes—when I am gone."

The man's neighbour laid a restraining hand on his shoulder.

"And Marshal Tavannes will pay you finely," he said.

But Maudron, the man who had offered, shook off the hand.

"If I take the message!" he muttered in a grim aside. "Do you think me mad?" And then aloud he cried, "Ay, I'll take your message! Give me the paper."

"You swear you will take it?"

The man had no intention of taking it, but he perjured himself and went forward. The others would have pressed round too, half in envy, half in scorn; but Tavannes by a gesture stayed them.

"Gentlemen, I ask a minute only," he said. "A minute for a dying man is not much. Your friends had as much."

And the fellows, acknowledging the claim and assured that their victim could not escape, let Maudron go round the table to him.

The man was in haste and ill at ease, conscious of his evil intentions and the fraud he was practising; and at once greedy to have, yet ashamed of the bargain he was making. His attention was divided between the slip of paper, on which his eyes fixed themselves, and the attitude of his comrades; he paid little heed to Count Hannibal, whom he knew to be unarmed. Only when Tavannes seemed to ponder on his message, and to be fain to delay, "Go on," he muttered with brutal frankness; "your time is up!"

Tavannes started, the paper slipped from his fingers. Maudron saw a chance of getting it without committing himself, and quick as the thought leapt up in his mind he stooped, and grasped the paper, and would have leapt back with it! But quick as he, and quicker, Tavannes too stooped, gripped him by the waist, and with a prodigious effort, and a yell in which all the man's stormy nature, restrained to a part during the last few minutes, broke forth, he flung the ill-fated wretch head first through the window.

The movement carried Tavannes himself—even while his victim's scream rang through the chamber—into the embrasure. An instant he hung on the verge; then, as the men, a moment thunderstruck, sprang forward to avenge their comrade, he leapt out, jumping for the struggling body that had struck the mud, and now lay in it face downwards.

He alighted on it, and drove it deep into the quaking slime; but he himself bounded off right-handed. The peril was appalling, the possibility untried, the chance one which only a doomed man would have taken. But he reached the straw-bale, and it gave him a momentary, a precarious footing. He could not regain his balance, he could not even for an instant stand upright on it. But from its support he leapt on convulsively, and, as a pike, flung from above, wounded him in the shoulder, he fell his length in the slough—but forward, with his outstretched hands resting on soil of a harder nature. They sank, it is true, to the elbow, but he dragged his body forward on them, and forward, and freeing one by a last effort of strength— he could not free both, and, as it was, half his face was submerged—he reached out another yard, and gripped a balk of wood, which projected from the corner of the building for the purpose of fending off the stream in flood-time.

The men at the window shrieked with rage as he slowly drew himself from the slough, and stood from head to foot a pillar of mud. Shout as they might, they had no firearms, and, crowded together in the narrow embrasure, they could take no aim with their pikes. They could only look on in furious impotence, flinging curses at him until he passed from their view, behind the angle of the building.

Here for a score of yards a strip of hard foreshore ran between mud and wall. He struggled along it until he reached the end of the wall; then with a shuddering glance at the black heaving pit from which he had escaped, and which yet gurgled above the body of the hapless Maudron—a tribute to horror which even his fierce nature could not withhold—he turned and painfully climbed the river-bank. The pike-wound in his shoulder was slight, but the effort had been supreme; the sweat poured from his brow, his visage was grey and drawn. Nevertheless, when he had put fifty paces between himself and the buildings of the Arsenal he paused, and turned. He saw that the men had run to other windows which looked that way; and his face lightened and his form dilated with triumph.

He shook his fist at them. "Ho, fools!" he cried, "you kill not Tavannes so! Till our next meeting at Montfaucon, fare you well!"

CHAPTER XV
THE BROTHER OF ST. MAGLOIRE

As the exertion of power is for the most part pleasing, so the exercise of that which a woman possesses over a man is especially pleasant. When in addition a risk of no ordinary kind has been run, and the happy issue has been barely expected—above all when the momentary gain seems an augury of final victory—it is impossible that a feeling akin to exultation should not arise in the mind, however black the horizon, and however distant the fair haven.

The situation in which Count Hannibal left Mademoiselle de Vrillac will be remembered. She had prevailed over him; but in return he had bowed her to the earth, partly by subtle threats, and partly by sheer savagery. He had left her weeping, with the words "Madame de Tavannes" ringing doom in her ears, and the dark phantom of his will pointing onward to an inevitable future. Had she abandoned hope, it would have been natural.

But the girl was of a spirit not long nor easily cowed; and Tavannes had not left her half an hour before the reflection, that so far the honours of the day were hers, rose up to console her. In spite of his power and her impotence, she had imposed her will upon his; she had established an influence over him, she had discovered a scruple which stayed him, and a limit beyond which he would not pass. In the result she might escape; for the conditions which he had accepted with an ill grace might prove beyond his fulfilling. She might escape! True, many in her place would have feared a worse fate and harsher handling. But there lay half the merit of her victory. It had left her not only in a better position, but with a new confidence in her power over her adversary. He would insist on the bargain struck between them; within its four corners she could look for no indulgence. But if the conditions proved to be beyond his power, she believed that he would spare her: with an ill grace, indeed, with such ferocity and coarse reviling as her woman's pride might scarcely support. But he would spare her.

And if the worst befell her? She would still have the consolation of knowing that from the cataclysm which had overwhelmed her friends she had ransomed those most dear to her. Owing to the position of her chamber, she saw nothing of the excesses to which Paris gave itself up during the remainder of that day, and to which it returned with unabated zest on the following morning. But the Carlats and her women learned from the guards below what was passing; and quaking and cowering in their corners fixed frightened eyes on her, who was their stay and hope. How could she prove false to them? How doom them to perish, had there been no question of her lover?

Of him she sat thinking by the hour together. She recalled with solemn tenderness the moment in which he had devoted himself to the death which came but halfway to seize them; nor was she slow to forgive his subsequent withdrawal, and his attempt to rescue her in spite of herself. She found the impulse to die glorious; the withdrawal—for the actor was her lover—a thing done for her, which he would not have done for himself, and which she quickly forgave him. The revulsion of feeling which had conquered her at the time, and led her to tear herself from him, no longer moved her much while all in his action that might have seemed in other eyes less than heroic, all in his conduct—in a crisis demanding the highest—that smacked of common or mean, vanished, for she still clung to him. Clung to him, not so much with the passion of the mature woman, as with the maiden and sentimental affection of one who has now no hope of possessing, and for whom love no longer spells life, but sacrifice.

She had leisure for these musings, for she was left to herself all that day, and until late on the following day. Her own servants waited on her, and it was known that below stairs Count Hannibal's riders kept sullen ward behind barred doors and shuttered windows, refusing admission to all who came. Now and again echoes of the riot which filled the streets with bloodshed reached her ears: or word of the more striking occurrences was brought to her by Madame Carlat. And early on this second day, Monday, it was whispered that M. de Tavannes had not returned, and that the men below were growing uneasy.

At last, when the suspense below and above was growing tense, it was broken. Footsteps and voices were heard ascending the stairs, the trampling and hubbub were followed by a heavy knock; perforce the door was opened. While Mademoiselle, who had risen, awaited with a beating heart she knew not what, a cowled father, in the dress of the monks of St. Magloire, stood on the threshold, and, crossing himself, muttered the words of benediction. He entered slowly.

No sight could have been more dreadful to Mademoiselle; for it set at naught the conditions which she had so hardly exacted. What if Count Hannibal were behind, were even now mounting the stairs, prepared to force her to a marriage before this shaveling? Or ready to proceed, if she refused, to the last extremity? Sudden terror taking her by the throat choked her; her colour fled, her hand flew to her breast. Yet, before the door had closed on Bigot, she had recovered herself.

"This intrusion is not by M. de Tavannes' orders!" she cried, stepping forward haughtily. "This person has no business here. How dare you admit him?"

The Norman showed his bearded visage a moment at the door.

"My lord's orders," he muttered sullenly. And he closed the door on them.

She had a Huguenot's hatred of a cowl; and, in this crisis, her reasons for fearing it. Her eyes blazed with indignation.

"Enough!" she cried, pointing, with a gesture of dismissal, to the door. "Go back to him who sent you! If he will insult me, let him do it to my face! If he will perjure himself, let him forswear himself in person. Or, if you come on your own account," she continued, flinging prudence to the winds, "as your brethren came to Philippa de Luns, to offer me the choice you offered her, I give you her answer! If I had thought of myself only, I had not lived so long! And rather than bear your presence or hear your arguments—"

She came to a sudden, odd, quavering pause on the word; her lips remained parted, she swayed an instant on her feet. The next moment Madame Carlat, to whom the visitor had turned his shoulder, doubted her eyes, for Mademoiselle was in the monk's arms!

"Clotilde! Clotilde!" he cried, and held her to him.

For the monk was M. de Tignonville! Under the cowl was the lover with whom Mademoiselle's thoughts had been engaged. In this disguise, and armed with Tavannes' note to Madame St. Lo—which the guards below knew for Count Hannibal's hand, though they were unable to decipher the contents—he had found no difficulty in making his way to her.

He had learned before he entered that Tavannes was abroad, and was aware, therefore, that he ran little risk. But his betrothed, who knew nothing of his adventures in the interval, saw in him one who came to her at the greatest risk, across unnumbered perils, through streets swimming with blood. And though she had never embraced him save in the crisis of the massacre, though she had never called him by his Christian name, in the joy of this meeting she abandoned herself to him, she clung to him weeping, she forgot for the time his defection, and thought only of him who had returned to her so gallantly, who brought into the room a breath of Poitou, and the sea, and the old days, and the old life; and at the sight of whom the horrors of the last two days fell from her—for the moment.

And Madame Carlat wept also, and in the room was a sound of weeping. The least moved was, for a certainty, M. de Tignonville himself, who, as we know, had gone through much that day. But even his heart swelled, partly with pride, partly with thankfulness that he had returned to one who loved him so well. Fate had been kinder to him than he deserved; but he need not confess that now. When he had brought off the *coup* which he had in his mind, he would hasten to forget that he had entertained other ideas.

Mademoiselle had been the first to be carried away; she was also the first to recover herself.

"I had forgotten," she cried suddenly, "I had forgotten," and she wrested herself from his embrace with violence, and stood panting, her face white, her eyes affrighted. "I must not! And you—I had forgotten that too! To be here, Monsieur, is the worst office you can do me. You must go! Go, Monsieur, in mercy I beg of you, while it is possible. Every moment you are here, every moment you spend in this house, I shudder."

"You need not fear for me," he said, in a tone of bravado. He did not understand.

"I fear for myself!" she answered. And then, wringing her hands, divided between her love for him and her fear for herself, "Oh, forgive me!" she said. "You do not know that he has promised to spare me, if he cannot produce you, and—and—a minister? He has granted me that; but I thought when you entered that he had gone back on his word, and sent a priest, and it maddened me! I could not bear to think that I had gained nothing. Now you understand, and you will pardon me, Monsieur? If he cannot produce you I am saved. Go then, leave me, I beg, without a moment's delay."

He laughed derisively as he turned back his cowl and squared his shoulders.

"All that is over!" he said, "over and done with, sweet! M. de Tavannes is at this moment a prisoner in the Arsenal. On my way hither I fell in with

M. de Biron, and he told me. The Grand Master, who would have had me join his company, had been all night at Marshal Tavannes' hotel, where he had been detained longer than he expected. He stood pledged to release Count Hannibal on his return, but at my request he consented to hold him one hour, and to do also a little thing for me."

The glow of hope which had transfigured her face faded slowly.

"It will not help," she said, "if he find you here."

"He will not! Nor you!"

"How, Monsieur?"

"In a few minutes," he explained—he could not hide his exultation, "a message will come from the Arsenal in the name of Tavannes, bidding the monk he sent to you bring you to him. A spoken message, corroborated by my presence, should suffice: '*Bid the monk who is now with Mademoiselle,*' it will run, '*bring her to me at the Arsenal, and let four pikes guard them hither.*' When I begged M. de Biron to do this, he laughed. 'I can do better,' he said. 'They shall bring one of Count Hannibal's gloves, which he left on my table. Always supposing my rascals have done him no harm, which God forbid, for I am answerable.'"

Tignonville, delighted with the stratagem which the meeting with Biron had suggested, could see no flaw in it. She could, and though she heard him to the end, no second glow of hope softened the lines of her features. With a gesture full of dignity, which took in not only Madame Carlat and the waiting-woman who stood at the door, but the absent servants—

"And what of these?" she said. "What of these? You forget them, Monsieur. You do not think, you cannot have thought, that I would abandon them? That I would leave them to such mercy as he, defeated, might extend to them? No, you forgot them."

He did not know what to answer, for the jealous eyes of the frightened waiting-woman, fierce with the fierceness of a hunted animal, were on him. The Carlat and she had heard, could hear. At last—

"Better one than none!" he muttered, in a voice so low that if the servants caught his meaning it was but indistinctly. "I have to think of you."

"And I of them," she answered firmly. "Nor is that all. Were they not here, it could not be. My word is passed—though a moment ago, Monsieur, in the joy of seeing you I forgot it. And how," she continued, "if I keep not my word, can I expect him to keep his? Or how, if I am ready to break the bond, on this happening which I never expected, can I hold him to conditions which he loves as little—as little as I love him?"

Her voice dropped piteously on the last words; her eyes, craving her lover's pardon, sought his. But rage, not pity or admiration, was the feeling roused in Tignonville's breast. He stood staring at her, struck dumb by folly so immense. At last—

"You cannot mean this," he blurted out. "You cannot mean, Mademoiselle, that you intend to stand on that! To keep a promise wrung from you by force, by treachery, in the midst of such horrors as he and his have brought upon us! It is inconceivable!"

She shook her head. "I promised," she said.

"You were forced to it."

"But the promise saved our lives."

"From murderers! From assassins!" he protested.

She shook her head. "I cannot go back," she said firmly; "I cannot."

"Then you are willing to marry him," he cried in ignoble anger. "That is it! Nay, you must wish to marry him! For, as for his conditions, Mademoiselle," the young man continued, with an insulting laugh, "you cannot think seriously of them. *He* keep conditions and you in his power! He, Count Hannibal! But for the matter of that, and were he in the mind to keep them, what are they? There are plenty of ministers. I left one only this morning. I could lay my hand on one in five minutes. He has only to find one, therefore—and to find me!"

"Yes, Monsieur," she cried, trembling with wounded pride, "it is for that reason I implore you to go. The sooner you leave me, the sooner you place yourself in a position of security, the happier for me! Every moment that you spend here, you endanger both yourself and me!"

"If you will not be persuaded—"

"I shall not be persuaded," she answered firmly, "and you do but"—alas! her pride began to break down, her voice to quiver, she looked piteously at him—"by staying here make it harder for me to—to—"

"Hush!" cried Madame Carlat. "Hush!" And as they started and turned towards her—she was at the end of the chamber by the door, almost out of earshot—she raised a warning hand. "Listen!" she muttered, "some one has entered the house."

"'Tis my messenger from Biron," Tignonville answered sullenly. And he drew his cowl over his face, and, hiding his hands in his sleeves, moved towards the door. But on the threshold he turned and held out his arms. He could not go thus. "Mademoiselle! Clotilde!" he cried with passion, "for the last time, listen to me, come with me. Be persuaded!"

"Hush!" Madame Carlat interposed again, and turned a scared face on them. "It is no messenger! It is Tavannes himself: I know his voice." And she wrung her hands. "*Oh, mon Dieu, mon Dieu,* what are we to do?" she continued, panic-stricken. And she looked all ways about the room.

CHAPTER XVI
AT CLOSE QUARTERS

Fear leapt into Mademoiselle's eyes, but she commanded herself. She signed to Madame Carlat to be silent, and they listened, gazing at one another, hoping against hope that the woman was mistaken. A long moment they waited, and some were beginning to breathe again, when the strident tones of Count Hannibal's voice rolled up the staircase, and put an end to doubt. Mademoiselle grasped the table and stood supporting herself by it.

"What are we to do?" she muttered. "What are we to do?" and she turned distractedly towards the women. The courage which had supported her in her lover's absence had abandoned her now. "If he finds him here I am lost! I am lost!"

"He will not know me," Tignonville muttered. But he spoke uncertainly; and his gaze, shifting hither and thither, belied the boldness of his words.

Madame Carlat's eyes flew round the room; on her for once the burden seemed to rest. Alas! the room had no second door, and the windows looked on a courtyard guarded by Tavannes' people. And even now Count Hannibal's step rang on the stair! his hand was almost on the latch. The woman wrung her hands; then, a thought striking her, she darted to a corner where Mademoiselle's robes hung on pegs against the wall.

"Here!" she cried, raising them. "Behind these! He may not be seen here! Quick, Monsieur, quick! Hide yourself!"

It was a forlorn hope—the suggestion of one who had not thought out the position; and, whatever its promise, Mademoiselle's pride revolted against it.

"No," she cried. "Not there!" while Tignonville, who knew that the step was useless, since Count Hannibal must have learned that a monk had entered, held his ground.

"You could not deny yourself?" he muttered hurriedly.

"And a priest with me?" she answered; and she shook her head.

There was no time for more, and even as Mademoiselle spoke Count Hannibal's knuckles tapped the door. She cast a last look at her lover. He had turned his back on the window; the light no longer fell on his face. It was possible that he might pass unrecognized, if Tavannes' stay was brief; at any rate, the risk must be run. In a half stifled voice she bade her woman, Javette, open the door. Count Hannibal bowed low as he entered; and he deceived the others. But he did not deceive her. He had not crossed the threshold before she repented that she had not acted on Tignonville's suggestion, and denied herself. For what could escape those hard keen eyes, which swept the room, saw all, and seemed to see nothing—those eyes in which there dwelt even now a glint of cruel humour? He might deceive others, but she who panted within his grasp, as the wild bird palpitates in the hand of the fowler, was not deceived! He saw, he knew! although, as he bowed, and smiling, stood upright, he looked only at her.

"I expected to be with you before this," he said courteously, "but I have been detained. First, Mademoiselle, by some of your friends, who were reluctant to part with me; then by some of your enemies, who, finding me in no handsome case, took me for a Huguenot escaped from the river, and drove me to shifts to get clear of them. However, now I am come, I have news."

"News?" she muttered with dry lips. It could hardly be good news.

"Yes, Mademoiselle, of M. de Tignonville," he answered. "I have little doubt that I shall be able to produce him this evening, and so to satisfy one of your scruples. And as I trust that this good father," he went on, turning to the ecclesiastic, and speaking with the sneer from which he seldom refrained, Catholic as he was, when he mentioned a priest, "has by this time succeeded in removing the other, and persuading you to accept his ministrations—"

"No!" she cried impulsively.

"No?" with a dubious smile, and a glance from one to the other. "Oh, I had hoped better things. But he still may? He still may. I am sure he may. In which case, Mademoiselle, your modesty must pardon me if I plead urgency, and fix the hour after supper this evening for the fulfilment of your promise."

She turned white to the lips. "After supper?" she gasped.

"Yes, Mademoiselle, this evening. Shall I say—at eight o'clock?"

In horror of the thing which menaced her, of the thing from which only two hours separated her, she could find no words but those which she had already used. The worst was upon her; worse than the worst could not befall her.

"But he has not persuaded me!" she cried, clenching her hands in passion. "He has not persuaded me!"

"Still he may, Mademoiselle."

"He will not!" she cried wildly. "He will not!"

The room was going round with her. The precipice yawned at her feet; its naked terrors turned her brain. She had been pushed nearer, and nearer, and nearer; struggle as she might, she was on the verge. A mist rose before her eyes, and though they thought she listened she understood nothing of what was passing. When she came to herself, after the lapse of a minute, Count Hannibal was speaking.

"Permit him another trial," he was saying in a tone of bland irony. "A short time longer, Mademoiselle! One more assault, father! The weapons of the Church could not be better directed or to a more worthy object; and, successful, shall not fail of due recognition and an earthly reward."

And while she listened, half fainting, with a humming in her ears, he was gone. The door closed on him, and the three—Mademoiselle's woman had withdrawn when she opened to him—looked at one another. The girl parted her lips to speak, but she only smiled piteously; and it was M. de Tignonville who broke the silence, in a tone which betrayed rather relief than any other feeling.

"Come, all is not lost yet," he said briskly. "If I can escape from the house—"

"He knows you," she answered.

"What?"

"He knows you," Mademoiselle repeated in a tone almost apathetic. "I read it in his eyes. He knew you at once: and knew, too," she added bitterly, "that he had here under his hand one of the two things he required."

"Then why did he hide his knowledge?" the young man retorted sharply.

"Why?" she answered. "To induce me to waive the other condition in the hope of saving you. Oh!" she continued in a tone of bitter raillery, "he has the cunning of hell, of the priests! You are no match for him, Monsieur. Nor I; nor any of us. And"—with a gesture of despair—"he will be my master! He will break me to his will and to his hand! I shall be his! His, body and soul, body and soul!" she continued drearily, as she sank into a chair and, rocking herself to and fro, covered her face. "I shall be his! His till I die!"

The man's eyes burned, and the pulse in his temples beat wildly.

"But you shall not!" he exclaimed. "I may be no match for him in cunning, you say well. But I can kill him. And I will!" He paced up and down. "I will!"

"You should have done it when he was here," she answered, half in scorn, half in earnest.

"It is not too late," he cried; and then he stopped, silenced by the opening door. It was Javette who entered. They looked at her, and before she spoke were on their feet. Her face, white and eager, marking something besides fear, announced that she brought news. She closed the door behind her, and in a moment it was told.

"Monsieur can escape, if he is quick," she cried in a low tone; and they saw that she trembled with excitement. "They are at supper. But he must be quick! He must be quick!"

"Is not the door guarded?"

"It is, but—"

"And he knows! Your mistress says that he knows that I am here."

For a moment Javette looked startled. "It is possible," she muttered. "But he has gone out."

Madame Carlat clapped her hands. "I heard the door close," she said, "three minutes ago."

"And if Monsieur can reach the room in which he supped last night, the window that was broken is only blocked"—she swallowed once or twice in her excitement—"with something he can move. And then Monsieur is in the street, where his cowl will protect him."

"But Count Hannibal's men?" he asked eagerly.

"They are eating in the lodge by the door."

"Ha! And they cannot see the other room from there?"

Javette nodded. Her tale told, she seemed to be unable to add a word. Mademoiselle, who knew her for a craven, wondered that she had found courage either to note what she had or to bring the news. But as Providence had been so good to them as to put it into this woman's head to act as she had, it behoved them to use the opportunity—the last, the very last opportunity they might have.

She turned to Tignonville. "Oh, go!" she cried feverishly. "Go, I beg! Go now, Monsieur! The greatest kindness you can do me is to place yourself as quickly as possible beyond his reach." A faint colour, the flush of hope, had returned to her cheeks. Her eyes glittered.

"Right, Mademoiselle!" he cried, obedient for once, "I go! And do you be of good courage."

He held her hand: an instant, then, moving to the door, he opened it and listened. They all pressed behind him to hear. A murmur of voices, low and distant, mounted the staircase and bore out the girl's tale; apart from this the house was silent. Tignonville cast a last look at Mademoiselle, and, with a gesture of farewell, glided a-tiptoe to the stairs and began to descend, his face hidden in his cowl. They watched him reach the angle of the staircase, they watched him vanish beyond it; and still they listened, looking at one another when a board creaked or the voices below were hushed for a moment.

CHAPTER XVII
THE DUEL

At the foot of the staircase Tignonville paused. The droning Norman voices of the men on guard issued from an open door a few paces before him on the left. He caught a jest, the coarse chuckling laughter which attended it, and the gurgle of applause which followed; and he knew that at any moment one of the men might step out and discover him. Fortunately the door of the room with the shattered window was almost within reach of his hand on the right side of the passage, and he stepped softly to it. He stood an instant hesitating, his hand on the latch; then, alarmed by a movement in the guard-room, as if some were rising, he pushed the door in a panic, slid into the room, and shut the door behind him. He was safe, and he had made no noise; but at the table, at supper, with his back to him and his face to the partly closed window, sat Count Hannibal!

The young man's heart stood still. For a long minute he gazed at the Count's back, spellbound and unable to stir. Then, as Tavannes ate on without looking round, he began to take courage. Possibly he had entered so quietly that he had not been heard, or possibly his entrance was taken for that of a servant. In either case, there was a chance that he might retire after the same fashion; and he had actually raised the latch, and was drawing the door to him with infinite precaution, when Tavannes' voice struck him, as it were, in the face.

"Pray do not admit the draught, M. de Tignonville," he said, without looking round. "In your cowl you do not feel it, but it is otherwise with me."

The unfortunate Tignonville stood transfixed, glaring at the back of the other's head. For an instant he could not find his voice. At last—

"Curse you!" he hissed in a transport of rage. "Curse you! You did know, then? And she was right."

"If you mean that I expected you, to be sure, Monsieur," Count Hannibal answered. "See, your place is laid. You will not feel the air from without there. The very becoming dress which you have adopted secures you from cold. But—do you not find it somewhat oppressive this summer weather?"

"Curse you!" the young man cried, trembling.

Tavannes turned and looked at him with a dark smile. "The curse may fall," he said, "but I fancy it will not be in consequence of your petitions, Monsieur. And now, were it not better you played the man?"

"If I were armed," the other cried passionately, "you would not insult me!"

"Sit down, sir, sit down," Count Hannibal answered sternly. "We will talk of that presently. In the mean time I have something to say to you. Will you not eat?"

But Tignonville would not.

"Very well," Count Hannibal answered; and he went on with his supper. "I am indifferent whether you eat or not. It is enough for me that you are one of the two things I lacked an hour ago; and that I have you, M. de Tignonville. And through you I look to obtain the other."

"What other?" Tignonville cried.

"A minister," Tavannes answered, smiling. "A minister. There are not many left in Paris—of your faith. But you met one this morning, I know."

"I? I met one?"

"Yes, Monsieur, you! And can lay your hand on him in five minutes, you know."

M. de Tignonville gasped. His face turned a shade paler.

"You have a spy," he cried. "You have a spy upstairs!"

Tavannes raised his cup to his lips, and drank. When he had set it down—

"It may be," he said, and he shrugged his shoulders. "I know, it boots not how I know. It is my business to make the most of my knowledge—and of yours!"

M. de Tignonville laughed rudely. "Make the most of your own," he said; "you will have none of mine."

"That remains to be seen," Count Hannibal answered. "Carry your mind back two days, M. de Tignonville. Had I gone to Mademoiselle de Vrillac last Saturday and said to her 'Marry me, or promise to marry me,' what answer would she have given?"

"She would have called you an insolent!" the young man replied hotly. "And I—"

"No matter what you would have done!" Tavannes said. "Suffice it that she would have answered as you suggest. Yet to-day she has given me her promise."

"Yes," the young man retorted, "in circumstances in which no man of honour—"

"Let us say in peculiar circumstances."

"Well?"

"Which still exist! Mark me, M. de Tignonville," Count Hannibal continued, leaning forward and eyeing the young man with meaning, "*which still exist!* And may have the same effect on another's will as on hers! Listen! Do you hear?" And rising from his seat with a darkening face, he pointed to the partly shuttered window, through which the measured tramp of a body of men came heavily to the ear. "Do you hear, Monsieur? Do you understand? As it was yesterday it is to-day! They killed the President La Place this morning! And they are searching! They are still searching! The river is not yet full, nor the gibbet glutted! I have but to open that window and denounce you, and your life would hang by no stronger thread than the life of a mad dog which they chase through the streets!"

The younger man had risen also. He stood confronting Tavannes, the cowl fallen back from his face, his eyes dilated.

"You think to frighten me!" he cried. "You think that I am craven enough to sacrifice her to save myself. You—"

"You were craven enough to draw back yesterday, when you stood at this window and waited for death!" Count Hannibal answered brutally. "You flinched then, and may flinch again!"

"Try me!" Tignonville retorted, trembling with passion. "Try me!" And then, as the other stared at him and made no movement, "But you dare not!" he cried. "You dare not!"

"No?"

"No! For if I die you lose her!" Tignonville replied in a voice of triumph. "Ha, ha! I touch you there!" he continued. "You dare not, for my safety is part of the price, and is more to you than it is to myself! You may threaten, M. de Tavannes, you may bluster, and shout and point to the window"—and he mocked, with a disdainful mimicry, the other's gesture—"but my safety is more to you than to me! And 'twill end there!"

"You believe that?"

"I know it!"

In two strides Count Hannibal was at the window. He seized a great piece of the boarding which closed one-half of the opening; he wrenched it away. A flood of evening light burst in through the aperture, and fell on and heightened the flushed passion of his features, as he turned again to his opponent.

"Then if you know it," he cried vehemently, "in God's name act upon it!" And he pointed to the window.

"Act upon it?"

"Ay, act upon it!" Tavannes repeated, with a glance of flame. "The road is open! If you would save your mistress, behold the way! If you would save her from the embrace she abhors, from the eyes under which she trembles, from the hand of a master, there lies the way! And it is not her glove only you will save, but herself, her soul, her body! So," he continued, with a certain wildness, and in a tone wherein contempt and bitterness were mingled, "to the lions, brave lover! Will you your life for her honour? Will you death that she may live a maid? Will you your head to save her finger? Then, leap down! leap down! The lists are open, the sand is strewed! Out of your own mouth I have it that if you perish she is saved! Then out, Monsieur! Cry 'I am a Huguenot!' And God's will be done!"

Tignonville was livid. "Rather, your will!" he panted. "Your will, you devil! Nevertheless—"

"You will go! Ha! ha! You will go!"

For an instant it seemed that he would go. Stung by the challenge, wrought on by the contempt in which Tavannes held him, he shot a look of hate at the tempter; he caught his breath, and laid his hand on the edge of the shuttering as if he would leap out.

But it goes hard with him who has once turned back from the foe. The evening light, glancing cold on the burnished pike-points of a group of archers who stood near, caught his eye and went chill to his heart. Death, not in the arena, not in the sight of shouting thousands, but in this darkening street, with an enemy laughing from the window, death with no revenge to follow, with no certainty that after all she would be safe, such a death could be compassed only by pure love—the love of a child for a parent, of a parent for a child, of a man for the one woman in the world!

He recoiled. "You would not spare her!" he cried, his face damp with sweat—for he knew now that he would not go. "You want to be rid of me! You would fool me, and then—"

"Out of your own mouth you are convict!" Count Hannibal retorted gravely. "It was you who said it! But still I swear it! Shall I swear it to you?"

But Tignonville recoiled another step and was silent.

"No? O *preux chevalier*, O gallant knight! I knew it! Do you think that I did not know with whom I had to deal?" And Count Hannibal burst into harsh laughter, turning his back on the other, as if he no longer counted. "You will neither die with her nor for her! You were better in her petticoats and she in your breeches! Or no, you are best as you are, good father! Take my advice, M. de Tignonville, have done with arms; and with a string of beads, and soft words, and talk of Holy Mother Church, you will fool the women as surely as the best of them! They are not all like my cousin, a flouting, gibing, jeering woman—you had poor fortune there, I fear?"

"If I had a sword!" Tignonville hissed, his face livid with rage. "You call me coward, because I will not die to please you. But give me a sword, and I will show you if I am a coward!"

Tavannes stood still. "You are there, are you?" he said in an altered tone. "I—"

"Give me a sword," Tignonville repeated, holding out his open trembling hands. "A sword! A sword! 'Tis easy taunting an unarmed man, but—"

"You wish to fight?"

"I ask no more! No more! Give me a sword," he urged, his voice quivering with eagerness. "It is you who are the coward!"

Count Hannibal stared at him. "And what am I to get by fighting you?" he reasoned slowly. "You are in my power. I can do with you as I please. I can call from this window and denounce you, or I can summon my men—"

"Coward! Coward!"

"Ay? Well, I will tell you what I will do," with a subtle smile. "I will give you a sword, M. de Tignonville, and I will meet you foot to foot here, in this room, on a condition."

"What is it? What is it?" the young man cried with incredible eagerness. "Name your condition!"

"That if I get the better of you, you find me a minister."

"I find you a—"

"A minister. Yes, that is it. Or tell me where I can find one."

The young man recoiled. "Never!" he said.

"You know where to find one."

"Never! Never!"

"You can lay your hand on one in five minutes, you know."

"I will not."

"Then I shall not fight you!" Count Hannibal answered coolly; and he turned from him, and back again. "You will pardon me if I say, M. de Tignonville, that you are in as many minds about fighting as about dying! I do not think that you would have made your fortune at Court. Moreover, there is a thing which I fancy you have not considered. If we fight you may kill me, in which case the condition will not help me much. Or I—which is more likely—" he added, with a harsh smile, "may kill you, and again I am no better placed."

The young man's pallid features betrayed the conflict in his breast. To do him justice, his hand itched for the sword-hilt—he was brave enough for that; he hated, and only so could he avenge himself. But the penalty if he had the worse! And yet what of it? He was in hell now, in a hell of humiliation, shame, defeat, tormented by this fiend! 'Twas only to risk a lower hell.

At last, "I will do it!" he cried hoarsely. "Give me a sword and look to yourself."

"You promise?"

"Yes, yes, I promise!"

"Good," Count Hannibal answered suavely, "but we cannot fight so, we must have more light."

And striding to the door he opened it, and calling the Norman bade him move the table and bring candles—a dozen candles; for in the narrow streets the light was waning, and in the half-shuttered room it was growing dusk. Tignonville, listening with a throbbing brain, wondered that the attendant expressed no surprise and said no word—until Tavannes added to his orders one for a pair of swords.

Then, "Monsieur's sword is here," Bigot answered in his half-intelligible patois. "He left it here yester morning."

"You are a good fellow, Bigot," Tavannes answered, with a gaiety and good-humour which astonished Tignonville. "And one of these days you shall marry Suzanne."

The Norman smiled sourly and went in search of the weapon.

"You have a poniard?" Count Hannibal continued in the same tone of unusual good temper, which had already struck Tignonville. "Excellent! Will you strip, then, or—as we are? Very good, Monsieur; in the unlikely event of fortune declaring for you, you will be in a better condition to take care of yourself. A man running through the streets in his shirt is exposed to inconveniences!" And he laughed gaily.

While he laughed the other listened; and his rage began to give place to wonder. A man who regarded as a pastime a sword and dagger conflict between four walls, who, having his adversary in his power, was ready to discard the advantage, to descend into the lists, and to risk life for a whim, a fancy—such a man was outside his experience, though in Poitou in those days of war were men reckoned brave. For what, he asked himself as he waited, had Tavannes to gain by fighting? The possession of Mademoiselle? But Mademoiselle, if his passion for her overwhelmed him, was in his power; and if his promise were a barrier—which seemed inconceivable in the light of his reputation—he had only to wait, and to-morrow, or the next day, or the next, a minister would be found, and without risk he could gain that for which he was now risking all.

Tignonville did not know that it was in the other's nature to find pleasure in such utmost ventures. Nevertheless the recklessness to which Tavannes' action bore witness had its effect upon him. By the time the young man's sword arrived something of his passion for the conflict had evaporated; and though the touch of the hilt restored his determination, the locked door, the confined space, and the unaccustomed light went a certain distance towards substituting despair for courage.

The use of the dagger in the duels of that day, however, rendered despair itself formidable. And Tignonville, when he took his place, appeared anything but a mean antagonist. He had removed his robe and cowl, and lithe and active as a cat he stood as it were on springs, throwing his weight now on this foot and now on that, and was continually in motion. The table bearing the candles had been pushed against the window, the boarding of which had been replaced by Bigot before he left the room. Tignonville had this, and consequently the lights, on his dagger hand; and he plumed himself on the advantage, considering his point the more difficult to follow.

Count Hannibal did not seem to notice this, however. "Are you ready?" he asked. And then—

"On guard!" he cried, and he stamped the echo to the word. But, that done, instead of bearing the other down with a headlong rush characteristic of the man—as Tignonville feared—he held off warily, stooping low; and when his slow opening was met by one as cautious, he began to taunt his antagonist.

"Come!" he cried, and feinted half-heartedly. "Come, Monsieur, are we going to fight, or play at fighting?"

"Fight yourself, then!" Tignonville answered, his breath quickened by excitement and growing hope. "'Tis not I hold back!" And he lunged, but was put aside.

"Ça! ça!" Tavannes retorted; and he lunged and parried in his turn, but loosely and at a distance.

After which the two moved nearer the door, their eyes glittering as they watched one another, their knees bent, the sinews of their backs straining for the leap. Suddenly Tavannes thrust, and leapt away, and as his antagonist thrust in return the Count swept the blade aside with a strong parry, and for a moment seemed to be on the point of falling on Tignonville with the poniard. But Tignonville retired his right foot nimbly, which brought them front to front again. And the younger man laughed.

"Try again, M. le Comte!" he said. And, with the word, he dashed in himself quick as light; for a second the blades ground on one another, the daggers hovered, the two suffused faces glared into one another; then the pair disengaged again.

The blood trickled from a scratch on Count Hannibal's neck; half an inch to the right and the point had found his throat. And Tignonville, elated, laughed anew, and swaying from side to side on his hips, watched with growing confidence for a second chance. Lithe as one of the leopards Charles kept at the Louvre, he stooped lower and lower, and more and more with each moment took the attitude of the assailant, watching for an opening; while Count Hannibal, his face dark and his eyes vigilant, stood increasingly on the defence. The light was waning a little, the wicks of the candles were burning long; but neither noticed it or dared to remove his eyes from the other's. Their laboured breathing found an echo on the farther side of the door, but this again neither observed.

"Well?" Count Hannibal said at last. "Are you coming?"

"When I please," Tignonville answered; and he feinted but drew back.

The other did the same, and again they watched one another, their eyes seeming to grow smaller and smaller. Gradually a smile had birth on Tignonville's lips. He thrust! It was parried! He thrust again—parried! Tavannes, grown still more cautious, gave a yard. Tignonville pushed on, but did not allow confidence to master caution. He began, indeed, to taunt his adversary; to flout and jeer him. But it was with a motive.

For suddenly, in the middle of a sentence, he repeated the peculiar thrust which had been successful before. This time, however, Tavannes was ready. He put aside the blade with a quick parade, and instead of making a riposte sprang within the other's guard. The two came face to face and breast to shoulder, and struck furiously with their daggers. Count Hannibal was outside his opponent's sword and had the advantage. Tignonville's dagger fell, but glanced off the metalwork of the other's hilt; Tavannes' fell swift and hard between the young man's eyes. The Huguenot flung up his hands and staggered back, falling his length on the floor.

In an instant Count Hannibal was on his breast, and had knocked away his dagger. Then—

"You own yourself vanquished?" he cried.

The young man, blinded by the blood which trickled down his face, made a sign with his hands. Count Hannibal rose to his feet again, and stood a moment looking at his foe without speaking. Presently he seemed to be satisfied. He nodded, and going to the table dipped a napkin in water. He brought it, and carefully supporting Tignonville's head, laved his brow.

"It is as I thought," he said, when he had stanched the blood. "You are not hurt, man. You are stunned. It is no more than a bruise."

The young man was coming to himself. "But I thought—" he muttered, and broke off to pass his hand over his face. Then he got up slowly, reeling a little, "I thought it was the point," he muttered.

"No, it was the pommel," Tavannes answered dryly. "It would not have served me to kill you. I could have done that ten times."

Tignonville groaned, and, sitting down at the table, held the napkin to his aching head. One of the candles had been overturned in the struggle and lay on the floor, flaring in a little pool of grease. Tavannes set his heel upon it; then, striding to the farther end of the room, he picked up Tignonville's dagger and placed it beside his sword on the table. He looked about to see if aught else remained to do, and, finding nothing, he returned to Tignonville's side.

"Now, Monsieur," he said in a voice hard and constrained, "I must ask you to perform your part of the bargain."

A groan of anguish broke from the unhappy man. And yet he had set his life on the cast; what more could he have done?

"You will not harm him?" he muttered.

"He shall go safe," Count Hannibal replied gravely.

"And—" he fought a moment with his pride, then blurted out the words, "you will not tell her—that it was through me—you found him?"

"I will not," Tavannes answered in the same tone. He stooped and picked up the other's robe and cowl, which had fallen from a chair—so that as he spoke his eyes were averted. "She shall never know through me," he said.

And Tignonville, his face hidden in his hands, told him.

CHAPTER XVIII
ANDROMEDA, PERSEUS BEING ABSENT

Little by little—while they fought below—the gloom had thickened, and night had fallen in the room above. But Mademoiselle would not have candles brought. Seated in the darkness, on the uppermost step of the stairs, her hands clasped about her knees, she listened and listened, as if by that action she could avert misfortune; or as if, by going so far forward to meet it, she could turn aside the worst. The women shivering in the darkness about her would fain have struck a light and drawn her back into the room, for they felt safer there. But she was not to be moved. The laughter and chatter of the men in the guard-room, the coming and going of Bigot as he passed, below but out of sight, had no terrors for her; nay, she breathed more freely on the bare open landing of the staircase than in the close confines of a room which her fears made hateful to her. Here at least she could listen, her face unseen; and listening she bore the suspense more easily.

A turn in the staircase, with the noise which proceeded from the guard-room, rendered it difficult to hear what happened in the closed room below. But she thought that if an alarm were raised there she must hear it; and as the moments passed and nothing happened, she began to feel confident that her lover had made good his escape by the window.

Presently she got a fright. Three or four men came from the guard-room and went, as it seemed to her, to the door of the room with the shattered casement. She told herself that she had rejoiced too soon, and her heart stood still. She waited for a rush of feet, a cry, a struggle. But except an uncertain muffled sound which lasted for some minutes, and was followed by a dull shock, she heard nothing more. And presently the men went back whispering, the noise in the guard-room which had been partially hushed broke forth anew, and perplexed but relieved she breathed again. Surely he had escaped by this time. Surely by this time he was far away, in the Arsenal, or in some place of refuge! And she might take courage, and feel that for this day the peril was overpast.

"Mademoiselle will have the lights now?" one of the women ventured.

"No! no!" she answered feverishly, and she continued to crouch where she was on the stairs, bathing herself and her burning face in the darkness and coolness of the stairway. The air entered freely through a window at her elbow, and the place was fresher, were that all, than the room she had left. Javette began to whimper, but she paid no heed to her; a man came and went along the passage below, and she heard the outer door unbarred, and the jarring tread of three or four men who passed through it. But all without disturbance; and afterwards the house was quiet again. And as on this Monday evening the prime virulence of the massacre had begun to abate—though it held after a fashion to the end of the week—Paris without was quiet also. The sounds which had chilled her heart at intervals during two days were no longer heard. A feeling almost of peace, almost of comfort—a drowsy feeling, that was three parts a reaction from excitement—took possession of her. In the darkness her head sank lower and lower on her knees. And half an hour passed, while Javette whimpered, and Madame Carlat slumbered, her broad back propped against the wall.

Suddenly Mademoiselle opened her eyes, and saw, three steps below her, a strange man whose upward way she barred. Behind him came Carlat, and behind him Bigot, lighting both; and in the confusion of her thoughts as she rose to her feet the three, all staring at her in a common amazement, seemed a company. The air entering through the open window beside her blew the flame of the candle this way and that, and added to the nightmare character of the scene; for by the shifting light the men seemed to laugh one moment and scowl the next, and their shadows were now high and now low on the wall. In truth, they were as much amazed at coming on her in that place as she at their appearance; but they were awake, and she newly roused from sleep; and the advantage was with them.

"What is it?" she cried in a panic. "What is it?"

"If Mademoiselle will return to her room?" one of the men said courteously.

"But—what is it?" She was frightened.

"If Mademoiselle—"

Then she turned without more and went back into the room, and the three followed, and her woman and Madame Carlat. She stood resting one hand on the table while Javette with shaking fingers lighted the candles. Then—

"Now, Monsieur," she said in a hard voice, "if you will tell me your business?"

"You do not know me?" The stranger's eyes dwelt kindly and pitifully on her.

She looked at him steadily, crushing down the fears which knocked at her heart.

"No," she said. "And yet I think I have seen you."

"You saw me a week last Sunday," the stranger answered sorrowfully. "My name is La Tribe. I preached that day, Mademoiselle, before the King of Navarre. I believe that you were there."

For a moment she stared at him in silence, her lips parted. Then she laughed, a laugh which set the teeth on edge.

"Oh, he is clever!" she cried. "He has the wit of the priests! Or the devil! But you come too late, Monsieur! You come too late! The bird has flown."

"Mademoiselle—"

"I tell you the bird has flown!" she repeated vehemently. And her laugh of joyless triumph rang through the room. "He is clever, but I have outwitted him! I have—"

She paused and stared about her wildly, struck by the silence; struck too by something solemn, something pitiful in the faces that were turned on her. And her lip began to quiver.

"What?" she muttered. "Why do you look at me so? He has not"—she turned from one to another—"he has not been taken?"

"M. Tignonville?"

She nodded.

"He is below."

"Ah!" she said.

They expected to see her break down, perhaps to see her fall. But she only groped blindly for a chair and sat. And for a moment there was silence in the room. It was the Huguenot minister who broke it in a tone formal and solemn.

"Listen, all present!" he said slowly. "The ways of God are past finding out. For two days in the midst of great perils I have been preserved by His hand and fed by His bounty, and I am told that I shall live if, in this matter, I do the will of those who hold me in their power. But be assured—and hearken all," he continued, lowering his voice to a sterner note. "Rather than marry this woman to this man against her will—if indeed in His sight such marriage can be—rather than save my life by such base compliance, I will die not once but ten times! See. I am ready! I will make no defence!" And he opened his arms as if to welcome the stroke. "If there be trickery here, if there has been practising below, where they told me this and that, it shall not avail! Until I hear from Mademoiselle's own lips that she is willing, I will not say over her so much as Yea, yea, or Nay, nay!"

"She is willing!"

La Tribe turned sharply, and beheld the speaker. It was Count Hannibal, who had entered a few seconds earlier, and had taken his stand within the door.

"She is willing!" Tavannes repeated quietly. And if, in this moment of the fruition of his schemes, he felt his triumph, he masked it under a face of sombre purpose. "Do you doubt me, man?"

"From her own lips!" the other replied, undaunted—and few could say as much—by that harsh presence. "From no other's!"

"Sirrah, you—"

"I can die. And you can no more, my lord!" the minister answered bravely. "You have no threat can move me."

"I am not sure of that," Tavannes answered, more blandly. "But had you listened to me and been less anxious to be brave, M. La Tribe, where no danger is, you had learned that here is no call for heroics! Mademoiselle is willing, and will tell you so."

"With her own lips?"

Count Hannibal raised his eyebrows. "With her own lips, if you will," he said. And then, advancing a step and addressing her, with unusual gravity, "Mademoiselle de Vrillac," he said, "you hear what this gentleman requires. Will you be pleased to confirm what I have said?"

She did not answer, and in the intense silence which held the room in its freezing grasp a woman choked, another broke into weeping. The colour ebbed from the cheeks of more than one; the men fidgeted on their feet.

Count Hannibal looked round, his head high. "There is no call for tears," he said; and whether he spoke in irony or in a strange obtuseness was known only to himself. "Mademoiselle is in no hurry—and rightly—to answer a question so momentous. Under the pressure of utmost peril, she passed her word; the more reason that, now the time has come to redeem it, she should do so at leisure and after thought. Since she gave her promise, Monsieur, she has had more than one opportunity of evading its fulfilment. But she is a Vrillac, and I know that nothing is farther from her thoughts."

He was silent a moment; and then, "Mademoiselle," he said, "I would not hurry you."

Her eyes were closed, but at that her lips moved. "I am—willing," she whispered. And a fluttering sigh, of relief, of pity, of God knows what, filled the room.

"You are satisfied, M. La Tribe?"

"I do not—"

"Man!" With a growl as of a tiger, Count Hannibal dropped the mask. In two strides he was at the minister's side, his hand gripped his shoulder; his face, flushed with passion, glared into his. "Will you play with lives?" he hissed. "If you do not value your own, have you no thought of others? Of these? Look and count! Have you no bowels? If she will save them, will not you?"

"My own I do not value."

"Curse your own!" Tavannes cried in furious scorn. And he shook the other to and fro. "Who thought of your life? Will you doom these? Will you give them to the butcher?"

"My lord," La Tribe answered, shaken in spite of himself, "if she be willing—"

"She is willing."

"I have nought to say. But I caught her words indistinctly. And without her consent—"

"She shall speak more plainly. Mademoiselle—"

She anticipated him. She had risen, and stood looking straight before her, seeing nothing.

"I am willing," she muttered with a strange gesture, "if it must be."

He did not answer.

"If it must be," she repeated slowly, and with a heavy sigh. And her chin dropped on her breast. Then, abruptly, suddenly—it was a strange thing to see—she looked up. A change as complete as the change which had come over Count Hannibal a minute before came over her. She sprang to his side; she clutched his arm and devoured his face with her eyes. "You are not deceiving me?" she cried. "You have Tignonville below? You—oh, no, no!" And she fell back from him, her eyes distended, her voice grown suddenly shrill and defiant, "You have not! You are deceiving me! He has escaped, and you have lied to me!"

"I?"

"Yes, you have lied to me!" It was the last fierce flicker of hope when hope seemed dead: the last clutch of the drowning at the straw that floated before the eyes.

He laughed harshly. "You will be my wife in five minutes," he said, "and you give me the lie? A week, and you will know me better! A month, and—but we will talk of that another time. For the present," he continued, turning to La Tribe, "do you, sir, tell her that the gentleman is below. Perhaps she will believe you. For you know him."

La Tribe looked at her sorrowfully; his heart bled for her. "I have seen M. de Tignonville," he said. "And M. le Comte says truly. He is in the same case with ourselves, a prisoner."

"You have seen him?" she wailed.

"I left him in the room below, when I mounted the stairs."

Count Hannibal laughed, the grim mocking laugh which seemed to revel in the pain it inflicted.

"Will you have him for a witness?" he cried. "There could not be a better, for he will not forget. Shall I fetch him?"

She bowed her head, shivering. "Spare me that," she said. And she pressed her hands to her eyes while an uncontrollable shudder passed over her frame. Then she stepped forward: "I am ready," she whispered. "Do with me as you will!"

When they had all gone out and closed the door behind them, and the two whom the minister had joined were left together, Count Hannibal continued for a time to pace the room, his hands clasped at his back, and his head sunk somewhat on his chest. His thoughts appeared to run in a new channel, and one, strange to say, widely diverted from his bride and from that which he had just done. For he did not look her way, or, for a time, speak to her. He stood once to snuff a candle, doing it with an absent face: and once to look, but still absently, and as if he read no word of it, at the marriage writing which lay, the ink still wet, upon the table. After each of these interruptions he resumed his steady pacing to and fro, to and fro, nor did his eye wander once in the direction of her chair.

And she waited. The conflict of emotions, the strife between hope and fear, the final defeat had stunned her; had left her exhausted, almost apathetic. Yet not quite, nor wholly. For when in his walk he came a little nearer to her, a chill perspiration broke out on her brow, and shudderings crept over her; and when he passed farther from her—and then only, it seemed—she breathed again. But the change lay beneath the surface, and cheated the eye. Into her attitude, as she sat, her hands clasped on her lap, her eyes fixed, came no apparent change or shadow of movement.

Suddenly, with a dull shock, she became aware that he was speaking.

"There was need of haste," he said, his tone strangely low and free from emotion, "for I am under bond to leave Paris to-morrow for Angers, whither I bear letters from the King. And as matters stood, there was no one with whom I could leave you. I trust Bigot; he is faithful, and you may trust him, Madame, fair or foul! But he is not quick-witted. Badelon, also, you may trust. Bear it in mind. Your woman Javette is not faithful; but as her life is guaranteed she must stay with us until she can be securely placed. Indeed, I must take all with me—with one exception—for the priests and monks rule Paris, and they do not love me, nor would spare aught at my word."

He was silent a few moments. Then he resumed in the same tone, "You ought to know how we, Tavannes, stand. It is by Monsieur and the Queen-Mother; and *contra* the Guises. We have all been in this matter; but the latter push and we are pushed, and the old crack will reopen. As it is, I cannot answer for much beyond the reach of my arm. Therefore, we take all with us except M. de Tignonville, who desires to be conducted to the Arsenal."

She had begun to listen with averted eyes. But as he continued to speak surprise awoke in her, and something stronger than surprise—amazement, stupefaction. Slowly her eyes came to him, and when he ceased to speak—

"Why do you tell me these things?" she muttered, her dry lips framing the words with difficulty.

"Because it behoves you to know them," he answered, thoughtfully tapping the table. "I have no one, save my brother, whom I can trust."

She would not ask him why he trusted her, nor why he thought he could trust her. For a moment or two she watched him, while he, with his eyes lowered, stood in deep thought. At last he looked up and his eyes met hers.

"Come!" he said abruptly, and in a different tone, "we must end this! Is it to be a kiss or a blow between us?"

She rose, though her knees shook under her; and they stood face to face, her face white as paper.

"What—do you mean?" she whispered.

"Is it to be a kiss or a blow?" he repeated. "A husband must be a lover, Madame, or a master, or both! I am content to be the one or the other, or both, as it shall please you. But the one I will be."

"Then, a thousand times, a blow," she cried, her eyes flaming, "from you!"

He wondered at her courage, but he hid his wonder. "So be it!" he answered. And before she knew what he would be at, he struck her sharply across the cheek with the glove which he held in his hand. She recoiled with a low cry, and her cheek blazed scarlet where he had struck it.

"So be it!" he continued sombrely. "The choice shall be yours, but you will come to me daily for the one or the other. If I cannot be lover, Madame, I will be master. And by this sign I will have you know it, daily, and daily remember it."

She stared at him, her bosom rising and falling, in an astonishment too deep for words. But he did not heed her. He did not look at her again. He had already turned to the door, and while she looked he passed through it, he closed it behind him. And she was alone.

CHAPTER XIX
IN THE ORLÉANNAIS

"But you fear him?"

"Fear him?" Madame St. Lo answered; and, to the surprise of the Countess, she made a little face of contempt. "No; why should I fear him? I fear him no more than the puppy leaping at old Sancho's bridle fears his tall playfellow! Or than the cloud you see above us fears the wind before which it flies!" She pointed to a white patch, the size of a man's hand, which hung above the hill on their left hand and formed the only speck in the blue summer sky. "Fear him? Not I!" And, laughing gaily, she put her horse at a narrow rivulet which crossed the grassy track on which they rode.

"But he is hard?" the Countess murmured in a low voice, as she regained her companion's side.

"Hard?" Madame St. Lo rejoined with a gesture of pride. "Ay, hard as the stones in my jewelled ring! Hard as flint, or the nether millstone—to his enemies! But to women? Bah! Who ever heard that he hurt a woman?"

"Why, then, is he so feared?" the Countess asked, her eyes on the subject of their discussion—a solitary figure riding some fifty paces in front of them.

"Because he counts no cost!" her companion answered. "Because he killed Savillon in the court of the Louvre, though he knew his life the forfeit. He would have paid the forfeit too, or lost his right hand, if Monsieur, for his brother the Marshal's sake, had not intervened. But Savillon had whipped his dog, you see. Then he killed the Chevalier de Millaud, but 'twas in fair fight, in the snow, in their shirts. For that, Millaud's son lay in wait for him with two, in the passage under the Châtelet; but Hannibal wounded one, and the others saved themselves. Undoubtedly he is feared!" she added with the same note of pride in her voice.

The two who talked, rode at the rear of the little company which had left Paris at daybreak two days before, by the Porte St. Jacques. Moving steadily south-westward by the lesser roads and bridle-tracks—for Count Hannibal seemed averse from the great road—they had lain the second night in a village three leagues from Bonneval. A journey of two days on fresh horses is apt to change scenery and eye alike; but seldom has an alteration—in themselves and all about them—as great as that which blessed this little company, been wrought in so short a time. From the stifling wynds and evil-smelling lanes of Paris, they had passed to the green uplands, the breezy woods and babbling streams of the upper Orléannais; from sights and sounds the most appalling, to the solitude of the sandy heath, haunt of the great bustard, or the sunshine of the hillside, vibrating with the songs of larks; from an atmosphere of terror and gloom to the freedom of God's earth and sky. Numerous enough—they numbered a score of armed men—to defy the lawless bands which had their lairs in the huge forest of Orleans, they halted where they pleased: at mid-day under a grove of chestnut-trees, or among the willows beside a brook; at night, if they willed it, under God's heaven. Far, not only from Paris, but from the great road, with its gibbets and pillories—the great road which at that date ran through a waste, no peasant living willingly within sight of it—they rode in the morning and in the evening, resting in the heat of the day. And though they had left Paris with much talk of haste, they rode more at leisure with every league.

For whatever Tavannes' motive, it was plain that he was in no hurry to reach his destination. Nor for that matter were any of his company. Madame St. Lo, who had seized the opportunity of escaping from the capital under her cousin's escort, was in an ill-humour with cities, and declaimed much on the joys of a cell in the woods. For the time the coarsest nature and the dullest rider had had enough of alarums and conflicts.

The whole company, indeed, though it moved in some fashion of array with an avant and a rear-guard, the ladies riding together, and Count Hannibal proceeding solitary in the midst, formed as peaceful a band, and one as innocently diverted, as if no man of them had ever grasped pike or blown a match. There was an old rider among them who had seen the sack of Rome, and the dead face of the great Constable the idol of the Free Companies. But he had a taste for simples and much skill in them; and when Madame had once seen Badelon on his knees in the grass searching for plants, she lost her fear of him. Bigot, with his low brow and matted hair, was the abject slave of Suzanne, Madame St. Lo's woman, who twitted him mercilessly on his Norman *patois*, and poured the vials of her scorn on him a dozen times a day. In all, with La Tribe and the Carlats, Madame St. Lo's servants, and the Countess's following, they numbered not far short of two score; and when they halted at noon, and under the shadow of some leafy tree, ate their mid-day meal, or drowsed to the tinkle of Madame St. Lo's lute, it was difficult to believe that Paris existed, or that these same people had so lately left its blood-stained pavements.

They halted this morning a little earlier than usual. Madame St. Lo had barely answered her companion's question before the subject of their discussion swung himself from old Sancho's back, and stood waiting to assist them to dismount. Behind him, where the green valley through which the road passed narrowed to a rocky gate, an old mill stood among willows at the foot of a mound. On the mound behind it a ruined castle which had stood siege in the Hundred Years' War raised its grey walls; and beyond this the stream which turned the mill poured over rocks with a cool rushing sound that proved irresistible. The men, their horses watered and hobbled, went off, shouting like boys, to bathe below the falls; and after a moment's hesitation Count Hannibal rose from the grass on which he had flung himself.

"Guard that for me, Madame," he said. And he dropped a packet, bravely sealed and tied with a silk thread, into the Countess's lap. "'Twill be safer than leaving it in my clothes. Ohé!" And he turned to Madame St. Lo. "Would you fancy a life that was all gipsying, cousin?" And if there was irony in his voice, there was desire in his eyes.

"There is only one happy man in the world," she answered, with conviction.

"By name?"

"The hermit of Compiégne."

"And in a week you would be wild for a masque!" he said cynically. And turning on his heel he followed the men.

Madame St. Lo sighed complacently. "Heigho!" she said. "He's right! We are never content, *ma mie*! When I am trifling in the Gallery my heart is in the greenwood. And when I have eaten black bread and drank spring water for a fortnight I do nothing but dream of Zamet's, and white mulberry tarts! And you are in the same case. You have saved your round white neck, or it has been saved for you, by not so much as the thickness of Zamet's pie-crust—I declare my mouth is beginning to water for it!—and instead of being thankful and making the best of things, you are thinking of poor Madame d'Yverne, or dreaming of your calf-love!"

The girl's face—for a girl she was, though they called her Madame—began to work. She struggled a moment with her emotion, and then broke down, and fell to weeping silently. For two days she had sat in public and not given way. But the reference to her lover was too much for her strength.

Madame St. Lo looked at her with eyes which were not unkindly.

"Sits the wind in that quarter?" she murmured. "I thought so! But there, my dear, if you don't put that packet in your gown you'll wash out the address! Moreover, if you ask me, I don't think the young man is worth it. It is only that what we have not got—we want!"

But the young Countess had borne to the limit of her powers. With an incoherent word she rose to her feet, and walked hurriedly away. The thought of what was and of what might have been, the thought of the lover who still—though he no longer seemed, even to her, the perfect hero—held a place in her heart, filled her breast to overflowing. She longed for some spot where she could weep unseen; where the sunshine and the blue sky would not mock her grief; and seeing in front of her a little clump of alders, which grew beside the stream, in a bend that in winter was marshy, she hastened towards it.

Madame St. Lo saw her figure blend with the shadow of the trees.

"Quite *à la* Ronsard, I give my word!" she murmured. "And now she is out of sight! *La, la*! I could play at the game myself, and carve sweet sorrow on the barks of trees, if it were not so lonesome! And if I had a man!"

And gazing pensively at the stream and the willows, my lady tried to work herself into a proper frame of mind; now murmuring the name of one gallant, and now, finding it unsuited, the name of another. But the soft inflection would break into a giggle, and finally into a yawn; and, tired of the attempt, she began to pluck grass and throw it from her. By-and-by she discovered that Madame Carlat and the women, who had their place a little apart, had disappeared; and affrighted by the solitude and silence—for neither of which she was made—she sprang up and stared about her, hoping to discern them. Right and left, however, the sweep of hillside curved upward to the skyline, lonely and untenanted; behind her the castled rock frowned down on the rugged gorge and filled it with dispiriting shadow. Madame St. Lo stamped her foot on the turf.

"The little fool!" she murmured pettishly. "Does she think that I am to be murdered that she may fatten on sighs? Oh, come up, Madame, you must be dragged out of this!" And she started briskly towards the alders, intent on gaining company as quickly as possible.

She had gone about fifty yards, and had as many more to traverse when she halted. A man, bent double, was moving stealthily along the farther side of the brook, a little in front of her. Now she saw him, now she lost him; now she caught a glimpse of him again, through a screen of willow branches. He moved with the utmost caution, as a man moves who is pursued or in danger; and for a moment she deemed him a peasant whom the bathers had disturbed and who was bent on escaping. But when he came opposite to the alder-bed she saw that that was his point, for he crouched down, sheltered by a willow, and gazed eagerly among the trees, always with his back to her; and then he waved his hand to some one in the wood.

Madame St. Lo drew in her breath. As if he had heard the sound—which was impossible—the man dropped down where he stood, crawled a yard or two on his face, and disappeared.

Madame stared a moment, expecting to see him or hear him. Then, as nothing happened, she screamed. She was a woman of quick impulses, essentially feminine; and she screamed three or four times, standing where she was, her eyes on the edge of the wood. "If that does not bring her out, nothing will!" she thought.

It brought her. An instant, and the Countess appeared, and hurried in dismay to her side.

"What is it?" the younger woman asked, glancing over her shoulder; for all the valley, all the hills were peaceful, and behind Madame St. Lo—but the lady had not discovered it—the servants who had returned were laying the meal. "What is it?" she repeated anxiously.

"Who was it?" Madame St. Lo asked curtly. She was quite calm now.

"Who was—who?"

"The man in the wood?"

The Countess stared a moment, then laughed. "Only the old soldier they call Badelon, gathering simples. Did you think that he would harm me?"

"It was not old Badelon whom I saw!" Madame St. Lo retorted. "It was a younger man, who crept along the other side of the brook, keeping under cover. When I first saw him he was there," she continued, pointing to the place. "And he crept on and on until he came opposite to you. Then he waved his hand."

"To me?"

Madame nodded.

"But if you saw him, who was he?" the Countess asked.

"I did not see his face," Madame St. Lo answered. "But he waved to you. That I saw."

The Countess had a thought which slowly flooded her face with crimson. Madame St. Lo saw the change, saw the tender light which on a sudden softened the other's eyes; and the same thought occurred to her. And having a mind to punish her companion for her reticence—for she did not doubt that the girl knew more than she acknowledged—she proposed that they should return and find Badelon, and learn if he had seen the man.

"Why?" Madame Tavannes asked. And she stood stubbornly, her head high. "Why should we?"

"To clear it up," the elder woman answered mischievously. "But perhaps, it were better to tell your husband and let his men search the coppice."

The colour left the Countess's face as quickly as it had come. For a moment she was tongue-tied. Then—

"Have we not had enough of seeking and being sought?" she cried, more bitterly than befitted the occasion. "Why should we hunt him? I am not timid, and he did me no harm. I beg, Madame, that you will do me the favour of being silent on the matter."

"Oh, if you insist? But what a pother—"

"I did not see him, and he did not see me," Madame de Tavannes answered vehemently. "I fail, therefore, to understand why we should harass him, whoever he be. Besides, M. de Tavannes is waiting for us."

"And M. de Tignonville—is following us!" Madame St. Lo muttered under her breath. And she made a face at the other's back.

She was silent, however. They returned to the others and nothing of import, it would seem, had happened. The soft summer air played on the meal laid under the willows as it had played on the meal of yesterday laid under the chestnut-trees. The horses grazed within sight, moving now and again, with a jingle of trappings or a jealous neigh: the women's chatter vied with the unceasing sound of the mill-stream. After dinner, Madame St. Lo touched the lute, and Badelon—Badelon who had seen the sack of the Colonna's Palace, and been served by cardinals on the knee—fed a water-rat, which had its home in one of the willow-stumps, with carrot-parings. One by one the men laid themselves to sleep with their faces on their arms; and to the eyes all was as all had been yesterday in this camp of armed men living peacefully.

But not to the Countess! She had accepted her life, she had resigned herself, she had marvelled that it was no worse. After the horrors of Paris the calm of the last two days had fallen on her as balm on a wound. Worn out in body and mind, she had rested, and only rested; without thought, almost without emotion, save for the feeling, half fear, half curiosity, which stirred her in regard to the strange man, her husband. Who on his side left her alone.

But the last hour had wrought a change. Her eyes were grown restless, her colour came and went. The past stirred in its shallow—ah, so shallow—grave; and dead hopes and dead forebodings, strive as she might, thrust out hands to plague and torment her. If the man who sought to speak with her by stealth, who dogged her footsteps and hung on the skirts of her party, were Tignonville—her lover, who at his own request had been escorted to the Arsenal before their departure from Paris—then her plight was a sorry one. For what woman, wedded as she had been wedded, could think otherwise than indulgently of his persistence? And yet, lover and husband! What peril, what shame the words had often spelled! At the thought only she trembled and her colour ebbed. She saw, as one who stands on the brink of a precipice, the depth which yawned before her. She asked herself, shivering, if she would ever sink to *that*.

All the loyalty of a strong nature, all the virtue of a good woman, revolted against the thought. True, her husband—husband she must call him—had not deserved her love; but his bizarre magnanimity, the gloomy, disdainful kindness with which he had crowned possession, even the unity of their interests, which he had impressed upon her in so strange a fashion, claimed a return in honour.

To be paid—how? how? That was the crux which perplexed, which frightened, which harassed her. For, if she told her suspicions, she exposed her lover to capture by one who had no longer a reason to be merciful. And if she sought occasion to see Tignonville and so to dissuade him, she did it at deadly risk to herself. Yet what other course lay open to her if she would not stand by? If she would not play the traitor? If she—

"Madame,"—it was her husband, and he spoke to her suddenly,—"are you not well?" And, looking up guiltily, she found his eyes fixed curiously on hers.

Her face turned red and white and red again, and she faltered something and looked from him, but only to meet Madame St. Lo's eyes. My lady laughed softly in sheer mischief.

"What is it?" Count Hannibal asked sharply.

But Madame St. Lo's answer was a line of Ronsard.

CHAPTER XX
ON THE CASTLE HILL

Thrice she hummed it, bland and cwas very nice in company, obliged her to squeal. The uproar which ensued, the men backing the man and the women the woman, brought Tavannes to his feet. He did not speak, but a glance from his eyes was enough. There was not one who failed to see that something was amiss with him, and a sudden silence fell on the party.

He turned to the Countess. "You wished to see the castle?" he said. "You had better go now, but not alone." He cast his eyes over the company, and summoned La Tribe, who was seated with the Carlats. "Go with Madame," he said curtly. "She has a mind to climb the hill. Bear in mind, we start at three, and do not venture out of hearing."

"I understand, M. le Comte," the minister answered. He spoke quietly, but there was a strange light in his face as he turned to go with her.

None the less he was silent until Madame's lagging feet—for all her interest in the expedition was gone—had borne her a hundred paces from the company. Then—

"Who knoweth our thoughts and forerunneth all our desires," he murmured. And when she turned to him, astonished, "Madame," he continued, "I have prayed, ah, how I have prayed, for this opportunity of speaking to you! And it has come. I would it had come this morning, but it has come. Do not start or look round; many eyes are on us, and, alas! I have that to say to you which it will move you to hear, and that to ask of you which it must task your courage to perform."

She began to tremble, and stood looking up the green slope to the broken grey wall which crowned its summit.

"What is it?" she whispered, commanding herself with an effort. "What is it? If it have aught to do with M. Tignonville—"

"It has not!"

In her surprise—for although she had put the question she had felt no doubt of the answer—she started and turned to him.

"It has not?" she exclaimed almost incredulously.

"No."

"Then what is it, Monsieur?" she replied, a little haughtily. "What can there be that should move me so?"

"Life or death, Madame," he answered solemnly. "Nay, more; for since Providence has given me this chance of speaking to you, a thing of which I despaired, I know that the burden is laid on us, and that it is guilt or it is innocence, according as we refuse the burden or bear it."

"What is it, then?" she cried impatiently. "What is it?"

"I tried to speak to you this morning."

"Was it you, then, whom Madame St. Lo saw stalking me before dinner?"

"It was."

She clasped her hands and heaved a sigh of relief. "Thank God, Monsieur!" she replied. "You have lifted a weight from me. I fear nothing in comparison of that. Nothing!"

"Alas!" he answered sombrely, "there is much to fear, for others if not for ourselves! Do you know what that is which M. de Tavannes bears always in his belt? What it is he carries with such care? What it was he handed to you to keep while he bathed to-day?"

"Letters from the King."

"Yes, but the import of those letters?"

"No."

"And yet, should they be written in letters of blood!" the minister exclaimed, his face kindling. "They should scorch the hands that hold them and blister the eyes that read them. They are the fire and the sword! They are the King's order to do at Angers as they have done in Paris. To slay all of the religion who are found there—and they are many! To spare none, to have mercy neither on the old man nor the unborn child! See yonder hawk!" he continued, pointing with a shaking hand to a falcon which hung light and graceful above the valley, the movement of its wings invisible. "How it disports itself in the face of the sun! How easy its way, how smooth its flight! But see, it drops upon its prey in the rushes beside the brook, and the end of its beauty is slaughter! So is it with yonder company!" His finger sank until it indicated the little camp seated toy-like in the green meadow four hundred feet below them, with every man and horse, and the very camp-kettle, clear-cut and visible, though diminished by distance to fairy-like proportions. "So it is with yonder company!" he repeated sternly.

"They play and are merry, and one fishes and another sleeps! But at the end of the journey is death. Death for their victims, and for them the judgment!"

She stood, as he spoke, in the ruined gateway, a walled grass-plot behind her, and at her feet the stream, the smiling valley, the alders, and the little camp. The sky was cloudless, the scene drowsy with the stillness of an August afternoon. But his words went home so truly that the sunlit landscape before the eyes added one more horror to the picture he called up before the mind.

The Countess turned white and sick. "Are you sure?" she whispered at last.

"Quite sure."

"Ah, God!" she cried, "are we never to have peace?" And turning from the valley, she walked some distance into the grass court, and stood. After a time, she turned to him; he had followed her doggedly, pace for pace. "What do you want me to do?" she cried, despair in her voice. "What can I do?"

"Were the letters he bears destroyed—"

"The letters?"

"Yes, were the letters destroyed," La Tribe answered relentlessly, "he could do nothing! Nothing! Without that authority the magistrates of Angers would not move. He could do nothing. And men and women and children—men and women and children whose blood will otherwise cry for vengeance, perhaps for vengeance on us who might have saved them—will live! Will live!" he repeated, with a softening eye. And with an all-embracing gesture he seemed to call to witness the open heavens, the sunshine and the summer breeze which wrapped them round. "Will live!"

She drew a deep breath. "And you have brought me here," she said, "to ask me to do this?"

"I was sent here to ask you to do this."

"Why me? Why me?" she wailed, and she held out her open hands to him, her face wan and colourless. "You come to me, a woman! Why to me?"

"You are his wife!"

"And he is my husband!"

"Therefore he trusts you," was the unyielding, the pitiless answer. "You, and you alone, have the opportunity of doing this."

She gazed at him in astonishment. "And it is you who say that?" she faltered, after a pause. "You who made us one, who now bid me betray him, whom I have sworn to love? To ruin him whom I have sworn to honour?"

"I do!" he answered solemnly. "On my head be the guilt, and on yours the merit."

"Nay, but—" she cried quickly, and her eyes glittered with passion—"do you take both guilt and merit! You are a man," she continued, her words coming quickly in her excitement, "he is but a man! Why do you not call him aside, trick him apart on some pretence or other, and when there are but you two, man to man, wrench the warrant from him? Staking your life against his, with all those lives for prize? And save them or perish? Why I, even I, a woman, could find it in my heart to do that, were he not my husband! Surely you, you who are a man, and young—"

"Am no match for him in strength or arms," the minister answered sadly. "Else would I do it! Else would I stake my life, Heaven knows, as gladly to save their lives as I sit down to meat! But I should fail, and if I failed all were lost. Moreover," he continued solemnly, "I am certified that this task has been set for you. It was not for nothing, Madame, nor to save one poor household that you were joined to this man; but to ransom all these lives and this great city. To be the Judith of our faith, the saviour of Angers, the—"

"Fool! Fool!" she cried. "Will you be silent?" And she stamped the turf passionately, while her eyes blazed in her white face. "I am no Judith, and no madwoman as you are fain to make me. Mad?" she continued, overwhelmed with agitation, "My God, I would I were, and I should be free from this!" And, turning, she walked a little way from him with the gesture of one under a crushing burden.

He waited a minute, two minutes, three minutes, and still she did not return. At length she came back, her bearing more composed; she looked at him, and her eyes seized his and seemed as if they would read his soul.

"Are you sure," she said, "of what you have told me? Will you swear that the contents of these letters are as you say?"

"As I live," he answered gravely. "As God lives."

"And you know—of no other way, Monsieur? Of no other way?" she repeated slowly and piteously.

"Of none, Madame, of none, I swear."

She sighed deeply, and stood sunk in thought. Then, "When do we reach Angers?" she asked heavily.

"The day after to-morrow."

"I have—until the day after to-morrow?"

"Yes. To-night we lie near Vendôme."

"And to-morrow night?"

"Near a place called La Flèche. It is possible," he went on with hesitation—for he did not understand her—"that he may bathe to-morrow, and may hand the packet to you, as he did to-day when I vainly sought speech with you. If he does that—"

"Yes?" she said, her eyes on his face.

"The taking will be easy. But when he finds you have it not"—he faltered anew—"it may go hard with you."

She did not speak.

"And there, I think, I can help you. If you will stray from the party, I will meet you and destroy the letter. That done—and would God it were done already—I will take to flight as best I can, and you will raise the alarm and say that I robbed you of it! And if you tear your dress—"

"No," she said.

He looked a question.

"No!" she repeated in a low voice. "If I betray him I will not lie to him! And no other shall pay the price! If I ruin him it shall be between him and me, and no other shall have part in it!"

He shook his head. "I do not know," he murmured, "what he may do to you!"

"Nor I," she said proudly. "That will be for him."

Curious eyes had watched the two as they climbed the hill. For the path ran up the slope to the gap which served for gate, much as the path leads up to the Castle Beautiful in old prints of the Pilgrim's journey, and Madame St. Lo had marked the first halt and the second, and, noting every gesture, had lost nothing of the interview save the words. But until the two, after pausing a moment, passed out of sight she made no sign. Then she laughed. And as Count Hannibal, at whom the laugh was aimed, did not heed her, she laughed again. And she hummed the line of Ronsard.

Still he would not be roused, and, piqued, she had recourse to words.

"I wonder what you would do," she said, "if the old lover followed us, and she went off with him!"

"She would not go," he answered coldly, and without looking up.

"But if he rode off with her?"

"She would come back on her feet!"

Madame St. Lo's prudence was not proof against that. She had the woman's inclination to hide a woman's secret; and she had not intended, when she laughed, to do more than play with the formidable man with whom so few dared to play. Now, stung by his tone and his assurance, she must needs show him that his trustfulness had no base. And, as so often happens in the circumstances, she went a little farther than the facts bore her.

"Any way, he has followed us so far!" she cried viciously.

"M. de Tignonville?"

"Yes. I saw him this morning while you were bathing. She left me and went into the little coppice. He came down the other side of the brook, stooping and running, and went to join her."

"How did he cross the brook?"

Madame St. Lo blushed. "Old Badelon was there, gathering simples," she said. "He scared him. And he crawled away."

"Then he did not cross?"

"No. I did not say he did!"

"Nor speak to her?"

"No. But if you think it will pass so next time—you do not know much of women!"

"Of women generally, not much," he answered, grimly polite. "Of this woman a great deal!"

"You looked in her big eyes, I suppose!" Madame St. Lo cried with heat. "And straightway fell down and worshipped her!" She liked rather than disliked the Countess; but she was of the lightest, and the least opposition drove her out of her course. "And you think you know her! And she, if she could save you from death by opening an eye, would go with a patch on it till her dying day! Take my word for it, Monsieur, between her and her lover you will come to harm."

Count Hannibal's swarthy face darkened a tone, and his eyes grew a very little smaller.

"I fancy that he runs the greater risk," he muttered.

"You may deal with him, but, for her—"

"I can deal with her. You deal with some women with a whip—"

"You would whip me, I suppose?"

"Yes," he said quietly. "It would do you good, Madame. And with other women otherwise. There are women who, if they are well frightened, will not deceive you. And there are others who will not deceive you though they are frightened. Madame de Tavannes is of the latter kind."

"Wait! Wait and see!" Madame cried in scorn.

"I am waiting."

"Yes! And whereas if you had come to me I could have told her that about M. de Tignonville which would have surprised her, you will go on waiting and waiting and waiting until one fine day you'll wake up and find Madame gone, and—"

"Then I'll take a wife I can whip!" he answered, with a look which apprised her how far she had carried it. "But it will not be you, sweet cousin. For I have no whip heavy enough for your case."

CHAPTER XXI
SHE WOULD, AND WOULD NOT

We noted some way back the ease with which women use one concession as a stepping-stone to a second; and the lack of magnanimity, amounting almost to unscrupulousness, which the best display in their dealings with a retiring foe. But there are concessions which touch even a good woman's conscience; and Madame de Tavannes, free by the tenure of a blow, and with that exception treated from hour to hour with rugged courtesy, shrank appalled before the task which confronted her.

To ignore what La Tribe had told her, to remain passive when a movement on her part might save men, women, and children from death, and a whole city from massacre—this was a line of conduct so craven, so selfish, that from the first she knew herself incapable of it. But to take the only other course open to her, to betray her husband and rob him of that, the loss of which might ruin him, this needed not courage only, not devotion only, but a hardness proof against reproaches as well as against punishment. And the Countess was no fanatic. No haze of bigotry glorified the thing she contemplated, or dressed it in colours other than its own. Even while she acknowledged the necessity of the act and its ultimate righteousness, even while she owned the obligation which lay upon her to perform it, she saw it as he would see it, and saw herself as he would see her.

True, he had done her a great wrong; and this in the eyes of some might pass for punishment. But he had saved her life where many had perished; and, the wrong done, he had behaved to her with fantastic generosity. In return for which she was to ruin him? It was not hard to imagine what he would say of her, and of the reward with which she had requited him.

She pondered over it as they rode that evening, with the weltering sun in their eyes and the lengthening shadows of the oaks falling athwart the bracken which fringed the track. Across breezy heaths and over downs, through green bottoms and by hamlets, from which every human creature fled at their approach, they ambled on by twos and threes; riding in a world of their own, so remote, so different from the real world—from which they came and to which they must return—that she could have wept in anguish, cursing God for the wickedness of man which lay so heavy on creation. The gaunt troopers riding at ease with swinging legs and swaying stirrups—and singing now a refrain from Ronsard, and now one of those verses of Marot's psalms which all the world had sung three decades before—wore their most lamb-like aspect. Behind them Madame St. Lo chattered to Suzanne of a riding mask which had not been brought, or planned expedients, if nothing sufficiently in the mode could be found at Angers. And the other women talked and giggled, screamed when they came to fords, and made much of steep places, where the men must help them. In time of war death's shadow covers but a day, and sorrow out of sight is out of mind. Of all the troop whom the sinking sun left within sight of the lofty towers and vine-clad hills of Vendôme, three only wore faces attuned to the cruel August week just ending; three only, like dark beads strung far apart on a gay nun's rosary, rode, brooding and silent, in their places. The Countess was one—the others were the two men whose thoughts she filled, and whose eyes now and again sought her, La Tribe's with sombre fire in their depths, Count Hannibal's fraught with a gloomy speculation, which belied his brave words to Madame St. Lo.

He, moreover, as he rode, had other thoughts; dark ones, which did not touch her. And she, too, had other thoughts at times, dreams of her young lover, spasms of regret, a wild revolt of heart, a cry out of the darkness which had suddenly whelmed her. So that of the three only La Tribe was single-minded.

This day they rode a long league after sunset, through a scattered oak-wood, where the rabbits sprang up under their horses' heads and the squirrels made angry faces at them from the lower branches. Night was hard upon them when they reached the southern edge of the forest, and looked across the dusky open slopes to a distant light or two which marked where Vendôme stood.

"Another league," Count Hannibal muttered; and he bade the men light fires where they were, and unload the packhorses. "'Tis pure and dry here," he said. "Set a watch, Bigot, and let two men go down for water. I hear frogs below. You do not fear to be moonstruck, Madame?"

"I prefer this," she answered in a low voice.

"Houses are for monks and nuns!" he rejoined heartily. "Give me God's heaven."

"The earth is His, but we deface it," she murmured, reverting to her thoughts, and unconscious that it was to him she spoke.

He looked at her sharply, but the fire was not yet kindled; and in the gloaming her face was a pale blot undecipherable. He stood a moment, but she did not speak again; and Madame St. Lo bustling up, he moved away to give an order. By-and-by the fires burned up, and showed the pillared aisle in which they sat, small groups dotted here and there on the floor of Nature's cathedral. Through the shadowy Gothic vaulting, the groining of many boughs which met overhead, a rare star twinkled, as through some clerestory window; and from the dell below rose in the night, now the monotonous chanting of the frogs, and now, as some great bull-frog took the note, a diapason worthy of a Brescian organ. The darkness walled all in; the night was still; a falling caterpillar sounded. Even the rude men at the farthest fire stilled their voices at times; awed, they knew not why, by the silence and vastness of the night.

The Countess long remembered that vigil—for she lay late awake; the cool gloom, the faint wood-rustlings, the distant cry of fox or wolf, the soft glow of the expiring fires that at last left the world to darkness and the stars; above all, the silent wheeling of the planets, which spoke indeed of a supreme Ruler, but crushed the heart under a sense of its insignificance, and of the insignificance of all human revolutions.

"Yet, I believe!" she cried, wrestling upwards, wrestling with herself. "Though I have seen what I have seen, yet I believe!"

And though she had to bear what she had to bear, and do that from which her soul shrank! The woman, indeed, within her continued to cry out against this tragedy ever renewed in her path, against this necessity for choosing evil, or good, ease for herself or life for others. But the moving heavens, pointing onward to a time when good and evil alike should be past, strengthened a nature essentially noble; and before she slept no shame and no suffering seemed—for the moment at least—too great a price to pay for the lives of little children. Love had been taken from her life; the pride which would fain answer generosity with generosity—that must go, too!

She felt no otherwise when the day came, and the bustle of the start and the common round of the journey put to flight the ideals of the night. But things fell out in a manner she had not pictured. They halted before noon on the north bank of the Loir, in a level meadow with lines of poplars running this way and that, and filling all the place with the soft shimmer of leaves. Blue succory, tiny mirrors of the summer sky, flecked the long grass, and the women picked bunches of them, or, Italian fashion, twined the blossoms in their hair. A road ran across the meadow to a ferry, but the ferryman, alarmed by the aspect of the party, had conveyed his boat to the other side and hidden himself.

Presently Madame St. Lo espied the boat, clapped her hands and must have it. The poplars threw no shade, the flies teased her, the life of a hermit—in a meadow—was no longer to her taste.

"Let us go on the water!" she cried. "Presently you will go to bathe, Monsieur, and leave us to grill!"

"Two livres to the man who will fetch the boat!" Count Hannibal cried.

In less than half a minute three men had thrown off their boots, and were swimming across, amid the laughter and shouts of their fellows. In five minutes the boat was brought.

It was not large and would hold no more than four. Tavannes' eye fell on Carlat.

"You understand a boat," he said. "Go with Madame St. Lo. And you, M. La Tribe."

"But you are coming?" Madame St. Lo cried, turning to the Countess. "Oh, Madame," with a curtsey, "you are not? You—"

"Yes, I will come," the Countess answered.

"I shall bathe a short distance up the stream," Count Hannibal said. He took from his belt the packet of letters, and as Carlat held the boat for Madame St. Lo to enter, he gave it to the Countess, as he had given it to her yesterday. "Have a care of it, Madame," he said in a low voice, "and do not let it pass out of your hands. To lose it may be to lose my head."

The colour ebbed from her cheeks. In spite of herself her shaking hand put back the packet. "Had you not better then—give it to Bigot?" she faltered.

"He is bathing."

"Let him bathe afterwards."

"No," he answered almost harshly; he found a species of pleasure in showing her that, strange as their relations were, he trusted her. "No; take it, Madame. Only have a care of it."

She took it then, hid it in her dress, and he turned away; and she turned towards the boat. La Tribe stood beside the stern, holding it for her to enter, and as her fingers rested an instant on his arm their eyes met. His were alight, his arm even quivered; and she shuddered.

She avoided looking at him a second time, and this was easy, since he took his seat in the bows beyond Carlat, who handled the oars. Silently the boat glided out on the surface of the stream, and floated downwards, Carlat now and again touching an oar, and Madame St. Lo chattering gaily in a voice which carried far on the water. Now it was a flowering rush she must have, now a green bough to shield her face from the sun's reflection; and now they must lie in some cool, shadowy pool under fern-clad banks, where the fish rose heavily, and the trickle of a rivulet fell down over stones.

It was idyllic. But not to the Countess. Her face burned, her temples throbbed, her fingers gripped the side of the boat in the vain attempt to steady her pulses. The packet within her dress scorched her. The great city and its danger, Tavannes and his faith in her, the need of action, the irrevocableness of action hurried through her brain. The knowledge that she must act now—or never—pressed upon her with distracting force. Her hand felt the packet, and fell again nerveless.

"The sun has caught you, *ma mie*," Madame St. Lo said. "You should ride in a mask as I do."

"I have not one with me," she muttered, her eyes on the water.

"And I but an old one. But at Angers—"

The Countess heard no more; on that word she caught La Tribe's eye. He was beckoning to her behind Carlat's back, pointing imperiously to the water, making signs to her to drop the packet over the side. When she did not obey—she felt sick and faint—she saw through a mist his brow grow dark. He menaced her secretly. And still the packet scorched her; and twice her hand went to it, and dropped again empty.

On a sudden Madame St. Lo cried out. The bank on one side of the stream was beginning to rise more boldly above the water, and at the head of the steep thus formed she had espied a late rosebush in bloom; nothing would now serve but she must land at once and plunder it. The boat was put in therefore, she jumped ashore, and began to scale the bank.

"Go with Madame!" La Tribe cried, roughly nudging Carlat in the back. "Do you not see that she cannot climb the bank? Up, man, up!"

The Countess opened her mouth to cry "No!" but the word died half-born on her lips; and when the steward looked at her, uncertain what she had said, she nodded.

"Yes, go!" she muttered. She was pale.

"Yes, man, go!" cried the minister, his eyes burning. And he almost pushed the other out of the boat.

The next second the craft floated from the bank, and began to drift downwards. La Tribe waited until a tree interposed and hid them from the two whom they had left; then he leaned forward.

"Now, Madame!" he cried imperiously. "In God's name, now!"

"Oh!" she cried. "Wait! Wait! I want to think."

"To think?"

"He trusted me!" she wailed. "He trusted me! How can I do it?" Nevertheless, and even while she spoke, she drew forth the packet.

"Heaven has given you the opportunity!"

"If I could have stolen it!" she answered.

"Fool!" he returned, rocking himself to and fro, and fairly beside himself with impatience. "Why steal it? It is in your hands! You have it! It is Heaven's own opportunity, it is God's opportunity given to you!"

For he could not read her mind nor comprehend the scruple which held her hand. He was single-minded. He had but one aim, one object. He saw the haggard faces of brave men hopeless; he heard the dying cries of women and children. Such an opportunity of saving God's elect, of redeeming the innocent, was in his eyes a gift from Heaven. And having these thoughts and seeing her hesitate—hesitate when every movement caused him agony, so imperative was haste, so precious the opportunity—he could bear the suspense no longer. When she did not answer he stooped forward, until his knees touched the thwart on which Carlat had sat; then, without a word, he flung himself forward, and, with one hand far extended, grasped the packet.

Had he not moved, she would have done his will; almost certainly she would have done it. But, thus attacked, she resisted instinctively; she clung to the letters.

"No!" she cried. "No! Let go, Monsieur!" And she tried to drag the packet from him.

"Give it me!"

"Let go, Monsieur! Do you hear?" she repeated. And, with a vigorous jerk, she forced it from him—he had caught it by the edge only—and held it behind her. "Go back, and—"

"Give it me!" he panted.

"I will not!"

"Then throw it overboard!"

"I will not!" she cried again, though his face, dark with passion, glared into hers, and it was clear that the man, possessed by one idea only, was no longer master of himself. "Go back to your place!"

"Give it me," he gasped, "or I will upset the boat!" And, seizing her by the shoulder, he reached over her, striving to take hold of the packet which she held behind her. The boat rocked; and, as much in rage as fear, she screamed.

A cry uttered wholly in rage answered hers; it came from Carlat. La Tribe, however, whose whole mind was fixed on the packet, did not heed, nor would have heeded, the steward. But the next moment a second cry, fierce as that of a wild beast, clove the air from the lower and farther bank; and the Huguenot, recognizing Count Hannibal's voice, involuntarily desisted and stood erect. A moment the boat rocked perilously under him; then—for unheeded it had been drifting that way—it softly touched the bank on which Carlat stood staring and aghast.

La Tribe's chance was gone; he saw that the steward must reach him before he could succeed in a second attempt. On the other hand, the undergrowth on the bank was thick, he could touch it with his hand, and if he fled at once he might escape.

He hung an instant irresolute; then, with a look which went to the Countess's heart, he sprang ashore, plunged among the alders, and in a moment was gone.

"After him! After him!" thundered Count Hannibal. "After him, man!" and Carlat, stumbling down the steep slope and through the rough briars, did his best to obey. But in vain. Before he reached the water's edge, the noise of the fugitive's retreat had grown faint. A few seconds and it died away.

CHAPTER XXII
PLAYING WITH FIRE

The impulse of La Tribe's foot as he landed had driven the boat into the stream. It drifted slowly downward, and if naught intervened, would take the ground on Count Hannibal's side, a hundred and fifty yards below him. He saw this, and walked along the bank, keeping pace with it, while the Countess sat motionless, crouching in the stern of the craft, her fingers strained about the fatal packet. The slow glide of the boat, as almost imperceptibly it approached the low bank; the stillness of the mirror-like surface on which it moved, leaving only the faintest ripple behind it; the silence—for under the influence of emotion Count Hannibal too was mute—all were in tremendous contrast with the storm which raged in her breast.

Should she—should she even now, with his eyes on her, drop the letters over the side? It needed but a movement. She had only to extend her hand, to relax the tension of her fingers, and the deed was done. It needed only that; but the golden sands of opportunity were running out—were running out fast. Slowly and more slowly, silently and more silently, the boat slid in towards the bank on which he stood, and still she hesitated. The stillness, and the waiting figure, and the watching eyes now but a few feet distant, weighed on her and seemed to paralyze her will. A foot, another foot! A moment and it would be too late, the last of the sands would have run out. The bow of the boat rustled softly through the rushes; it kissed the bank. And her hand still held the letters.

"You are not hurt?" he asked curtly. "The scoundrel might have drowned you. Was he mad?"

She was silent. He held out his hand, and she gave him the packet.

"I owe you much," he said, a ring of gaiety, almost of triumph, in his tone. "More than you guess, Madame. God made you for a soldier's wife, and a mother of soldiers. What? You are not well, I am afraid?"

"If I could sit down a minute," she faltered. She was swaying on her feet.

He supported her across the belt of meadow which fringed the bank, and made her recline against a tree. Then as his men began to come up—for the alarm had reached them—he would have sent two of them in the boat to fetch Madame St. Lo to her. But she would not let him.

"Your maid, then?" he said.

"No, Monsieur, I need only to be alone a little! Only to be alone," she repeated, her face averted; and believing this he sent the men away, and, taking the boat himself, he crossed over, took in Madame St. Lo and Carlat, and rowed them to the ferry. Here the wildest rumours were current. One held that the Huguenot had gone out of his senses; another, that he had watched for this opportunity of avenging his brethren; a third, that his intention had been to carry off the Countess and hold her to ransom. Only Tavannes himself, from his position on the farther bank, had seen the packet of letters, and the hand which withheld them; and he said nothing. Nay, when some of the men would have crossed to search for the fugitive, he forbade them, he scarcely knew why, save that it might please her; and when the women would have hurried to join her and hear the tale from her lips he forbade them also.

"She wishes to be alone," he said curtly.

"Alone?" Madame St. Lo cried, in a fever of curiosity. "You'll find her dead, or worse! What? Leave a woman alone after such a fright as that!"

"She wishes it."

Madame laughed cynically; and the laugh brought a tinge of colour to his brow.

"Oh, does she?" she sneered. "Then I understand! Have a care, have a care, or one of these days, Monsieur, when you leave her alone, you'll find them together!"

"Be silent!"

"With pleasure," she returned. "Only when it happens don't say that you were not warned. You think that she does not hear from him—"

"How can she hear?" The words were wrung from him.

Madame St. Lo's contempt passed all limits. "How can she!" she retorted. "You trail a woman across France, and let her sit by herself, and lie by herself, and all but drown by herself, and you ask how she hears from her lover? You leave her old servants about her, and you ask how she communicates with him?"

"You know nothing!" he snarled.

"I know this," she retorted. "I saw her sitting this morning, and smiling and weeping at the same time! Was she thinking of you, Monsieur? Or of him? She was looking at the hills through tears; a blue mist hung over them, and I'll wager she saw some one's eyes gazing and some one's hand beckoning out of the blue!"

"Curse you!" he cried, tormented in spite of himself. "You love to make mischief!"

"No!" she answered swiftly. "For 'twas not I made the match. But go your way, go your way, Monsieur, and see what kind of a welcome you'll get!"

"I will," Count Hannibal growled. And he started along the bank to rejoin his wife.

The light in his eyes had died down. Yet would they have been more sombre, and his face more harsh, had he known the mind of the woman to whom he was hastening. The Countess had begged to be left alone; alone, she found the solitude she had craved a cruel gift. She had saved the packet. She had fulfilled her trust. But only to experience, the moment the deed was done, the full poignancy of remorse. Before the act, while the choice had lain with her, the betrayal of her husband had loomed large; now she saw that to treat him as she had treated him was the true betrayal, and that even for his own sake, and to save him from a fearful sin, it had become her to destroy the letters.

Now, it was no longer her duty to him which loomed large, but her duty to the innocent, to the victims of the massacre which she might have stayed, to the people of her faith whom she had abandoned, to the women and children whose death-warrant she had preserved. Now, she perceived that a part more divine had never fallen to woman, nor a responsibility so heavy been laid upon woman. Nor guilt more dread!

She writhed in misery, thinking of it. What had she done? She could hear afar off the sounds of the camp; an occasional outcry, a snatch of laughter. And the cry and the laughter rang in her ears, a bitter mockery. This summer camp, to what was it the prelude? This forbearance on her husband's part, in what would it end? Were not the one and the other cruel make-believes? Two days, and the men who laughed beside the water would slay and torture with equal zest. A little, and the husband who now chose to be generous would show himself in his true colours. And it was for the sake of such as these that she had played the coward. That she had laid up for herself endless remorse. That henceforth the cries of the innocent would haunt her dreams.

Racked by such thoughts she did not hear his step, and it was his shadow falling across her feet which first warned her of his presence. She looked up, saw him, and involuntarily recoiled. Then, seeing the change in his face—

"Oh! Monsieur," she stammered, affrighted, her hand pressed to her side, "I ask your pardon! You startled me!"

"So it seems," he answered. And he stood over her regarding her dryly.

"I am not quite—myself yet," she murmured. His look told her that her start had betrayed her feelings.

Alas! the plan of taking a woman by force has drawbacks, and among others this one: that he must be a sanguine husband who deems her heart his, and a husband without jealousy, whose suspicions are not aroused by the faintest flush or the lightest word. He knows that she is his unwillingly, a victim, not a mistress; and behind every bush beside the road and behind every mask in the crowd he espies a rival.

Moreover, where women are in question, who is always strong? Or who can say how long he will pursue this plan or that? A man of sternest temper, Count Hannibal had set out on a path of conduct carefully and deliberately chosen; knowing—and he still knew—that if he abandoned it he had little to hope, if the less to fear. But the proof of fidelity which the Countess had just given him had blown to a white heat the smouldering flame in his heart, and Madame St. Lo's gibes, which should have fallen as cold water alike on his hopes and his passion, had but fed the desire to know the best. For all that, he might not have spoken now, if he had not caught her look of affright; strange as it sounds, that look, which of all things should have silenced him and warned him that the time was not yet, stung him out of patience. Suddenly the man in him carried him away.

"You still fear me, then?" he said, in a voice hoarse and unnatural. "Is it for what I do or for what I leave undone that you hate me, Madame? Tell me, I beg, for—"

"For neither!" she said, trembling. His eyes, hot and passionate, were on her, and the blood had mounted to his brow. "For neither! I do not hate you, Monsieur!"

"You fear me then? I am right in that."

"I fear—that which you carry with you," she stammered, speaking on impulse and scarcely knowing what she said.

He started, and his expression changed. "So?" he exclaimed. "So? You know what I carry, do you? And from whom? From whom," he continued in a tone of menace, "if you please, did you get that knowledge?"

"From M. La Tribe," she muttered. She had not meant to tell him. Why had she told him?

He nodded. "I might have known it," he said. "I more than suspected it. Therefore I should be the more beholden to you for saving the letters. But"—he paused and laughed harshly—"it was out of no love for me you saved them. That too I know."

She did not answer or protest; and when he had waited a moment in vain expectation of her protest, a cruel look crept into his eyes.

"Madame," he said slowly, "do you never reflect that you may push the part you play too far? That the patience, even of the worst of men, does not endure for ever?"

"I have your word!" she answered.

"And you do not fear?"

"I have your word," she repeated. And now she looked him bravely in the face, her eyes full of the courage of her race.

The lines of his mouth hardened as he met her look. "And what have I of yours?" he said in a low voice. "What have I of yours?"

Her face began to burn at that, her eyes fell and she faltered.

"My gratitude," she murmured, with an upward look that prayed for pity. "God knows, Monsieur, you have that!"

"God knows I do not want it!" he answered. And he laughed derisively. "Your gratitude!" And he mocked her tone rudely and coarsely. "Your gratitude!" Then for a minute—for so long a time that she began to wonder and to quake—he was silent. At last, "A fig for your gratitude," he said. "I want your love! I suppose—cold as you are, and a Huguenot—you can love like other women!"

It was the first, the very first time he had used the word to her; and though it fell from his lips like a threat, though he used it as a man presents a pistol, she flushed anew from throat to brow. But she did not quail.

"It is not mine to give," she said.

"It is his?"

"Yes, Monsieur," she answered, wondering at her courage, at her audacity, her madness. "It is his."

"And it cannot be mine—at any time?"

She shook her head, trembling.

"Never?" And, suddenly reaching forward, he gripped her wrist in an iron grasp. There was passion in his tone. His eyes burned her.

Whether it was that set her on another track, or pure despair, or the cry in her ears of little children and of helpless women, something in a moment inspired her, flashed in her eyes and altered her voice. She raised her head and looked him firmly in the face.

"What," she said, "do you mean by love?"

"You!" he answered brutally.

"Then—it may be, Monsieur," she returned. "There is a way if you will."

"A way!"

"If you will!"

As she spoke she rose slowly to her feet; for in his surprise he had released her wrist. He rose with her, and they stood confronting one another on the strip of grass between the river and the poplars.

"If I will?" His form seemed to dilate, his eyes devoured her. "If I will?"

"Yes," she replied. "If you will give me the letters that are in your belt, the packet which I saved to-day—that I may destroy them—I will be yours freely and willingly."

He drew a deep breath, still devouring her with his eyes.

"You mean it?" he said at last.

"I do." She looked him in the face as she spoke, and her cheeks were white, not red. "Only—the letters! Give me the letters."

"And for them you will give me your love?"

Her eyes flickered, and involuntarily she shivered. A faint blush rose and dyed her cheeks.

"Only God can give love," she said, her tone low.

"And yours is given?"

"Yes."

"To another?"

"I have said it."

"It is his. And yet for these letters—"

"For these lives!" she cried proudly.

"You will give yourself?"

"I swear it," she answered, "if you will give them to me! If you will give them to me," she repeated. And she held out her hands; her face, full of passion, was bright with a strange light. A close observer might have thought her distraught; still excited by the struggle in the boat, and barely mistress of herself.

But the man whom she tempted, the man who held her price at his belt, after one searching look at her turned from her; perhaps because he could not trust himself to gaze on her. Count Hannibal walked a dozen paces from her and returned, and again a dozen paces and returned; and again a third time, with something fierce and passionate in his gait. At last he stopped before her.

"You have nothing to offer for them," he said, in a cold, hard tone. "Nothing that is not mine already, nothing that is not my right, nothing that I cannot take at my will. My word?" he continued, seeing her about to interrupt him. "True, Madame, you have it, you had it. But why need I keep my word to you, who tempt me to break my word to the King?"

She made a weak gesture with her hands. Her head had sunk on her breast—she seemed dazed by the shock of his contempt, dazed by his reception of her offer.

"You saved the letters?" he continued, interpreting her action. "True, but the letters are mine, and that which you offer for them is mine also. You have nothing to offer. For the rest, Madame," he went on, eyeing her cynically, "you surprise me! You, whose modesty and virtue are so great, would corrupt your husband, would sell yourself, would dishonour the love of which you boast so loudly, the love that only God gives!" He laughed derisively as he quoted her words. "Ay, and, after showing at how low a price you hold yourself, you still look, I doubt not, to me to respect you, and to keep my word. Madame!" in a terrible voice, "do not play with fire! You saved my letters, it is true! And for that, for this time, you shall go free, if God will help me to let you go! But tempt me not! Tempt me not!" he repeated, turning from her and turning back again with a gesture of despair, as if he mistrusted the strength of the restraint which he put upon himself. "I am no more than other men! Perhaps I am less. And you—you who prate of love, and know not what love is—could love! could love!"

He stopped on that word as if the word choked him—stopped, struggling with his passion. At last, with a half-stifled oath, he flung away from her, halted and hung a moment, then, with a swing of rage, went off again violently. His feet as he strode along the river-bank trampled the flowers, and slew the pale water forget-me-not, which grew among the grasses.

CHAPTER XXIII
A MIND, AND NOT A MIND

La Tribe tore through the thicket, imagining Carlat and Count Hannibal hot on his heels. He dared not pause even to listen. The underwood tripped him, the lissom branches of the alders whipped his face and blinded him; once he fell headlong over a moss-grown stone, and picked himself up groaning. But the hare hard-pushed takes no account of the briars, nor does the fox heed the mud through which it draws itself into covert. And for the time he was naught but a hunted beast. With elbows pinned to his sides, or with hands extended to ward off the boughs, with bursting lungs and crimson face, he plunged through the tangle, now slipping downwards, now leaping upwards, now all but prostrate, now breasting a mass of thorns. On and on he ran, until he came to the verge of the wood, saw before him an open meadow devoid of shelter or hiding-place, and with a groan of despair cast himself flat. He listened. How far were they behind him?

He heard nothing—nothing, save the common noises of the wood, the angry chatter of a disturbed blackbird as it flew low into hiding, or the harsh notes of a flock of starlings as they rose from the meadow. The hum of bees filled the air, and the August flies buzzed about his sweating brow, for he had lost his cap. But behind him—nothing. Already the stillness of the wood had closed upon his track.

He was not the less panic-stricken. He supposed that Tavannes' people were getting to horse, and calculated that, if they surrounded and beat the wood, he must be taken. At the thought, though he had barely got his breath, he rose, and keeping within the coppice crawled down the slope towards the river. Gently, when he reached it, he slipped into the water, and stooping below the level of the bank, his head and shoulders hidden by the bushes, he waded down stream until he had put another hundred and fifty yards between himself and pursuit. Then he paused and listened. Still he heard nothing, and he waded on again, until the water grew deep. At this point he marked a little below him a clump of trees on the farther side; and reflecting that that side—if he could reach it unseen—would be less suspect, he swam across, aiming for a thorn bush which grew low to the water. Under its shelter he crawled out, and, worming himself like a snake across the few yards of grass which intervened, he stood at length within the shadow of the trees. A moment he paused to shake himself, and then, remembering that he was still within a mile of the camp, he set off, now walking, and now running in the direction of the hills which his party had crossed that morning.

For a time he hurried on, thinking only of escape. But when he had covered a mile or two, and escape seemed probable, there began to mingle with his thankfulness a bitter—a something which grew more bitter with each moment. Why had he fled and left the work undone? Why had he given way to unworthy fear, when the letters were within his grasp? True, if he had lingered a few seconds longer, he would have failed to make good his escape; but what of that if in those seconds he had destroyed the letters, he had saved Angers, he had saved his brethren? Alas! he had played the coward. The terror of Tavannes' voice had unmanned him. He had saved himself and left the flock to perish; he, whom God had set apart by many and great signs for this work!

He had commonly courage enough. He could have died at the stake for his convictions. But he had not the presence of mind which is proof against a shock, nor the cool judgment which, in the face of death, sees to the end of two roads. He was no coward, but now he deemed himself one, and in an agony of remorse he flung himself on his face in the long grass. He had known trials and temptations, but hitherto he had held himself erect; now, like Peter, he had betrayed his Lord.

He lay an hour groaning in the misery of his heart, and then he fell on the text "Thou art Peter, and on this rock—" and he sat up. Peter had betrayed his trust through cowardice—as he had. But Peter had not been held unworthy. Might it not be so with him? He rose to his feet, a new light in his eyes. He would return! He would return, and at all costs, even at the cost of surrendering himself, he would obtain access to the letters. And then—not the fear of Count Hannibal, not the fear of instant death, should turn him from his duty.

He had cast himself down in a woodland glade which lay near the path along which he had ridden that morning. But the mental conflict from which he rose had shaken him so violently that he could not recall the side on which he had entered the clearing, and he turned himself about, endeavouring to remember. At that moment the light jingle of a bridle struck his ear; he caught through the green bushes the flash and sparkle of harness. They had tracked him then, they were here! So had he clear proof that this second chance was to be his. In a happy fervour he stood forward where the pursuers could not fail to see him.

Or so he thought. Yet the first horseman, riding carelessly with his face averted and his feet dangling, would have gone by and seen nothing if his horse, more watchful, had not shied. The man turned then; and for a moment the two stared at one another between the pricked ears of the horse. At last—

"M. de Tignonville!" the minister ejaculated.

"La Tribe!"

"It is truly you?"

"Well—I think so," the young man answered.

The minister lifted up his eyes and seemed to call the trees and the clouds and the birds to witness.

"Now," he cried, "I know that I am chosen! And that we were instruments to do this thing from the day when the hen saved us in the haycart in Paris! Now I know that all is forgiven and all is ordained, and that the faithful of Angers shall to-morrow live and not die!" And with a face radiant, yet solemn, he walked to the young man's stirrup.

An instant Tignonville looked sharply before him. "How far ahead are they?" he asked. His tone, hard and matter-of-fact, was little in harmony with the other's enthusiasm.

"They are resting a league before you, at the ferry. You are in pursuit of them?"

"Yes."

"Not alone?"

"No." The young man's look as he spoke was grim. "I have five behind me—of your kidney, M. la Tribe. They are from the Arsenal. They have lost one his wife, and one his son. The three others—"

"Yes?"

"Sweethearts," Tignonville answered dryly. And he cast a singular look at the minister.

But La Tribe's mind was so full of one matter, he could think only of that.

"How did you hear of the letters?" he asked.

"The letters?"

"Yes."

"I do not know what you mean."

La Tribe stared. "Then why are you following him?" he asked.

"Why?" Tignonville echoed, a look of hate darkening his face. "Do you ask why we follow—" But on the name he seemed to choke and was silent.

By this time his men had come up, and one answered for him.

"Why are we following Hannibal de Tavannes?" he said sternly. "To do to him as he has done to us! To rob him as he has robbed us—of more than gold! To kill him as he has killed ours, foully and by surprise! In his bed if we can! In the arms of his wife if God wills it!"

The speaker's face was haggard from brooding and lack of sleep, but his eyes glowed and burned, as his fellows growled assent.

"'Tis simple why we follow," a second put in. "Is there a man of our faith who will not, when he hears the tale, rise up and stab the nearest of this black brood—though it be his brother? If so, God's curse on him!"

"Amen! Amen!"

"So, and so only," cried the first, "shall there be faith in our land! And our children, our little maids, shall lie safe in their beds!"

"Amen! Amen!"

The speaker's chin sank on his breast, and with his last word the light died out of his eyes. La Tribe looked at him curiously, then at the others. Last of all at Tignonville, on whose face he fancied that he surprised a faint smile. Yet Tignonville's tone when he spoke was grave enough.

"You have heard," he said. "Do you blame us?"

"I cannot," the minister answered, shivering. "I cannot." He had been for a while beyond the range of these feelings; and in the greenwood, under God's heaven, with the sunshine about him, they jarred on him. Yet he could not blame men who had suffered as these had suffered; who were maddened, as these were maddened, by the gravest wrongs which it is possible for one man to inflict on another. "I dare not," he continued sorrowfully. "But in God's name I offer you a higher and a nobler errand."

"We need none," Tignonville muttered impatiently.

"Yet many others need you," La Tribe answered in a tone of rebuke. "You are not aware that the man you follow bears a packet from the King for the hands of the magistrates of Angers?"

"Ha! Does he?"

"Bidding them do at Angers as his Majesty has done in Paris?"

The men broke into cries of execration. "But he shall not see Angers!" they swore. "The blood that he has shed shall choke him by the way! And as he would do to others it shall be done to him."

La Tribe shuddered as he listened, as he looked. Try as he would, the thirst of these men for vengeance appalled him.

"How?" he said. "He has a score and more with him and you are only six."

"Seven now," Tignonville answered with a smile.

"True, but—"

"And he lies to-night at La Flèche? That is so?"

"It was his intention this morning."

"At the old King's Inn at the meeting of the great roads?"

"It was mentioned," La Tribe admitted, with a reluctance he did not comprehend. "But if the night be fair he is as like as not to lie in the fields."

One of the men pointed to the sky. A dark bank of cloud fresh risen from the ocean, and big with tempest, hung low in the west.

"See! God will deliver him into our hands!" he cried.

Tignonville nodded. "If he lie there," he said, "He will." And then to one of his followers, as he dismounted, "Do you ride on," he said, "and stand guard that we be not surprised. And do you, Perrot, tell Monsieur. Perrot here, as God wills it," he added, with the faint smile which did not escape the minister's eye, "married his wife from the great inn at La Flèche, and he knows the place."

"None better," the man growled. He was a sullen, brooding knave, whose eyes when he looked up surprised by their savage fire.

La Tribe shook his head. "I know it, too," he said. "'Tis strong as a fortress, with a walled court, and all the windows look inwards. The gates are closed an hour after sunset, no matter who is without. If you think, M. de Tignonville, to take him there—"

"Patience, Monsieur, you have not heard me," Perrot interposed. "I know it after another fashion. Do you remember a rill of water which runs through the great yard and the stables?"

La Tribe nodded.

"Grated with iron at either end and no passage for so much as a dog? You do? Well, Monsieur, I have hunted rats there, and where the water passes under the wall is a culvert, a man's height in length. In it is a stone, one of those which frame the grating at the entrance, which a strong man can remove—and the man is in!"

"Ay, in! But where?" La Tribe asked, his eyebrows drawn together.

"Well said, Monsieur, where?" Perrot rejoined in a tone of triumph. "There lies the point. In the stables, where will be sleeping men, and a snorer on every truss? No, but in a fairway between two stables where the water at its entrance runs clear in a stone channel; a channel deepened in one place that they may draw for the chambers above with a rope and a bucket. The rooms above are the best in the house, four in one row, opening all on the gallery; which was uncovered, in the common fashion until Queen-Mother Jezebel, passing that way to Nantes, two years back, found the chambers draughty; and that end of the gallery was closed in against her return. Now, Monsieur, he and his Madame will lie there; and he will feel safe, for there is but one way to those four rooms—through the door which shuts off the covered gallery from the open part. But—" he glanced up an instant and La Tribe caught the smouldering fire in his eyes—"we shall not go in by the door."

"The bucket rises through a trap?"

"In the gallery? To be sure, monsieur. In the corner beyond the fourth door. There shall he fall into the pit which he dug for others, and the evil that he planned rebound on his own head!"

La Tribe was silent.

"What think you of it?" Tignonville asked.

"That it is cleverly planned," the minister answered.

"No more than that?"

"No more until I have eaten."

"Get him something!" Tignonville replied in a surly tone. "And we may as well eat, ourselves. Lead the horses into the wood. And do you, Perrot, call Tuez-les-Moines, who is forward. Two hours' riding should bring us to La Flèche. We need not leave here, therefore, until the sun is low. To dinner! To dinner!"

Probably he did not feel the indifference he affected, for his face as he ate grew darker, and from time to time he shot a glance, barbed with suspicion, at the minister. La Tribe on his side remained silent, although the men ate apart. He was in doubt, indeed, as to his own feelings. His instinct and his reason were at odds. Through all, however, a single purpose, the rescue of Angers, held good, and gradually other things fell into their places. When the meal was at an end, and Tignonville challenged him, he was ready.

"Your enthusiasm seems to have waned," the younger man said with a sneer, "since we met, monsieur! May I ask now if you find any fault with the plan?"

"With the plan, none."

"If it was Providence brought us together, was it not Providence furnished me with Perrot who knows La Flèche? If it was Providence brought the danger of the faithful in Angers to your knowledge, was it not Providence set us on the road—without whom you had been powerless?"

"I believe it!"

"Then, in His name, what is the matter?" Tignonville rejoined with a passion of which the other's manner seemed an inadequate cause. "What will you! What is it?"

"I would take your place," La Tribe answered quietly.

"My place?"

"Yes."

"What, are we too many?"

"We are enough without you, M. Tignonville," the minister answered. "These men, who have wrongs to avenge, God will justify them."

Tignonville's eyes sparkled with anger. "And have I no wrongs to avenge?" he cried. "Is it nothing to lose my mistress, to be robbed of my wife, to see the woman I love dragged off to be a slave and a toy? Are these no wrongs?"

"He spared your life, if he did not save it," the minister said solemnly. "And hers. And her servants."

"To suit himself."

La Tribe spread out his hands.

"To suit himself! And for that you wish him to go free?" Tignonville cried in a voice half-choked with rage. "Do you know that this man, and this man alone, stood forth in the great Hall of the Louvre, and when even the King flinched, justified the murder of our people? After that is he to go free?"

"At your hands," La Tribe answered quietly. "You alone of our people must not pursue him." He would have added more, but Tignonville would not listen.

Brooding on his wrongs behind the wall of the Arsenal, he had let hatred eat away his more generous instincts. Vain and conceited, he fancied that the world laughed at the poor figure he had cut; and the wound in his vanity festered until nothing would serve but to see the downfall of his enemy. Instant pursuit, instant vengeance—only these, he fancied, could restore him in his fellows' eyes.

In his heart he knew what would become him better. But vanity is a potent motive: and his conscience, even when supported by La Tribe, struggled but weakly. From neither would he hear more.

"You have travelled with him, until you side with him!" he cried violently. "Have a care, monsieur, have a care, lest we think you papist!" And walking over to the men, he bade them saddle; adding a sour word which turned their eyes, in no friendly gaze, on the minister.

After that La Tribe said no more. Of what use would it have been?

But as darkness came on and cloaked the little troop, and the storm which the men had foreseen began to rumble in the west, his distaste for the business waxed. The summer lightning which presently began to play across the sky revealed not only the broad gleaming stream, between which and a wooded hill their road ran, but the faces of his companions; and these, in their turn, shed a grisly light on the bloody enterprise towards which they were set. Nervous and ill at ease, the minister's mind dwelt on the stages of that enterprise: the stealthy entrance through the waterway, the ascent through the trap, the surprise, the slaughter in the sleeping-chamber. And either because he had lived for days in the victim's company, or was swayed by the arguments he had addressed to another, the prospect shook his soul.

In vain he told himself that this was the oppressor; he saw only the man, fresh roused from sleep, with the horror of impending dissolution in his eyes. And when the rider, behind whom he sat, pointed to a faint spark of light, at no great distance before them, and whispered that it was St. Agnes's Chapel, hard by the inn, he could have cried with the best Catholic of them all, "Inter pontem et fontem, Domine!" Nay, some such words did pass his lips.

For the man before him turned halfway in his saddle. "What?" he asked.

But the Huguenot did not explain.

CHAPTER XXIV
AT THE KING'S INN

The Countess sat up in the darkness of the chamber. She had writhed since noon under the stings of remorse; she could bear them no longer. The slow declension of the day, the evening light, the signs of coming tempest which had driven her company to the shelter of the inn at the crossroads, all had racked her, by reminding her that the hours were flying, and that soon the fault she had committed would be irreparable. One impulsive attempt to redeem it she had made; but it had failed, and, by rendering her suspect, had made reparation more difficult. Still, by daylight it had seemed possible to rest content with the trial made; not so now, when night had fallen, and the cries of little children and the haggard eyes of mothers peopled the darkness of her chamber. She sat up, and listened with throbbing temples.

To shut out the lightning which played at intervals across the heavens, Madame St. Lo, who shared the room, had covered the window with a cloak; and the place was dark. To exclude the dull roll of the thunder was less easy, for the night was oppressively hot, and behind the cloak the casement was open. Gradually, too, another sound, the hissing fall of heavy rain, began to make itself heard, and to mingle with the regular breathing which proved that Madame St. Lo slept.

Assured of this fact, the Countess presently heaved a sigh, and slipped from the bed. She groped in the darkness for her cloak, found it, and donned it over her night gear. Then, taking her bearings by her bed, which stood with its head to the window and its foot to the entrance, she felt her way across the floor to the door, and after passing her hands a dozen times over every part of it, she found the latch, and raised it. The door creaked, as she pulled it open, and she stood arrested; but the sound went no farther, for the roofed gallery outside, which looked by two windows on the courtyard, was full of outdoor noises, the rushing of rain and the running of spouts and eaves. One of the windows stood wide, admitting the rain and wind, and as she paused, holding the door open, the draught blew the cloak from her. She stepped out quickly and shut the door behind her. On her left was the blind end of the passage; she turned to the right. She took one step into the darkness and stood motionless. Beside her, within a few feet of her, some one had moved, with a dull sound as of a boot on wood; a sound so near her that she held her breath, and pressed herself against the wall.

She listened. Perhaps some of the servants—it was a common usage—had made their beds on the floor. Perhaps one of the women had stirred in the room against the wall of which she crouched. Perhaps—but, even while she reassured herself, the sound rose anew at her feet.

Fortunately at the same instant the glare of the lightning flooded all, and showed the passage, and showed it empty. It lit up the row of doors on her right and the small windows on her left, and discovered facing her the door which shut off the rest of the house. She could have thanked—nay, she did thank God for that light. If the sound she had heard recurred she did not hear it; for, as the thunder which followed hard on the flash crashed overhead and rolled heavily eastwards, she felt her way boldly along the passage, touching first one door, and then a second, and then a third.

She groped for the latch of the last, and found it, but, with her hand on it, paused. In order to summon up her courage, she strove to hear again the cries of misery and to see again the haggard eyes which had driven her hither. And if she did not wholly succeed, other reflections came to her aid. This storm, which covered all smaller noises, and opened, now and again, God's lantern for her use, did it not prove that He was on her side, and that she might count on His protection? The thought at least was timely, and with a better heart she gathered her wits. Waiting until the thunder burst over her head, she opened the door, slid within it, and closed it. She would fain have left it ajar, that in case of need she might escape the more easily. But the wind, which beat into the passage through the open window, rendered the precaution too perilous.

She went forward two paces into the room, and as the roll of the thunder died away she stooped forward and listened with painful intensity for the sound of Count Hannibal's breathing. But the window was open, and the hiss of the rain persisted; she could hear nothing through it, and fearfully she took another step forward. The window should be before her; the bed in the corner to the left. But nothing of either could she make out. She must wait for the lightning.

It came, and for a second or more the room shone. The window, the low truckle-bed, the sleeper, she saw all with dazzling clearness, and before the flash had well passed she was crouching low, with the hood of her cloak dragged about her face. For the glare had revealed Count Hannibal; but not asleep! He lay on his side, his face towards her; lay with open eyes, staring at her.

Or had the light tricked her? The light must have tricked her, for in the interval between the flash and the thunder, while she crouched quaking, he did not move or call. The light must have deceived her. She felt so certain of it that she found courage to remain where she was until another flash came and showed him sleeping with closed eyes.

She drew a breath of relief at that, and rose slowly to her feet. But she dared not go forward until a third flash had confirmed the second. Then, while the thunder burst overhead and rolled away, she crept on until she stood beside the pillow, and, stooping, could hear the sleeper's breathing.

Alas! the worst remained to be done. The packet, she was sure of it, lay under his pillow. How was she to find it, how remove it without rousing him? A touch might awaken him. And yet, if she would not return empty-handed, if she would not go back to the harrowing thoughts which had tortured her through the long hours of the day, it must be done, and done now.

She knew this, yet she hung irresolute a while, blenching before the manual act, listening to the persistent rush and downpour of the rain. Then a second time she drew courage from the storm. How timely had it broken. How signally had it aided her! How slight had been her chance without it! And so at last, resolutely but with a deft touch, she slid her fingers between the pillow and the bed, slightly pressing down the latter with her other hand. For an instant she fancied that the sleeper's breathing stopped, and her heart gave a great bound. But the breathing went on the next instant—if it had stopped—and dreading the return of the lightning, shrinking from being revealed so near him, and in that act—for which the darkness seemed more fitting—she groped farther, and touched something. Then, as her fingers closed upon it and grasped it, and his breath rose hot to her burning cheek, she knew that the real danger lay in the withdrawal.

At the first attempt he uttered a kind of grunt and moved, throwing out his hand. She thought that he was going to awake, and had hard work to keep herself where she was; but he did not move, and she began again with so infinite a precaution that the perspiration ran down her face and her hair within the hood hung dank on her neck. Slowly, oh so slowly, she drew back the hand, and with it the packet; so slowly, and yet so resolutely, being put to it, that when the dreaded flash surprised her, and she saw his harsh swarthy face, steeped in the mysterious aloofness of sleep, within a hand's breadth of hers, not a muscle of her arm moved, nor did her hand quiver.

It was done—at last! With a burst of gratitude, of triumph, of exultation, she stood erect. She realized that it was done, and that here in her hand she held the packet. A deep gasp of relief, of joy, of thankfulness, and she glided towards the door.

She groped for the latch, and in the act fancied his breathing was changed. She paused, and bent her head to listen. But the patter of the rain, drowning all sounds save those of the nearest origin, persuaded her that she was mistaken, and, finding the latch, she raised it, slipped like a shadow into the passage, and closed the door behind her.

That done she stood arrested, all the blood in her body running to her heart. She must be dreaming! The passage in which she stood—the passage which she had left in black darkness—was alight; was so far lighted, at least, that to eyes fresh from the night, the figures of three men, grouped at the farther end, stood out against the glow of the lanthorn which they appeared to be trimming—for the two nearest were stooping over it. These two had their backs to her, the third his face; and it was the sight of this third man which had driven the blood to her heart. He ended at the waist! It was only after a few seconds, it was only when she had gazed at him awhile in speechless horror, that he rose another foot from the floor, and she saw that he had paused in the act of ascending through a trapdoor. What the scene meant, who these men were, or what their entrance portended, with these questions her brain refused at the moment to grapple. It was much that—still remembering who might hear her, and what she held—she did not shriek aloud.

Instead, she stood in the gloom at her end of the passage, gazing with all her eyes until she had seen the third man step clear of the trap. She could see him; but the light intervened and blurred his view of her. He stooped, almost as soon as he had cleared himself, to help up a fourth man, who rose with a naked knife between his teeth. She saw then that all were armed, and something stealthy in their bearing, something cruel in their eyes as the light of the lanthorn fell now on one dark face and now on another, went to her heart and chilled it. Who were they, and why were they here? What was their purpose? As her reason awoke, as she asked herself these questions, the fourth man stooped in his turn, and gave his hand to a fifth. And on that she lost her self-control, and cried out. For the last man to ascend was La Tribe—La Tribe, from whom she had parted that morning.

The sound she uttered was low, but it reached the men's ears, and the two whose backs were towards her turned as if they had been pricked. He who held the lanthorn raised it, and the five glared at her and she at them. Then a second cry, louder and more full of surprise, burst from her lips. The nearest man, he who held the lanthorn high that he might view her, was Tignonville, was her lover!

"*Mon Dieu!*" she whispered. "What is it? What is it?"

Then, not till then, did he know her. Until then the light of the lanthorn had revealed only a cloaked and cowled figure, a gloomy phantom which shook the heart of more than one with superstitious terror. But they knew her now—two of them; and slowly, as in a dream, Tignonville came forward.

The mind has its moments of crisis, in which it acts upon instinct rather than upon reason. The girl never knew why she acted as she did; why she asked no questions, why she uttered no exclamations, no remonstrances; why, with a finger on her lips and her eyes on his, she put the packet into his hands.

He took it from her, too, as mechanically as she gave it—with the hand which held his bare blade. That done, silent as she, with his eyes set hard, he would have gone by her. The sight of her *there*, guarding the door of him who had stolen her from him, exasperated his worst passions. But she moved to hinder him, and barred the way. With her hand raised she pointed to the trapdoor.

"Go!" she whispered, her tone stern and low, "you have what you want! Go!"

"No!" And he tried to pass her.

"Go!" she repeated in the same tone. "You have what you need." And still she held her hand extended; still without faltering she faced the five men, while the thunder, growing more distant, rolled sullenly eastward, and the midnight rain, pouring from every spout and dripping eave about the house, wrapped the passage in its sibilant hush. Gradually her eyes dominated his, gradually her nobler nature and nobler aim subdued his weaker parts. For she understood now; and he saw that she did, and had he been alone he would have slunk away, and said no word in his defence.

But one of the men, savage and out of patience, thrust himself between them.

"Where is he?" he muttered. "What is the use of this? Where is he?" And his bloodshot eyes—it was Tuez-les-Moines—questioned the doors, while his hand, trembling and shaking on the haft of his knife, bespoke his eagerness. "Where is he? Where is he, woman? Quick, or—"

"I shall not tell you," she answered.

"You lie," he cried, grinning like a dog. "You will tell us! Or we will kill you too! Where is he? Where is he?"

"I shall not tell you," she repeated, standing before him in the fearlessness of scorn. "Another step and I rouse the house! M. de Tignonville, to you who know me, I swear that if this man does not retire—"

"He is in one of these rooms?" was Tignonville's answer. "In which? In which?"

"Search them!" she answered, her voice low, but biting in its contempt. "Try them. Rouse my women, alarm the house! And when you have his people at your throats—five as they will be to one of you—thank your own mad folly!"

Tuez-les-Moines' eyes glittered. "You will not tell us?" he cried.

"No!"

"Then—"

But as the fanatic sprang on her, La Tribe flung his arms round him and dragged him back. "It would be madness," he cried. "Are you mad, fool? Have done!" he panted, struggling with him. "If Madame gives the alarm—and he may be in any one of these four rooms, you cannot be sure which—we are undone." He looked for support to Tignonville, whose movement to protect the girl he had anticipated, and who had since listened sullenly. "We have obtained what we need. Will you requite Madame, who has gained it for us at her own risk—"

"It is Monsieur I would requite," Tignonville muttered grimly.

"By using violence to her?" the minister retorted passionately. He and Tuez were still gripping one another. "I tell you, to go on is to risk what we have got! And I for one—"

"Am chicken-hearted!" the young man sneered. "Madame—" He seemed to choke on the word. "Will you swear that he is not here?"

"I swear that if you do not go I will raise the alarm!" she hissed—all their words were sunk to that stealthy note. "Go! if you have not stayed too long already. Go! Or see!" And she pointed to the trapdoor, from which the face and arms of a sixth man had that moment risen—the face dark with perturbation, so that her woman's wit told her at once that something was amiss. "See what has come of your delay already!"

"The water is rising," the man muttered earnestly. "In God's name come, whether you have done it or not, or we cannot pass out again. It is within a foot of the crown of the culvert now, and it is rising."

"Curse on the water!" Tuez-les-Moines answered in a frenzied whisper. "And on this Jezebel. Let us kill her and him! What matter afterwards?" And he tried to shake off La Tribe's grasp.

But the minister held him desperately. "Are you mad? Are you mad?" he answered. "What can we do against thirty? Let us be gone while we can. Let us be gone! Come."

"Ay, come," Perrot cried, assenting reluctantly. He had taken no side hitherto. "The luck is against us! 'Tis no use to-night, man!" And he turned with an air of sullen resignation. Letting his legs drop through the trap, he followed the bearer of the tidings out of sight. Another made up his mind to go, and went. Then only Tignonville, holding the lanthorn, and La Tribe, who feared to release Tuez-les-Moines, remained with the fanatic.

The Countess's eyes met her old lover's, and whether old memories overcame her, or, now that the danger was nearly past, she began to give way, she swayed a little on her feet. But he did not notice it. He was sunk in black rage—rage against her, rage against himself.

"Take the light," she muttered unsteadily. "And—and he must follow!"

"And you?"

But she could bear it no longer. "Oh, go," she wailed. "Go! Will you never go? If you love me, if you ever loved me, I implore you to go."

He had betrayed little of a lover's feeling. But he could not resist that appeal, and he turned silently. Seizing Tuez-les-Moines by the other arm, he drew him by force to the trap.

"Quiet, fool," he muttered savagely when the man would have resisted, "and go down! If we stay to kill him, we shall have no way of escape, and his life will be dearly bought. Down, man, down!" And between them, in a struggling silence, with now and then an audible rap, or a ring of metal, the two forced the desperado to descend.

La Tribe followed hastily. Tignonville was the last to go. In the act of disappearing he raised his lanthorn for a last glimpse of the Countess. To his astonishment the passage was empty; she was gone. Hard by him a door stood an inch or two ajar, and he guessed that it was hers, and swore under his breath, hating her at that moment. But he did not guess how nicely she had calculated her strength; how nearly exhaustion had overcome her; or that, even while he paused—a fatal pause had he known it—eyeing the dark opening of the door, she lay as one dead, on the bed within. She had fallen in a swoon, from which she did not recover until the sun had risen, and marched across one quarter of the heavens.

Nor did he see another thing, or he might have hastened his steps. Before the yellow light of his lanthorn faded from the ceiling of the passage, the door of the room farthest from the trap slid open. A man, whose eyes, until darkness swallowed him, shone strangely in a face extraordinarily softened, came out on tip-toe. This man stood awhile, listening. At length, hearing those below utter a cry of dismay, he awoke to sudden activity. He opened with a turn of the key the door which stood at his elbow, the door which led to the other part of the house. He vanished through it. A second later a sharp whistle pierced the darkness of the courtyard, and brought a dozen sleepers to their senses and their feet. A moment, and the courtyard hummed with voices, above which one voice rang clear and insistent. With a startled cry the inn awoke.

CHAPTER XXV
THE COMPANY OF THE BLEEDING HEART

"But why," Madame St. Lo asked, sticking her arms akimbo, "why stay in this forsaken place a day and a night, when six hours in the saddle would set us in Angers?"

"Because," Tavannes replied coldly—he and his cousin were walking before the gateway of the inn—"the Countess is not well, and will be the better, I think, for staying a day."

"She slept soundly enough! I'll answer for that!"

He shrugged his shoulders.

"She never raised her head this morning, though my women were shrieking 'Murder!' next door, and—Name of Heaven!" Madame resumed, after breaking off abruptly, and shading her eyes with her hand, "what comes here? Is it a funeral? Or a pilgrimage? If all the priests about here are as black, no wonder M. Rabelais fell out with them!"

The inn stood without the walls for the convenience of those who wished to take the road early: a little also, perhaps, because food and forage were cheaper, and the wine paid no town-dues. Four great roads met before the house, along the most easterly of which the sombre company which had caught Madame St. Lo's attention could be seen approaching. At first Count Hannibal supposed with his companion that the travellers were conveying to the grave the corpse of some person of distinction; for the *cortége* consisted mainly of priests and the like mounted on mules, and clothed for the most part in black. Black also was the small banner which waved above them, and bore in place of arms the emblem of the Bleeding Heart. But a second glance failed to discover either litter or bier; and a nearer approach showed that the travellers, whether they wore the tonsure or not, bore weapons of one kind or another.

Suddenly Madame St. Lo clapped her hands, and proclaimed in great astonishment that she knew them.

"Why, there is Father Boucher, the Curé of St. Benoist!" she said, "and Father Pezelay of St. Magloire. And there is another I know, though I cannot remember his name! They are preachers from Paris! That is who they are! But what can they be doing here? Is it a pilgrimage, think you?"

"Ay, a pilgrimage of Blood!" Count Hannibal answered between his teeth. And, turning to him to learn what moved him, she saw the look in his eyes which portended a storm. Before she could ask a question, however, the gloomy company, which had first appeared in the distance, moving, an inky blot, through the hot sunshine of the summer morning, had drawn near, and was almost abreast of them. Stepping from her side, he raised his hand and arrested the march.

"Who is master here?" he asked haughtily.

"I am the leader," answered a stout pompous Churchman, whose small malevolent eyes belied the sallow fatuity of his face. "I, M. de Tavannes, by your leave."

"And you, by your leave," Tavannes sneered, "are—"

"Archdeacon and Vicar of the Bishop of Angers and Prior of the Lesser Brethren of St. Germain, M. le Comte. Visitor also of the Diocese of Angers," the dignitary continued, puffing out his cheeks, "and Chaplain to the Lieutenant-Governor of Saumur, whose unworthy brother I am."

"A handsome glove, and well embroidered!" Tavannes retorted in a tone of disdain. "The hand I see yonder!" He pointed to the lean parchment mask of Father Pezelay, who coloured ever so faintly, but held his peace under the sneer. "You are bound for Angers?" Count Hannibal continued. "For what purpose, Sir Prior?"

"His Grace the Bishop is absent, and in his absence—"

"You go to fill his city with strife! I know you! Not you!" he continued, contemptuously turning from the Prior, and regarding the third of the principal figures of the party. "But you! You were the Curé who got the mob together last All Souls'."

"I speak the words of Him Who sent me!" answered the third Churchman, whose brooding face and dull-curtained eyes gave no promise of the fits of frenzied eloquence which had made his pulpit famous in Paris.

"Then Kill and Burn are His alphabet!" Tavannes retorted, and heedless of the start of horror which a saying so near blasphemy excited among the Churchmen, he turned to Father Pezelay. "And you! You, too, I know!" he continued. "And you know me! And take this from me. Turn, father! Turn! Or worse than a broken head—you bear the scar, I see—will befall you. These good persons, whom you have moved, unless I am in error, to take this journey, may not know me; but you do, and can tell them. If they will to Angers, they must to Angers. But if I find trouble in Angers when I come, I will hang some one high. Don't scowl at me, man!"—in truth, the look of hate in Father Pezelay's eyes was enough to provoke the exclamation. "Some one, and it shall not be a bare patch on the crown will save his windpipe from squeezing!"

A murmur of indignation broke from the preachers' attendants; one or two made a show of drawing their weapons. But Count Hannibal paid no heed to them, and had already turned on his heel when Father Pezelay spurred his mule a pace or two forward. Snatching a heavy brass cross from one of the acolytes, he raised it aloft, and in the voice which had often thrilled the heated congregation of St. Magloire, he called on Tavannes to pause.

"Stand, my lord!" he cried. "And take warning! Stand, reckless and profane, whose face is set hard as a stone, and his heart as a flint, against High Heaven and Holy Church! Stand and hear! Behold the word of the Lord is gone out against this city, even against Angers, for the unbelief thereof! Her place shall be left unto her desolate, and her children shall be dashed against the stones! Woe unto you, therefore, if you gainsay it, or fall short of that which is commanded! You shall perish as Achan, the son of Charmi, and as Saul! The curse that has gone out against you shall not tarry, nor your days continue! For the Canaanitish woman that is in your house, and for the thought that is in your heart, the place that was yours is given to another! Yea, the sword is even now drawn that shall pierce your side!"

"You are more like to split my ears!" Count Hannibal answered sternly. "And now mark me! Preach as you please here. But a word in Angers, and though you be shaven twice over, I will have you silenced after a fashion which will not please you! If you value your tongue therefore, father—Oh, you shake off the dust, do you? Well, pass on! 'Tis wise, perhaps."

And undismayed by the scowling brows, and the cross ostentatiously lifted to heaven, he gazed after the procession as it moved on under its swaying banner, now one and now another of the acolytes looking back and raising his hands to invoke the bolt of Heaven on the blasphemer. As the *cortége* passed the huge watering-troughs, and the open gateway of the inn, the knot of persons congregated there fell on their knees. In answer the Churchmen raised their banner higher, and began to sing the *Eripe me, Domine*! and to its strains, now vengeful, now despairing, now rising on a wave of menace, they passed slowly into the distance, slowly towards Angers and the Loire.

Suddenly Madame St. Lo twitched his sleeve. "Enough for me!" she cried passionately. "I go no farther with you!"

"Ah?"

"No farther!" she repeated. She was pale, she shivered. "Many thanks, my cousin, but we part company here. I do not go to Angers. I have seen horrors enough. I will take my people, and go to my aunt by Tours and the east road. For you, I foresee what will happen. You will perish between the hammer and the anvil."

"Ah?"

"You play too fine a game," she continued, her face quivering. "Give over the girl to her lover, and send away her people with her. And wash your hands of her and hers. Or you will see her fall, and fall beside her! Give her to him, I say—give her to him!"

"My wife?"

"Wife?" she echoed, for, fickle, and at all times swept away by the emotions of the moment, she was in earnest now. "Is there a tie," and she pointed after the vanishing procession, "that they cannot unloose? That they will not unloose? Is there a life which escapes if they doom it? Did the Admiral escape? Or Rochefoucauld? Or Madame de Luns in old days? I tell you they go to rouse Angers against you, and I see beforehand what will happen. She will perish, and you with her. Wife? A pretty wife, at whose door you took her lover last night."

"And at your door!" he answered quietly, unmoved by the gibe.

But she did not heed. "I warned you of that!" she cried. "And you would not believe me. I told you he was following. And I warn you of this. You are between the hammer and the anvil, M. le Comte! If Tignonville does not murder you in your bed—"

"I hold him in my power."

"Then Holy Church will fall on you and crush you. For me, I have seen enough and more than enough. I go to Tours by the east road."

He shrugged his shoulders. "As you please," he said.

She flung away in disgust with him. She could not understand a man who played fast and loose at such a time. The game was too fine for her, its danger too apparent, the gain too small. She had, too, a woman's dread of the Church, a woman's belief in the power of the dead hand to punish. And in half an hour her orders were given. In two hours her people were gathered, and she departed by the eastward road, three of Tavannes' riders reinforcing her servants for a part of the way. Count Hannibal stood to watch them start, and noticed Bigot riding by the side of Suzanne's mule. He smiled; and presently, as he turned away, he did a thing rare with him — he laughed outright.

A laugh which reflected a mood rare as itself. Few had seen Count Hannibal's eye sparkle as it sparkled now; few had seen him laugh as he laughed, walking to and fro in the sunshine before the inn. His men watched him, and wondered, and liked it little, for one or two who had overheard his altercation with the Churchmen had reported it, and there was shaking of heads over it. The man who had singed the Pope's beard and chucked cardinals under the chin was growing old, and the most daring of the others had no mind to fight with foes whose weapons were not of this world.

Count Hannibal's gaiety, however, was well grounded, had they known it. He was gay, not because he foresaw peril, and it was his nature to love peril; not—in the main, though a little, perhaps—because he knew that the woman whose heart he desired to win had that night stood between him and death; not, though again a little, perhaps, because she had confirmed his choice by conduct which a small man might have deprecated, but which a great man loved; but chiefly, because the events of the night had placed in his grasp two weapons by the aid of which he looked to recover all the ground he had lost—lost by his impulsive departure from the pall of conduct on which he had started.

Those weapons were Tignonville, taken like a rat in a trap by the rising of the water; and the knowledge that the Countess had stolen the precious packet from his pillow. The knowledge—for he had lain and felt her breath upon his cheek, he had lain and felt her hand beneath his pillow, he had lain while the impulse to fling his arms about her had been almost more than he could tame! He had lain and suffered her to go, to pass out safely as she had passed in. And then he had received his reward in the knowledge that, if she robbed him, she robbed him not for herself; and that where it was a question of his life she did not fear to risk her own.

When he came, indeed, to that point, he trembled. How narrowly had he been saved from misjudging her! Had he not lain and waited, had he not possessed himself in patience, he might have thought her in collusion with the old lover whom he found at her door, and with those who came to slay him. Either he might have perished unwarned; or escaping that danger, he might have detected her with Tignonville and lost for all time the ideal of a noble woman.

He had escaped that peril. More, he had gained the weapons we have indicated; and the sense of power, in regard to her, almost intoxicated him.

Surely if he wielded those weapons to the best advantage, if he strained generosity to the uttermost, the citadel of her heart must yield at last!

He had the defect of his courage and his nature, a tendency to do things after a flamboyant fashion. He knew that her act would plunge him in perils which she had not foreseen. If the preachers roused the Papists of Angers, if he arrived to find men's swords whetted for the massacre and the men themselves awaiting the signal, then if he did not give that signal there would be trouble. There would be trouble of the kind in which the soul of Hannibal de Tavannes revelled, trouble about the ancient cathedral and under the black walls of the Angevin castle; trouble amid which the hearts of common men would be as water.

Then, when things seemed at their worst, he would reveal his knowledge. Then, when forgiveness must seem impossible, he would forgive. With the flood of peril which she had unloosed rising round them, he would say, "Go!" to the man who had aimed at his life; he would say to her, "I know, and I forgive!" That, that only, would fitly crown the policy on which he had decided from the first, though he had not hoped to conduct it on lines so splendid as those which now dazzled him.

CHAPTER XXVI
TEMPER

It was his gaiety, that strange unusual gaiety, still continuing, which on the following day began by perplexing and ended by terrifying the Countess. She could not doubt that he had missed the packet on which so much hung and of which he had indicated the importance. But if he had missed it, why, she asked herself, did he not speak? Why did he not cry the alarm, search and question and pursue? Why did he not give her that opening to tell the truth, without which even her courage failed, her resolution died within her?

Above all, what was the secret of his strange merriment? Of the snatches of song which broke from him, only to be hushed by her look of astonishment? Of the parades which his horse, catching the infection, made under him, as he tossed his riding-cane high in the air and caught it?

Ay, what? Why, when he had suffered so great a loss, when he had been robbed of that of which he must give account—why did he cast off his melancholy and ride like the youngest? She wondered what the men thought, and looking, saw them stare, saw that they watched him stealthily, saw that they laid their heads together. What were they thinking of it? She could not tell; and slowly a terror, more insistent than any to which the extremity of violence would have reduced her, began to grip her heart.

Twenty hours of rest had lifted her from the state of collapse into which the events of the night had cast her; still her limbs at starting had shaken under her. But the cool freshness of the early summer morning, and the sight of the green landscape and the winding Loir, beside which their road ran, had not failed to revive her spirits; and if he had shown himself merely gloomy, merely sunk in revengeful thoughts, or darting hither and thither the glance of suspicion, she felt that she could have faced him, and on the first opportunity could have told him the truth.

But his new mood veiled she knew not what. It seemed, if she comprehended it at all, the herald of some bizarre, some dreadful vengeance, in harmony with his fierce and mocking spirit. Before it her heart became as water. Even her colour little by little left her cheeks. She knew that he had only to look at her now to read the truth; that it was written in her face, in her shrinking figure, in the eyes which now guiltily sought and now avoided his. And feeling sure that he did read it and know it, she fancied that he licked his lips, as the cat which plays with the mouse; she fancied that he gloated on her terror and her perplexity.

This, though the day and the road were warrants for all cheerful thoughts. On one side vineyards clothed the warm red slopes, and rose in steps from the valley to the white buildings of a convent. On the other the stream wound through green flats where the black cattle stood knee-deep in grass, watched by wild-eyed and half-naked youths. Again the travellers lost sight of the Loir, and crossing a shoulder, rode through the dim aisles of a beech-forest, through deep rustling drifts of last year's leaves. And out again and down again they passed, and turning aside from the gateway, trailed along beneath the brown machicolated wall of an old town, from the crumbling battlements of which faces half-sleepy, half-suspicious, watched them as they moved below through the glare and heat. Down to the river-level again, where a squalid anchorite, seated at the mouth of a cave dug in the bank, begged of them, and the bell of a monastery on the farther bank tolled slumberously the hour of Nones.

And still he said nothing, and she, cowed by his mysterious gaiety, yet spurning herself for her cowardice, was silent also. He hoped to arrive at Angers before nightfall. What, she wondered, shivering, would happen there? What was he planning to do to her? How would he punish her? Brave as she was, she was a woman, with a woman's nerves; and fear and anticipation got upon them; and his silence—his silence which must mean a thing worse than words!

And then on a sudden, piercing all, a new thought. Was it possible that he had other letters? If his bearing were consistent with anything, it was consistent with that. Had he other genuine letters, or had he duplicate letters, so that he had lost nothing, but instead had gained the right to rack and torture her, to taunt and despise her?

That thought stung her into sudden self-betrayal. They were riding along a broad dusty track which bordered a stone causey raised above the level of winter floods. Impulsively she turned to him.

"You have other letters!" she cried. "You have other letters!" And freed for the moment from her terror, she fixed her eyes on his and strove to read his face.

He looked at her, his mouth grown hard. "What do you mean, Madame?" he asked,

"You have other letters?"

"For whom?"

"From the King, for Angers!"

He saw that she was going to confess, that she was going to derange his cherished plan; and unreasonable anger awoke in the man who had been more than willing to forgive a real injury.

"Will you explain?" he said between his teeth. And his eyes glittered unpleasantly. "What do you mean?"

"You have other letters," she cried, "besides those which I stole."

"Which you stole?" He repeated the words without passion. Enraged by this unexpected turn, he hardly knew how to take it.

"Yes, I!" she cried. "I! I took them from under your pillow!"

He was silent a minute. Then he laughed and shook his head.

"It will not do, Madame," he said, his lip curling. "You are clever, but you do not deceive me."

"Deceive you?"

"Yes."

"You do not believe that I took the letters?" she cried in great amazement.

"No," he answered, "and for a good reason." He had hardened his heart now. He had chosen his line, and he would not spare her.

"Why, then?" she cried. "Why?"

"For the best of all reasons," he answered. "Because the person who stole the letters was seized in the act of making his escape, and is now in my power."

"The person—who stole the letters?" she faltered.

"Yes, Madame."

"Do you mean M. de Tignonville?"

"You have said it."

She turned white to the lips, and trembling, could with difficulty sit her horse. With an effort she pulled it up, and he stopped also. Their attendants were some way ahead.

"And you have the letters?" she whispered, her eyes meeting his. "You have the letters?"

"No, but I have the thief!" Count Hannibal answered with sinister meaning. "As I think you knew, Madame," he continued ironically, "a while back before you spoke."

"I? Oh no, no!" and she swayed in her saddle. "What—what are you—going to do?" she muttered after a moment's stricken silence.

"To him?"

"Yes."

"The magistrates will decide, at Angers."

"But he did not do it! I swear he did not."

Count Hannibal shook his head coldly.

"I swear, Monsieur, I took the letters!" she repeated piteously. "Punish me!" Her figure, bowed like an old woman's over the neck of her horse, seemed to crave his mercy.

Count Hannibal smiled.

"You do not believe me?"

"No," he said. And then, in a tone which chilled her, "If I did believe you," he continued, "I should still punish him!" She was broken; but he would see if he could not break her further. He would try if there were no weak spot in her armour. He would rack her now, since in the end she must go free. "Understand, Madame," he continued in his harshest tone, "I have had enough of your lover. He has crossed my path too often. You are my wife, I am your husband. In a day or two there shall be an end of this farce and of him."

"He did not take them!" she wailed, her face sinking lower on her breast. "He did not take them! Have mercy!"

"Any way, Madame, they are gone!" Tavannes answered. "You have taken them between you; and as I do not choose that you should pay, he will pay the price."

If the discovery that Tignonville had fallen into her husband's hands had not sufficed to crush her, Count Hannibal's tone must have done so. The shoot of new life which had raised its head after those dreadful days in Paris, and—for she was young—had supported her under the weight which the peril of Angers had cast on her shoulders, died, withered under the heel of his brutality. The pride which had supported her, which had won Tavannes' admiration and exacted his respect, sank, as she sank herself, bowed to her horse's neck, weeping bitter tears before him. She abandoned herself to her misery, as she had once abandoned herself in the upper room in Paris.

And he looked at her. He had willed to crush her; he had his will, and he was not satisfied. He had bowed her so low that his magnanimity would now have its full effect, would shine as the sun into a dark world; and yet he was not happy. He could look forward to the morrow, and say, "She will understand me, she will know me!" and, lo, the thought that she wept for her lover stabbed him, and stabbed him anew; and he thought, "Rather would she death from him, than life from me! Though I give her creation, it will not alter her! Though I strike the stars with my head, it is he who fills her world."

The thought spurred him to further cruelty, impelled him to try if, prostrate as she was, he could not draw a prayer from her.

"You don't ask after him?" he scoffed. "He may be before or behind? Or wounded or well? Would you not know, Madame? And what message he sent you? And what he fears, and what hope he has? And his last wishes? And—for while there is life there is hope—would you not learn where the key of his prison lies to-night? How much for the key to-night, Madame?"

Each question fell on her like the lash of a whip; but as one who has been flogged into insensibility, she did not wince. That drove him on: he felt a mad desire to hear her prayers, to force her lower, to bring her to her knees. And he sought about for a keener taunt. Their attendants were almost out of sight before them; the sun, declining apace, was in their eyes.

"In two hours we shall be in Angers," he said. "Mon Dieu, Madame, it was a pity, when you two were taking letters, you did not go a step farther. You were surprised, or I doubt if I should be alive to-day!"

Then she did look up. She raised her head and met his gaze with such wonder in her eyes, such reproach in her tear-stained face, that his voice sank on the last word.

"You mean—that I would have murdered you?" she said. "I would have cut off my hand first. What I did"—and now her voice was as firm as it was low—"what I did, I did to save my people. And if it were to be done again, I would do it again!"

"You dare to tell me that to my face?" he cried, hiding feelings which almost choked him. "You would do it again, would you? Mon Dieu, Madame, you need to be taught a lesson!"

And by chance, meaning only to make the horses move on again, he raised his whip. She thought that he was going to strike her, and she flinched at last. The whip fell smartly on her horse's quarters, and it sprang forward. Count Hannibal swore between his teeth.

He had turned pale, she red as fire. "Get on! Get on!" he cried harshly. "We are falling behind!" And riding at her heels, flipping her horse now and then, he forced her to trot on until they overtook the servants.

CHAPTER XXVII
THE BLACK TOWN

It was late evening when, riding wearily on jaded horses, they came to the outskirts of Angers, and saw before them the term of their journey. The glow of sunset had faded, but the sky was still warm with the last hues of day; and against its opal light the huge mass of the Angevin castle, which even in sunshine rises dark and forbidding above the Mayenne, stood up black and sharply defined. Below it, on both banks of the river, the towers and spires of the city soared up from a sombre huddle of ridge-roofs, broken here by a round-headed gateway, crumbling and pigeon-haunted, that dated from St. Louis, and there by the gaunt arms of a windmill.

The city lay dark under a light sky, keeping well its secrets. Thousands were out of doors enjoying the evening coolness in alley and court, yet it betrayed the life which pulsed in its arteries only by the low murmur which rose from it. Nevertheless, the Countess at sight of its roofs tasted the first moment of happiness which had been hers that day. She might suffer, but she had saved. Those roofs would thank her! In that murmur were the voices of women and children she had redeemed! At the sight and at the thought a wave of love and tenderness swept all bitterness from her breast. A profound humility, a boundless thankfulness took possession of her. Her head sank lower above her horse's mane; but this time it sank in reverence, not in shame.

Could she have known what was passing beneath those roofs which night was blending in a common gloom—could she have read the thoughts which at that moment paled the cheeks of many a stout burgher, whose gabled house looked on the great square, she had been still more thankful. For in attics and back rooms women were on their knees at that hour, praying with feverish eyes; and in the streets men—on whom their fellows, seeing the winding-sheet already at the chin, gazed askance—smiled, and showed brave looks abroad, while their hearts were sick with fear.

For darkly, no man knew how, the news had come to Angers. It had been known, more or less, for three days. Men had read it in other men's eyes. The tongue of a scold, the sneer of an injured woman had spread it, the birds of the air had carried it. From garret window to garret window across the narrow lanes of the old town it had been whispered at dead of night; at convent grilles, and in the timber-yards beside the river. Ten thousand, fifty thousand, a hundred thousand, it was rumoured, had perished in Paris. In Orleans, all. In Tours this man's sister; at Saumur that man's son. Through France the word had gone forth that the Huguenots must die; and in the busy town the same roof-tree sheltered fear and hate, rage and cupidity. On one side of the party-wall murder lurked fierce-eyed; on the other, the victim lay watching the latch, and shaking at a step. Strong men tasted the bitterness of death, and women clasping their babes to their breasts smiled sickly into children's eyes.

The signal only was lacking. It would come, said some, from Saumur, where Montsoreau, the Duke of Anjou's Lieutenant-Governor and a Papist, had his quarters. From Paris, said others, directly from the King. It might come at any hour now, in the day or in the night; the magistrates, it was whispered, were in continuous session, awaiting its coming. No wonder that from lofty gable windows, and from dormers set high above the tiles, haggard faces looked northward and eastward, and ears sharpened by fear imagined above the noises of the city the ring of the iron shoes that carried doom.

Doubtless the majority desired — as the majority in France have always desired — peace. But in the purlieus about the cathedral and in the lanes where the sacristans lived, in convent parlours and college courts, among all whose livelihood the new faith threatened, was a stir as of a hive deranged. Here was grumbling against the magistrates — why wait? There, stealthy plannings and arrangements; everywhere a grinding of weapons and casting of slugs. Old grudges, new rivalries, a scholar's venom, a priest's dislike, here was final vent for all. None need leave this feast unsated!

It was a man of this class, sent out for the purpose, who first espied Count Hannibal's company approaching. He bore the news into the town, and by the time the travellers reached the city gate, the dusky street within, on which lights were beginning to twinkle from booths and casements, was alive with figures running to meet them and crying the news as they ran. The travellers, weary and road-stained, had no sooner passed under the arch than they found themselves the core of a great crowd which moved with them and pressed about them; now unbonneting, and now calling out questions, and now shouting, "Vive le Roi! Vive le Roi!" Above the press, windows burst into light; and over all, the quaint leaning gables of the old timbered houses looked down on the hurry and tumult.

They passed along a narrow street in which the rabble, hurrying at Count Hannibal's bridle, and often looking back to read his face, had much ado to escape harm; along this street and before the yawning doors of a great church whence a breath heavy with incense and burning wax issued to meet them. A portion of the congregation had heard the tumult and struggled out, and now stood close-packed on the steps under the double vault of the portal. Among them the Countess's eyes, as she rode by, a sturdy man-at-arms on either hand, caught and held one face. It was the face of a tall, lean man in dusty black; and though she did not know him she seemed to have an equal attraction for him; for as their eyes met he seized the shoulder of the man next him and pointed her out. And something in the energy of the gesture, or in the thin lips and malevolent eyes of the man who pointed, chilled the Countess's blood and shook her, she knew not why.

Until then, she had known no fear save of her husband. But at that a sense of the force and pressure of the crowd—as well as of the fierce passions, straining about her, which a word might unloose—broke upon her; and looking to the stern men on either side she fancied that she read anxiety in their faces.

She glanced behind. Boot to boot, the Count's men came on, pressing round her women and shielding them from the exuberance of the throng. In their faces too she thought that she traced uneasiness. What wonder if the scenes through which she had passed in Paris began to recur to her mind, and shook nerves already overwrought?

She began to tremble. "Is there—danger?" she muttered, speaking in a low voice to Bigot, who rode on her right hand. "Will they do anything?"

The Norman snorted. "Not while he is in the saddle," he said, nodding towards his master, who rode a pace in front of them, his reins loose. "There be some here know him!" Bigot continued, in his drawling tone. "And more will know him if they break line. Have no fear, Madame, he will bring you safe to the inn. Down with the Huguenots?" he continued, turning from her and addressing a rogue who, holding his stirrup, was shouting the cry till he was crimson. "Then why not away, and—"

"The King! The King's word and leave!" the man answered.

"Ay, tell us!" shrieked another, looking upward, while he waved his cap; "have we the King's leave?"

"You'll bide *his* leave!" the Norman retorted, indicating the Count with his thumb. "Or 'twill be up with you—on the three-legged horse!"

"But he comes from the King!" the man panted.

"To be sure. To be sure!"

"Then—"

"You'll bide his time! That's all!" Bigot answered, rather it seemed for his own satisfaction than the other's enlightenment. "You'll all bide it, you dogs!" he continued in his beard, as he cast his eye over the weltering crowd. "Ha! so we are here, are we? And not too soon, either."

He fell silent as they entered an open space, overlooked on one side by the dark façade of the cathedral, on the other three sides by houses more or less illumined. The rabble swept into this open space with them and before them, filled much of it in an instant, and for a while eddied and swirled this way and that, thrust onward by the worshippers who had issued from the church and backwards by those who had been first in the square, and had no mind to be hustled out of hearing. A stranger, confused by the sea of excited faces, and deafened by the clamour of "Vive le Roi!" "Vive Anjou!" mingled with cries against the Huguenots, might have fancied that the whole city was arrayed before him. But he would have been wide of the mark. The scum, indeed—and a dangerous scum—frothed and foamed and spat under Tavannes' bridle-hand; and here and there among them, but not of them, the dark-robed figure of a priest moved to and fro; or a Benedictine, or some smooth-faced acolyte egged on to the work he dared not do. But the decent burghers were not there. They lay bolted in their houses; while the magistrates, with little heart to do aught except bow to the mob—or other their masters for the time being—shook in their council chamber.

There is not a city of France which has not seen it; which has not known the moment when the mass impended, and it lay with one man to start it or stay its course. Angers within its houses heard the clamour, and from the child, clinging to its mother's skirt, and wondering why she wept, to the Provost, trembled, believing that the hour had come. The Countess heard it too, and understood it. She caught the savage note in the voice of the mob— that note which means danger—and, her heart beating wildly, she looked to her husband. Then, fortunately for her, fortunately for Angers, it was given to all to see that in Count Hannibal's saddle sat a man.

He raised his hand for silence, and in a minute or two—not at once, for the square was dusky—it was obtained. He rose in his stirrups, and bared his head.

"I am from the King!" he cried, throwing his voice to all parts of the crowd. "And this is his Majesty's pleasure and good will! That every man hold his hand until to-morrow on pain of death, or worse! And at noon his further pleasure will be known! Vive le Roi!"

And he covered his head again.

"Vive le Roi!" cried a number of the foremost. But their shouts were feeble and half-hearted, and were quickly drowned in a rising murmur of discontent and ill-humour, which, mingled with cries of "Is that all? Is there no more? Down with the Huguenots!" rose from all parts. Presently these cries became merged in a persistent call, which had its origin, as far as could be discovered, in the darkest corner of the square. A call for "Montsoreau! Montsoreau! Give us Montsoreau!"

With another man, or had Tavannes turned or withdrawn, or betrayed the least anxiety, words had become actions, disorder a riot; and that in the twinkling of an eye. But Count Hannibal, sitting his horse, with his handful of riders behind him, watched the crowd, as little moved by it as the Armed Knight of Notre Dame. Only once did he say a word. Then, raising his hand as before to gain a hearing—

"You ask for Montsoreau?" he thundered. "You will have Montfaucon if you do not quickly go to your homes!"

At which, and at the glare of his eye, the more timid took fright. Feeling his gaze upon them, seeing that he had no intention of withdrawing, they began to sneak away by ones and twos. Soon others missed them and took the alarm, and followed. A moment and scores were streaming away through lanes and alleys and along the main street. At last the bolder and more turbulent found themselves a remnant. They glanced uneasily at one another and at Tavannes, took fright in their turn, and plunging into the current hastened away, raising now and then as they passed through the streets a cry of "Vive Montsoreau! Montsoreau!"—which was not without its menace for the morrow.

Count Hannibal waited motionless until no more than half a dozen groups remained in the open. Then he gave the word to dismount; for, so far, even the Countess and her women had kept their saddles, lest the movement which their retreat into the inn must have caused should be misread by the mob. Last of all he dismounted himself, and with lights going before him and behind, and preceded by Bigot, bearing his cloak and pistols, he escorted the Countess into the house. Not many minutes had elapsed since he had called for silence; but long before he reached the chamber looking over the square from the first floor, in which supper was being set for them, the news had flown through the length and breadth of Angers that for this night the danger was past. The hawk had come to Angers, and lo! it was a dove.

Count Hannibal strode to one of the open windows and looked out. In the room, which was well lighted, were people of the house, going to and fro, setting out the table; to Madame, standing beside the hearth—which held its summer dressing of green boughs—while her woman held water for her to wash, the scene recalled with painful vividness the meal at which she had been present on the morning of the St. Bartholomew—the meal which had ushered in her troubles. Naturally her eyes went to her husband, her mind to the horror in which she had held him then; and with a kind of shock—perhaps because the last few minutes had shown him in a new light—she compared her old opinion of him with that which, much as she feared him, she now entertained.

This afternoon, if ever, within the last few hours, if at all, he had acted in a way to justify that horror and that opinion. He had treated her—brutally; he had insulted and threatened her, had almost struck her. And yet—and yet Madame felt that she had moved so far from the point which she had once occupied that the old attitude was hard to understand. Hardly could she believe that it was on this man, much as she still dreaded him, that she had looked with those feelings of repulsion.

She was still gazing at him with eyes which strove to see two men in one, when he turned from the window. Absorbed in thought, she had forgotten her occupation, and stood, the towel suspended in her half-dried hands. Before she knew what he was doing he was at her side; he bade the woman hold the bowl, and he rinsed his hands. Then he turned, and without looking at the Countess, he dried his hands on the farther end of the towel which she was still using.

She blushed faintly. A something in the act, more intimate and more familiar than had ever marked their intercourse, set her blood running strangely. When he turned away and bade Bigot unbuckle his spur-leathers, she stepped forward.

"I will do it!" she murmured, acting on a sudden and unaccountable impulse. And as she knelt, she shook her hair about her face to hide its colour.

"Nay, Madame, but you will soil your fingers!" he said coldly.

"Permit me," she muttered half coherently. And though her fingers shook, she pursued and performed her task.

When she rose he thanked her; and then the devil in the man, or the Nemesis he had provoked when he took her by force from another—the Nemesis of jealousy, drove him to spoil all.

"And for whose sake, Madame?" he added, with a jeer; "mine or M. de Tignonville's?" And with a glance between jest and earnest, he tried to read her thoughts.

She winced as if he had indeed struck her, and the hot colour fled her cheeks.

"For his sake!" she said, with a shiver of pain. "That his life may be spared!" And she stood back humbly, like a beaten dog. Though, indeed, it was for the sake of Angers, in thankfulness for the past rather than in any desperate hope of propitiating her husband, that she had done it!

Perhaps he would have withdrawn his words. But before he could answer, the host, bowing to the floor, came to announce that all was ready, and that the Provost of the City, for whom M. le Comte had sent, was in waiting below.

"Let him come up!" Tavannes answered, grave and frowning. "And see you, close the room, sirrah! My people will wait on us. Ah!" as the Provost, a burly man, with a face framed for jollity, but now pale and long, entered and approached him with many salutations. "How comes it, M. le Prévôt—you are the Prévôt, are you not?"

"Yes, M. le Comte."

"How comes it that so great a crowd is permitted to meet in the streets? And that at my entrance, though I come unannounced, I find half of the city gathered together?"

The Provost stared. "Respect, M. le Comte," he said, "for His Majesty's letters, of which you are the bearer, no doubt induced some to come together."

"Who said I brought letters?"

"Who—?"

"Who said I brought letters?" Count Hannibal repeated in a strenuous voice. And he ground his chair half about and faced the astonished magistrate. "Who said I brought letters?"

"Why, my lord," the Provost stammered, "it was everywhere yesterday—"

"Yesterday?"

"Last night, at latest—that letters were coming from the King."

"By my hand?"

"By your lordship's hand—whose name is so well known here," the magistrate added, in the hope of clearing the great man's brow.

Count Hannibal laughed darkly. "My hand will be better known by-and-by," he said. "See you, sirrah, there is some practice here. What is this cry of Montsoreau that I hear?"

"Your lordship knows that he is His Grace's lieutenant-governor in Saumur."

"I know that, man. But is he here?"

"He was at Saumur yesterday, and 'twas rumoured three days back that he was coming here to extirpate the Huguenots. Then word came of your lordship and of His Majesty's letters, and 'twas thought that M. de Montsoreau would not come, his authority being superseded."

"I see. And now your rabble think that they would prefer M. Montsoreau. That is it, is it?"

The magistrate shrugged his shoulders and opened his hands.

"Pigs!" he said. And having spat on the floor, he looked apologetically at the lady. "True pigs!"

"What connections has he here?" Tavannes asked.

"He is a brother of my lord the Bishop's vicar, who arrived yesterday."

"With a rout of shaven heads who have been preaching and stirring up the town!" Count Hannibal cried, his face growing red. "Speak, man; is it so? But I'll be sworn it is!"

"There has been preaching," the Provost answered reluctantly.

"Montsoreau may count his brother, then, for one. He is a fool, but with a knave behind him, and a knave who has no cause to love us! And the Castle? 'Tis held by one of M. de Montsoreau's creatures, I take it?"

"Yes, my lord."

"With what force?"

The magistrate shrugged his shoulders, and looked doubtfully at Badelon, who was keeping the door. Tavannes followed the glance with his usual impatience. "Mon Dieu, you need not look at him!" he cried. "He has sacked St. Peter's and singed the Pope's beard with a holy candle! He has been served on the knee by Cardinals; and is Turk or Jew, or monk or Huguenot as I please. And Madame"—for the Provost's astonished eyes, after resting awhile on the old soldier's iron visage, had passed to her—"is Huguenot, so you need have no fear of her! There, speak, man," with impatience, "and cease to think of your own skin!"

The Provost drew a deep breath, and fixed his small eyes on Count Hannibal.

"If I knew, my lord, what you—why, my own sister's son"—he paused, his face began to work, his voice shook—"is a Huguenot! Ay, my lord, a Huguenot! And they know it!" he continued, a flush of rage augmenting the emotion which his countenance betrayed. "Ay, they know it! And they push me on at the Council, and grin behind my back; Lescot, who was Provost two years back, and would match his son with my daughter; and Thuriot, who prints for the University! They nudge one another, and egg me on, till half the city thinks it is I who would kill the Huguenots! I!" Again his voice broke. "And my own sister's son a Huguenot! And my girl at home white-faced for—for his sake."

Tavannes scanned the man shrewdly. "Perhaps she is of the same way of thinking?" he said.

The Provost started, and lost one half of his colour. "God forbid!" he cried, "saving Madame's presence! Who says so, my lord, lies!"

"Ay, lies not far from the truth."

"My lord!"

"Pish, man, Lescot has said it, and will act on it. And Thuriot, who prints for the University! Would you 'scape them? You would? Then listen to me. I want but two things. First, how many men has Montsoreau's fellow in the Castle? Few, I know, for he is a niggard, and if he spends, he spends the Duke's pay."

"Twelve. But five can hold it."

"Ay, but twelve dare not leave it! Let them stew in their own broth! And now for the other matter. See, man, that before daybreak three gibbets, with a ladder and two ropes apiece, are set up in the square. And let one be before this door. You understand? Then let it be done! The rest," he added with a ferocious smile, "you may leave to me."

The magistrate nodded rather feebly. "Doubtless," he said, his eye wandering here and there, "there are rogues in Angers. And for rogues the gibbet! But saving your presence, my lord, it is a question whether—"

But M. de Tavannes' patience was exhausted. "Will you do it?" he roared. "That is the question. And the only question."

The Provost jumped, he was so startled. "Certainly, my lord, certainly!" he muttered humbly. "Certainly, I will!" And bowing frequently, but saying no more, he backed himself out of the room.

Count Hannibal laughed grimly after his fashion, and doubtless thought that he had seen the last of the magistrate for that night. Great was his wrath, therefore, when, less than a minute later—and before Bigot had carved for him—the door opened, and the Provost appeared again. He slid in, and without giving the courage he had gained on the stairs time to cool, plunged into his trouble.

"It stands this way, M. le Comte," he bleated. "If I put up the gibbets and a man is hanged, and you have letters from the King, 'tis a rogue the less, and no harm done. But if you have no letters from His Majesty, then it is on my shoulders they will put it, and 'twill be odd if they do not find a way to hang me to right him."

Count Hannibal smiled grimly. "And your sister's son?" he sneered. "And your girl who is white-faced for his sake, and may burn on the same bonfire with him? And—"

"Mercy! Mercy!" the wretched Provost cried. And he wrung his hands. "Lescot and Thuriot—"

"Perhaps we may hang Lescot and Thuriot—"

"But I see no way out," the Provost babbled. "No way! No way!"

"I am going to show you one," Tavannes retorted. "If the gibbets are not in place by sunrise, I shall hang you from this window. That is one way out; and you'll be wise to take the other! For the rest and for your comfort, if I have no letters, it is not always to paper that the King commits his inmost heart."

The magistrate bowed. He quaked, he doubted, but he had no choice.

"My lord," he said, "I put myself in your hands. It shall be done, certainly it shall be done. But, but—" and shaking his head in foreboding, he turned to the door. At the last moment, when he was within a pace of it, the Countess rose impulsively to her feet. She called to him.

"M. le Prévôt, a minute, if you please," she said. "There may be trouble to-morrow; your daughter may be in some peril. You will do well to send her to me. My lord"—and on the word her voice, uncertain before, grew full and steady—"will see that I am safe. And she will be safe with me."

The Provost saw before him only a gracious lady, moved by a thoughtfulness unusual in persons of her rank. He was at no pains to explain the flame in her cheek, or the soft light which glowed in her eyes, as she looked at him across her formidable husband. He was only profoundly grateful—moved even to tears. Humbly thanking her, he accepted her offer for his child, and withdrew wiping his eyes. When he was gone, and the door had closed behind him, Tavannes turned to the Countess, who still kept her feet.

"You are very confident this evening," he sneered. "Gibbets do not frighten you, it seems, madame. Perhaps if you knew for whom the one before the door is intended?"

She met his look with a searching gaze, and spoke with a ring of defiance in her tone. "I do not believe it!" she said. "I do not believe it! You who save Angers will not destroy him!" And then her woman's mood changing, with courage and colour ebbing together, "Oh no, you will not! You will not!" she wailed. And she dropped on her knees before him, and holding up her clasped hands, "God will put it in your heart to spare him—and me!"

He rose with a stifled oath, took two steps from her, and in a tone hoarse and constrained, "Go!" he said. "Go, or sit! Do you hear, Madame? You try my patience too far!"

But when she had gone his face was radiant. He had brought her, he had brought all, to the point at which he aimed. To-morrow his triumph awaited him. To-morrow he who had cast her down would raise her up.

He did not foresee what a day would bring forth.

CHAPTER XXVIII
IN THE LITTLE CHAPTER-HOUSE

The sun was an hour high, and in Angers the shops and booths, after the early fashion of the day, were open or opening. Through all the gates country folk were pressing into the gloomy streets of the Black Town with milk and fruit; and at doors and windows housewives cheapened fish, or chaffered over the fowl for the pot. For men must eat, though there be gibbets in the Place Ste.-Croix: gaunt gibbets, high and black and twofold, each, with its dangling ropes, like a double note of interrogation.

But gibbets must eat also; and between ground and noose was so small a space in those days that a man dangled almost before he knew it. The sooner, then, the paniers were empty, and the clown, who pays for all, was beyond the gates, the better he, for one, would be pleased. In the market, therefore, was hurrying. Men cried their wares in lowered voices, and tarried but a little for the oldest customer. The bargain struck, the more timid among the buyers hastened to shut themselves into their houses again; the bolder, who ventured to the Place to confirm the rumour with their eyes, talked in corners and in lanes, avoided the open, and eyed the sinister preparations from afar. The shadow of the things which stood before the cathedral affronting the sunlight with their gaunt black shapes lay across the length and breadth of Angers. Even in the corners where men whispered, even in the cloisters where men bit their nails in impotent anger, the stillness of fear ruled all. Whatever Count Hannibal had it in his mind to tell the city, it seemed unlikely—and hour by hour it seemed less likely—that any would contradict him.

He knew this as he walked in the sunlight before the inn, his spurs ringing on the stones as he made each turn, his movements watched by a hundred peering eyes. After all, it was not hard to rule, nor to have one's way in this world. But then, he went on to remember, not every one had his self-control, or that contempt for the weak and unsuccessful which lightly took the form of mercy. He held Angers safe, curbed by his gibbets. With M. de Montsoreau he might have trouble; but the trouble would be slight, for he knew Montsoreau, and what it was the Lieutenant-Governor valued above profitless bloodshed.

He might have felt less confident had he known what was passing at that moment in a room off the small cloister of the Abbey of St. Aubin, a room known at Angers as the Little Chapter-house. It was a long chamber with a groined roof and stone walls, panelled as high as a tall man might reach with dark chestnut wood. Gloomily lighted by three grated windows, which looked on a small inner green, the last resting-place of the Benedictines, the room itself seemed at first sight no more than the last resting-place of worn-out odds and ends. Piles of thin sheepskin folios, dog's-eared and dirty, the rejected of the choir, stood against the walls; here and there among them lay a large brass-bound tome on which the chains that had fettered it to desk or lectern still rusted. A broken altar cumbered one corner: a stand bearing a curious—and rotting—map filled another. In the other two corners a medley of faded scutcheons and banners, which had seen their last Toussaint procession, mouldered slowly into dust—into much dust. The air of the room was full of it.

In spite of which the long oak table that filled the middle of the chamber shone with use: so did the great metal standish which it bore. And though the seven men who sat about the table seemed, at a first glance and in that gloomy light, as rusty and faded as the rubbish behind them, it needed but a second look at their lean jaws and hungry eyes to be sure of their vitality.

He who sat in the great chair at the end of the table was indeed rather plump than thin. His white hands, gay with rings, were well cared for; his peevish chin rested on a falling-collar of lace worthy of a Cardinal. But though the Bishop's Vicar was heard with deference, it was noticeable that when he had ceased to speak his hearers looked to the priest on his left, to Father Pezelay, and waited to hear his opinion before they gave their own. The Father's energy, indeed, had dominated the Angerins, clerks and townsfolk alike, as it had dominated the Parisian *dévotes* who knew him well. The vigour which hate inspires passes often for solid strength; and he who had seen with his own eyes the things done in Paris spoke with an authority to which the more timid quickly and easily succumbed.

Yet gibbets are ugly things; and Thuriot, the printer, whose pride had been tickled by a summons to the conclave, began to wonder if he had done wisely in coming. Lescot, too, who presently ventured a word.

"But if M. de Tavannes' order be to do nothing," he began doubtfully, "you would not, reverend Father, have us resist his Majesty's will?"

"God forbid, my friend!" Father Pezelay answered with unction. "But his Majesty's will is to do—to do for the glory of God and the saints and His Holy Church! How? Is that which was lawful at Saumur unlawful here? Is that which was lawful at Tours unlawful here? Is that which the King did in Paris—to the utter extermination of the unbelieving and the purging of that Sacred City—against his will here? Nay, his will is to do—to do as they have done in Paris and in Tours and in Saumur! But his Minister is unfaithful! The woman whom he has taken to his bosom has bewildered him with her charms and her sorceries, and put it in his mind to deny the mission he bears."

"You are sure, beyond chance of error, that he bears letters to that effect, good Father?" the printer ventured.

"Ask my lord's Vicar! He knows the letters and the import of them!"

"They are to that effect," the Archdeacon answered, drumming on the table with his fingers and speaking somewhat sullenly. "I was in the Chancellery, and I saw them. They are duplicates of those sent to Bordeaux."

"Then the preparations he has made must be against the Huguenots," Lescot, the ex-Provost, said with a sigh of relief. And Thuriot's face lightened also. "He must intend to hang one or two of the ringleaders, before he deals with the herd."

"Think it not!" Father Pezelay cried in his high shrill voice. "I tell you the woman has bewitched him, and he will deny his letters!"

For a moment there was silence. Then, "But dare he do that, reverend Father?" Lescot asked slowly and incredulously. "What? Suppress the King's letters?"

"There is nothing he will not dare! There is nothing he has not dared!" the priest answered vehemently, the recollection of the scene in the great guard-room of the Louvre, when Tavannes had so skilfully turned the tables on him, instilling venom into his tone. "She who lives with him is the devil's. She has bewitched him with her spells and her Sabbaths! She bears the mark of the Beast on her bosom, and for her the fire is even now kindling!"

The laymen who were present shuddered. The two canons who faced them crossed themselves, muttering, "Avaunt, Satan!"

"It is for you to decide," the priest continued, gazing on them passionately, "whether you will side with him or with the Angel of God! For I tell you it was none other executed the Divine judgments at Paris! It was none other but the Angel of God held the sword at Tours! It is none other holds the sword here! Are you for him or against him? Are you for him, or for the woman with the mark of the Beast? Are you for God or against God? For the hour draws near! The time is at hand! You must choose! You must choose!" And, striking the table with his hand, he leaned forward, and with glittering eyes fixed each of them in turn, as he cried, "You must choose! You must choose!" He came to the Archdeacon last.

The Bishop's Vicar fidgeted in his chair, his face a shade more shallow, his cheeks hanging a trifle more loosely, than ordinary.

"If my brother were here!" he muttered. "If M. de Montsoreau had arrived!"

But Father Pezelay knew whose will would prevail if Montsoreau met Tavannes at his leisure. To force Montsoreau's hand, therefore, to surround him on his first entrance with a howling mob already committed to violence, to set him at their head and pledge him before he knew with whom he had to do—this had been, this still was, the priest's design.

But how was he to pursue it while those gibbets stood? While their shadows lay even on the chapter table, and darkened the faces of his most forward associates? That for a moment staggered the priest; and had not private hatred, ever renewed by the touch of the scar on his brow, fed the fire of bigotry he had yielded, as the rabble of Angers were yielding, reluctant and scowling, to the hand which held the city in its grip. But to have come so far on the wings of hate, and to do nothing! To have come avowedly to preach a crusade, and to sneak away cowed! To have dragged the Bishop's Vicar hither, and fawned and cajoled and threatened by turns—and for nothing! These things were passing bitter—passing bitter, when the morsel of vengeance he had foreseen smacked so sweet on the tongue.

For it was no common vengeance, no layman's vengeance, coarse and clumsy, which the priest had imagined in the dark hours of the night, when his feverish brain kept him wakeful. To see Count Hannibal roll in the dust had gone but a little way towards satisfying him. No! But to drag from his arms the woman for whom he had sinned, to subject her to shame and torture in the depths of some convent, and finally to burn her as a witch—it was that which had seemed to the priest in the night hours a vengeance sweet in the mouth.

But the thing seemed unattainable in the circumstances. The city was cowed; the priest knew that no dependence was to be placed on Montsoreau, whose vice was avarice and whose object was plunder. To the Archdeacon's feeble words, therefore, "We must look," the priest retorted sternly, "not to M. de Montsoreau, reverend Father, but to the pious of Angers! We must cry in the streets, 'They do violence to God! They wound God and His Mother!' And so, and so only, shall the unholy thing be rooted out!"

"Amen!" the Curé of St.-Benoist muttered, lifting his head; and his dull eyes glowed awhile. "Amen! Amen!" Then his chin sank again upon his breast.

But the Canons of Angers looked doubtfully at one another, and timidly at the speakers; the meat was too strong for them. And Lescot and Thuriot shuffled in their seats. At length, "I do not know," Lescot muttered timidly.

"You do not know?"

"What can be done!"

"The people will know!" Father Pezelay retorted "Trust them!"

"But the people will not rise without a leader."

"Then will I lead them!"

"Even so, reverend Father—I doubt," Lescot faltered. And Thuriot nodded assent. Gibbets were erected in those days rather for laymen than for the Church.

"You doubt!" the priest cried. "You doubt!" His baleful eyes passed from one to the other; from them to the rest of the company. He saw that with the exception of the Curé of St.-Benoist all were of a mind. "You doubt! Nay, but I see what it is! It is this," he continued slowly and in a different tone, "the King's will goes for nothing in Angers! His writ runs not here. And Holy Church cries in vain for help against the oppressor. I tell you, the sorceress who has bewitched him has bewitched you also. Beware! beware, therefore, lest it be with you as with him! And the fire that shall consume her, spare not your houses!"

The two citizens crossed themselves, grew pale and shuddered. The fear of witchcraft was great in Angers, the peril, if accused of it, enormous. Even the Canons looked startled.

"If—if my brother were here," the Archdeacon repeated feebly, "something might be done!"

"Vain is the help of man!" the priest retorted sternly, and with a gesture of sublime dismissal. "I turn from you to a mightier than you!" And, leaning his head on his hands, he covered his face.

The Archdeacon and the churchmen looked at him, and from him their scared eyes passed to one another. Their one desire now was to be quit of the matter, to have done with it, to escape; and one by one with the air of whipped curs they rose to their feet, and in a hurry to be gone muttered a word of excuse shamefacedly and got themselves out of the room. Lescot and the printer were not slow to follow, and in less than a minute the two strange preachers, the men from Paris, remained the only occupants of the chamber; save, to be precise, a lean official in rusty black, who throughout the conference had sat by the door.

Until the last shuffling footstep had ceased to sound in the still cloister no one spoke. Then Father Pezelay looked up, and the eyes of the two priests met in a long gaze.

"What think you?" Pezelay muttered at last.

"Wet hay," the other answered dreamily, "is slow to kindle, yet burns if the fire be big enough. At what hour does he state his will?"

"At noon."

"In the Council Chamber?"

"It is so given out."

"It is three hundred yards from the Place Ste.-Croix and he must go guarded," the Curé of St.-Benoist continued in the same dull fashion. "He cannot leave many in the house with the woman. If it were attacked in his absence—"

"He would return, and—" Father Pezelay shook his head, his cheek turned a shade paler. Clearly, he saw with his mind's eye more than he expressed.

"*Hoc est corpus*," the other muttered, his dreamy gaze on the table. "If he met us then, on his way to the house and we had bell, book, and candle, would he stop?"

"He would not stop!" Father Pezelay rejoined.

"He would not?"

"I know the man!"

"Then—" but the rest St. Benoist whispered, his head drooping forward; whispered so low that even the lean man behind him, listening with greedy ears, failed to follow the meaning of his superior's words. But that he spoke plainly enough for his hearer Father Pezelay's face was witness. Astonishment, fear, hope, triumph, the lean pale face reflected all in turn; and, underlying all, a subtle malignant mischief, as if a devil's eyes peeped through the holes in an opera mask.

When the other was at last silent, Pezelay drew a deep breath.

"'Tis bold! Bold! Bold!" he muttered. "But have you thought? He who bears the—"

"Brunt?" the other whispered, with a chuckle. "He may suffer? Yes, but it will not be you or I! No, he who was last here shall be first there! The Archdeacon-Vicar—if we can persuade him—who knows but that even for him the crown of martyrdom is reserved?" The dull eyes flickered with unholy amusement.

"And the alarm that brings him from the Council Chamber?"

"Need not of necessity be real. The pinch will be to make use of it. Make use of it—and the hay will burn!"

"You think it will?"

"What can one man do against a thousand? His own people dare not support him."

Father Pezelay turned to the lean man who kept the door, and, beckoning to him, conferred a while with him in a low voice.

"A score or so I might get," the man answered presently, after some debate. "And well posted, something might be done. But we are not in Paris, good father, where the Quarter of the Butchers is to be counted on, and men know that to kill Huguenots is to do God service! Here"—he shrugged his shoulders contemptuously—"they are sheep."

"It is the King's will," the priest answered, frowning on him darkly.

"Ay, but it is not Tavannes'," the man in black answered with a grimace. "And he rules here to-day."

"Fool!" Pezelay retorted. "He has not twenty with him. Do you do as I say, and leave the rest to Heaven!"

"And to you, good master?" the other answered. "For it is not all you are going to do," he continued, with a grin, "that you have told me. Well, so be it! I'll do my part, but I wish we were in Paris. St. Genevieve is ever kind to her servants."

CHAPTER XXIX
THE ESCAPE

In a small back room on the second floor of the inn at Angers, a mean, dingy room which looked into a narrow lane, and commanded no prospect more informing than a blind wall, two men sat, fretting; or, rather, one man sat, his chin resting on his hand, while his companion, less patient or more sanguine, strode ceaselessly to and fro. In the first despair of capture—for they were prisoners—they had made up their minds to the worst, and the slow hours of two days had passed over their heads without kindling more than a faint spark of hope in their breasts. But when they had been taken out and forced to mount and ride—at first with feet tied to the horses' girths—they had let the change, the movement, and the open air fan the flame. They had muttered a word to one another, they had wondered, they had reasoned. And though the silence of their guards—from whose sour vigilance the keenest question drew no response—seemed of ill-omen, and, taken with their knowledge of the man into whose hands they had fallen, should have quenched the spark, these two, having special reasons, the one the buoyancy of youth, the other the faith of an enthusiast, cherished the flame. In the breast of one indeed it had blazed into a confidence so arrogant that he now took all for granted, and was not content.

"It is easy for you to say 'Patience!'" he cried, as he walked the floor in a fever. "You stand to lose no more than your life, and if you escape go free at all points! But he has robbed me of more than life! Of my love, and my self-respect, curse him! He has worsted me not once, but twice and thrice! And if he lets me go now, dismissing me with my life, I shall—I shall kill him!" he concluded, through his teeth.

"You are hard to please!"

"I shall kill him!"

"That were to fall still lower!" the minister answered, gravely regarding him. "I would, M. de Tignonville, you remembered that you are not yet out of jeopardy. Such a frame of mind as yours is no good preparation for death, let me tell you!"

"He will not kill us!" Tignonville cried. "He knows better than most men how to avenge himself!"

"Then he is above most!" La Tribe retorted. "For my part I wish I were sure of the fact, and I should sit here more at ease."

"If we could escape, now, of ourselves!" Tignonville cried. "Then we should save not only life, but honour! Man, think of it! If we could escape, not by his leave, but against it! Are you sure that this is Angers?"

"As sure as a man can be who has only seen the Black Town once or twice!" La Tribe answered, moving to the casement—which was not glazed—and peering through the rough wooden lattice. "But if we could escape we are strangers here. We know not which way to go, nor where to find shelter. And for the matter of that," he continued, turning from the window with a shrug of resignation, "'tis no use to talk of it while yonder foot goes up and down the passage, and its owner bears the key in his pocket."

"If we could get out of his power as we came into it!" Tignonville cried.

"Ay, if! But it is not every floor has a trap!"

"We could take up a board."

The minister raised his eyebrows.

"We could take up a board!" the younger man repeated; and he stepped the mean chamber from end to end, his eyes on the floor. "Or—yes, *mon Dieu*!" with a change of attitude, "we might break through the roof?" And, throwing back his head, he scanned the cobwebbed surface of laths which rested on the unceiled joists.

"Umph!"

"Well, why not, Monsieur? Why not break through the ceiling?" Tignonville repeated, and in a fit of energy he seized his companion's shoulder and shook him. "Stand on the bed, and you can reach it."

"And the floor which rests on it!"

"*Par Dieu*, there is no floor! 'Tis a cockloft above us! See there! And there!" And the young man sprang on the bed, and thrust the rowel of a spur through the laths. La Tribe's expression changed. He rose slowly to his feet.

"Try again!" he said.

Tignonville, his face red, drove the spur again between the laths, and worked it to and fro until he could pass his fingers into the hole he had made. Then he gripped and bent down a length of one of the laths, and, passing his arm as far as the elbow through the hole, moved it this way and that. His eyes, as he looked down at his companion through the falling rubbish, gleamed with triumph.

"Where is your floor now?" he asked.

"You can touch nothing?"

"Nothing. It's open. A little more and I might touch the tiles." And he strove to reach higher.

For answer La Tribe gripped him. "Down! Down, Monsieur," he muttered. "They are bringing our dinner."

Tignonville thrust back the lath as well as he could, and slipped to the floor; and hastily the two swept the rubbish from the bed. When Badelon, attended by two men, came in with the meal he found La Tribe at the window blocking much of the light, and Tignonville laid sullenly on the bed. Even a suspicious eye must have failed to detect what had been done; the three who looked in suspected nothing and saw nothing. They went out, the key was turned again on the prisoners, and the footsteps of two of the men were heard descending the stairs.

"We have an hour, now!" Tignonville cried; and leaping, with flaming eyes, on the bed, he fell to hacking and jabbing and tearing at the laths amid a rain of dust and rubbish. Fortunately the stuff, falling on the bed, made little noise; and in five minutes, working half-choked and in a frenzy of impatience, he had made a hole through which he could thrust his arms, a hole which extended almost from one joist to its neighbour. By this time the air was thick with floating lime; the two could scarcely breathe, yet they dared not pause. Mounting on La Tribe's shoulders—who took his stand on the bed—the young man thrust his head and arms through the hole, and, resting his elbows on the joists, dragged himself up, and with a final effort of strength landed nose and knees on the timbers, which formed his supports. A moment to take breath, and press his torn and bleeding fingers to his lips; then, reaching down, he gave a hand to his companion and dragged him to the same place of vantage.

They found themselves in a long narrow cockloft, not more than six feet high at the highest, and insufferably hot. Between the tiles, which sloped steeply on either hand, a faint light filtered in, disclosing the giant rooftree running the length of the house, and at the farther end of the loft the main tie-beam, from which a network of knees and struts rose to the rooftree.

Tignonville, who seemed possessed by unnatural energy, stayed only to put off his boots. Then "Courage!" he panted, "all goes well!" and, carrying his boots in his hands, he led the way, stepping gingerly from joist to joist until he reached the tie-beam. He climbed on it, and, squeezing himself between the struts, entered a second loft, similar to the first. At the farther end of this a rough wall of bricks in a timber-frame lowered his hopes; but as he approached it, joy! Low down in the corner where the roof descended, a small door, square, and not more than two feet high, disclosed itself.

The two crept to it on hands and knees and listened. "It will lead to the leads, I doubt?" La Tribe whispered. They dared not raise their voices.

"As well that way as another!" Tignonville answered recklessly. He was the more eager, for there is a fear which transcends the fear of death. His eyes shone through the mask of dust, the sweat ran down to his chin, his breath came and went noisily. "Naught matters if we can escape him!" he panted. And he pushed the door recklessly. It flew open; the two drew back their faces with a cry of alarm.

They were looking, not into the sunlight, but into a grey dingy garret open to the roof, and occupying the upper part of a gable-end somewhat higher than the wing in which they had been confined. Filthy truckle-beds and ragged pallets covered the floor, and, eked out by old saddles and threadbare horserugs, marked the sleeping quarters either of the servants or of travellers of the meaner sort. But the dinginess was naught to the two who knelt looking into it, afraid to move. Was the place empty? That was the point; the question which had first stayed, and then set their pulses at the gallop.

Painfully their eyes searched each huddle of clothing, scanned each dubious shape. And slowly, as the silence persisted, their heads came forward until the whole floor lay within the field of sight. And still no sound! At last Tignonville stirred, crept through the doorway, and rose up, peering round him. He nodded, and, satisfied that all was safe, the minister followed him.

They found themselves a pace or so from the head of a narrow staircase, leading downwards. Without moving, they could see the door which closed it below. Tignonville signed to La Tribe to wait, and himself crept down the stairs. He reached the door, and, stooping, set his eye to the hole through which the string of the latch passed. A moment he looked, and then, turning on tiptoe, he stole up again, his face fallen.

"You may throw the handle after the hatchet!" he muttered. "The man on guard is within four yards of the door." And in the rage of disappointment he struck the air with his hand.

"Is he looking this way?"

"No. He is looking down the passage towards our room. But it is impossible to pass him."

La Tribe nodded, and moved softly to one of the lattices which lighted the room. It might be possible to escape that way, by the parapet and the tiles. But he found that the casement was set high in the roof, which sloped steeply from its sill to the eaves. He passed to the other window, in which a little wicket in the lattice stood open. He looked through it. In the giddy void white pigeons were wheeling in the dazzling sunshine, and, gazing down, he saw far below him, in the hot square, a row of booths, and troops of people moving to and fro like pigmies; and—and a strange thing, in the middle of all! Involuntarily, as if the persons below could have seen his face at the tiny dormer, he drew back.

He beckoned to M. Tignonville to come to him; and when the young man complied, he bade him in a whisper look down. "See!" he muttered. "There!"

The younger man saw and drew in his breath. Even under the coating of dust his face turned a shade greyer.

"You had no need to fear that he would let us go!" the minister muttered, with half-conscious irony.

"No."

"Nor I! There are two ropes." And La Tribe breathed a few words of prayer. The object which had fixed his gaze was a gibbet: the only one of the three which could be seen from their eyrie.

Tignonville, on the other hand, turned sharply away, and with haggard eyes stared about the room. "We might defend the staircase," he muttered. "Two men might hold it for a time."

"We have no food."

"No." Suddenly he gripped La Tribe's arm. "I have it!" he cried. "And it may do! It must do!" he continued, his face working. "See!" And lifting from the floor one of the ragged pallets, from which the straw protruded in a dozen places, he set it flat on his head.

It drooped at each corner—it had seen much wear—and, while it almost hid his face, it revealed his grimy chin and mortar-stained shoulders. He turned to his companion.

La Tribe's face glowed as he looked. "It may do!" he cried. "It's a chance! But you are right! It may do!"

Tignonville dropped the ragged mattress, and tore off his coat; then he rent his breeches at the knee, so that they hung loose about his calves.

"Do you the same!" he cried. "And quick, man, quick! Leave your boots! Once outside we must pass through the streets under these"—he took up his burden again and set it on his head—"until we reach a quiet part, and there we—"

"Can hide! Or swim the river!" the minister said. He had followed his companion's example, and now stood under a similar burden. With breeches rent and whitened, and his upper garments in no better case, he looked a sorry figure.

Tignonville eyed him with satisfaction, and turned to the staircase.

"Come," he cried, "there is not a moment to be lost. At any minute they may enter our room and find it empty! You are ready? Then, not too softly, or it may rouse suspicion! And mumble something at the door."

He began himself to scold, and, muttering incoherently, stumbled down the staircase, the pallet on his head rustling against the wall on each side. Arrived at the door, he fumbled clumsily with the latch, and, when the door gave way, plumped out with an oath—as if the awkward burden he bore were the only thing on his mind. Badelon—he was on duty—stared at the apparition; but the next moment he sniffed the pallet, which was none of the freshest, and, turning up his nose, he retreated a pace. He had no suspicion; the men did not come from the part of the house where the prisoners lay, and he stood aside to let them pass. In a moment, staggering, and going a little unsteadily, as if they scarcely saw their way, they had passed by him, and were descending the staircase.

So far well! Unfortunately, when they reached the foot of that flight they came on the main passage of the first-floor. It ran right and left, and Tignonville did not know which way he must turn to reach the lower staircase. Yet he dared not hesitate; in the passage, waiting about the doors, were four or five servants, and in the distance he caught sight of three men belonging to Tavannes' company. At any moment, too, an upper servant might meet them, ask what they were doing, and detect the fraud. He turned at random, therefore—to the left as it chanced—and marched along bravely, until the very thing happened which he had feared. A man came from a room plump upon them, saw them, and held up his hands in horror.

"What are you doing?" he cried in a rage and with an oath. "Who set you on this?"

Tignonville's tongue clave to the roof of his mouth. La Tribe from behind muttered something about the stable.

"And time too!" the man said. "Faugh! But how come you this way? Are you drunk? Here!" He opened the door of a musty closet beside him, "Pitch them in here, do you hear? And take them down when it is dark. Faugh. I wonder you did not carry the things though her ladyship's room at once! If my lord had been in and met you! Now then, do as I tell you! Are you drunk?"

With a sullen air Tignonville threw in his mattress. La Tribe did the same. Fortunately the passage was ill-lighted, and there were many helpers and strange servants in the inn. The butler only thought them ill-looking fellows who knew no better.

"Now be off!" he continued irascibly. "This is no place for your sort. Be off!" And, as they moved, "Coming! Coming!" he cried in answer to a distant summons; and he hurried away on the errand which their appearance had interrupted.

Tignonville would have gone to work to recover the pallets, for the man had left the key in the door. But as he went to do so the butler looked back, and the two were obliged to make a pretence of following him. A moment, however, and he was gone; and Tignonville turned anew to regain them. A second time fortune was adverse; a door within a pace of him opened, a woman came out. She recoiled from the strange figure; her eyes met his. Unluckily the light from the room behind her fell on his face, and with a shrill cry she named him.

One second and all had been lost, for the crowd of idlers at the other end of the passage had caught her cry, and were looking that way. With presence of mind Tignonville clapped his hand on her mouth, and, huddling her by force into the room, followed her, with La Tribe at his heels.

It was a large room, in which seven or eight people, who had been at prayers when the cry startled them, were rising from their knees. The first thing they saw was Javette on the threshold, struggling in the grasp of a wild man, ragged and begrimed; they deemed the city risen and the massacre upon them. Carlat threw himself before his mistress, the Countess in her turn sheltered a young girl, who stood beside her and from whose face the last trace of colour had fled. Madame Carlat and a waiting-woman ran shrieking to the window; another instant and the alarm would have gone abroad.

Tignonville's voice stopped it. "Don't you know me?" he cried, "Madame! you at least! Carlat! Are you all mad?"

The words stayed them where they stood in an astonishment scarce less than their alarm. The Countess tried twice to speak; the third time—

"Have you escaped?" she muttered.

Tignonville nodded, his eyes bright with triumph. "So far," he said. "But they may be on our heels at any moment! Where can we hide?"

The Countess, her hand pressed to her side, looked at Javette.

"The door, girl!" she whispered. "Lock it!"

"Ay, lock it! And they can go by the back-stairs," Madame Carlat answered, awaking suddenly to the situation. "Through my closet! Once in the yard they may pass out through the stables."

"Which way?" Tignonville asked impatiently. "Don't stand looking at me, but—"

"Through this door!" Madame Carlat answered, hurrying to it.

He was following when the Countess stepped forward and interposed between him and the door.

"Stay!" she cried; and there was not one who did not notice a new decision in her voice, a new dignity in her bearing. "Stay, Monsieur, we may be going too fast. To go out now and in that guise—may it not be to incur greater peril than you incur here? I feel sure that you are in no danger of your life at present. Therefore, why run the risk—"

"In no danger, Madame!" he cried, interrupting her in astonishment. "Have you seen the gibbet in the Square? Do you call that no danger?"

"It is not erected for you."

"No?"

"No, Monsieur," she answered firmly, "I swear it is not. And I know of reasons, urgent reasons, why you should not go. M. de Tavannes"—she named her husband nervously, as conscious of the weak spot—"before he rode abroad laid strict orders on all to keep within, since the smallest matter might kindle the city. Therefore, M. de Tignonville, I request, nay I entreat," she continued with greater urgency, as she saw his gesture of denial, "you to stay here until he returns."

"And you, Madame, will answer for my life?"

She faltered. For a moment, a moment only, her colour ebbed. What if she deceived herself? What if she surrendered her old lover to death? What if—but the doubt was of a moment only. Her duty was plain.

"I will answer for it," she said, with pale lips, "if you remain here. And I beg, I implore you—by the love you once had for me, M. de Tignonville," she added desperately, seeing that he was about to refuse, "to remain here."

"Once!" he retorted, lashing himself into ignoble rage. "By the love I once had! Say, rather, the love I have, Madame—for I am no woman-weathercock to wed the winner, and hold or not hold, stay or go, as he commands! You, it seems," he continued with a sneer, "have learned the wife's lesson well! You would practise on me now, as you practised on me the other night when you stood between him and me! I yielded then, I spared him. And what did I get by it? Bonds and a prison! And what shall I get now? The same! No, Madame," he continued bitterly, addressing himself as much to the Carlats and the others as to his old mistress. "I do not change! I loved! I love! I was going and I go! If death lay beyond that door"—and he pointed to it—"and life at his will were certain here, I would pass the threshold rather than take my life of him!" And, dragging La Tribe with him, with a passionate gesture he rushed by her, opened the door, and disappeared in the next room.

The Countess took one pace forward, as if she would have followed him, as if she would have tried further persuasion. But as she moved a cry rooted her to the spot. A rush of feet and the babel of many voices filled the passage with a tide of sound, which drew rapidly nearer. The escape was known! Would the fugitives have time to slip out below?

Some one knocked at the door, tried it, pushed and beat on it. But the Countess and all in the room had run to the windows and were looking out.

If the two had not yet made their escape they must be taken. Yet no; as the Countess leaned from the window, first one dusty figure and then a second darted from a door below, and made for the nearest turning, out of the Place Ste.-Croix. Before they gained it, four men, of whom, Badelon, his grey locks flying, was first, dashed out in pursuit, and the street rang with cries of "Stop him! Seize him! Seize him!" Some one—one of the pursuers or another—to add to the alarm let off a musket, and in a moment, as if the report had been a signal, the Place was in a hubbub, people flocked into it with mysterious quickness, and from a neighbouring roof—whence, precisely, it was impossible to say—the crackling fire of a dozen arquebuses alarmed the city far and wide.

Unfortunately, the fugitives had been baulked at the first turning. Making for a second, they found it choked, and, swerving, darted across the Place towards St.-Maurice, seeking to lose themselves in the gathering crowd. But the pursuers clung desperately to their skirts, overturning here a man and there a child; and then in a twinkling, Tignonville, as he ran round a booth, tripped over a peg and fell, and La Tribe stumbled over him and fell also. The four riders flung themselves fiercely on their prey, secured them, and began to drag them with oaths and curses towards the door of the inn.

The Countess had seen all from her window; had held her breath while they ran, had drawn it sharply when they fell. Now, "They have them!" she muttered, a sob choking her, "they have them!" And she clasped her hands. If he had followed her advice! If he had only followed her advice!

But the issue proved less certain than she deemed it. The crowd, which grew each moment, knew nothing of pursuers or pursued. On the contrary, a cry went up that the riders were Huguenots, and that the Huguenots were rising and slaying the Catholics; and as no story was too improbable for those days, and this was one constantly set about, first one stone flew, and then another, and another. A man with a staff darted forward and struck Badelon on the shoulder, two or three others pressed in and jostled the riders; and if three of Tavannes' following had not run out on the instant and faced the mob with their pikes, and for a moment forced them to give back, the prisoners would have been rescued at the very door of the inn. As it was they were dragged in, and the gates were flung to and barred in the nick of time. Another moment, almost another second, and the mob had seized them. As it was, a hail of stones poured on the front of the inn, and amid the rising yells of the rabble there presently floated heavy and slow over the city the tolling of the great bell of St.-Maurice.

CHAPTER XXX
SACRILEGE!

M. de Montsoreau, Lieutenant-Governor of Saumur almost rose from his seat in his astonishment.

"What! No letters?" he cried, a hand on either arm of the chair.

The Magistrates stared, one and all. "No letters?" they muttered.

And "No letters?" the Provost chimed in more faintly.

Count Hannibal looked smiling round the Council table. He alone was unmoved.

"No," he said. "I bear none."

M. de Montsoreau, who, travel-stained and in his corselet, had the second place of honour at the foot of the table, frowned.

"But, M. le Comte," he said, "my instructions from Monsieur were to proceed to carry out his Majesty's will in co-operation with you, who, I understood, would bring letters *de par le Roi.*"

"I had letters," Count Hannibal answered negligently. "But on the way I mislaid them."

"Mislaid them?" Montsoreau cried, unable to believe his ears; while the smaller dignitaries of the city, the magistrates and churchmen who sat on either side of the table, gaped open-mouthed. It was incredible! It was unbelievable! Mislay the King's letters! Who had ever heard of such a thing?

"Yes, I mislaid them. Lost them, if you like it better."

"But you jest!" the Lieutenant-Governor retorted, moving uneasily in his chair. He was a man more highly named for address than courage; and, like most men skilled in finesse, he was prone to suspect a trap. "You jest, surely, Monsieur! Men do not lose his Majesty's letters, by the way."

"When they contain his Majesty's will, no," Tavannes answered, with a peculiar smile.

"You imply, then?"

Count Hannibal shrugged his shoulders, but had not answered when Bigot entered and handed him his sweetmeat box; he paused to open it and select a prune. He was long in selecting; but no change of countenance led any of those at the table to suspect that inside the lid of the box was a message—a scrap of paper informing him that Montsoreau had left fifty spears in the suburb without the Saumur gate, besides those whom he had brought openly into the town. Tavannes read the note slowly while he seemed to be choosing his fruit. And then—

"Imply?" he answered. "I imply nothing, M. de Montsoreau."

"But—"

"But that sometimes his Majesty finds it prudent to give orders which he does not mean to be carried out. There are things which start up before the eye," Tavannes continued, negligently tapping the box on the table, "and there are things which do not; sometimes the latter are the more important. You, better than I, M. de Montsoreau, know that the King in the Gallery at the Louvre is one, and in his closet is another."

"Yes."

"And that being so—"

"You do not mean to carry the letters into effect?"

"Had I the letters, certainly, my friend. I should be bound by them. But I took good care to lose them," Tavannes added naïvely. "I am no fool."

"Umph!"

"However," Count Hannibal continued, with an airy gesture, "that is my affair. If you, M. de Montsoreau, feel inclined, in spite of the absence of my letters, to carry yours into effect, by all means do so—after midnight of to-day."

M. de Montsoreau breathed hard. "And why," he asked, half sulkily and half ponderously, "after midnight only, M. le Comte?"

"Merely that I may be clear of all suspicion of having lot or part in the matter," Count Hannibal answered pleasantly. "After midnight of to-night by all means do as you please. Until midnight, by your leave, we will be quiet."

The Lieutenant-Governor moved doubtfully in his chair, the fear—which Tavannes had shrewdly instilled into his mind—that he might be disowned if he carried out his instructions, struggling with his avarice and his self-importance. He was rather crafty than bold; and such things had been, he knew. Little by little, and while he sat gloomily debating, the notion of dealing with one or two and holding the body of the Huguenots to ransom—a notion which, in spite of everything, was to bear good fruit for Angers—began to form in his mind. The plan suited him: it left him free to face either way, and it would fill his pockets more genteelly than would open robbery. On the other hand, he would offend his brother and the fanatical party, with whom he commonly acted. They were looking to see him assert himself. They were looking to hear him declare himself. And—

Harshly Count Hannibal's voice broke in on his thoughts; harshly, a something sinister in its tone.

"Where is your brother?" he said. And it was evident that he had not noted his absence until then. "My lord's Vicar of all people should be here!" he continued, leaning forward and looking round the table. His brow was stormy.

Lescot squirmed under his eye; Thuriot turned pale and trembled. It was one of the canons of St.-Maurice, who at length took on himself to answer.

"His lordship requested, M. le Comte," he ventured, "that you would excuse him. His duties—"

"Is he ill?"

"He—"

"Is he ill, sirrah?" Tavannes roared. And while all bowed before the lightning of his eye, no man at the table knew what had roused the sudden tempest. But Bigot knew, who stood by the door, and whose ear, keen as his master's, had caught the distant report of a musket shot. "If he be not ill," Tavannes continued, rising and looking round the table in search of signs of guilt, "and there be foul play here, and he the player, the Bishop's own hand shall not save him! By Heaven it shall not! Nor yours!" he continued, looking fiercely at Montsoreau. "Nor your master's!"

The Lieutenant-Governor sprang to his feet. "M. le Comte," he stammered, "I do not understand this language! Nor this heat, which may be real or not! All I say is, if there be foul play here—"

"If!" Tavannes retorted. "At least, if there be, there be gibbets too! And I see necks!" he added, leaning forward. "Necks!" And then, with a look of flame, "Let no man leave this table until I return," he cried, "or he will have to deal with me. Nay," he continued, changing his tone abruptly, as the prudence, which never entirely left him—and perhaps the remembrance of the other's fifty spearmen—sobered him in the midst of his rage, "I am hasty. I mean not you, M. de Montsoreau! Ride where you will; ride with me, if you will, and I will thank you. Only remember, until midnight Angers is mine!"

He was still speaking when he moved from the table, and, leaving all staring after him, strode down the room. An instant he paused on the threshold and looked back; then he passed out, and clattered down the stone stairs. His horse and riders were waiting, but, his foot in the stirrup, he stayed for a word with Bigot.

"Is it so?" he growled.

The Norman did not speak, but pointed towards the Place Ste.-Croix, whence an occasional shot made answer for him.

In those days the streets of the Black City were narrow and crooked, overhung by timber houses, and hampered by booths; nor could Tavannes from the old Town Hall—now abandoned—see the Place Ste.-Croix. But that he could cure. He struck spurs to his horse, and, followed by his ten horsemen, he clattered noisily down the paved street. A dozen groups hurrying the same way sprang panic-stricken to the walls, or saved themselves in doorways. He was up with them, he was beyond them! Another hundred yards, and he would see the Place.

And then, with a cry of rage, he drew rein a little, discovering what was before him. In the narrow gut of the way a great black banner, borne on two poles, was lurching towards him. It was moving in the van of a dark procession of priests, who, with their attendants and a crowd of devout, filled the street from wall to wall. They were chanting one of the penitential psalms, but not so loudly as to drown the uproar in the Place beyond them.

They made no way, and Count Hannibal swore furiously, suspecting treachery. But he was no madman, and at the moment the least reflection would have sent him about to seek another road. Unfortunately, as he hesitated a man sprang with a gesture of warning to his horse's head and seized it; and Tavannes, mistaking the motive of the act, lost his self-control. He struck the fellow down, and, with a reckless word, rode headlong into the procession, shouting to the black robes to make way, make way! A cry, nay, a shriek of horror, answered him and rent the air. And in a minute the thing was done. Too late, as the Bishop's Vicar, struck by his horse, fell screaming under its hoofs—too late, as the consecrated vessels which he had been bearing rolled in the mud, Tavannes saw that they bore the canopy and the Host!

He knew what he had done, then. Before his horse's iron shoes struck the ground again, his face—even his face—had lost its colour. But he knew also that to hesitate now, to pause now, was to be torn in pieces; for his riders, seeing that which the banner had veiled from him, had not followed him, and he was alone, in the middle of brandished fists and weapons. He hesitated not a moment. Drawing a pistol, he spurred onwards, his horse plunging wildly among the shrieking priests; and though a hundred hands, hands of acolytes, hands of shaven monks, clutched at his bridle or gripped his boot, he got clear of them. Clear, carrying with him the memory of one face seen an instant amid the crowd, one face seen, to be ever remembered—the face of Father Pezelay, white, evil, scarred, distorted by wicked triumph.

Behind him, the thunder of "Sacrilege! Sacrilege!" rose to Heaven, and men were gathering. In front the crowd which skirmished about the inn was less dense, and, ignorant of the thing that had happened in the narrow street, made ready way for him, the boldest recoiling before the look on his face. Some who stood nearest to the inn, and had begun to hurl stones at the window and to beat on the doors—which had only the minute before closed on Badelon and his prisoners—supposed that he had his riders behind him; and these fled apace. But he knew better even than they the value of time; he pushed his horse up to the gates, and hammered them with his boot while be kept his pistol-hand towards the Place and the cathedral, watching for the transformation which he knew would come!

And come it did; on a sudden, in a twinkling! A white-faced monk, frenzy in his eyes, appeared in the midst of the crowd. He stood and tore his garments before the people, and, stooping, threw dust on his head. A second and a third followed his example; then from a thousand throats the cry of "Sacrilege! Sacrilege!" rolled up, while clerks flew wildly hither and thither shrieking the tale, and priests denied the Sacraments to Angers until it should purge itself of the evil thing.

By that time Count Hannibal had saved himself behind the great gates, by the skin of his teeth. The gates had opened to him in time. But none knew better than he that Angers had no gates thick enough, nor walls of a height, to save him for many hours from the storm he had let loose!

CHAPTER XXXI
THE FLIGHT FROM ANGERS

But that only the more roused the devil in the man; that, and the knowledge that he had his own headstrong act to thank for the position. He looked on the panic-stricken people who, scared by the turmoil without, had come together in the courtyard, wringing their hands and chattering; and his face was so dark and forbidding that fear of him took the place of all other fear, and the nearest shrank from contact with him. On any other entering as he had entered, they would have hailed questions; they would have asked what was amiss, and if the city were rising, and where were Bigot and his men. But Count Hannibal's eye struck curiosity dumb. When he cried from his saddle, "Bring me the landlord!" the trembling man was found, and brought, and thrust forward almost without a word.

"You have a back gate?" Tavannes said, while the crowd leaned forward to catch his words.

"Yes, my lord," the man faltered.

"Into the street which leads to the ramparts?"

"Ye-yes, my lord."

"Then"—to Badelon—"saddle! You have five minutes. Saddle as you never saddled before," he continued in a low tone, "or—" His tongue did not finish the threat, but his hand waved the man away. "For you"—he held Tignonville an instant with his lowering eye—"and the preaching fool with you, get arms and mount! You have never played aught but the woman yet; but play me false now, or look aside but a foot from the path I bid you take, and you thwart me no more, Monsieur! And you, Madame," he continued, turning to the Countess, who stood bewildered at one of the doors, the Provost's daughter clinging and weeping about her, "you have three minutes to get your women to horse! See you, if you please, that they take no longer!"

She found her voice with difficulty. "And this child?" she said. "She is in my care."

"Bring her," he muttered with a scowl of impatience. And then, raising his voice as he turned on the terrified gang of hostlers and inn servants who stood gaping round him, "Go help!" he thundered. "Go help! And quickly!" he added, his face growing a shade darker as a second bell began to toll from a neighbouring tower, and the confused babel in the Place Ste.-Croix settled into a dull roar of "*Sacrilège! sacrilège.*" — "Hasten!"

Fortunately it had been his first intention to go to the Council attended by the whole of his troop; and eight horses stood saddled in the stalls. Others were hastily pulled out and bridled, and the women were mounted. La Tribe, at a look from Tavannes, took behind him the Provost's daughter, who was helpless with terror. Between the suddenness of the alarm, the uproar without, and the panic within, none but a man whose people served him at a nod and dreaded his very gesture could have got his party mounted in time. Javette would fain have swooned, but she dared not. Tignonville would fain have questioned, but he shrank from the venture. The Countess would fain have said something, but she forced herself to obey and no more. Even so the confusion in the courtyard, the mingling of horses and men and trappings and saddle-bags, would have made another despair; but wherever Count Hannibal, seated in his saddle in the middle, turned his face, chaos settled into a degree of order, servants, ceasing to listen to the yells and cries outside, ran to fetch, women dropped cloaks from the gallery, and men loaded muskets and strapped on bandoliers.

Until at last — but none knew what those minutes of suspense cost him — he saw all mounted, and, pistol in hand, shepherded them to the back gates. As he did so he stooped for a few scowling words with Badelon, whom he sent to the van of the party: then he gave the word to open. It was done; and even as Montsoreau's horsemen, borne on the bosom of a second and more formidable throng, swept raging into the already crowded square, and the cry went up for "a ram! a ram!" to batter in the gates, Tavannes, hurling his little party before him, dashed out at the back, and putting to flight a handful of rascals who had wandered to that side, cantered unmolested down the lane to the ramparts. Turning eastward at the foot of the frowning Castle, he followed the inner side of the wall in the direction of the gate by which he had entered the preceding evening.

To gain this his party had to pass the end of the Rue Toussaint, which issues from the Place Ste.-Croix and runs so straight that the mob seething in front of the inn had only to turn their heads to see them. The danger incurred at this point was great; for a party as small as Tavannes' and encumbered with women would have had no chance if attacked within the walls.

Count Hannibal knew it. But he knew also that the act which he had committed rendered the north bank of the Loire impossible for him. Neither King nor Marshal, neither Charles of Valois nor Gaspard of Tavannes, would dare to shield him from an infuriated Church, a Church too wise to forgive certain offences. His one chance lay in reaching the southern bank of the Loire—roughly speaking, the Huguenot bank—and taking refuge in some town, Rochelle or St. Jean d'Angely, where the Huguenots were strong, and whence he might take steps to set himself right with his own side.

But to cross the great river which divides France into two lands widely differing he must leave the city by the east gate; for the only bridge over the Loire within forty miles of Angers lay eastward from the town, at Ponts de Cé, four miles away. To this gate, therefore, past the Rue Toussaint, he whirled his party daringly; and though the women grew pale as the sounds of riot broke louder on the ear, and they discovered that they were approaching instead of leaving the danger—and though Tignonville for an instant thought him mad, and snatched at the Countess's rein—his men-at-arms, who knew him, galloped stolidly on, passed like clockwork the end of the street, and, reckless of the stream of persons hurrying in the direction of the alarm, heedless of the fright and anger their passage excited, pressed steadily on. A moment and the gate through which they had entered the previous evening appeared before them. And—a sight welcome to one of them—it was open.

They were fortunate indeed, for a few seconds later they had been too late. The alarm had preceded them. As they dashed up, a man ran to the chains of the portcullis and tried to lower it. He failed to do so at the first touch, and, quailing, fled from Badelon's levelled pistol. A watchman on one of the bastions of the wall shouted to them to halt or he would fire: but the riders yelled in derision, and thundering through the echoing archway, emerged into the open, and saw, extended before them, in place of the gloomy vistas of the Black Town, the glory of the open country and the vine-clad hills, and the fields about the Loire yellow with late harvest.

The women gasped their relief, and one or two who were most out of breath would have pulled up their horses and let them trot, thinking the danger at an end. But a curt savage word from the rear set them flying again, and down and up and on again they galloped, driven forward by the iron hand which never relaxed its grip of them. Silent and pitiless he whirled them before him until they were within a mile of the long Ponts de Cé—a series of bridges rather than one bridge—and the broad shallow Loire lay plain before them, its sandbanks grilling in the sun, and grey lines of willows marking its eyots. By this time some of the women, white with fatigue, could only cling to their saddles with their hands; while others were red-hot, their hair unrolled, and the perspiration mingled with the dust on their faces. But he who drove them had no pity for weakness in an emergency. He looked back and saw, a half-mile behind them, the glitter of steel following hard on their heels: and "Faster! faster!" he cried, regardless of their prayers: and he beat the rearmost of the horses with his scabbard. A waiting-woman shrieked that she should fall, but he answered ruthlessly, "Fall then, fool!" and the instinct of self-preservation coming to her aid, she clung and bumped and toiled on with the rest until they reached the first houses of the town about the bridges, and Badelon raised his hand as a signal that they might slacken speed.

The bewilderment of the start had been so great that it was then only, when they found their feet on the first link of the bridge, that two of the party, the Countess and Tignonville, awoke to the fact that their faces were set southwards. To cross the Loire in those days meant much to all: to a Huguenot, very much. It chanced that these two rode on to the bridge side by side, and the memory of their last crossing—the remembrance that, on their journey north a month before, they had crossed it hand-in-hand with the prospect of passing their lives together, and with no faintest thought of the events which were to ensue, flashed into the mind of each of them. It deepened the flush which exertion had brought to the woman's cheek, then left it paler than before. A minute earlier she had been wroth with her old lover; she had held him accountable for the outbreak in the town and this hasty retreat; now her anger died as she looked and she remembered. In the man, shallower of feeling and more alive to present contingencies, the uppermost emotion as he trod the bridge was one of surprise and congratulation.

He could not at first believe in their good fortune. "*Mon Dieu!*" he cried, "we are crossing!" And then again in a lower tone, "We are crossing! We are crossing!" And he looked at her.

It was impossible that she should not look back; that she who had ceased to be angry should not feel and remember; impossible that her answering glance should not speak to his heart. Below them, as on that day a month earlier, when they had crossed the bridges going northward, the broad shallow river ran its course in the sunshine, its turbid currents gleaming and flashing about the sandbanks and osier-beds. To the eye, the landscape, save that the vintage was farther advanced and the harvest in part gathered in, was the same. But how changed were their relations, their prospects, their hopes, who had then crossed the river hand-in-hand, planning a life to be passed together.

The young man's rage boiled up at the thought. Too vividly, too sharply it showed him the wrongs which he had suffered at the hands of the man who rode behind him, the man who even now drove him on and ordered him and insulted him. He forgot that he might have perished in the general massacre if Count Hannibal had not intervened. He forgot that Count Hannibal had spared him once and twice. He laid on his enemy's shoulders the guilt of all, the blood of all: and, as quick on the thought of his wrongs and his fellows' wrongs followed the reflection that with every league they rode southwards the chance of requital grew, he cried again, and this time joyously—

"We are crossing! A little, and we shall be in our own land!"

The tears filled the Countess's eyes as she looked westwards and southwards.

"Vrillac is there!" she cried; and she pointed. "I smell the sea!"

"Ay!" he answered, almost under his breath. "It lies there! And no more than thirty leagues from us! With fresh horses we might see it in two days!"

Badelon's voice broke in on them. "Forward!" he cried, as the party reached the southern bank. "*En avant!*" And, obedient to the word, the little company, refreshed by the short respite, took the road out of Ponts de Cé at a steady trot. Nor was the Countess the only one whose face glowed, being set southwards, or whose heart pulsed to the rhythm of the horses' hoofs that beat out "Home!" Carlat's and Madame Carlat's also. Javette even, hearing from her neighbour that they were over the Loire, plucked up courage; while La Tribe, gazing before him with moistened eyes, cried "Comfort" to the scared and weeping girl who clung to his belt. It was singular to see how all sniffed the air as if already it smacked of the sea and of the south; and how they of Poitou sat their horses as if they asked nothing better than to ride on and on and on until the scenes of home arose about them. For them the sky had already a deeper blue, the air a softer fragrance, the sunshine a purity long unknown.

Was it wonderful, when they had suffered so much on that northern bank? When their experience during the month had been comparable only with the direst nightmare? Yet one among them, after the first impulse of relief and satisfaction, felt differently. Tignonville's gorge rose against the sense of compulsion, of inferiority. To be driven forward after this fashion, whether he would or no, to be placed at the back of every base-born man-at-arms, to have no clearer knowledge of what had happened or of what was passing, or of the peril from which they fled, than the women among whom he rode—these things kindled anew the sullen fire of hate. North of the Loire there had been some excuse for his inaction under insult; he had been in the man's country and power. But south of the Loire, within forty leagues of Huguenot Niort, must he still suffer, still be supine?

His rage was inflamed by a disappointment he presently underwent. Looking back as they rode clear of the wooden houses of Ponts de Cé, he missed Tavannes and several of his men; and he wondered if Count Hannibal had remained on his own side of the river. It seemed possible; and in that event La Tribe and he and Carlat might deal with Badelon and the four who still escorted them. But when he looked back a minute later, Tavannes was within sight, following the party with a stern face; and not Tavannes only. Bigot, with two of the ten men who hitherto had been missing, was with him.

It was clear, however, that they brought no good news, for they had scarcely ridden up before Count Hannibal cried, "Faster! faster!" in his harshest voice, and Bigot urged the horses to a quicker trot. Their course lay almost parallel with the Loire in the direction of Beaupréau; and Tignonville began to fear that Count Hannibal intended to recross the river at Nantes, where the only bridge below Angers spanned the stream. With this in view it was easy to comprehend his wish to distance his pursuers before he recrossed.

The Countess had no such thought. "They must be close upon us!" she murmured, as she urged her horse in obedience to the order.

"Whoever they are!" Tignonville muttered bitterly. "If we knew what had happened, or who followed, we should know more about it, Madame. For that matter, I know what I wish he would do. And our heads are set for it."

"What?"

"Make for Vrillac!" he answered, a savage gleam in his eyes.

"For Vrillac?"

"Yes."

"Ah, if he would!" she cried, her face turning pale. "If he would. He would be safe there!"

"Ay, quite safe!" he answered with a peculiar intonation. And he looked at her askance.

He fancied that his thought, the thought which had just flashed into his brain, was her thought; that she had the same notion in reserve, and that they were in sympathy. And Tavannes, seeing them talking together, and noting her look and the fervour of her gesture, formed the same opinion, and retired more darkly into himself. The downfall of his plan for dazzling her by a magnanimity unparalleled and beyond compare, a plan dependent on the submission of Angers—his disappointment in this might have roused the worst passions of a better man. But there was in this man a pride on a level at least with his other passions: and to bear himself in this hour of defeat and flight so that if she could not love him she must admire him, checked in a strange degree the current of his rage.

When Tignonville presently looked back he found that Count Hannibal and six of his riders had pulled up and were walking their horses far in the rear. On which he would have done the same himself; but Badelon called over his shoulder the eternal "Forward, Monsieur, *en avant!*" and sullenly, hating the man and his master more deeply every hour, Tignonville was forced to push on, with thoughts of vengeance in his heart.

Trot, trot! Trot, trot! Through a country which had lost its smiling wooded character and grew more sombre and less fertile the farther they left the Loire behind them. Trot, trot! Trot, trot!—for ever, it seemed to some. Javette wept with fatigue, and the other women were little better. The Countess herself spoke seldom except to cheer the Provost's daughter; who, poor girl, flung suddenly out of the round of her life and cast among strangers, showed a better spirit than might have been expected. At length, on the slopes of some low hills, which they had long seen before them, a cluster of houses and a church appeared; and Badelon, drawing rein, cried—

"Beaupréau, Madame! We stay an hour!"

It was six o'clock. They had ridden some hours without a break. With sighs and cries of pain the women dropped from their clumsy saddles, while the men laid out such food—it was little—as had been brought, and hobbled the horses that they might feed. The hour passed rapidly, and when it had passed Badelon was inexorable. There was wailing when he gave the word to mount again; and Tignonville, fiercely resenting this dumb, reasonless flight, was at heart one of the mutineers. But Badelon said grimly that they might go on and live, or stay and die, as it pleased them; and once more they climbed painfully to their saddles, and jogged steadily on through the sunset, through the gloaming, through the darkness, across a weird, mysterious country of low hills and narrow plains which grew more wild and less cultivated as they advanced. Fortunately the horses had been well saved during the long leisurely journey to Angers, and now went well and strongly. When they at last unsaddled for the night in a little dismal wood within a mile of Clisson, they had placed some forty miles between themselves and Angers.

CHAPTER XXXII
THE ORDEAL BY STEEL

The women for the most part fell like sacks and slept where they alighted, dead weary. The men, when they had cared for the horses, followed the example; for Badelon would suffer no fire. In less than half an hour, a sentry who stood on guard at the edge of the wood, and Tignonville and La Tribe, who talked in low voices with their backs against a tree, were the only persons who remained awake, with the exception of the Countess. Carlat had made a couch for her, and screened it with cloaks from the wind and the eye; for the moon had risen and where the trees stood sparsest its light flooded the soil with pools of white. But Madame had not yet retired to her bed. The two men, whose voices reached her, saw her from time to time moving restlessly to and fro between the road and the little encampment. Presently she came and stood over them.

"He led His people out of the wilderness," La Tribe was saying; "out of the trouble of Paris, out of the trouble of Angers, and always, always southward. If you do not in this, Monsieur, see His finger—"

"And Angers?" Tignonville struck in, with a faint sneer. "Has He led that out of trouble? A day or two ago you would risk all to save it, my friend. Now, with your back safely turned on it, you think all for the best."

"We did our best," the minister answered humbly. "From the day we met in Paris we have been but instruments."

"To save Angers?"

"To save a remnant."

On a sudden the Countess raised her hand. "Do you not hear horses, Monsieur?" she cried. She had been listening to the noises of the night, and had paid little heed to what the two were saying.

"One of ours moved," Tignonville answered listlessly. "Why do you not lie down, Madame?"

Instead of answering, "Whither is he going?" she asked. "Do you know?"

"I wish I did know," the young man answered peevishly. "To Niort, it may be. Or presently he will double back and recross the Loire."

"He would have gone by Cholet to Niort," La Tribe said. "The direction is rather that of Rochelle. God grant we be bound thither!"

"Or to Vrillac," the Countess cried, clasping her hands in the darkness. "Can it be to Vrillac he is going?"

The minister shook his head.

"Ah, let it be to Vrillac!" she cried, a thrill in her voice. "We should be safe there. And he would be safe."

"Safe?" echoed a fourth and deeper voice. And out of the darkness beside them loomed a tall figure.

The minister looked and leapt to his feet. Tignonville rose more slowly.

The voice was Tavannes'. "And where am I to be safe?" he repeated slowly, a faint ring of saturnine amusement in his tone.

"At Vrillac!" she cried. "In my house, Monsieur!"

He was silent a moment. Then, "Your house, Madame? In which direction is it, from here?"

"Westwards," she answered impulsively, her voice quivering with eagerness and emotion and hope. "Westwards, Monsieur—on the sea. The causeway from the land is long, and ten can hold it against ten hundred."

"Westwards? And how far westwards?"

Tignonville answered for her; in his tone throbbed the same eagerness, the same anxiety, which spoke in hers. Nor was Count Hannibal's ear deaf to it.

"Through Challans," he said, "thirteen leagues."

"From Clisson?"

"Yes, Monsieur le Comte."

"And by Commequiers less," the Countess cried.

"No, it is a worse road," Tignonville answered quickly; "and longer in time."

"But we came—"

"At our leisure, Madame. The road is by Challans, if we wish to be there quickly."

"Ah!" Count Hannibal said. In the darkness it was impossible to see his face or mark how he took it. "But being there, I have few men."

"I have forty will come at call," she cried with pride. "A word to them, and in four hours or a little more—"

"They would outnumber mine by four to one," Count Hannibal answered coldly, dryly, in a voice like ice-water flung in their faces. "Thank you, Madame; I understand. To Vrillac is no long ride; but we will not ride it at present." And he turned sharply on his heel and strode from them.

He had not covered thirty paces before she overtook him in the middle of a broad patch of moonlight, and touched his arm. He wheeled swiftly, his hand halfway to his hilt. Then he saw who it was.

"Ah," he said, "I had forgotten, Madame. You have come—"

"No!" she cried passionately; and standing before him she shook back the hood of her cloak that he might look into her eyes. "You owe me no blow to-day. You have paid me, Monsieur. You have struck me already, and foully, like a coward. Do you remember," she continued rapidly, "the hour after our marriage, and what you said to me? Do you remember what you told me? And whom to trust and whom to suspect, where lay our interest and where our foes'? You trusted me then! What have I done that you now dare—ay, dare, Monsieur," she repeated fearlessly, her face pale and her eyes glittering with excitement, "to insult me? That you treat me as—Javette? That you deem me capable of *that*? Of luring you into a trap, and in my own house, or the house that was mine, of—"

"Treating me as I have treated others."

"You have said it!" she cried. She could not herself understand why his distrust had wounded her so sharply, so home, that all fear of him was gone. "You have said it, and put that between us which will not be removed. I could have forgiven blows," she continued, breathless in her excitement, "so you had thought me what I am. But now you will do well to watch me! You will do well to leave Vrillac on one side. For were you there, and raised your hand against me—not that that touches me, but it will do—and there are those, I tell you, would fling you from the tower at my word."

"Indeed?"

"Ay, indeed! And indeed, Monsieur!"

Her face was in moonlight, his was in shadow.

"And this is your new tone, Madame, is it?" he said, slowly and after a pregnant pause. "The crossing of a river has wrought so great a change in you?"

"No!" she cried.

"Yes," he said. And, despite herself, she flinched before the grimness of his tone. "You have yet to learn one thing, however: that I do not change. That, north or south, I am the same to those who are the same to me. That what I have won on the one bank I will hold on the other, in the teeth of all, and though God's Church be thundering on my heels! I go to Vrillac—"

"You—go?" she cried. "You go?"

"I go," he repeated, "to-morrow. And among your own people I will see what language you will hold. While you were in my power I spared you. Now that you are in your own land, now that you lift your hand against me, I will show you of what make I am. If blows will not tame you, I will try that will suit you less. Ay, you wince, Madame! You had done well had you thought twice before you threatened, and thrice before you took in hand to scare Tavannes with a parcel of clowns and fisherfolk. To-morrow, to Vrillac and your duty! And one word more, Madame," he continued, turning back to her truculently when he had gone some paces from her. "If I find you plotting with your lover by the way I will hang not you, but him. I have spared him a score of times; but I know him, and I do not trust him."

"Nor me," she said, and with a white, set face she looked at him in the moonlight. "Had you not better hang me now?"

"Why?"

"Lest I do you an injury!" she cried with passion; and she raised her hand and pointed northward. "Lest I kill you some night, Monsieur! I tell you, a thousand men on your heels are less dangerous than the woman at your side—if she hate you."

"Is it so?" he cried. His hand flew to his hilt; his dagger flashed out. But she did not move, did not flinch, only she set her teeth; and her eyes, fascinated by the steel, grew wider.

His hand sank slowly. He held the weapon to her, hilt foremost; she took it mechanically.

"You think yourself brave enough to kill me, do you?" he sneered. "Then take this, and strike, if you dare. Take it—strike, Madame! It is sharp, and my arms are open." And he flung them wide, standing within a pace of her. "Here, above the collar-bone, is the surest for a weak hand. What, afraid?" he continued, as, stiffly clutching the weapon which he had put into her hand, she glared at him, trembling and astonished. "Afraid, and a Vrillac! Afraid, and 'tis but one blow! See, my arms are open. One blow home, and you will never lie in them. Think of that. One blow home, and you may lie in his. Think of that! Strike, then, Madame," he went on, piling taunt on taunt, "if you dare, and if you hate me. What, still afraid! How shall I give you heart? Shall I strike you? It will not be the first time by ten. I keep count, you see," he continued mockingly. "Or shall I kiss you? Ay, that may do. And it will not be against your will, either, for you have that in your hand will save you in an instant. Even"—he drew a foot nearer—"now! Even—" And he stooped until his lips almost touched hers.

She sprang back. "Oh, do not!" she cried. "Oh, do not!" And, dropping the dagger, she covered her face with her hands, and burst into weeping.

He stooped coolly, and, after groping some time for the poniard, drew it from the leaves among which it had fallen. He put it into the sheath, and not until he had done that did he speak. Then it was with a sneer.

"I have no need to fear overmuch," he said. "You are a poor hater, Madame. And poor haters make poor lovers. 'Tis his loss! If you will not strike a blow for him, there is but one thing left. Go, dream of him!"

And, shrugging his shoulders contemptuously, he turned on his heel.

CHAPTER XXXIII
THE AMBUSH

The start they made at daybreak was gloomy and ill-omened, through one of those white mists which are blown from the Atlantic over the flat lands of Western Poitou. The horses, looming gigantic through the fog, winced as the cold harness was girded on them. The men hurried to and fro with saddles on their heads, and stumbled over other saddles, and swore savagely. The women turned mutinous and would not rise; or, being dragged up by force, shrieked wild, unfitting words, as they were driven to the horses. The Countess looked on and listened, and shuddered, waiting for Carlat to set her on her horse. She had gone during the last three weeks through much that was dreary, much that was hopeless; but the chill discomfort of this forced start, with tired horses and wailing women, would have darkened the prospect of home had there been no fear or threat to cloud it.

He whose will compelled all stood a little apart and watched all, silent and gloomy. When Badelon, after taking his orders and distributing some slices of black bread to be eaten in the saddle, moved off at the head of his troop, Count Hannibal remained behind, attended by Bigot and the eight riders who had formed the rearguard so far. He had not approached the Countess since rising, and she had been thankful for it. But now, as she moved away, she looked back and saw him still standing; she marked that he wore his corselet, and in one of those revulsions of feeling—which outrun man's reason—she who had tossed on her couch through half the night, in passionate revolt against the fate before her, took fire at his neglect and his silence; she resented on a sudden the distance he kept, and his scorn of her. Her breast heaved, her colour came, involuntarily she checked her horse, as if she would return to him, and speak to him. Then the Carlats and the others closed up behind her, Badelon's monotonous "Forward, Madame, *en avant!*" proclaimed the day's journey begun, and she saw him no more.

Nevertheless, the motionless figure, looming Homeric through the fog, with gleams of wet light reflected from the steel about it, dwelt long in her mind. The road which Badelon followed, slowly at first, and with greater speed as the horses warmed to their work, and the women, sore and battered resigned themselves to suffering, wound across a flat expanse broken by a few hills. These were little more than mounds, and for the most part were veiled from sight by the low-lying sea-mist, through which gnarled and stunted oaks rose mysterious, to fade as strangely. Weird trees they were, with branches unlike those of this world's trees, rising in a grey land without horizon or limit, through which our travellers moved, weary phantoms in a clinging nightmare. At a walk, at a trot, more often at a jaded amble, they pushed on behind Badelon's humped shoulders. Sometimes the fog hung so thick about them that they saw only those who rose and fell in the saddles immediately before them; sometimes the air cleared a little, the curtain rolled up a space, and for a minute or two they discerned stretches of unfertile fields, half-tilled and stony, or long tracts of gorse and broom, with here and there a thicket of dwarf shrubs or a wood of wind-swept pines. Some looked and saw these things; more rode on sulky and unseeing, supporting impatiently the toils of a flight from they knew not what.

To do Tignonville justice, he was not of these. On the contrary, he seemed to be in a better temper on this day and, where so many took things unheroically, he showed to advantage. Avoiding the Countess and riding with Carlat, he talked and laughed with marked cheerfulness; nor did he ever fail, when the mist rose, to note this or that landmark, and confirm Badelon in the way he was going.

"We shall be at Lége by noon!" he cried more than once, "and if M. le Comte persists in his plan, may reach Vrillac by late sunset. By way of Challans!"

And always Carlat answered, "Ay, by Challans, Monsieur, so be it!"

He proved, too, so far right in his prediction that noon saw them drag, a weary train, into the hamlet of Lége, where the road from Nantes to Olonne runs southward over the level of Poitou. An hour later Count Hannibal rode in with six of his eight men, and, after a few minutes' parley with Badelon, who was scanning the horses, he called Carlat to him. The old man came.

"Can we reach Vrillac to-night?" Count Hannibal asked curtly.

"By Challans, my lord," the steward answered, "I think we can. We call it seven hours' riding from here."

"And that route is the shortest?"

"In time, M. le Comte, the road being better."

Count Hannibal bent his brows. "And the other way?" he said.

"Is by Commequiers, my lord. It is shorter in distance."

"By how much?"

"Two leagues. But there are fordings and a salt marsh; and with Madame and the women—"

"It would be longer?"

The steward hesitated. "I think so," he said slowly, his eyes wandering to the grey misty landscape, against which the poor hovels of the village stood out naked and comfortless. A low thicket of oaks sheltered the place from south-westerly gales. On the other three sides it lay open.

"Very good," Tavannes said curtly. "Be ready to start in ten minutes. You will guide us."

But when the ten minutes had elapsed and the party were ready to start, to the astonishment of all the steward was not to be found. To peremptory calls for him no answer came; and a hurried search through the hamlet proved equally fruitless. The only person who had seen him since his interview with Tavannes turned out to be M. de Tignonville; and he had seen him mount his horse five minutes before, and move off—as he believed—by the Challans road.

"Ahead of us?"

"Yes, M. le Comte," Tignonville answered, shading his eyes and gazing in the direction of the fringe of trees. "I did not see him take the road, but he was beside the north end of the wood when I saw him last. Thereabouts!" and he pointed to a place where the Challans road wound round the flank of the wood. "When we are beyond that point, I think we shall see him."

Count Hannibal growled a word in his beard, and, turning in his saddle, looked back the way he had come. Half a mile away, two or three dots could be seen approaching across the plain. He turned again.

"You know the road?" he said, curtly addressing the young man.

"Perfectly. As well as Carlat."

"Then lead the way, Monsieur, with Badelon. And spare neither whip nor spur. There will be need of both, if we would lie warm to-night."

Tignonville nodded assent and, wheeling his horse, rode to the head of the party, a faint smile playing about his mouth. A moment, and the main body moved off behind him, leaving Count Hannibal and six men to cover the rear. The mist, which at noon had risen for an hour or two, was closing down again, and they had no sooner passed clear of the wood than the trees faded out of sight behind them. It was not wonderful that they could not see Carlat. Objects a hundred paces from them were completely hidden.

Trot, trot! Trot, trot! through a grey world so featureless, so unreal that the riders, now dozing in the saddle, and now awaking, seemed to themselves to stand still, as in a nightmare. A trot and then a walk, and then a trot again; and all a dozen times repeated, while the women bumped along in their wretched saddles, and the horses stumbled, and the men swore at them.

Ha! La Garnache at last, and a sharp turn southward to Challans. The Countess raised her head, and began to look about her. There, should be a church, she knew; and there, the old ruined tower built by wizards, or the Carthaginians, so old tradition ran; and there, to the westward, the great salt marshes towards Noirmoutier. The mist hid all, but the knowledge that they were there set her heart beating, brought tears to her eyes, and lightened the long road to Challans.

At Challans they halted half an hour, and washed out the horses' mouths with water and a little *guignolet*—the spirit of the country. A dose of the cordial was administered to the women; and a little after seven they began the last stage of the journey, through a landscape which even the mist could not veil from the eyes of love. There rose the windmill of Soullans! There the old dolmen, beneath which the grey wolf that ate the two children of Tornic had its lair. For a mile back they had been treading my lady's land; they had only two more leagues to ride, and one of those was crumbling under each dogged footfall. The salt flavour, which is new life to the shore-born, was in the fleecy reek which floated by them, now thinner, now more opaque; and almost they could hear the dull thunder of the Biscay waves falling on the rocks.

Tignonville looked back at her and smiled. She caught the look; she fancied that she understood it and his thoughts. But her own eyes were moist at the moment with tears, and what his said, and what there was of strangeness in his glance, half-warning, half-exultant, escaped her. For there, not a mile before them, where the low hills about the fishing village began to rise from the dull inland level—hills green on the land side, bare and scarped towards the sea and the island—she espied the wayside chapel at which the nurse of her early childhood had told her beads. Where it stood, the road from Commequiers and the road she travelled became one: a short mile thence, after winding among the hillocks, it ran down to the beach and the causeway—and to her home.

At the sight she bethought herself of Carlat, and calling to M. de Tignonville, she asked him what he thought of the steward's continued absence.

"He must have outpaced us!" he answered, with an odd laugh.

"But he must have ridden hard to do that."

He reined back to her. "Say nothing!" he muttered under his breath. "But look ahead, Madame, and see if we are expected!"

"Expected? How can we be expected?" she cried. The colour rushed into her face.

He put his finger to his lip, and looked warningly at Badelon's humped shoulders, jogging up and down in front of them. Then, stooping towards her, in a lower tone, "If Carlat has arrived before us, he will have told them," he said.

"Have told them?"

"He came by the other road, and it is quicker."

She gazed at him in astonishment, her lips parted; and slowly she understood, and her eyes grew hard.

"Then why," she said, "did you say it was longer. Had we been overtaken, Monsieur, we had had you to thank for it, it seems!"

He bit his lip. "But we have not been overtaken," he rejoined. "On the contrary, you have me to thank for something quite different."

"As unwelcome, perhaps!" she retorted. "For what?"

"Softly, Madame."

"For what?" she repeated, refusing to lower her voice. "Speak, Monsieur, if you please." He had never seen her look at him in that way.

"For the fact," he answered, stung by her look and tone, "that when you arrive you will find yourself mistress in your own house! Is that nothing?"

"You have called in my people?"

"Carlat has done so, or should have," he answered. "Henceforth," he continued, a ring of exultation in his voice, "it will go hard with M. le Comte, if he does not treat you better than he has treated you hitherto. That is all!"

"You mean that it will go hard with him in any case?" she cried, her bosom rising and falling.

"I mean, Madame—But there they are! Good Carlat! Brave Carlat! He has done well!"

"Carlat?"

"Ay, there they are! And you are mistress in your own land! At last you are mistress, and you have me to thank for it! See!" And heedless in his exultation whether Badelon understood or not, he pointed to a place before them where the road wound between two low hills. Over the green shoulder of one of these, a dozen bright points caught and reflected the last evening light; while as he spoke a man rose to his feet on the hillside above, and began to make signs to persons below. A pennon, too, showed an instant over the shoulder, fluttered, and was gone.

Badelon looked as they looked. The next instant he uttered a low oath, and dragged his horse across the front of the party.

"Pierre!" he cried to the man on his left, "ride for your life! To my lord, and tell him we are ambushed!" And as the trained soldier wheeled about and spurred away, the sacker of Rome turned a dark scowling face on Tignonville. "If this be your work," he hissed, "we shall thank you for it in hell! For it is where most of us will lie to-night! They are Montsoreau's spears, and they have those with them are worse to deal with than themselves!" Then in a different tone, and throwing off all disguise, "Men to the front!" he shouted. "And you, Madame, to the rear quickly, and the women with you! Now, men, forward, and draw! Steady! Steady! They are coming!"

There was an instant of confusion, disorder, panic; horses jostling one another, women screaming and clutching at men, men shaking them off and forcing their way to the van. Fortunately the enemy did not fall on at once, as Badelon expected, but after showing themselves in the mouth of the valley, at a distance of three hundred paces, hung for some reason irresolute. This gave Badelon time to array his seven swords in front; but real resistance was out of the question, as he knew. And to none seemed less in question than to Tignonville.

When the truth, and what he had done, broke on the young man, he sat a moment motionless with horror. It was only when Badelon had twice summoned him with opprobrious words that he awoke to the relief of action. Even after that he hung an instant trying to meet the Countess's eyes, despair in his own; but it was not to be. She had turned her head, and was looking back, as if thence only and not from him could help come. It was not to him she turned; and he saw it, and the justice of it. And silent, grim, more formidable even than old Badelon, the veteran fighter, who knew all the tricks and shifts of the *mêlée*, he spurred to the flank of the line.

"Now, steady!" Badelon cried again, seeing that the enemy were beginning to move. "Steady! Ha! Thank God, my lord! My lord is coming! Stand! Stand!" The distant sound of galloping hoofs had reached his ear in the nick of time. He stood in his stirrups and looked back. Yes, Count Hannibal was coming, riding a dozen paces in front of his men. The odds were still desperate—for he brought but six—the enemy were still three to one. But the thunder of his hoofs as he came up checked for a moment the enemy's onset; and before Montsoreau's people got started again Count Hannibal had ridden up abreast of the women, and the Countess, looking at him, knew that, desperate as was their strait, she had not looked behind in vain. The glow of battle, the stress of the moment, had displaced the cloud from his face; the joy of the born fighter lightened in his eye. His voice rang clear and loud above the press.

"Badelon! wait you and two with Madame!" he cried. "Follow at fifty paces' distance, and, when we have broken them, ride through! The others with me! Now forward, men, and show your teeth! A Tavannes! A Tavannes! A Tavannes! We carry it yet!"

And he dashed forward, leading them on, leaving the women behind; and down the sward to meet him, thundering in double line, came Montsoreau's men-at-arms, and with the men-at-arms, a dozen pale, fierce-eyed men in the Church's black, yelling the Church's curses. Madame's heart grew sick as she heard, as she waited, as she judged him by the fast-failing light a horse's length before his men—with only Tignonville beside him.

She held her breath—would the shock never come? If Badelon had not seized her rein and forced her forward, she would not have moved. And then, even as she moved, they met! With yells and wild cries and a mare's savage scream, the two bands crashed together in a huddle of fallen or rearing horses, of flickering weapons, of thrusting men, of grapples hand-to-hand. What happened, what was happening to any one, who it was fell, stabbed through and through by four, or who were those who still fought single combats, twisting round one another's horses, those on her right and on her left, she could not tell. For Badelon dragged her on with whip and spur, and two horsemen—who obscured her view—galloped in front of her, and rode down bodily the only man who undertook to bar her passage. She had a glimpse of that man's face, as his horse, struck in the act of turning, fell sideways on him; and she knew it, in its agony of terror, though she had seen it but once. It was the face of the man whose eyes had sought hers from the steps of the church in Angers; the lean man in black, who had turned soldier of the Church—to his misfortune.

Through? Yes, through, the way was clear before them! The fight with its screams and curses died away behind them. The horses swayed and all but sank under them. But Badelon knew it no time for mercy; iron-shod hoofs rang on the road behind, and at any moment the pursuers might be on their heels. He flogged on until the cots of the hamlet appeared on either side of the way; on, until the road forked and the Countess with strange readiness cried "The left!"—on, until the beach appeared below them at the foot of a sharp pitch, and beyond the beach the slow heaving grey of the ocean.

The tide was high. The causeway ran through it, a mere thread lipped by the darkling waves, and at the sight a grunt of relief broke from Badelon. For at the end of the causeway, black against the western sky, rose the gateway and towers of Vrillac; and he saw that, as the Countess had said, it was a place ten men could hold against ten hundred!

They stumbled down the beach, reached the causeway and trotted along it; more slowly now, and looking back. The other women had followed by hook or by crook, some crying hysterically, yet clinging to their horses and even urging them; and in a medley, the causeway clear behind them and no one following, they reached the drawbridge, and passed under the arch of the gate beyond.

There friendly hands, Carlat's foremost, welcomed them and aided them to alight, and the Countess saw, as in a dream, the familiar scene, all unfamiliar: the gate, where she had played, a child, aglow with lantern-light and arms. Men, whose rugged faces she had known in infancy, stood at the drawbridge chains and at the winches. Others blew matches and handled primers, while old servants crowded round her, and women looked at her, scared and weeping. She saw it all at a glance—the lights, the black shadows, the sudden glow of a match on the groining of the arch above. She saw it, and turning swiftly, looked back the way she had come; along the dusky causeway to the low, dark shore, which night was stealing quickly from their eyes. She clasped her hands.

"Where is Badelon?" she cried. "Where is he? Where is he?"

One of the men who had ridden before her answered that he had turned back.

"Turned back!" she repeated. And then, shading her eyes, "Who is coming?" she asked, her voice insistent. "There is some one coming. Who is it? Who is it?"

Two were coming out of the gloom, travelling slowly and painfully along the causeway. One was La Tribe, limping; the other a rider, slashed across the forehead, and sobbing curses.

"No more!" she muttered. "Are there no more?"

The minister shook his head. The rider wiped the blood from his eyes, and turned up his face that he might see the better. But he seemed to be dazed, and only babbled strange words in a strange *patois*.

She stamped her foot in passion. "More lights!" she cried. "Lights! How can they find their way? And let six men go down the *digue*, and meet them. Will you let them be butchered between the shore and this?"

But Carlat, who had not been able to collect more than a dozen men, shook his head; and before she could repeat the order, sounds of battle, shrill, faint, like cries of hungry seagulls, pierced the darkness which shrouded the farther end of the causeway. The women shrank inward over the threshold, while Carlat cried to the men at the chains to be ready, and to some who stood at loopholes above, to blow up their matches and let fly at his word. And then they all waited, the Countess foremost, peering eagerly into the growing darkness. They could see nothing.

A distant scuffle, an oath, a cry, silence! The same, a little nearer, a little louder, followed this time, not by silence, but by the slow tread of a limping horse. Again a rush of feet, the clash of steel, a scream, a laugh, all weird and unreal, issuing from the night; then out of the darkness into the light, stepping slowly with hanging head, moved a horse, bearing on its back a man—or was it a man?—bending low in the saddle, his feet swinging loose. For an instant the horse and the man seemed to be alone, a ghostly pair; then at their heels came into view two figures, skirmishing this way and that; and now coming nearer, and now darting back into the gloom. One, a squat figure, stooping low, wielded a sword with two hands; the other covered him with a half-pike. And then beyond these—abruptly as it seemed—the night gave up to sight a swarm of dark figures pressing on them and after them, driving them before them.

Carlat had an inspiration. "Fire!" he cried; and four arquebuses poured a score of slugs into the knot of pursuers. A man fell, another shrieked and stumbled, the rest gave back. Only the horse came on spectrally, with hanging head and shining eyeballs, until a man ran out and seized its head, and dragged it, more by his strength than its own, over the drawbridge. After it Badelon, with a gaping wound in his knee, and Bigot, bleeding from a dozen hurts, walked over the bridge, and stood on either side of the saddle, smiling foolishly at the man on the horse.

"Leave me!" he muttered. "Leave me!" He made a feeble movement with his hand, as if it held a weapon; then his head sank lower. It was Count Hannibal. His thigh was broken, and there was a lance-head in his arm. The Countess looked at him, then beyond him, past him into the darkness.

"Are there no more?" she whispered tremulously. "No more? Tignonville—my—"

Badelon shook his head. The Countess covered her face and wept.

CHAPTER XXXIV
WHICH WILL YOU, MADAME?

It was in the grey dawning of the next day, at the hour before the sun rose, that word of M. de Tignonville's fate came to them in the castle. The fog which had masked the van and coming of night hung thick on its retreating skirts, and only reluctantly and little by little gave up to sight and daylight a certain thing which night had left at the end of the causeway. The first man to see it was Carlat, from the roof of the gateway; and he rubbed eyes weary with watching, and peered anew at it through the mist, fancying himself back in the Place Ste.-Croix at Angers, supposing for a wild moment the journey a dream, and the return a nightmare. But rub as he might, and stare as he might, the ugly outlines of the thing he had seen persisted—nay, grew sharper as the haze began to lift from the grey, slow-heaving floor of sea. He called another man and bade him look.

"What is it?" he said. "D'you see, there? Below the village?"

"'Tis a gibbet," the man answered, with a foolish laugh; they had watched all night. "God keep us from it."

"A gibbet?"

"Ay!"

"But what is it for? What is it doing there?"

"It is there to hang those they have taken, very like," the man answered, stupidly practical. And then other men came up, and stared at it and growled in their beards. Presently there were eight or ten on the roof of the gateway looking towards the land and discussing the thing; and by-and-by a man was descried approaching along the causeway with a white flag in his hand.

At that Carlat bade one fetch the minister. "He understands things," he muttered, "and I misdoubt this. And see," he cried after the messenger, "that no word of it come to Mademoiselle!" Instinctively in the maiden home he reverted to the maiden title.

The messenger went, and came again bringing La Tribe, whose head rose above the staircase at the moment the envoy below came to a halt before the gate. Carlat signed to the minister to come forward; and La Tribe, after sniffing the salt air, and glancing at the long, low, misty shore and the stiff ugly shape which stood at the end of the causeway, looked down and met the envoy's eyes. For a moment no one spoke. Only the men who had remained on the gateway, and had watched the stranger's coming, breathed hard.

At last, "I bear a message," the man announced loudly and clearly, "for the lady of Vrillac. Is she present?"

"Give your message!" La Tribe replied.

"It is for her ears only."

"Do you want to enter?"

"No!" The man answered so hurriedly that more than one smiled. He had the bearing of a lay clerk of some precinct, a verger or sacristan; and after a fashion the dress of one also, for he was in dusty black and wore no sword, though he was girded with a belt. "No!" he repeated, "but if Madame will come to the gate, and speak to me—"

"Madame has other fish to fry," Carlat blurted out. "Do you think that she has naught to do but listen to messages from a gang of bandits?"

"If she does not listen she will repent it all her life!" the fellow answered hardily. "That is part of my message."

There was a pause while La Tribe considered the matter. In the end, "From whom do you come?" he asked.

"From His Excellency the Lieutenant-Governor of Saumur," the envoy answered glibly, "and from my Lord Bishop of Angers, him assisting by his Vicar; and from others gathered lawfully, who will as lawfully depart if their terms are accepted. Also from M. de Tignonville, a gentleman, I am told, of these parts, now in their hands and adjudged to die at sunset this day if the terms I bring be not accepted."

There was a long silence on the gate. The men looked down fixedly; not a feature of one of them moved, for no one was surprised. "Wherefore is he to die?" La Tribe asked at last.

"For good cause shown."

"Wherefore?"

"He is a Huguenot."

The minister nodded. "And the terms?" Carlat muttered.

"Ay, the terms!" La Tribe repeated, nodding afresh. "What are they?"

"They are for Madame's ear only," the messenger made answer.

"Then they will not reach it!" Carlat broke forth in wrath. "So much for that! And for yourself, see you go quickly before we make a target of you!"

"Very well, I go," the envoy answered sullenly. "But—"

"But what?" La Tribe cried, gripping Carlat's shoulder to quiet him. "But what? Say what you have to say, man! Speak out, and have done with it!'

"I will say it to her and to no other."

"Then you will not say it!" Carlat cried again. "For you will not see her. So you may go. And the black fever in your vitals."

"Ay, go!" La Tribe added more quietly.

The man turned away with a shrug of the shoulders, and moved off a dozen paces, watched by all on the gate with the same fixed attention. But presently he paused; he returned.

"Very well," he said, looking up with an ill grace. "I will do my office here, if I cannot come to her. But I hold also a letter from M. de Tignonville, and that I can deliver to no other hands than hers!" He held it up as he spoke, a thin scrap of greyish paper, the fly-leaf of a missal perhaps. "See!" he continued, "and take notice! If she does not get this, and learns when it is too late that it was offered—"

"The terms," Carlat growled impatiently. "The terms! Come to them!"

"You will have them?" the man answered, nervously passing his tongue over his lips. "You will not let me see her, or speak to her privately?"

"No."

"Then hear them. His Excellency is informed that one Hannibal de Tavannes, guilty of the detestable crime of sacrilege and of other gross crimes, has taken refuge here. He requires that the said Hannibal de Tavannes be handed to him for punishment, and, this being done before sunset this evening, he will yield to you free and uninjured the said M. de Tignonville, and will retire from the lands of Vrillac. But if you refuse"— the man passed his eye along the line of attentive faces which fringed the battlement—"he will at sunset hang the said Tignonville on the gallows raised for Tavannes, and will harry the demesne of Vrillac to its farthest border!"

There was a long silence on the gate. Some, their gaze still fixed on him, moved their lips as if they chewed. Others looked aside, met their fellows' eyes in a pregnant glance, and slowly returned to him. But no one spoke.

At his back the flush of dawn was flooding the east, and spreading and waxing brighter. The air was growing warm; the shore below, from grey, was turning green.

In a minute or two the sun, whose glowing marge already peeped above the low hills of France, would top the horizon.

The man, getting no answer, shifted his feet uneasily. "Well," he cried, "what answer am I to take?"

Still no one moved.

"I've done my part. Will no one give her the letter?" he cried. And he held it up. "Give me my answer, for I am going."

"Take the letter!" The words came from the rear of the group in a voice that startled all. They turned, as though some one had struck them, and saw the Countess standing beside the hood which covered the stairs. They guessed that she had heard all or nearly all; but the glory of the sunrise, shining full on her at that moment, lent a false warmth to her face, and life to eyes woefully and tragically set. It was not easy to say whether she had heard or not. "Take the letter," she repeated.

Carlat looked helplessly over the parapet.

"Go down!"

He cast a glance at La Tribe, but he got none in return, and he was preparing to do her bidding when a cry of dismay broke from those who still had their eyes bent downwards. The messenger, waving the letter in a last appeal, had held it too loosely; a light air, as treacherous, as unexpected, had snatched it from his hand, and bore it—even as the Countess, drawn by the cry, sprang to the parapet—fifty paces from him. A moment it floated in the air, eddying, rising, falling; then, light as thistledown, it touched the water and began to sink.

The messenger uttered frantic lamentations, and stamped the causeway in his rage. The Countess only looked, and looked, until the rippling crest of a baby wave broke over the tiny venture, and with its freight of tidings it sank from sight.

The man, silent now, stared a moment, then shrugged his shoulders.

"Well, 'tis fortunate it was his," he cried brutally, "and not His Excellency's, or my back had suffered! And now," he added impatiently, "by your leave, what answer?"

What answer? Ah, God, what answer? The men who leant on the parapet, rude and coarse as they were, felt the tragedy of the question and the dilemma, guessed what they meant to her, and looked everywhere save at her.

What answer? Which of the two was to live? Which die—shamefully? Which? Which?

"Tell him—to come back—an hour before sunset," she muttered.

They told him and he went; and one by one the men began to go too, and stole from the roof, leaving her standing alone, her face to the shore, her hands resting on the parapet. The light breeze which blew off the land stirred loose ringlets of her hair, and flattened the thin robe against her sunlit figure. So had she stood a thousand times in old days, in her youth, in her maidenhood. So in her father's time had she stood to see her lover come riding along the sands to woo her! So had she stood to welcome him on the eve of that fatal journey to Paris! Thence had others watched her go with him. The men remembered—remembered all; and one by one they stole shamefacedly away, fearing lest she should speak or turn tragic eyes on them.

True, in their pity for her was no doubt of the end, or thought of the victim who must suffer—of Tavannes. They, of Poitou, who had not been with him, knew nothing of him; they cared as little. He was a northern man, a stranger, a man of the sword, who had seized her—so they heard—by the sword. But they saw that the burden of choice was laid on her; there, in her sight and in theirs, rose the gibbet; and, clowns as they were, they discerned the tragedy of her *rôle*, play it as she might, and though her act gave life to her lover.

When all had retired save three or four, she turned and saw these gathered at the head of the stairs in a ring about Carlat, who was addressing them in a low eager voice. She could not catch a syllable, but a look hard and almost cruel flashed into her eyes as she gazed; and raising her voice she called the steward to her.

"The bridge is up," she said, her tone hard, "but the gates? Are they locked?"

"Yes, Madame."

"The wicket?"

"No, not the wicket." And Carlat looked another way.

"Then go, lock it, and bring the keys to me!" she replied. "Or stay!" Her voice grew harder, her eyes spiteful as a cat's. "Stay, and be warned that you play me no tricks! Do you hear? Do you understand? Or old as you are, and long as you have served us, I will have you thrown from this tower, with as little pity as Isabeau flung her gallants to the fishes. I am still mistress here, never more mistress than this day. Woe to you if you forget it."

He blenched and cringed before her, muttering incoherently.

"I know," she said, "I read you! And now the keys. Go, bring them to me! And if by chance I find the wicket unlocked when I come down, pray, Carlat, pray! For you will have need of prayers."

He slunk away, the men with him; and she fell to pacing the roof feverishly. Now and then she extended her arms, and low cries broke from her, as from a dumb creature in pain. Wherever she looked, old memories rose up to torment her and redouble her misery. A thing she could have borne in the outer world, a thing which might have seemed tolerable in the reeking air of Paris or in the gloomy streets of Angers wore here its most appalling aspect. Henceforth, whatever choice she made, this home, where even in those troublous times she had known naught but peace, must bear a damning stain! Henceforth this day and this hour must come between her and happiness, must brand her brow, and fix her with a deed of which men and women would tell while she lived! Oh, God—pray? Who said, pray?

"I!" And La Tribe with tears in his eyes held out the keys to her. "I, Madame," he continued solemnly, his voice broken with emotion. "For in man is no help. The strongest man, he who rode yesterday a master of men, a very man of war in his pride and his valour—see him, now, and—"

"Don't!" she cried, sharp pain in her voice. "Don't!" And she stopped him with her hand, her face averted. After an interval, "You come from him?" she muttered faintly.

"Yes."

"Is he—hurt to death, think you?" She spoke low, and kept her face hidden from him.

"Alas, no!" he answered, speaking the thought in his heart. "The men who are with him seem confident of his recovery."

"Do they know?"

"Badelon has had experience."

"No, no. Do they know of this?" she cried. "Of this!" And she pointed with a gesture of loathing to the black gibbet on the farther strand.

He shook his head. "I think not," he muttered. And after a moment, "God help you!" he added fervently. "God help and guide you, Madame!"

She turned on him suddenly, fiercely. "Is that all you can do?" she cried. "Is that all the help you can give? You are a man. Go down, lead them out; drive off these cowards who drain our life's blood, who trade on a woman's heart! On them! Do something, anything, rather than lie in safety here—here!"

The minister shook his head sadly. "Alas, Madame!" he said, "to sally were to waste life. They outnumber us three to one. If Count Hannibal could do no more than break through last night, with scarce a man unwounded—"

"He had the women!"

"And we have not him!"

"He would not have left us!" she cried hysterically.

"I believe it."

"Had they taken me, do you think he would have lain behind walls? Or skulked in safety here, while—while—" Her voice failed her.

He shook his head despondently.

"And that is all you can do?" she cried, and turned from him, and to him again, extending her arms, in bitter scorn. "All you will do? Do you forget that twice he spared your life? That in Paris once, and once in Angers, he held his hand? That always, whether he stood or whether he fled, he held himself between us and harm? Ay, always? And who will now raise a hand for him? Who?"

"Madame!"

"Who? Who? Had he died in the field," she continued, her voice shaking with grief, her hands beating the parapet—for she had turned from him—"had he fallen where he rode last night, in the front, with his face to the foe, I had viewed him tearless, I had deemed him happy! I had prayed dry-eyed for him who—who spared me all these days and weeks! Whom I robbed and he forgave me! Whom I tempted, and he forbore me! Ay, and who spared not once or twice him for whom he must now—he must now—" And unable to finish the sentence she beat her hands again and passionately on the stones.

"Heaven knows, Madame," the minister cried vehemently, "Heaven knows, I would advise you if I could."

"Why did he wear his corselet?" she wailed, as if she had not heard him. "Was there no spear could reach his breast, that he must come to this? No foe so gentle he would spare him this? Or why did *he* not die with me in Paris when we waited? In another minute death might have come and saved us this."

With the tears running down his face he tried to comfort her.

"Man that is a shadow," he said, "passeth away—what matter how? A little while, a very little while, and we shall pass!"

"With his curse upon us!" she cried. And, shuddering, she pressed her hands to her eyes to shut out the sight her fancy pictured.

He left her for a while, hoping that in solitude she might regain control of herself. When he returned he found her seated, and outwardly more composed; her arms resting on the parapet-wall, her eyes bent steadily on the long stretch of hard sand which ran northward from the village. By that route her lover had many a time come to her; there she had ridden with him in the early days; and that way they had started for Paris on such a morning and at such an hour as this, with sunshine about them, and larks singing hope above the sand-dunes, and with wavelets creaming to the horses' hoofs!

Of all which La Tribe, a stranger, knew nothing. The rapt gaze, the unchanging attitude only confirmed his opinion of the course she would adopt. He was thankful to find her more composed; and in fear of such a scene as had already passed between them, he stole away again. He returned by-and-by, but with the greatest reluctance, and only because Carlat's urgency would take no refusal.

He came this time to crave the key of the wicket, explaining that—rather to satisfy his own conscience and the men than with any hope of success—he proposed to go halfway along the causeway, and thence by signs invite a conference.

"It is just possible," he added, hesitating—he feared nothing so much as to raise hopes in her—"that by the offer of a money ransom, Madame—"

"Go," she said, without turning her head. "Offer what you please. But"—bitterly—"have a care of them! Montsoreau is very like Monetreau! Beware of the bridge!"

He went and came again in half an hour. Then, indeed, though she had spoken as if hope was dead in her, she was on her feet at the first sound of his tread on the stairs; her parted lips and her white face questioned him. He shook his head.

"There is a priest," he said in broken tones, "with them, whom God will judge. It is his plan, and he is without mercy or pity."

"You bring nothing from—him?"

"They will not suffer him to write again."

"You did not see him?"

"No."

CHAPTER XXXV
AGAINST THE WALL

In a room beside the gateway, into which, as the nearest and most convenient place, Count Hannibal had been carried from his saddle, a man sat sideways in the narrow embrasure of a loophole, to which his eyes seemed glued. The room, which formed part of the oldest block of the château, and was ordinarily the quarters of the Carlats, possessed two other windows, deep-set indeed, yet superior to that through which Bigot—for he it was—peered so persistently. But the larger windows looked southwards, across the bay—at this moment the noon-high sun was pouring his radiance through them; while the object which held Bigot's gaze and fixed him to his irksome seat, lay elsewhere. The loophole commanded the causeway leading shorewards; through it the Norman could see who came and went, and even the cross-beam of the ugly object which rose where the causeway touched the land.

On a flat truckle-bed behind the door lay Count Hannibal, his injured leg protected from the coverlid by a kind of cage. His eyes were bright with fever, and his untended beard and straggling hair heightened the wildness of his aspect. But he was in possession of his senses; and as his gaze passed from Bigot at the window to the old Free Companion, who sat on a stool beside him, engaged in shaping a piece of wood into a splint, an expression almost soft crept into his harsh face.

"Old fool!" he said. And his voice, though changed, had not lost all its strength and harshness. "Did the Constable need a splint when you laid him under the tower at Gaeta?"

The old man lifted his eyes from his task, and glanced through the nearest window.

"It is long from noon to night," he said quietly, "and far from cup to lip, my lord!"

"It would be if I had two legs," Tavannes answered, with a grimace, half-snarl, half-smile. "As it is—where is that dagger? It leaves me every minute."

It had slipped from the coverlid to the ground. Badelon took it up, and set it on the bed within reach of his master's hand.

Bigot swore fiercely. "It would be farther still," he growled, "if you would be guided by me, my lord. Give me leave to bar the door, and 'twill be long before these fisher clowns force it. Badelon and I—"

"Being in your full strength," Count Hannibal murmured cynically.

"Could hold it. We have strength enough for that," the Norman boasted, though his livid face and his bandages gave the lie to his words. He could not move without pain; and for Badelon, his knee was as big as two with plaisters of his own placing.

Count Hannibal stared at the ceiling. "You could not strike two blows!" he said. "Don't lie to me! And Badelon cannot walk two yards! Fine fighters!" he continued with bitterness, not all bitter. "Fine bars 'twixt a man and death! No, it is time to turn the face to the wall. And, since go I must, it shall not be said Count Hannibal dared not go alone! Besides—"

Bigot stopped him with an oath that was in part a cry of pain.

"D---n her!" he exclaimed in fury, "'tis she is that *besides*! I know it. 'Tis she has been our ruin from the day we saw her first, ay, to this day! 'Tis she has bewitched you until your blood, my lord, has turned to water. Or you would never, to save the hand that betrayed us, never to save a man—"

"Silence!" Count Hannibal cried, in a terrible voice. And rising on his elbow, he poised the dagger as if he would hurl it. "Silence, or I will spit you like the vermin you are! Silence, and listen! And you, old ban-dog, listen too, for I know you obstinate! It is not to save him. It is because I will die as I have lived, fearing nothing and asking nothing! It were easy to bar the door as you would have me, and die in the corner here like a wolf at bay, biting to the last. That were easy, old wolf-hound! Pleasant and good sport!"

"Ay! That were a death!" the veteran cried, his eyes brightening. "So I would fain die!"

"And I!" Count Hannibal returned, showing his teeth in a grim smile. "I too! Yet I will not! I will not! Because so to die were to die unwillingly, and give them triumph. Be dragged to death? No, old dog, if die we must, we will go to death! We will die grandly, highly, as becomes Tavannes! That when we are gone they may say, 'There died a man!'"

"*She* may say!" Bigot muttered, scowling.

Count Hannibal heard and glared at him, but presently thought better of it, and after a pause—

"Ay, she too!" he said. "Why not? As we have played the game—for her—so, though we lose, we will play it to the end; nor because we lose throw down the cards! Besides, man, die in the corner, die biting, and he dies too!"

"And why not?" Bigot asked, rising in a fury. "Why not? Whose work is it we lie here, snared by these clowns of fisherfolk? Who led us wrong and betrayed us? He die? Would the devil had taken him a year ago! Would he were within my reach now! I would kill him with my bare fingers! He die? And why not?"

"Why, because, fool, his death would not save me!" Count Hannibal answered coolly. "If it would, he would die! But it will not; and we must even do again as we have done. I have spared him—he's a white-livered hound!—both once and twice, and we must go to the end with it since no better can be! I have thought it out, and it must be. Only see you, old dog, that I have the dagger hid in the splint where I can reach it. And then, when the exchange has been made, and my lady has her silk glove again—to put in her bosom!"—with a grimace and a sudden reddening of his harsh features—"if master priest come within reach of my arm, I'll send him before me, where I go."

"Ay, ay!" said Badelon. "And if you fail of your stroke I will not fail of mine! I shall be there, and I will see to it he goes! I shall be there!"

"You?"

"Ay, why not?" the old man answered quietly. "I may halt on this leg for aught I know, and come to starve on crutches like old Claude Boiteux who was at the taking of Milan and now begs in the passage under the Châtelet."

"Bah, man, you will get a new lord!"

Badelon nodded. "Ay, a new lord with new ways!" he answered slowly and thoughtfully. "And I am tired. They are of another sort, lords now, than they were when I was young. It was a word and a blow then. Now I am old, with most it is—'Old hog, your distance! You scent my lady!' Then they rode, and hunted, and tilted year in and year out, and summer or winter heard the lark sing. Now they are curled, and paint themselves, and lie in silk and toy with ladies—who shamed to be seen at Court or board when I was a boy—and love better to hear the mouse squeak than the lark sing."

"Still, if I give you my gold chain," Count Hannibal answered quietly, "'twill keep you from that."

"Give it to Bigot," the old man answered. The splint he was fashioning had fallen on his knees, and his eyes were fixed on the distance of his youth. "For me, my lord, I am tired, and I go with you. I go with you. It is a good death to die biting before the strength be quite gone. Have the dagger too, if you please, and I'll fit it within the splint right neatly. But I shall be there—"

"And you'll strike home?" Tavannes cried eagerly. He raised himself on his elbow, a gleam of joy in his gloomy eyes.

"Have no fear, my lord. See, does it tremble?" He held out his hand. "And when you are sped, I will try the Spanish stroke—upwards with a turn ere you withdraw, that I learned from Ruiz—on the shaven pate. I see them about me now!" the old man continued, his face flushing, his form dilating. "It will be odd if I cannot snatch a sword and hew down three to go with Tavannes! And Bigot, he will see my lord the Marshal by-and-by; and as I do to the priest, the Marshal will do to Montsoreau. Ho! ho! He will teach him the *coup de Jarnac*, never fear!" And the old man's moustaches curled up ferociously.

Count Hannibal's eyes sparkled with joy. "Old dog!" he cried—and he held his hand to the veteran, who brushed it reverently with his lips—"we will go together then! Who touches my brother, touches Tavannes!"

"Touches Tavannes!" Badelon cried, the glow of battle lighting his bloodshot eyes. He rose to his feet. "Touches Tavannes! You mind at Jarnac—"

"Ah! At Jarnac!"

"When we charged their horse, was my boot a foot from yours, my lord?"

"Not a foot!"

"And at Dreux," the old man continued with a proud, elated gesture, "when we rode down the German pikemen—they were grass before us, leaves on the wind, thistledown—was it not I who covered your bridle hand, and swerved not in the *mêlée*?"

"It was! It was!"

"And at St. Quentin, when we fled before the Spaniard—it was his day, you remember, and cost us dear—"

"Ay, I was young then," Tavannes cried in turn, his eyes glistening. "St. Quentin! It was the tenth of August. And you were new with me, and seized my rein—"

"And we rode off together, my lord—of the last, of the last, as God sees me! And striking as we went, so that they left us for easier game."

"It was so, good sword! I remember it as if it had been yesterday!"

"And at Cerisoles, the Battle of the Plain, in the old Spanish wars, that was most like a joust of all the pitched fields I ever saw—at Cerisoles, where I caught your horse? You mind me? It was in the shock when we broke Guasto's line—"

"At Cerisoles?" Count Hannibal muttered slowly. "Why, man, I—"

"I caught your horse, and mounted you afresh? You remember, my lord? And at Landriano, where Leyva turned the tables on us again."

Count Hannibal stared. "Landriano?" he muttered bluntly. "'Twas in '29, forty years ago and more! My father, indeed—"

"And at Rome—at Rome, my lord? *Mon Dieu!* in the old days at Rome! When the Spanish company scaled the wall—Ruiz was first, I next—was it not my foot you held? And was it not I who dragged you up, while the devils of Swiss pressed us hard? Ah, those were days, my lord! I was young then, and you, my lord, young too, and handsome as the morning—"

"You rave!" Tavannes cried, finding his tongue at last. "Rome? You rave, old man! Why, I was not born in those days. My father even was a boy! It was in '27 you sacked it—five-and-forty years ago!"

The old man passed his hands over his heated face, and, as a man roused suddenly from sleep looks, he looked round the room. The light died out of his eyes—as a light blown out in a room; his form seemed to shrink, even while the others gazed at him, and he sat down.

"No, I remember," he muttered slowly. "It was Prince Philibert of Chalons, my lord of Orange."

"Dead these forty years!"

"Ay, dead these forty years! All dead!" the old man whispered, gazing at his gnarled hand, and opening and shutting it by turns. "And I grow childish! 'Tis time, high time, I followed them! It trembles now; but have no fear, my lord, this hand will not tremble then. All dead! Ay, all dead!"

He sank into a mournful silence; and Tavannes, after gazing at him awhile in rough pity, fell to his own meditations, which were gloomy enough. The day was beginning to wane, and with the downward turn, though the sun still shone brightly through the southern windows, a shadow seemed to fall across his thoughts. They no longer rioted in a turmoil of defiance as in the forenoon. In its turn, sober reflection marshalled the past before his eyes. The hopes of a life, the ambitions of a life, moved in sombre procession, and things done and things left undone, the sovereignty which Nostradamus had promised, the faces of men he had spared and of men he had not spared—and the face of one woman.

She would not now be his. He had played highly, and he would lose highly, playing the game to the end, that to-morrow she might think of him highly. Had she begun to think of him at all? In the chamber of the inn at Angers he had fancied a change in her, an awakening to life and warmth, a shadow of turning to him. It had pleased him to think so, at any rate. It pleased him still to imagine—of this he was more confident—that in the time to come, when she was Tignonville's, she would think of him secretly and kindly. She would remember him, and in her thoughts and in her memory he would grow to the heroic, even as the man she had chosen would shrink as she learned to know him.

It pleased him, that. It was almost all that was left to please him—that, and to die proudly as he had lived. But as the day wore on, and the room grew hot and close, and the pain in his thigh became more grievous, the frame of his mind altered. A sombre rage was born and grew in him, and a passion fierce and ill-suppressed. To end thus, with nothing done, nothing accomplished of all his hopes and ambitions! To die thus, crushed in a corner by a mean priest and a rabble of spearmen, he who had seen Dreux and Jarnac, had defied the King, and dared to turn the St. Bartholomew to his ends! To die thus, and leave her to that puppet! Strong man as he was, of a strength of will surpassed by few, it taxed him to the utmost to lie and make no sign. Once, indeed, he raised himself on his elbow with something between an oath and a snarl, and he seemed about to speak. So that Bigot came hurriedly to him.

"My lord?"

"Water!" he said. "Water, fool!" And, having drunk, he turned his face to the wall, lest he should name her or ask for her.

For the desire to see her before he died, to look into her eyes, to touch her hand once, only once, assailed his mind and all but whelmed his will. She had been with him, he knew it, in the night; she had left him only at daybreak. But then, in his state of collapse, he had been hardly conscious of her presence. Now to ask for her or to see her would stamp him coward, say what he might to her. The proverb, that the King's face gives grace, applied to her; and an overture on his side could mean but one thing, that he sought her grace. And that he would not do though the cold waters of death covered him more and more, and the coming of the end—in that quiet chamber, while the September sun sank to the appointed place—awoke wild longings and a wild rebellion in his breast. His thoughts were very bitter, as he lay, his loneliness of the uttermost. He turned his face to the wall.

In that posture he slept after a time, watched over by Bigot with looks of rage and pity. And on the room fell a long silence. The sun had lacked three hours of setting when he fell asleep. When he re-opened his eyes, and, after lying for a few minutes between sleep and waking, became conscious of his position, of the day, of the things which had happened, and his helplessness—an awakening which wrung from him an involuntary groan—the light in the room was still strong, and even bright. He fancied for a moment that he had merely dozed off and awaked again; and he continued to lie with his face to the wall, courting a return of slumber.

But sleep did not come, and little by little, as he lay listening and thinking and growing more restless, he got the fancy that he was alone. The light fell brightly on the wall to which his face was turned; how could that be if Bigot's broad shoulders still blocked the loophole? Presently, to assure himself, he called the man by name.

He got no answer.

"Badelon!" he muttered. "Badelon!"

Had he gone, too, the old and faithful? It seemed so, for again no answer came.

He had been accustomed all his life to instant service; to see the act follow the word ere the word ceased to sound. And nothing which had gone before, nothing which he had suffered since his defeat at Angers, had brought him to feel his impotence and his position—and that the end of his power was indeed come—as sharply as this. The blood rushed to his head; almost the tears to eyes which had not shed them since boyhood, and would not shed them now, weak as he was! He rose on his elbow and looked with a full heart; it was as he had fancied. Badelon's stool was empty; the embrasure—that was empty too. Through its narrow outlet he had a tiny view of the shore and the low rocky hill, of which the summit shone warm in the last rays of the setting sun.

The setting sun! Ay, for the lower part of the hill was growing cold; the shore at its foot was grey. Then he had slept long, and the time was come. He drew a deep breath and listened. But on all within and without lay silence, a silence marked, rather than broken, by the dull fall of a wave on the causeway. The day had been calm, but with the sunset a light breeze was rising.

He set his teeth hard, and continued to listen. An hour before sunset was the time they had named for the exchange. What did it mean? In five minutes the sun would be below the horizon; already the zone of warmth on the hillside was moving and retreating upwards. And Bigot and old Badelon? Why had they left him while he slept? An hour before sunset! Why, the room was growing grey, grey and dark in the corners, and—what was that?

He started, so violently that he jarred his leg, and the pain wrung a groan from him. At the foot of the bed, overlooked until then, a woman lay prone on the floor, her face resting on her outstretched arms. She lay without motion, her head and her clasped hands towards the loophole, her thick, clubbed hair hiding her neck. A woman! Count Hannibal stared, and, fancying he dreamed, closed his eyes, then looked again. It was no phantasm. It was the Countess; it was his wife!

He drew a deep breath, but he did not speak, though the colour rose slowly to his cheek. And slowly his eyes devoured her from head to foot, from the hands lying white in the light below the window to the shod feet; unchecked he took his fill of that which he had so much desired—the seeing her! A woman prone, with all of her hidden but her hands: a hundred acquainted with her would not have known her. But he knew her, and would have known her from a hundred, nay from a thousand, by her hands alone.

What was she doing here, and in this guise? He pondered; then he looked from her for an instant, and saw that while he had gazed at her the sun had set, the light had passed from the top of the hill; the world without and the room within were growing cold. Was that the cause she no longer lay quiet? He saw a shudder run through her, and a second; then it seemed to him—or was he going mad?—that she moaned, and prayed in half-heard words, and, wrestling with herself, beat her forehead on her arms, and then was still again, as still as death. By the time the paroxysm had passed, the last flush of sunset had faded from the sky, and the hills were growing dark.

CHAPTER XXXVI
HIS KINGDOM

Count Hannibal could not have said why he did not speak to her at once. Warned by an instinct vague and ill-understood, he remained silent, his eyes riveted on her, until she rose from the floor. A moment later she met his gaze, and he looked to see her start. Instead, she stood quiet and thoughtful, regarding him with a kind of sad solemnity, as if she saw not him only, but the dead; while first one tremor and then a second shook her frame.

At length "It is over!" she whispered. "Patience, Monsieur; have no fear, I will be brave. But I must give a little to him."

"To him!" Count Hannibal muttered, his face extraordinarily, pale.

She smiled with an odd passionateness. "Who was my lover!" she cried, her voice a-thrill. "Who will ever be my lover, though I have denied him, though I have left him to die! It was just. He who has so tried me knows it was just! He whom I have sacrificed—he knows it too, now! But it is hard to be—just," with a quavering smile. "You who take all may give him a little, may pardon me a little, may have—patience!"

Count Hannibal uttered a strangled cry, between a moan and a roar. A moment he beat the coverlid with his hands in impotence. Then he sank back on the bed.

"Water!" he muttered. "Water!"

She fetched it hurriedly, and, raising his head on her arm, held it to his lips. He drank, and lay back again with closed eyes. He lay so still and so long that she thought that he had fainted; but after a pause he spoke.

"You have done that?" he whispered; "you have done that?"

"Yes," she answered, shuddering. "God forgive me! I have done that! I had to do that, or—"

"And is it too late—to undo it?"

"It is too late." A sob choked her voice.

Tears—tears incredible, unnatural—welled from under Count Hannibal's closed eyelids, and rolled sluggishly down his harsh cheek to the edge of his beard.

"I would have gone," he muttered. "If you had spoken, I would have spared you this."

"I know," she answered unsteadily; "the men told me."

"And yet—"

"It was just. And you are my husband," she replied. "More, I am the captive of your sword, and as you spared me in your strength, my lord, I spared you in your weakness."

"Mon Dieu! Mon Dieu, Madame!" he cried, "at what a cost!"

And that arrested, that touched her in the depths of her grief and her horror; even while the gibbet on the causeway, which had burned itself into her eyeballs, hung before her. For she knew that it was the cost to *her* he was counting. She knew that for himself he had ever held life cheap, that he could have seen Tignonville suffer without a qualm. And the thoughtfulness for her, the value he placed on a thing—even on a rival's life—because its was dear to her, touched her home, moved her as few things could have moved her at that moment. She saw it of a piece with all that had gone before, with all that had passed between them, since that fatal Sunday in Paris. But she made no sign. More than she had said she would not say; words of love, even of reconciliation, had no place on her lips while he whom she had sacrificed awaited his burial.

And meantime the man beside her lay and found it incredible. "It was just," she had said. And he knew it; Tignonville's folly—that and that only had led them into the snare and caused his own capture. But what had justice to do with the things of this world? In his experience, the strong hand—that was justice, in France; and possession—that was law. By the strong hand he had taken her, and by the strong hand she might have freed herself.

And she had not. There was the incredible thing. She had chosen instead to do justice! It passed belief. Opening his eyes on a silence which had lasted some minutes, a silence rendered more solemn by the lapping water without, Tavannes saw her kneeling in the dusk of the chamber, her head bowed over his couch, her face hidden in her hands. He knew that she prayed, and feebly he deemed the whole a dream. No scene akin to it had had place in his life; and, weakened and in pain, he prayed that the vision might last for ever, that he might never awake.

But by-and-by, wrestling with the dread thought of what she had done, and the horror which would return upon her by fits and spasms, she flung out a hand, and it fell on him. He started, and the movement, jarring the broken limb, wrung from him a cry of pain. She looked up and was going to speak, when a scuffling of feet under the gateway arch, and a confused sound of several voices raised at once, arrested the words on her lips. She rose to her feet and listened. Dimly he could see her face through the dusk. Her eyes were on the door, and she breathed quickly.

A moment or two passed in this way, and then from the hurly-burly in the gateway the footsteps of two men—one limped—detached themselves and came nearer and nearer. They stopped without. A gleam of light shone under the door, and some one knocked.

She went to the door, and, withdrawing the bar, stepped quickly back to the bedside, where for an instant the light borne by those who entered blinded her. Then, above the lanthorn, the faces of La Tribe and Bigot broke upon her, and their shining eyes told her that they bore good news. It was well, for the men seemed tongue-tied. The minister's fluency was gone; he was very pale, and it was Bigot who in the end spoke for both. He stepped forward, and, kneeling, kissed her cold hand.

"My lady," he said, "you have gained all, and lost nothing. Blessed be God!"

"Blessed be God!" the minister wept. And from the passage without came the sound of laughter and weeping and many voices, with a flutter of lights and flying skirts, and women's feet.

She stared at him wildly, doubtfully, her hand at her throat.

"What?" she said, "he is not dead—M. de Tignonville?"

"No, he is alive," La Tribe answered, "he is alive." And he lifted up his hands as if he gave thanks.

"Alive?" she cried. "Alive! Oh, Heaven is merciful. You are sure? You are sure?"

"Sure, Madame, sure. He was not in their hands. He was dismounted in the first shock, it seems, and, coming to himself after a time, crept away and reached St. Gilles, and came hither in a boat. But the enemy learned that he had not entered with us, and of this the priest wove his snare. Blessed be God, who put it into your heart to escape it!"

The Countess stood motionless, and with closed eyes pressed her hands to her temples. Once she swayed as if she would fall her length, and Bigot sprang forward to support and save her. But she opened her eyes at that, sighed very deeply, and seemed to recover herself.

"You are sure?" she said faintly. "It is no trick?"

"No, Madame, it is no trick," La Tribe answered. "M. de Tignonville is alive, and here."

"Here!" She started at the word. The colour fluttered in her cheek. "But the keys," she murmured. And she passed her hand across her brow. "I thought—that I had them."

"He has not entered," the minister answered, "for that reason. He is waiting at the postern, where he landed. He came, hoping to be of use to you."

She paused a moment, and when she spoke again her aspect had undergone a subtle change. Her head was high, a flush had risen to her cheeks, her eyes were bright.

"Then," she said, addressing La Tribe, "do you, Monsieur, go to him, and pray him in my name to retire to St. Gilles, if he can do so without peril. He has no place here—now; and if he can go safely to his home it will be well that he do so. Add, if you please, that Madame de Tavannes thanks him for his offer of aid, but in her husband's house she needs no other protection."

Bigot's eyes sparkled with joy.

The minister hesitated. "No more, Madame?" he faltered. He was tender-hearted, and Tignonville was of his people.

"No more," she said gravely, bowing her head. "It is not M. de Tignonville I have to thank, but Heaven's mercy, that I do not stand here at this moment unhappy as I entered—a woman accursed, to be pointed at while I live. And the dead"—she pointed solemnly through the dark casement to the shore—"the dead lie there."

La Tribe went.

She stood a moment in thought, and then took the keys from the rough stone window-ledge on which she had laid them when she entered. As the cold iron touched her fingers she shuddered. The contact awoke again the horror and misery in which she had groped, a lost thing, when she last felt that chill.

"Take them," she said; and she gave them to Bigot. "Until my lord can leave his couch they will remain in your charge, and you will answer for all to him. Go, now, take the light; and in half an hour send Madame Carlat to me."

A wave broke heavily on the causeway and ran down seething to the sea; and another and another, filling the room with rhythmical thunders. But the voice of the sea was no longer the same in the darkness, where the Countess knelt in silence beside the bed—knelt, her head bowed on her clasped hands, as she had knelt before, but with a mind how different, with what different thoughts! Count Hannibal could see her head but dimly, for the light shed upwards by the spume of the sea fell only on the rafters. But he knew she was there, and he would fain, for his heart was full, have laid his hand on her hair.

And yet he would not. He would not, out of pride. Instead he bit on his harsh beard, and lay looking upward to the rafters, waiting what would come. He who had held her at his will now lay at hers, and waited. He who had spared her life at a price now took his own a gift at her hands, and bore it.

"*Afterwards, Madame de Tavannes—*"

His mind went back by some chance to those words—the words he had neither meant nor fulfilled. It passed from them to the marriage and the blow; to the scene in the meadow beside the river; to the last ride between La Flèche and Angers—the ride during which he had played with her fears and hugged himself on the figure he would make on the morrow. The figure? Alas! of all his plans for dazzling her had come—*this*! Angers had defeated him, a priest had worsted him. In place of releasing Tignonville after the fashion of Bayard and the Paladins, and in the teeth of snarling thousands, he had come near to releasing him after another fashion and at his own expense. Instead of dazzling her by his mastery and winning her by his magnanimity, he lay here, owing her his life, and so weak, so broken, that the tears of childhood welled up in his eyes.

Out of the darkness a hand, cool and firm, slid into his, clasped it tightly, drew it to warm lips, carried it to a woman's bosom.

"My lord," she murmured, "I was the captive of your sword, and you spared me. Him I loved you took and spared him too—not once or twice. Angers, also, and my people you would have saved for my sake. And you thought I could do this! Oh! shame, shame!" But her hand held his always.

"You loved him," he muttered.

"Yes, I loved him," she answered slowly and thoughtfully. "I loved him." And she fell silent a minute. Then, "And I feared you," she added, her voice low. "Oh, how I feared you—and hated you!"

"And now?"

"I do not fear him," she answered, smiling in the darkness. "Nor hate him. And for you, my lord, I am your wife and must do your bidding, whether I will or no. I have no choice."

He was silent.

"Is that not so?" she asked.

He tried weakly to withdraw his hand.

But she clung to it. "I must bear your blows or your kisses. I must be as you will and do as you will, and go happy or sad, lonely or with you, as you will! As you will, my lord! For I am your chattel, your property, your own. Have you not told me so?"

"But your heart," he cried fiercely, "is his! Your heart, which you told me in the meadow could never be mine!"

"I lied," she murmured, laughing tearfully, and her hands hovered over him. "It has come back! And it is on my lips."

And she leant over and kissed him. And Count Hannibal knew that he had entered into his kingdom, the sovereignty of a woman's heart.

An hour later there was a stir in the village on the mainland. Lanthorns began to flit to and fro. Sulkily men were saddling and preparing for the road. It was far to Challans, farther to Lège—more than one day, and many a weary league to Ponts de Cé and the Loire. The men who had ridden gaily southwards on the scent of spoil and revenge turned their backs on the castle with many a sullen oath and word. They burned a hovel or two, and stripped such as they spared, after the fashion of the day; and it had gone ill with the peasant woman who fell into their hands. Fortunately, under cover of the previous night every soul had escaped from the village, some to sea, and the rest to take shelter among the sand-dunes; and as the troopers rode up the path from the beach, and through the green valley, where their horses shied from the bodies of the men they had slain, there was not an eye to see them go.

Or to mark the man who rode last, the man of the white face—scarred on the temple—and the burning eyes, who paused on the brow of the hill, and, before he passed beyond, cursed with quivering lips the foe who had escaped him. The words were lost, as soon as spoken, in the murmur of the sea on the causeway; the sea, fit emblem of the Eternal, which rolled its tide regardless of blessing or cursing, good or ill will, nor spared one jot of ebb or flow because a puny creature had spoken to the night.